Erin —

DARKSHINE

R.D. Vallier

Yay! You won! :)

Happy Reading!

R.D. Vallier

Darkshine by R.D. Vallier

Published by Free Fire Press
www.freefirepress.com

Cover by Acid PopTart
www.acid-poptart.com

ISBN: 978-0997461916

For my husband, Joshua.
You are my magic.

CHAPTER ONE

In the dark crept something darker, but I dismissed it as merely shadows. A swaying branch perhaps, or a deer tensing until I finished stuffing the can with garbage. Something abnormal never crossed my mind, not even with my scalp prickling and my heart pounding. After all, excitement in this town meant the first gunshot of open season, and battered morels sizzling in oil. Muggings were rare here, murder nonexistent. Crimes occurred behind closed doors, and often by a man who swore he loved you.

I started back up the walkway, but froze mid-step when I entered the porch light's glow. It flickered, then dimmed, and I didn't feel the security I normally did. I felt *exposed*, as if the light was an agent of the shadows, highlighting my position for all the night to see. Behind me, wind chimes dinged in the gnarled oak tree. Woodsmoke drifted on the breeze. I released a shaky breath, but the cloud of mist didn't leave my lips; it *fled* with my body-heat, as if the night was a singing siren, her music luring my warmth away. Dread seeped into my marrow. Unseen eyes bore into the back of my skull. I rubbed my arms and summoned the courage to glance over my shoulder.

The sky was clouded, the darkness beyond the oak tree expanding into infinity. The world seemed empty. Hollow. If I listened closely I might have heard the shadows echo. But still, it was only blackness.

Stop being a goose, Miriam. The night is just

playing tricks with your imagination, I told myself, unaware the dark would soon make me tremble more than any nightmare. But right then, in a nowhere town in rural Appalachia, shivering on a cement walkway in flannel pajamas and fuzzy penguin slippers on a cloudy, winter night, I did not believe in magic or mystical creatures. I did not believe monsters lurked beneath my bed or in the woods around the farmhouse, and I *certainly* did not believe they lurked as neighbors or strangers or things darker than the darkness.

The backdoor's knob creaked in my hand. A shadow struck from the gloom and brushed my cheek, softer than a whisper. I recoiled as if a fist had swung. A moth fluttered up to the porch light and I cursed my foolishness, fear's bitter tang in my mouth. The moth circled the lightbulb twice, then rested upside down on the rim, its antennae twitching. I tilted my head. *Have I ever seen a moth so calm beside a light in the darkness?* I wondered. It was no larger than a half-dollar, and brown. When I stepped closer it spread its wings, exposing the yellow eyes on its back. My fingers itched to hold it, to feel its soft feet tap my skin. I reached up, my hand cupped. The powdered eyes on its back widened.

A chickadee buzzed my head; its wingtips scraped my wrist. I jumped back with an: "*eek*," yanking my hand away as the bird snatched the moth with its beak and zipped off into the night.

The porch light flickered. I darted through the backdoor and latched the deadbolt behind me.

"Damn, woman. You look like you've seen a ghost," my husband, Sam, said as I scurried into the living room from the kitchen. He was perched on the couch in a sweatsuit, his back stiff, the television remote in one hand and an iPhone on his thigh. He looked like the general of the living room, the commander of gadgets. His crewcut perfected the picture.

"No ghost," I said. On the flat screen the newscaster with the birthmark on his forehead reported about American soldiers injured in the Middle East. I clicked on the Christmas tree and slid the chain on the front door. The tree's lights shifted lazily from white to blue to green, and my heart began to steady. "A chickadee buzzed my head. It just startled me, is all."

"Chickadee? At this time of night?"

"It snatched a moth off the porch light."

Sam lifted his cigarette from the empty beer can on the coffee table and tapped off a stalk of ash. "Don't be stupid. It's too cold for moths. You're jumping at shadows again."

"I know—" *what I saw*, I almost said. My lips pressed tight as my mother's voice scolded me inside my head. *Never make waves, Mir. You already cause enough trouble. Don't cause any more. My poor heart can't take it.*

My face muscles relaxed and hung off my skull, heavy as dough. "You're probably right."

"Did you lock down the can's lid?" Sam asked, his eyes on the newscaster.

"Yes."

He spared me a glare. "Are you *sure?* I don't want raccoons spreading trash everywhere again. Makes us look bad to the neighbors."

That had happened once. Three years ago.

"It's locked. I tugged on the lid like you showed me."

He nodded curtly, my answer deemed acceptable.

Most nights I left the curtains open to display the Christmas tree, but tonight I pulled them shut to hide our home from the darkness. My right penguin slipper stared up at me, its stitched smile now pleading. A button eye had fallen off, probably on the walkway near the garbage can. Stuffing protruded from its socket. I glanced at the backdoor, remembering the hollow darkness, the heat-luring night.

Sorry, little penguin. Surgery must wait until daylight.

I headed for the stairs, then stopped on the lower landing. "Um, Sam?"

Smoke leaked out his nose. "What?"

My brow furrowed. *How do I ask for comfort without acting like a child who is afraid of the dark?* I leaned against the banister and traced a finger seductively along the wood. "Come to bed with me?"

Sam groaned as if I had asked him to re-shingle the roof. "I'm watching the news."

"I know. But we haven't seen each other much lately and—"

"We *live* together." His iPhone buzzed. He glanced at it, a ghost of a smile touching his lips. He tapped a quick text and sent it off, then noticed I still lingered. "I'll come up when the news is over, all right? *If* I'm tired."

Sam's iPhone buzzed as I headed up the staircase. "Can I get you anything before I go to bed?" I asked.

"Nuh-uh," he grunted.

"Love you." I stopped on the third step when he didn't answer. His fingers tapped away at the iPhone's screen. "Goodnight," I said.

When he didn't hear me the second time I crept upstairs alone.

I kicked off my slippers and clicked on the bedside lamp. Wind tapped the windowpane, and the floor vent whirred, straining to fight off the cold. A moth flittered out of the closet and circled the light, the shadows of its wings fluttering on the ceiling like a frightened heart.

"Don't you know it's too cold for moths?" I said, crawling beneath the blankets.

The moth perched on the lampshade, preened its antennae, then fluttered into the hallway as if eager to deliver a message.

CHAPTER TWO

The chickadee stood on the windowsill, staring in at me with its black, beady eyes. It had been there every morning since my incident with the moth three days ago, as if we had some prearranged appointment. I believed it was the same chickadee from that night as well, but had no proof. Instead, I dismissed its behavior as humans often do. *It is cold outside and it's seeking warmth through the window*. Nothing peculiar. Nothing odd. Life was normal, so carry on.

"Good morning, chickadee," I told the bird from across the bedroom, even though the sun wouldn't rise for another two and a half hours. The chickadee stared at me as I dressed for work, an intelligence behind those eyes beyond my comprehension. Inside, the window-frame was strung with bunches of dried flowers I had collected the year before—lavender, roses, yarrow—colorful reminders of warmth and sunshine, promises of spring. Outside, a gust of wind sprayed the chickadee with snowflakes. The bird didn't even flinch.

I must remember to buy birdseed on my way home from work. It's so miserable to be alone in the cold.

"Tell you what, chickadee," I said, tucking my T-shirt into my jeans. "If I make it through this day without murdering anybody, I'll bring you a treat. Deal?"

The chickadee stared at me, unmoving.

I fetched my sneakers from the closet.

They were old and dingy, and the double bow hadn't been untied since I bought them two years ago. I crammed my feet inside, wiggling to get my heels in. I stood four feet away from the bird, expecting it to flee from my sudden movement. Instead it watched me, feathers rustling in the wind. I crouched to its eye-level and inched closer to the window. Three feet away, then two, then one. The bird stood its ground. Brave little thing. I held my breath to keep from fogging the glass. If the bird hadn't blinked I would have thought it was dead, frozen on the windowsill. I admired its black cap, its gray body, the hint of tan outlining its wings. "Do you have a message for me?" I asked. The bird lunged at the glass and cursed in its tiny, chirping voice: "*chick-a-dee-dee-dee!*" Then flew up and over the house.

The outburst jolted me to my feet. The chickadee had left footprints on the sill, like two tiny pitchforks pressed into the snow.

I tugged my olive knitted cap over my ears, slid into my favorite overcoat and pranced downstairs, enjoying the weight of the layered, cranberry coattails flailing behind me. I had bought the coat seven years ago, and even on clearance it had been a splurge which made Sam blow his top. It was worth every penny and gripe, however. The satin-lined wool made me feel like a fairytale's winter princess, waiting to enter a ballroom carved from ice and be swept away in a swirl of silk and gold.

"We're out of milk."

Daydreams of tiaras and twirling ball-gowns disintegrated as I entered the kitchen. Sam leaned against the counter, scraping a spoon through a bowl of dry cornflakes. The deputy star on his chest gleamed beneath the fluorescent lighting. His collar was starched and creased. "You know I *hate* dry cereal."

I grabbed a banana from the Longaberger basket on the table. "I'll pick up some after work."

"And how exactly does your lack of foresight help me now?"

I leaned against the refrigerator, tracing a brown spot on the peel with my thumb. "It doesn't."

"Speak up. I don't understand mumbling," Sam said.

"It doesn't! I'm sorry, okay? I didn't mean to upset you."

Sam nodded, my apology acknowledged. He dumped the bowl of dry cornflakes into the sink and left to check his e-mail. I tossed the banana back into the basket, no longer hungry.

Computer keys tapped in the living room. My eyes narrowed as my blood-pressure rose. I wanted to march into the living room and tell Sam I was *not* sorry; his attitude was hurtful and unfair. But my mother's voice scolded me inside my head, insisting how *lucky* I was to have a husband with a respectable job; how *lucky* I was to have such an attractive man when most ignored my straggly brown hair and boyish figure; how *lucky* I was to marry a homeowner; how *lucky* I was he didn't beat me or cheat on me or mooch away all I had.

You're too damn sensitive, Miriam. Be grateful for what you have. I could almost see my mother in her wicker chair. A delicate gold cross hanging from her thick neck, her second glass of scotch in hand. *Be a good girl.*

Don't make waves.

"Be grateful for what you have. Don't make waves," I mumbled with a sigh, then glanced out the window above the kitchen sink. The chickadee stood on the sill, glaring in at me. It shook its head, as if disagreeing with my behavior. But that was ridiculous. Songbirds didn't understand English, let alone the complexities of human relationships.

"Odds are looking bad for your treat, bird."

The chickadee glared in response.

I scurried into the living room, away from the creepy bird and its accusations I imagined. Sam commanded the couch, his laptop on his thighs. He snapped it shut as I entered the room.

"Mad at me?" I asked as he shoved the laptop into its case and stood, slinging the strap over his shoulder.

"Stupid mistakes happen. I understand." He kissed my cheek, then murmured into my ear: "Although, you can always make me lasagna tonight to prove you're sorry."

"Tonight?" I had worked nearly every day for the last three weeks to earn time off for the holidays. Dirty dishes and cigarette butts cluttered the coffee table, junk mail was scattered everywhere, grime darkened the floors and baseboards, the laundry had developed a summit, and the whole house had the stale stench of smoke and neglect. "I planned to clean tonight," I blurted. "And I need to make the pie. And I need to wrap your family's presents. And I—"

A shadow passed over Sam's austere face.

"If I'm not worth the extra effort, just *say* so. But I honestly don't see the difficulty in some extra cooking. It's not like we have children to take up your time."

My heart winced. "You *are* worth the effort," I said. The shadow on Sam's face lingered. I forced a smile. "I'll pick up the noodles with the milk after work. You know I love making your mother's recipe."

Sam smirked and the eclipse passed. "Not as much as I love *you*," he said, and grabbed his truck keys off the hook on the wall.

A chickadee flapped off the porch when he opened the door.

CHAPTER THREE

My heart sank when Sam dropped me off at the shabby gas station, its square windows blazing like the gates of hell in the pre-morning gloom. Knowing I didn't have to return after my shift for five days helped to drag my feet through the door. I punched my timecard, tied my tacky, orange apron around my waist and said a quick hello-goodbye to the puffy-eyed night clerk who practically sleepwalked out the door. I had to survive eight hours today. Just eight hours. I plopped onto the stool behind the cash-register and watched the clock. Only seven hours and fifty-nine minutes to go, seven hours and fifty-nine minutes, seven hours and—Oh!—fifty-*eight* minutes, until freedom.

I gritted my teeth as the day dragged. Most people bought gas from the pumps and I never dealt with them. Winter was a bit of a treat since I didn't have to refill the squeegee buckets outside; the water just froze into a blue brick, anyway. Christmas Eve brought in excess out-of-towners, but the majority of customers were locals. Locals I served two to six days a week for the past three years. Locals who did not know my name despite the obnoxiously large *Miriam* stamped in caps across my heart. They stared through me as I rung up their gas and cigarettes and lottery tickets and booze. I asked them how their day was. How was the family? Any plans for the holidays? Are you sick of the snow yet? It was a rarity when I received more than a one-worded response.

I doodled roses and gnomes on discarded

receipts during the lulls, and numbed my feelings of inadequacy like an alcoholic, with inflated truths as my drink of choice. I silently praised myself for working steadily in a county with one of the highest unemployment rates in the United States. My minimum wage helped pay the mortgage and Sam's student loans, his diploma stashed somewhere with my box of oil paints and canvases, collecting a marriage's worth of dust. *Everyone* needed gas, I reasoned, from emergency workers to families. Thus my work helped America thrive and I had no reason for embarrassment or shame.

And yet, at the Sheriff's Christmas party this year, I had hid in the bathroom for twenty minutes after Sam gibed about my *monkey job* to all his snickering coworkers as they refilled their plastic cups with spiced wine.

At 1:59 P.M. I tugged my olive cap over my ears and buttoned my overcoat. Sixty-seconds later I waved goodbye to my relief and darted out the door, coattails flying.

I ambled down the rural, woodland roads, smiling. The F-250 was our only vehicle, and since Sam worked twelve hour shifts and hated relying on me to pick him up, I had a two mile hike home. I never minded, though. My step bounced as the gas station grew smaller behind me, leaving only the road and trees and the air's faint scent of woodsmoke. I could have gone to the Kroger in town for the lasagna noodles and milk, but I headed toward Keith's Corner Shop instead, a small mom-and-pop on the way home. The fifteen-percent markup was worth avoiding the Christmas Eve crowds.

The flurries had stopped hours ago and

the sun broke through the clouds, making the weather brisk but pleasant. A thin blanket of white covered the ground, and other than a few oaks clinging onto clumps of brown leaves, the trees were bare, watching the roads like skeleton guards. Cardinals darted between the branches, but otherwise the world was still, with the loud silence winter creates. During spring these woods breathed in shades of green, leaves dancing to a choir of songbirds. But for now their songs were a memory and a distant anticipation.

Except for one.

I had heard the birdsong before, but didn't know which species sang the four, crisp notes. High, low, high, low. The notes followed me for a full mile, the soloist hidden somewhere in the trees. *One of the cardinals, perhaps?* High, low, high, low. Do, bee, do, bee. The music rang in the winter stillness, sweet and tender, as if trying to coax the leaves from their buds.

A cowbell clanged against the glass door as I entered Keith's Corner Shop. Keith stood behind the beat-up wooden counter as always, wearing a faded OSU ball cap and a Realtree jacket, a lump of tobacco behind his lip. His weathered face smiled when I entered. The smile didn't touch his eyes, though. It never did.

"Mornin." Keith's voice crackled from decades of cigarettes and his sentences always trailed up, as if he was in a constant state of suspicion. "How's Sam a-doin'?"

"Good. I'm making him lasagna tonight," I replied, emphasizing my wifeliness. The star on Sam's chest had granted him instant acceptance from the community when we moved here, but I was merely an accessory on his arm like a cufflink or a watch. I had no status here or friends or roots or blood. I was not a church member; I had no children despite years of trying; and I occupied a job which could have been given to a *local.* Everyone was polite to my face, but I often caught people —like Keith, as I rounded an aisle corner—staring at me from the tail of their eyes. I often felt like an exotic animal, a gazelle perhaps, caught munching flowers on their grandmother's grave.

I wish I could blame the small-town atmosphere for the glares and unease, but growing up had never been any different. All my life an inner voice whispered I was an outcast, that I somehow didn't belong. *You always act as if you are hiding something,* my mother used to say. *Stop being so damn quiet.* Yet I knew people's unspoken dislike of me was more than my muteness. It was deeper. An unseen deformity, like that puppy all the litter-mates try to kill even though the breeder finds nothing wrong with it. Most days I ignored the stares, but some days it was so painfully obvious I ducked into public restrooms to make sure nothing was stuck to my face.

"Any plans tonight?" I asked Keith.

Keith sniffed. "Family," he mumbled, then flipped open a hunting magazine.

I sighed and wandered to the rear of the store. Shopping at Keith's reminded me of an archeology dig. I never knew what I would find or how long it had waited to be discovered. Metal shelving stretched across his small shop, crammed with everything from basic groceries to office supplies to children's toys to wigs to car fluids and car parts to deer gutting kits to greeting cards to tools. He also had an intimidating display of knives near the cash register, a small fridge of wilting fruits and vegetables, a small deli counter, and three floor-to-ceiling whirring refrigerators packed with bait and booze, namely Bud Ice.

I grabbed a half gallon of milk beside a small wall of beer cubes, then headed to the middle aisle. Pasta nestled between canned soups and bags of generic cat food which had probably been accumulating dust since the Kennedy assassination.

Cat food. That reminded me of the chickadee.

I grabbed a box of lasagna noodles, checked the expiration date (I still had eight days left, yippee!), and headed to the counter. "Do you sell bird seed?" I asked.

"All out."

I should have gone to Kroger, after all. I had told the chickadee that no bloodshed today meant a treat, and even though Sam would scoff at me for making a deal with a *dumb animal*, I intended to keep my promise. Beside the cash register was a basket of individually wrapped carrot cake slices. *Do chickadees even* like *carrot cake?* Apparently I would find out. "I'll take one of these, too."

Keith rang up my order. I headed out of the shop, plastic bag of groceries hanging off my wrist. The cowbell clanged as I opened the door. A brown moth fluttered inside and disappeared above the fluorescent lighting.

Do, bee, do, bee. Do, bee, do beeee.

"Hey, Keith?" He glowered at me, as if wondering why I didn't vanish from his town in the puff of voodoo smoke I most likely arrived in. "Do you know what species of bird makes this song? I've heard it all day."

Keith's face softened. He came around the counter and joined me in the doorway. "Aaaaah," he said, his smile touching his eyes. Apparently Keith was a bird man. I made a mental note for future conversations. "That there's a Carolina chickadee that is."

"*Chickadee?* I thought they sang their name."

Keith nodded, keeping his ear to the outside, listening to the high, low, high, low. Do, bee, do, bee. "Ah yup, their *chick-a-dee-dee-dee* is how they got their name, all right. But that's just one-uh their songs. The *see-me-I'm-here* is the other."

"See me I'm here?" I asked.

"That's the trick to rememberin' it. The notes kinda sound like those words if ya use yer 'magination some."

High, low, high, low. Do, bee, do, bee. See, me, I'm, here.

My eyebrows jumped. Once he pointed it out I couldn't *not* hear it, crisp and distinct.

See-me-I'm-here. See-me-I'm-here.

"I once heard an old Indian story bout them chickadees," he continued. "Said they're the strongest spirits in the wood, and I believe it."

I never would have related a tiny chickadee to strength. I turned to Keith, eyebrow raised. "Yeah? Why is that?"

"Cuz it don't matter how bad the winters get, those lil birds don't just survive, they *thrive*. Most other birds fly to warmer weather. Even big, tough bears will hide and sleep 'til the snow melts. But not chickadee. He's a brave'un. Heck, when the weatherman forecasts a nasty snowstorm it's hard a-keepin' my shelves stocked cuz we humans get so scared and crazy. But chickadee braves the storm, survives as if it were his playground, and keeps on a-singin'."

I glanced at Keith from the corner of my eye, a smile tugging at my lips. He seemed filled somehow, as if talking about birds ignited warmth beneath his Realtree jacket. I had always thought of chickadees as background noise, easily taken for granted, easily forgotten. Keith's story was like a map into a secret world. Maybe my chickadee friend was more special than I realized. Maybe it offered me a way to connect with this community, with something as simple as birding.

"A chickadee has visited my window every day for the past three days," I said.

"That's nice," Keith grumbled, and shuffled back to his counter. "Tell Sam hello."

My shoulders slumped. "I will," I mumbled. The cowbell clanged. "Merry Christmas."

I never saw Keith again.

CHAPTER FOUR

The remaining walk home was wooded, with a few houses and trailers tucked deep into the trees. My grocery bag's handle had snapped a quarter of a mile back and I now cradled the noodles, milk, and carrot cake in my arms like an infant. I had been scrutinizing my awkward interaction with Keith since I left his shop, trying to decide at which point I appeared the biggest idiot.

A narrow creek meandered along the roadside, but it wasn't the picturesque vision the local campgrounds touted in their brochures. The water was bright orange and acidic, cutting through the landscape like a blood-poisoned vein. Even after nine years of living near the acid mine drainage my heart sank at the sight. I thought about the hibernating fish that should have been nestled in the creek's pebbles, the frogs that would never bask on its summer banks, and the eggs that would never hatch. I thought of all the life that would never happen thanks to this toxic land, a byproduct of coal mining, desperate workers risking their lives, and good old corporate greed. The locals called the polluted waters Yellow Boy, but I secretly called it Agent Orange. Everywhere that water flowed brought destruction and death.

The poisoned creek snaked around overgrown slag piles which had merged with the forest during the past century, creating unnaturally shaped hills and valleys. I scanned the roadway, making sure I was alone, then followed the orange water into the woods. Bare branches scraped against my clothing as I pushed through a grove of paw paw trees between two slag hills and into the hidden clearing beyond.

I had never told anyone about this secret place. *And God forbid my husband finds out.* Sam would sneer and gibe and roll his eyes at the decomposing log blocking the abandoned mine shaft, dusted with snow. But, to me, this recess was more inviting than feather beds or day spas or stone hearths crackling with flame. It was my sacred haven, a time-out from a mundane life.

The mineshaft yawned from the hillside as if it had dozed off awaiting my return, waking to greet me with open arms. It blew a constant fifty-five degrees, warming me on my winter rests and cooling me in summer's heat. I set my groceries beside the paw paws and sat on the log, listening to the orange creek trickle faintly past the grove. Deer prints cut across the opening and disappeared into the brush; raccoon prints ran beside them. I never found human tracks, however, except for the ones I had left from the days before. Discarded bottles or food wrappers never littered the scenery. Nor was there graffiti spray-painted on the rock or carved into the trees. My shoulders relaxed. It was always just me, and it was the one place in the world where I believed that was enough.

See-me-I'm-here.

I guess today it isn't just me, after all. The sweet, crisp notes greeted me from the branches overhead. A chickadee stared down from twenty feet up. I doubted it was the same bird from my windowsill—I mean, what were the odds?—but I decided it was a good opportunity to see if carrot cake was chickadee-approved.

I fetched the carrot cake and unwrapped the cellophane, the warm scents of cinnamon and nutmeg tempting on a chilly Christmas Eve. I took a bite, moist and spicy, the frosting making my molar's cavity ache. "Do you like carrot cake, chickadee?" I asked, and threw a chunk to the ground.

The chickadee tilted its head, bounced on the branch, then flitted down and pecked eagerly at the morsel, shaking its head to rip out the carrot pieces. As pets went, this was the closest I would ever get. I had begged Sam for years to adopt, but he refused adamantly, insisting dogs were too much responsibility, cats were too snobbish, and birds were filthy rats with wings.

"How brave are you, spirit of the wood?" I crouched and held out the rest of the cake in my hand. The chickadee flew onto my wrist and pecked eagerly. I froze, my heart beating enthusiastically as I gaped at the wildlife at my fingertips, its tiny nails prickling my skin. The carrot cake had become a keyhole, a glimpse into a secret, untamable world. An unexplainable sense of home and belonging overwhelmed me. Tears pricked my eyes. I swallowed hard, feeling like a child again. A scared, lost child, who had finally collapsed into her father's arms after wandering aimlessly for so long. I let the tears drip off my chin, too terrified to wipe them away, too terrified any movement would scare away the chickadee, even though it seemed braver than a thousand armies armed to the teeth.

I don't know how long I crouched there or how long the chickadee pecked. Enough for my right foot to fall asleep, but not enough for the bird to fill. A brisk wind whipped the hair off my shoulder. A tear grew frigid on my cheek. The creek trickled outside the grove, its orange water flowing through the forest like a never ending funeral procession.

"Nature's veins are filled with poison, her flesh is rotting, and all the faeries are dead." My somber voice startled me. I hadn't intended to speak and had no idea where the words came from, or what they even meant.

The chickadee peered up at me. "The faeries aren't dead, Miriam. They just left the area."

My spine stiffened. The mineshaft puffed a gust of warm air. The chickadee stared at me and blinked its beady eyes.

"Did ... did you *say* something?" I asked.

The chickadee nodded. "I said the faeries aren't dead. Otherwise I would be unemployed."

I opened my mouth to speak, then closed it. My body tingled with excitement. My chest hummed as if ready to burst from holding in all the secrets of the world. Throughout my life I had felt like a stain on a carpet, an unwanted embarrassment the world tried to ignore. But in the span of a chickadee's tiny, chirping words, everything changed. Wildlife obviously didn't talk to just *anybody*. I must have been special somehow. I must have been—

The blood drained from my face. "Oh ... Oh my God." Wildlife did *not* talk to anybody. Chickadees didn't speak and faeries didn't exist. I was having a break with reality. I was more of a freak than anyone ever believed. I stood up slowly, every muscle tense, as if the chickadee had sprouted fangs and a rattler. "I'm going crazy."

The chickadee tilted its head. "How do you—*tweet!*"

I yanked my hand back; the chickadee tumbled into the snow. "I-I'm stressed about Sam," I muttered, "and working too much, and having to visit the in-laws tomorrow. The stress has made me snap."

"You aren't crazy," the chickadee said, shaking snowflakes off its tail. A tiny down feather seesawed in the air. I snatched my groceries and charged through the paw paw grove, branches snapping against my coat. Eyes felt everywhere. *People* felt everywhere. Hidden behind trees where people had never lurked before. I could almost hear them laughing and mocking. *There goes Sam's stupid wife. As crazy as she is worthless.*

The chickadee flew after me and landed on my shoulder. "You are different, Miriam."

I hugged the groceries against my chest, as if protecting my last shred of sanity. "You're not there! La! La! La! You're not there!"

"You *must* realize you are different," the chickadee continued, bobbing on my shoulder in rhythm to my stride. "Don't you feel lost? As if you can't find home?"

I fought back tears, refusing to allow this psychosis to manipulate my emotions. I was already Sam's odd wife, which had been fine when we were two outcasts in high school. But Sam was now well respected and determined to be elected Sheriff next election. He would kill me if I damaged his reputation and ruined his dream.

I raced past the slag piles and back onto the street. Gravel and road salt crunched beneath my sneakers. A brown mud-truck roared past us, smog billowing out the tailpipe, plastic testicles swaying beneath its hitch. The chickadee waited to speak until after it disappeared over a hill. "I am sorry I scared you, but how else was I supposed to communicate?" I pressed my lips tight and ignored the talking songbird on my shoulder. The *hallucination.* The chickadee sighed. "Fine. I will give you some time. But do me three favors: Avoid the moths, trust the spiders, and do *not* go out after dark."

"What is all that supposed to mean?" I cut the last word short, realizing curiosity had tricked me into joining this psychotic conversation. It didn't matter. The chickadee had already disappeared into the trees.

That was, if it had ever been there at all.

CHAPTER FIVE

I latched the deadbolt, shoved the milk in the refrigerator, then went straight to bed. Naps made me feel guilty, as if I was behaving lazy and disrespectful since Sam worked twelve hour days, sometimes six days a week. *The public appreciates hard workers,* he always said. *I need to prove I have what it takes if I want to be elected Sheriff.* I had a ton of chores and obligations to finish before Sam got home, but I would be utterly useless if my brain snapped and he found me comatose and dribbling in the corner.

Besides, I didn't need a *nap*, just a chance to rest my eyes, recollect myself, unwind. Chickadees did not speak English in the real world. That only happened in fairytales and nervous breakdowns. I was obviously sick, possibly in the early stages of schizophrenia. I remembered a talk-show which had said schizophrenia was most severe if it started in the late twenties. My psyche was prime breeding ground for the crazies.

I froze halfway up the stairs. *What if this* isn't *insanity? What if I'm having a stroke?* I sucked in my lips. I didn't dare go to the emergency room. Sam would be humiliated if the public saw his wife raving about birds insisting she was special and relaying secret information about moths and spiders. And if my ramblings spread through the county? I cringed. *The waves I'd cause would destroy his reputation.* I couldn't do that to Sam, not after all the time and hard work he put into his career. Who would elect a Sheriff married to a lunatic?

I couldn't remember if aspirin was for

strokes or heart attacks, but I took two anyway, then grabbed the cordless phone from the dresser and placed it beside my pillow so if I *was* on the verge of dying I could call 9-1-1. I tried to sleep, but the vision of the chickadee peering up from its carrot cake, a crumb stuck to its beak, repeated relentlessly in my head.

The faeries aren't dead, it had said.

My stomach knotted. My hallucination had spoken about imaginary creatures existing. That had to be a new record for insanity. I pushed the memory aside and visualized things I *knew* existed. The bed's brown and white striped comforter. Sam's gray-green eyes and crooked smile. The gold cross around my mother's neck.

When I opened my eyes I was calmer. Not rested—an enormous Brillo pad had somehow invaded my head—but the chickadee and the carrot cake seemed like a fading dream. I shuffled into the bathroom, rubbing my eyes. My heart jumped into my throat when I noticed the digital clock on the counter. *I slept over* two *hours? Holy crap!*

I bolted down the stairs, the clomps reverberating in the farmhouse. I needed to bake the pie for tomorrow, the in-laws' presents were still unwrapped, we had no clean clothes, and downstairs resembled a natural disaster. Sam typically strode through the door around 6:20, and I had promised lasagna for dinner.

"Okay, okay. You can do this. It's a matter of time management."

I cranked on the oven and started the first load of laundry. The skillet clanged against the burner. I set a stock pot to boil. Several minutes later noodles plopped into rolling water, and ground beef and chopped onion sizzled in the skillet. I popped open a jar of spaghetti sauce and prepared my cheeses. Thirty minutes later the oven door slammed shut on a raw lasagna.

Thankfully, I had made the pie crust the night before. I squinted, trying to read my mother-in-law's handwriting. *Cut sugar pumpkin into chunks. Simmer, covered in an inch of water for thirty minutes...? Or does that say twenty?* I had never made a pumpkin pie before, or had been allowed to help with Christmas dinner for that matter. God knew why my mother-in-law relented this year. Sam believed she was starting to trust me. I suspected it was a trap.

I boiled the raw pumpkin, mashed in the sugar and spices, filled the crust. I had twenty minutes until the lasagna finished baking and the pie went in. Perfect. I swapped the wet clothes for the dryer then scrambled upstairs and collected laundry for a second load, stomping on the remaining dirty clothing to make the mound appear as small as possible. Next I setup a gift wrapping station in the living room. The timer dinged as I taped the second gift closed. I yanked the lasagna from the oven and threw the pie inside. I glanced at the clock. 6:19. One minute to spare. I smirked, feeling smug about my efficiency.

My domestic panic grounded me, allowing no time to worry about talking birds or faeries or other such nonsense. I glanced occasionally out the living room window, but I never found a chickadee on the sill to glare or greet me. I never found a chickadee because the chickadee did not exist. Something must have been wrong with the piece of carrot cake I had eaten. Maybe it had expired, had mold spores which induced the hallucination and made me ill enough to sleep more than two hours when I needed to attend to my responsibilities.

I set the kitchen table with mismatched dishes and fetched the lasagna from the counter. When I turned around a wolf spider the size of a small tarantula stood on Sam's dinner plate. My throat clenched. Her shiny black eyes glimmered from four feet away with all the seeming knowledge of early predators and ancient gods. I set the lasagna cautiously back onto the countertop, my sight never leaving the spider. She stood as still as stone ... then lifted a single foot, as if choosing me from a crowd of one.

I reached for the plate with my fingertips, leaning my body and face as far back as possible without toppling over. I stretched my arms in front of me as if the plate smelled of rot and death, then slipped out the back door. My skin crawled. Something about spiders felt primeval and threatening, an instinct inherited from ancestors who had whispered warnings around campfires in drafty, soot-stained caves.

The wolf spider stood motionless, her shiny eyes on me, my wide eyes on her. Her leg remained up and pointing. "Enjoy your spider life but stay away," I said, and flung the spider into a shrub twenty feet away from the backdoor. I then hurried inside and rewashed the plate, scrubbing harder than probably necessary.

I clicked on the Christmas tree lights and continued wrapping presents. At 7:30 the driveway remained empty. My brow furrowed. I set the wrapped gifts beneath the tree. The dryer buzzed. I went to swap loads and stopped mid-step. I sniffed the air. It smelled like something was—

"No!"

I yanked open the oven, coughing as a dark cloud billowed into my face. The smoke detector screamed its high pitched *ree! ree! ree! ree!* The pie was black. Charred. *Ruined.*

I growled at my stupidity and flung open the kitchen window. I had forgotten to set the damn timer. Was this the trap I had suspected from my mother-in-law? Proof I was an incapable moron, over something as simple as baking a pie? I slammed the oven door closed, my eyes watering from smoke. I was several miles from the closest grocery store in rural Appalachia without a car on the night of Christmas Eve. How the hell would I get another sugar pumpkin?

The smoke detector pierced my eardrums with its shrieking *ree! ree! ree!* I climbed onto the table to reset it, my lips pursed. I *couldn't* get another *sugar* pumpkin, but I *did* have another pie crust in the freezer and canned pumpkin in the pantry. My mother-in-law would surely taste the difference, but I preferred she mock me for my inferior baking skill than mock me for being an incompetent wife.

The can-opener whirred. By eight o'clock a new pie baked in the oven, the timer set and ticking. Sam still wasn't home. Normally he called when he was late, often from paperwork or election schemes. I scratched the back of my neck. *The station would call me if anything bad happened, right?* Of course they would. I was his wife, after all. Yet instincts nagged at me, insisting something was wrong. *What if he is hurt and no one knows?* Maybe he had rolled his truck off a hillside. Maybe a drunk driver had plowed into him and sped away. Or maybe—

[something darker than the dark]

—a paroled felon he had arrested in the past now exacted revenge.

I gnawed my lower lip. Sam insisted personal and professional lives shouldn't mingle, and unless I was raped or murdered I should never call him at work—and even then I should only call the 9-1-1 line. I needed to relax, to trust Sam to be the responsible adult I knew he was. A daddy longlegs scurried across a cobweb above the sink. I wrung my hands. I needed to be a good girl and not cause waves.

Don't make waves. Don't make waves. Don't make-—

I grabbed the living room phone and dialed Sam's cell. It transferred straight to voicemail. His office line rang four times, then greeted me with another recording. I clenched the useless phone, my insides swirling with anxiety ... and a repressed, burning anger trying to claw through the emotional storm in my gut.

I went to return the phone to the living room table. A gray spider sat inside the cradle, one leg up, pointing at me. My breath caught in my throat. What the chickadee had said during my hallucination barreled back into my head: *Trust the spiders.*

The deadbolt unlatched with a triumphant *clack* and Sam sauntered through the front door. A wave of relief washed through me as I set the phone on the coffee table.

"Sorry I'm late." Sam pecked my lips, then shrugged off his jacket and tossed it onto the couch.

"It is an absolute nightmare at the station. Bogged down with reports thanks to Thompson's idiocy."

"Sounds terrible." I grabbed Sam's jacket from the couch and hung it in the coat closet. The gray spider faced me, its front leg still up and pointing. I opened my mouth to mention the spider to Sam, then closed it. If I was hallucinating, Sam would know when he saw nothing there. If I was sane and the spider existed, then he would squish it. Schizophrenia was a terrible fate, but I assumed squishing an agent of a magical world brought worse repercussions.

Sam unbuttoned his deputy's shirt. "I thought you planned to finally clean this sty," he said, frowning at the dusty baseboards and the papers cluttering the coffee table.

"I got a late start," I said, as we both drifted toward the kitchen. "I think I'm coming down with something."

Sam glared at me from the corner of his eye. "Are you trying to get out of seeing my family for Christmas?"

"No!"

"Good. Cuz—" He saw the set table and stopped short. "You made lasagna."

"Of course. You wanted me to," I said.

"I completely forgot." Sam checked the refrigerator, making sure I had remembered the milk, and grabbed a Bud Ice. "I'm full on Wendy's, so freeze it for when we get back," he said, and cracked the can's top.

My stomach muscles clenched as if expecting a punch. "But I—"

"Did you burn it or something?" He

slurped his beer. "The whole house smells like a goddamn crematorium."

I took a deep breath and fetched the freezer bags from the pantry. "No. I burnt the pie."

Sam gagged. "*What?* Jesus Christ, Miriam! My mother entrusted you with her recipe. *The* recipe!"

"I know! I'm sorry!" I said. "I made a second, but I had only canned pumpkin, so it—"

"My mother *never* uses canned *anything*," he snapped. "It's *tradition.*"

"I'm *sorry,*" I said. "It's Christmas Eve. What was I supposed to do? All the grocery stores are closed."

"You should have known you'd screw up, *like always*, and bought another pumpkin beforehand."

I glared at him, hurt. Sam rolled his eyes. "You are too damn sensitive," he said. "You know it's *true*. How hard is it for you to understand that—" My insides cringed, retreated, hid. Sam's gibes blew through me, leaving me standing like the naked stem of a dandelion. He kept talking, but his words floated around me like a burst of seeds on the wind. *Stupid. Wrong. Think.* My anger lunged at these taunts, but I caught its tail and shoved it down into my lowest darkness. Victory awarded me with a sinking sensation in my core, as if my suppressed resentment had turned to tar and everything good in me was drowning.

I focused on the lasagna as diligently as an agent defusing a bomb. On some level I acknowledged the sauced noodles, the knife and spatula breaking the melted cheese, the crispy chunks in the corner, the smoothness under my finger as the ziplock *clicked.* Yet numbness engulfed me, deadening my nerves, deadening me. Sam prattled about his patrol, but I registered no details. My dead hands placed two bags of lasagna in the freezer. My dead eyes regarded him vaguely, as if he weren't real but an image projected onto fog.

Of course I am crazy, I thought. *What sane person functions like this?*

"Are you even listening to me?" Sam asked.

"Of course." My heart bobbed in the tar, and I knew its only chance for freedom was if that inner darkness overflowed and devoured me with it. *And then what will be left to love?*

Sam finished his beer, showered, and plopped onto the couch with the evening news and a pack of Camel cigarettes. I curled up next to him in old flannel pajamas and my penguin slippers, its stuffing still protruding from the eye-socket. I sipped on a steaming mug of apple cider, distracting myself from burnt pies and chickadees and hallucinations and white-padded rooms.

A yellow spider crept onto the couch's armrest during the first commercial break. It lifted one leg, as if pointing me out. I leapt to my feet. "I'm going to bed."

"The news isn't done yet."

"Well, as I said, I felt lousy earlier and we have a long drive tomorrow." The yellow spider stared at me, pointing. I slinked behind the couch and trailed my finger seductively across Sam's shoulders. My voice dropped. "You can join me, if you *desire.*"

"Maybe when I get tired," he said, and

shrugged off my hand. The gray spider was still in the phone cradle, and still pointing. I sensed eyes everywhere, watching me from hidden crevices in clusters of eight. And I didn't know if they were real.

The faeries aren't dead, the chickadee had told me. *They just left the area.*

I shuddered as I hurried up the stairs, feeling that the spiders were pointing to the direction they had gone.

CHAPTER SIX

Dread woke me with a jolt, my heart pounding hard enough to hurt. The nightmare faded like steam when my eyes opened, leaving me feeling exposed and vulnerable without remembering why. I hugged a pillow to my chest, waiting for my breathing to steady. Warmth hummed through the floor vents. Downstairs, the kitchen clock faintly ticked. I watched Sam's shoulder rise and fall with his shallow breathing, illuminated from the light pushing through the crack in the bathroom door. My dread grew heavier, gouging a hole in my stomach, making me lonely, depressed. Homesick in my own home.

I rolled out of bed. My fuzzy socks swished across the bedroom's floorboards. The farmhouse was creaky, drafty, and as cold as the dead hands which had built it a century ago. I used the bathroom quickly—wincing against the toilet's cold porcelain—then left the door open wider than usual. *Maybe the extra light will scare away the monsters inside me.*

I huddled back beneath the blankets, warm with Sam's body-heat. He always slept as if his plug had been pulled, the lucky duck. I watched his shoulder rise and fall, wondering if his dreams were pleasant and adventurous or as dark as mine. I rolled onto my left side. Dread swirled in my gut. Worry tapped my bones. I flipped onto my stomach, back to my left side, then my right. I sighed, frustrated, then rolled onto my back and faced the ceiling.

Hundreds of powdered eyes stared down.

Blood drained from my face; my entrails turned to juice. Moths filled the ceiling like a powdered canopy, their numbers disappearing into the shadows. They stood motionless in the bathroom light, their yellow eyes staring down at me without a speck of white paint between. *Dear God. Do they fill the entire bedroom?*

"Sam!" I squeaked. He remained still and I took a deep breath. *The moths are another hallucination. If you wake him, he will know you are crazy. And then what?*

The moths' wings stretched. Their yellow eyes widened and glared. *We know who you are,* they said in a silent language I felt in my bones. *Your secret is exposed.*

I jumped from the bed and bolted out the bedroom door.

The unmistakable slap of cobwebs smacked my face when I hit the stairs, the strands crackling in my ears. I clawed my way through the dark; cobwebs grabbed my hair, my arms, my nightshirt, my feet. It didn't end, only thickened. I screamed and screamed and screamed.

"Miriam!" Sam called. "What the hell?" I heard the confused rustle of blankets and sleepy feet padding the ground. The stairwell flooded with light. "Holy shit!"

Cobwebs filled the stairwell from floor to ceiling, so thick it was as if I stood inside a solid fog. The cottony threads had filled my mouth when I screamed, sucking up all moisture and making it impossible to spit them off my tongue. Thousands of spiders scurried through the mass like eight-legged birds migrating through a cloud. Their feet tapped my flesh as they crawled up and out of my shirt, through my hair, over my pajamas and socks and face, racing up the stairwell toward the bedroom.

I pushed through the webs and stumbled into the living room, brushing spiders off of me, my chest heaving. Spiders scurried from beneath the front door, and through cracks in the floorboards and walls that I never knew existed. I froze, wide-eyed, as hundreds stormed the stairwell.

Whack! Whack! Whack!

The slapping snapped my attention back to Sam. *Sam!* Sam was in his tighty-whities smashing spiders with a shoe. Sam *saw* the spiders. *I'm not crazy. This is really happening.*

I heard the rustle of a thousand moth-wings take flight. Sam yelled a stream of confused curses as a brown cloud swarmed through the bedroom door. Moths flooded the stairwell, tangling themselves in the webs. Spiders lunged on the fluttering horde, some spinning them with silk. Hundreds of moths pushed forward. Their bodies piled. The cobwebs began to break and fall as the moths broke through the barrier. More spiders raced from the living room, the kitchen, scurrying up the steps. I realized then that I stood in the middle of a war. And I was the objective.

I wheeled around and fled out the kitchen's back door.

It was the middle of the night, but the sky was clear and the moon a few days from full, illuminating the world in silhouettes and grays. I sprinted down the gravel garden path in our back yard, past the tree-line at the edge of the property. My fuzzy socks and pajamas were a shoddy protection from the elements, but my blood pumped fiercely and shielded me from the cold.

I stopped beside a young tree to catch my breath, feeling guilty for abandoning my husband, silly for fearing insects, and relieved Sam saw them too. *Can an army of spiders defeat an army of moths?* I wondered. The lights upstairs illuminated the house. I watched Sam's silhouette throw open the bedroom window, and a flood of moths billow out.

My heart galloped. Frantically I scanned the darkness, seeing nothing, but even worse, *feeling* nothing. Night's siren had returned, luring away my warmth, withering it in the gloom. The moon no longer seemed to shine; instead the night sky encroached on its light. My breathing didn't send puffs of mist into the air; it abandoned my body to betray me to my enemies.

In the dark crept something darker, and it was hunting. It was hunting *me.* Ice water seeped into the marrow of my bones. I pivoted on my heel, unsure where to run, unsure what to do, unsure what was *happening.*

See-me-I'm-here.

A wave of relief rushed through me. The sweet notes sung behind me, somewhere in the trees. I hurried toward the music, tripping over branches, kicking snow, acting like the least graceful prey animal to ever flee through the woods. It took all of my willpower to restrain myself from running and risk snapping an ankle. For I heard the message—*see-me-I'm-here*—and knew answering was my one hope.

I panted at the base of a hill, surrounded by the shadows of skeleton-trees, and the cold, hollow chill of winter. The warmth from my breath and body had returned, as did the familiar glow of the moon. But I had no idea where I was. The woods were silent, filled with the crisp scents of frozen leaves, icicles, cedar. I hugged myself and trembled.

The chickadee landed on my shoulder. "You are safe for now."

"You're real," I told the bird. My voice was monotone. Stating a fact.

"Yes."

My face scrunched, then I dropped to my knees and started bawling. Shock, relief, bottled emotions, and repressed beliefs bubbled out of me like searing tar. Monsters, miracles, *magic.* All became validated in that instant, proving I stood on something bigger than myself and the reality I had always known.

Fairytales had taunted my imagination throughout my childhood. They made me believe anything was possible, from talking animals to granted wishes to flying carpets and candy homes. But as I aged, those adults who had seduced my imagination with these tales ripped them away. My mother insisted they were *just stories* and berated me for clinging onto them, for allowing my beliefs to run rampant down the road of impossibilities and dreams. I nodded and agreed to appease her, then skipped through the city park searching for enchanted castles and faerie rings among the bushes, and waited for our cat to speak every midnight on Christmas Eve. I wished on every shooting star, planted coins, kissed the frogs in the creek. Magic was everywhere. I *felt* it, humming on my skin like the wings of working bees on early summer flowers.

My mother's lectures had grown heavier

with age, though. Classmates berated me as well. Already isolated for inherent differences I never understood, I openly rebuked anything fantastic ... had even accepted it after a time. But in that moment, with a house of warring moths and spiders and a talking chickadee on my shoulder, I realized fairytales weren't *just* stories. They used to be reports, essays, eyewitness accounts.

Once upon a time, fairytales were warnings.

I wasn't crazy. Magic existed. Faeries were real. Animals talked and schemed. My instincts had been correct, and my body lightened with validation.

Then dread overcame me.

That also meant monsters existed. Magic could be used for evil. Insects had dangerous intentions, and the darkness prowled for prey. Sanity meant I was in danger, and I didn't know which fate was worse.

I knelt in the snow, trembling with all the passion of an abandoned child. Branches rattled overhead in the breeze and I realized I was too far out to hear our wind chime's ding. The chickadee snuggled against my neck, preening cobwebs from my hair. My gasps soon shifted to hiccups, and the tears stopped pouring down my cheeks. Adrenaline's heat left me; winter drilled into my chest. The snow had soaked through my socks and made my feet feel like sacks of burning sand.

"Go home," the chickadee said. I wondered vaguely if it was midnight, if it was still Christmas Eve. "You are freezing and your husband will worry."

My body stiffened. Darkness stood between me and Sam's protective embrace. It felt like a cruel, nighttime trap. A shooting star streaked across the sky and I wished I *was* insane, that there were no talking animals or things darker than the darkness. *Insanity is safer.*

The chickadee sensed my unease. "No darklings will hurt you tonight," the songbird said. "The spiders made sure to send their spies in the wrong direction."

"Darklings?"

"That's the polite name for them."

"What are they?" I asked.

"They are part of the Earth's magic. The *bad* part." The chickadee casually observed the sky. "Morning will be here in a few hours and darklings hunt only at night. The spiders have everything under control for now, but more of its agents are coming. *It* is coming. You must leave town."

"Why? What does this darkling want with me?"

"That is ... complicated. What's important is you leave."

"Me and Sam are going into the city for a few days tomorrow, but—"

"That will do," the chickadee said. "Your guide will arrive with more options."

"Guide? Who else is coming?"

The chickadee scratched its head. "I'm not sure exactly. A sudden change in the ranks has caused some issues. A raven in Kansas received orders from a golden eagle from the Sierra Nevada, ordering me to fly in from Indiana to find you."

I blinked. "Wait." I stood up, my feet numb with frozen fire. "Are you saying a bunch of talking birds flew across the United States to tell you to watch me?"

"Of course not. That's ridiculous," the chickadee said. "Eagles can't talk."

I opened my mouth, then closed it. I had a thousand questions to ask, but the whole idea of black magic and traveling messenger animals seeking someone as mundane as myself seemed so absurd I had trouble deciding where to begin.

The chickadee spoke before I formulated a thought. "We will talk more tomorrow. Now hurry back to the house before Sam calls a rescue squad." The chickadee flew up into the branches. "And don't worry. I'll watch out for you."

I started back through the woods, Keith's story about the chickadees's strength replaying in my mind. Perhaps it was foolish to trust my wellbeing to a songbird, but I trudged through the woods without jumping at a single shadow. The blood had settled in my veins, killing the heat and making me shiver. The way back seemed farther than when I was in a panic, but I soon found the farmhouse. It was impossible to miss. Every light inside glowed.

"Where the hell did you go?" Sam snapped as I slipped through the backdoor.

"S-sorry," I stammered, my teeth clacking. "I-I was covered in spiders an-and freaked out. I ran outside, brushing them off me, and got turned around in the woods."

Clumps of cobweb hung from the stairwell's ceiling, but Sam had cleared away most of the mess. Other than some smashed carcasses on the walls, no spiders or moths were in sight. "What *was* all that?" I asked, pretending confusion as I peeled the soaked socks off my feet. I never believed the farmhouse's floorboards would feel warm against my skin in December.

"A goddamn infestation." Sam rubbed his forehead and groaned. "I managed to scare the swarm away, so it will probably leave us alone for tonight. Let's go back to bed. You can finish cleaning the mess in the morning."

As we climbed the staircase I noticed the scores of smashed spiders—their blood smeared across the wall's paint, their bodies mashed into the crannies of the horsehair plaster. My heart sank as I realized it wasn't just a mess. It was a deserted battlefield, stained with blood for a cause I didn't understand, yet was somehow its catalyst. The steps creaked beneath my weight, and my heart grew heavy with guilt. I was passing the corpses of my murdered heroes.

I changed into dry pajamas and crawled into bed with Sam, waiting for his breathing to deepen, wondering about the future and chewing on my lip. Sam would be at my side for the next three days braving family obligations, but what about afterwards? Would my husband prove to be my knight in shining armor and stand against the supernatural if needed? If the darkling lunged, would he fight or faint or flee? He held his ground against moths and arachnids, but could he stand against black magic? Was my husband as brave as a spider?

Sam started snoring. I crept downstairs and fetched paper towels and a spray bottle of cleaner from the kitchen cupboards. By the light of the upstairs bathroom I removed the dead spiders from the floors and walls. I wrapped each body in its own strip of paper towel—the only palls I had to offer—and thanked each one for their sacrifice.

Thanked each one for my life.

CHAPTER SEVEN

"Will ya *hurry up*?" Sam said, our luggage slung over one of his shoulders, a gift-filled Hefty bag clenched in his fist. The boxwoods beneath my in-laws' front window were lined with wooden candy canes and strung with colorful lights, their bulbs dark in the daylight. Two blowup snowmen grinned and swayed on the grass, freshly dusted with snow. "Dinner was supposed to start at two o'clock."

"Isn't that technically still lunch?"

"Don't be a smart ass, Miriam."

I shut the truck door with my hip, clenching my scandalous canned pumpkin pie with both hands. I glanced both ways before leaving the truck, as if I was readying to cross rush hour traffic. Vehicles didn't zip along the suburban sidewalk, of course. Or, more importantly, darklings. (At least I didn't *think* there were any darklings here, since I hadn't the slightest idea what one looked like.) I scurried up the front walkway to catch up to Sam. Even in the daylight I felt shadows stalking me, waiting behind corners, creeping along my skin. The chickadee had said darklings hunted only at night, but it didn't specify if they *could* or *would.* Nocturnal predators hunted during the day if starving. How long until a ravenous darkling tracked me to the doorstep to tear the flesh off my bones? Instincts screamed for me to flee, but I couldn't abandon my husband without a word or trace. Nor could I tell Sam something evil hunted me in the dark —he would insist I was insane. *But what if Sam* sees *the darkling, meets it face to face?* I wondered. *Surely he will stand with me and fight and—*

"Watch it!" Sam caught my forearm as I stumbled over an uneven paver. The pie leapt into the air and landed precariously on my fingertips.

"It's a damn miracle you've lived this long with your clumsiness," Sam grumbled, hoisting me to my feet. I clenched the pie dish, imaginary shadows nipping at my heels.

"Good thing you're here to protect me, huh?" I said, shamelessly testing his loyalty.

Sam snorted, amused. "Someone's gotta."

Plus one, I thought, and smiled slightly.

"Merry Christmas!" Sam hollered as he flung open the front door. Cheers and dog barks trumpeted from the rear of the house. The home's warmth embraced us like a hug, swelling my heart with the scents of roasted ham and peppermint, apple stuffing and pine. Every year my mother-in-law's decorations made my heart glow. Frosted green garland spiraled around the banister, Santa figurines populated the shelves, velvet bows dressed every doorway, and crystal snowflakes dangled from the ceiling, reflecting beads of light from the Christmas tree's twinkling glow. Her decorations reminded me of every Christmas I never had in my childhood, with the shrieking mother, the empty liquor bottles, the cat piss rotting in the carpet. I had abandoned that life in search of a place where I was wanted and belonged, a place where I was allowed to be *happy.* At the tail of each year I sensed my quest had finally ended. I felt home seep from the spacing between my in-laws' glossy floorboards, and float along Elvis's drawl as he sang Silver

Bells. The spiraling garland seemed to whisper everything in the past was gone, buried, forgotten, and promised it was time to start anew.

"You made it!" Sam's mother called from the kitchen. My muscles tensed. I remembered these decorations were temporary, the aromas a trick. These twinkling Christmas lights were like those of an anglerfish, luring prey in a deep sea abyss. *The comfort here is not meant for you,* I reminded myself, and started the dance around the angler's jaws as Sam's mother, Charlene, waddled into the foyer.

"We almost started dinner without you." She hugged Sam as if he had just returned from war, the sleigh bells hanging off her sweatshirt jingling.

"Sorry, mama. I left a message on Rich's voicemail. I got called into the station for an hour this morning."

A Lhasa apso circled my legs like a beige mop, toenails clicking excitedly on the tile. "Hi, Ginger! I'm excited to see you too!" I said, and knelt to scratch her head.

Sam's mother cast me a strained smile. She reminded me of a gnome—short and squinty and most likely came from a hole in the ground. "Hello, Miriam."

I forced a smile and a "hello" in return. I had been dreading this visit since ... well ... last Christmas. But what better place to test Sam's protectiveness than in an angler's hunting ground?

"I'm so happy you made it," she said, her words meant just for Sam. She smirked. "Has your mother spoken with you yet, Miriam?"

"No." *Not since she kicked me out on my eighteenth birthday and I moved in with your son, as you already know,* I didn't say.

"How does a mother ignore her own *child?* Especially on *Christmas?*" Charlene said with a melodramatic sigh. I released a slow breath, knowing what she *meant* was: *What makes you think you're good enough for my son when even your mother hates you?* I looked to my knight in shining armor and watched him say nothing.

I scowled and drowned my annoyance in my inner tar. *Minus one.*

"Such a shame *you* can't be closer to *your* family," Charlene said to Sam. "You really must move closer."

"Sorry, mama," Sam said, dropping our bag of gifts and belongings at the bottom of the stairs. "I finally have a shot for Sheriff next election."

Charlene sighed loudly. I resisted the urge to roll my eyes, reminding myself her guilt trips were fruitless. Everyone knew Sam dreamed of being Sheriff since toddlerhood. He wanted nothing more. My brow furrowed as I scratched Ginger's rear, her back foot thumping. *But does that mean Sam wants it more than his marriage, too?*

"Is that my brother?" Sam's younger brother, Rich, hollered from the dining room, his voice as large as his barrel-chest. "Tell him to hurry up! I'm freakin' *starving!*"

We entered the dining room and were greeted with a jumble of Merry Christmases, hellos, and tardiness jibes. We seated ourselves at a table crammed with roasted ham, stuffing, creamed corn, green bean casserole, cranberries, mashed potatoes and gravy, sweet rolls, egg nog, sparkling cider. Sam's scarecrow of a father sat at the head of the table, quiet and brooding as always, eyeing the ham like a mongrel. Rich, and Rich's very pregnant wife, Cathy, sat to his left. Their chubby four year old daughter, Haley, squirmed in her chair between them, begging to turn the television back on, as if the blank screen was somehow suffocating the Grinch. I balanced my pumpkin pie on the edge of the table, its pan hanging halfway off the corner.

Sam's father grumbled about China made materials as he sliced the ham with an electric knife, then sat and stuffed his face with meat. Eggnog and cider poured into glasses. Utensils clinked against plates, food passed around the table. Discussions about work and politics and neighborhood gossip drifted from everyone's lips, but I was too focused on my meal to pay any attention. I sat stiff, as if my limbs were wood, and concentrated on every jab of my fork, every cut of meat, every lift of my glass, each chew, trying to act perfect and invisible, afraid any sudden movement would provoke the anglerfish into striking.

How do they see me? I wondered. Quiet? Rude? Aloof? I felt guilty for avoiding conversation, and hated my inability to be outgoing and joyful despite Charlene's quips and glares. *Her hatred of you should not matter,* I told myself. Yet it *did* matter, and I was too weak to fake any different. Too many times I had been bitten for reaching out during the last thirteen years. Too long I had been reminded I was tolerated in this family, not accepted.

A daddy longlegs scurried between the

wall and ceiling and disappeared behind the valance. Rich accidentally caught my eye from across the table and gave me a strained smile, his lips pressed tight. *I don't know what to say to you, but I don't want to appear rude, either,* his strained smile said. I returned the pressed smile, then poked a green bean with my fork.

Near the end of dinner I grabbed a roll from the basket and slathered on a lump of butter. Sam's mother cast her stare on me. I stiffened. *Did I grab the roll too fast?*

"I'm glad you remembered to make the pie," Charlene said, in a tone suggesting otherwise. My insides clenched. "It looks ... nice."

"I bet it tastes fantastic, too," Sam said. "She slaved most of last night on it." He winked at me as he spooned mashed potatoes into his mouth.

I smiled and bit my roll. *Plus one.* Some tension melted off my neck. *Why am I fretting? Of course my husband will stick with me if the darkling attacks.* Vying for Sheriff wasn't just a career move; it was a natural drive. Protectiveness stirred his blood, so why not do whatever was necessary to save his own wife?

How special you think you are, my mother mocked inside my head. *You're not the only thing in this world he loves, you know.*

My brow furrowed. This was true. Sam loved his work, his friends, his family, his truck, himself. Of course, none of those things had ever been threatened, either. But maybe ... *maybe ...* his family was an asset. If the darkling attacked during our visit, then Sam had more reasons to fight and defend. Safety in numbers, plus a home field advantage, had their benefits. *And if the darkling manages to take out my mother-in-law in the process?* I smirked as I daydreamed about Charlene disappearing forever into the darkness, then slipped Ginger a piece of ham beneath the table.

The chickadee flitted onto the windowsill and shook its head, as if answering my thoughts about staying to fight. *Is the guide out there, too?* I wondered, and quickly looked away.

"Getting excited?" I asked Cathy, addressing her stomach with my eyes.

"More nervous than anything else." She was a sandy-haired woman, like Sam's mother, with a long torso and a freckled moon-face. "I slept hardly a wink with Haley. I can't imagine how I'll manage *twins*."

"That's what grandmas are for," Charlene said proudly, slicing pieces of pumpkin pie for everyone. "Anyhow, twins are a blessing in this family." She cast me a frosty glare. "How else will I get any grandchildren?"

Maybe if your son was half as interested in sex as he is in his career, I didn't say.

"Have you two thought about checking your fertility?" Cathy asked. Sam's father grumbled about medical costs and insurance scams and illegal immigration. She ignored him and continued: "My friend's husband had a low sperm count, but the doctors fixed it and they had a baby boy thirteen months later."

"Hmph!" Charlene said. "No need to waste your money on tests, Sam. Thatchers are breeders. Always have been."

Rich guffawed and patted his wife's stomach. "Damn straight!"

Charlene lifted an eyebrow at me. "It's obvious where the issue lies."

Sam sighed. "Mama ... "

Charlene shrugged, passing small plates with pie pieces around the table. "I'm *just saying*, that's the problem with not knowing a child's father. No way to tell how many bad genes got through."

I turned to Sam, my mouth gaping. *Say something!* I tried to scream at him with my mind. *Defend and protect me!*

"If it isn't meant to be, it isn't meant to be." Sam yawned. "God, we had such a rough night. Strangest thing. We got infested." He chuckled. "You should have seen Miriam, screaming like it was the end of the world."

My lips pressed tight. Wind ruffled the chickadee's feathers on the sill.

Charlene lowered her fork. "Infested? Infested with what?"

"Spiders and moths," Sam said. "The swarm was *massive*. Unnatural. I smashed spiders and moths nonstop for at *least* an hour."

More like ten minutes, tops, I thought, and slipped Ginger more ham. I wondered if Sam emphasized the swarm because, on some level, he had sensed its supernatural element. Or maybe he was just boosting his own importance.

"That's because of bad housekeeping," Charlene said. "Learn how to keep a proper home and the problem will go away." She smirked at me. "I will give you tips if you need them, Miriam."

My blood simmered. I stalled for Sam to

defend me. When he remained silent I smiled politely and said: "I'm happy to hear them."

Charlene made a *mmmmph* sound—her mixture of acknowledging what I said while still dismissing me—and bit a piece of pie. She coughed lightly, swallowed with a wince, and set her fork on the table. "Well, *this* is an interesting take on our family's recipe."

I took a bite and my mouth puckered. Rich gagged and spat into his napkin. The bells on Charlene's sweatshirt jingled as she puffed her chest out triumphantly, behaving as if she had won a battle I never knew was declared. "Though, next time, *Miriam*, I'd suggest remembering to add the sugar."

CHAPTER EIGHT

The wrapping paper had been torn and tossed, and the tree lights twinkled in the corner. Haley pressed her nose against the television as Rudolph proved his worth to the North Pole. The rest of the family lounged around the living room, gabbing relentlessly for hours. I yawned on the couch, my head on Sam's shoulder as he babbled about college football with Rich and his father, and finished another Bud Ice. A chickadee occasionally darted past the window.

Charlene waddled in from the kitchen with an eggnog, her sweatshirt bells jingling, and plopped back into the recliner. "Christmas feels so strange without pie," she sighed for the fifth time since dinner. She would most likely continue for the next twenty years.

I gritted my teeth and pretended not to hear as I ripped the itchy care-tag off my new pajamas. They were as red as a throbbing headache, with obnoxious cartoon polar bears skiing down the stiff flannel. I despised them, but I knew to never slight a gift from Sam's parents, unless I wanted to be gibed to my grave. Besides, Sam's present had more than made up for it. A shiny silver bracelet encircled my wrist, a rose etched into the silver heart dangling off the chain. A stark contrast against the flannel with its loose threads and faint smell of chemicals. *It's not Tiffany's, but it still cost a whole paycheck*, he had said as he handed me the black velvet box. I beamed, loving his effort as much as his gift, for I knew that effort was the same he would use to protect me when the darkling showed.

"Wow! It's almost ten o'clock," Cathy said, struggling to push herself up from the couch. "We better go to bed, Haley. We have a big, big day tomorrow!"

"I don't wanna go to bed," Haley whined.

"Your nana will join you shortly, sweetie," Charlene said. "My blood sugar is just ... it's just so low."

I rolled my eyes and scratched beneath my waistband.

Haley slapped the carpet with her hands. "Noooo. I don't *wanna.*"

"Aw, duckling," Cathy soothed. "You get *another* Christmas with Grandma Ingrid tomorrow. Won't that be *fun?*"

Cathy clicked off the television and Haley shrieked like an air-raid siren. "Noooo! I hate Grandma Ingrid!"

I clenched my teeth, wanting to scream with her. *Grandma Ingrid* was actually Sam's grandmother, Charlene's mother. Every year the whole family took the three hour drive into West Virginia to visit her, but because of her Alzheimer's she never remembered. Last year she smeared Charlene's brownies across the wall and kept trying to slap me, insisting I was Margery, her late husband's mistress back in the sixties. The nursing home had cut our visit short and Charlene refused to speak to me for the remainder of our trip. It was the best Christmas I ever had.

Rich threw Haley over his shoulder and headed for the stairs. "No! No! No! No! *AAAAAH!*" she shrieked, pounding her fists on his back.

"Are we taking separate cars this year?" I asked Sam.

"Don't be ridiculous," Charlene snapped. "We will all squeeze into Rich's minivan."

"And we will listen to your new Wiggles sing-along CD the whole way there," Cathy said as she followed her husband and daughter upstairs. "Won't that be *fun*, duckling?"

"Nooooooo!"

I smiled wanly. "Sounds greeeat."

Haley cried herself to exhaustion forty-five minutes later, and soon after everyone else crawled off to bed. Sam clicked off the light and bellyflopped onto the guest mattress. I laid beside him, staring wide-eyed at the ceiling, fidgeting with a button on my new pajamas.

"Sam?"

"Mmwha?" he groaned into the pillow.

"If ... If I was ever in trouble and had to leave town fast, would you come with me?"

He snorted. "You a fugitive and never told me?"

I smiled in the dark. "No. But what if some bad guys try to kidnap me? Will you follow me? Fight if needed?"

"Of course. No one takes my girl." He yawned. "Now go to sleep."

I stared at the ceiling long after Sam started snoring, keeping my ears tuned to beyond the door, listening for creaking floorboards, latching bathroom knobs, water filling glasses. When I was positive the house was asleep I stuffed my feet into the wool socks

Rich and Cathy had bought me for Christmas, and crept downstairs.

The Christmas tree illuminated the living room in a soft, white glow, as if the branches were made of moonlight. I prepared a mug of cocoa, cracked open the curtains, and curled up on the couch, grateful for the solitude. The overhead vent purred and poured out warmth, protecting the house from the thin blanket of snow on the world. I absentmindedly rotated my new bracelet around my wrist as I gazed out the window. Outside appeared serene, a deception deeper than the garland's promise of comfort and home. I now knew the night was alive and plotting, conjuring strategies in its shadows. Hidden strangers vied to reach me, each with different wants, ideas, schemes. I chuckled at the silliness of it all. *Me.* A nobody girl in a nowhere town with a future promised to be as dull as my past.

I sipped my cocoa. *Well, why* shouldn't *a nobody like me have an adventure?* I wondered. *Even pawns can checkmate when played in the right hands.* I set the mug on the coffee table and stretched, knowing these thoughts were pointless. I would have no adventure, unless my husband was a part of it. I had said my vows to him, not to any talking bird or *guide*, whoever they might be. I chuckled, bitterly. All my life I had sought attention and acceptance, and now that it was coming I wanted it to go away.

The chickadee fluttered onto the windowsill and pecked the glass. *Tink!* I opened the backdoor and it flew onto my shoulder with a joyful *chirrup*. *Did the guide come too?* I wondered. I scanned the backyard, but found only patio furniture and shadows.

"Merry Christmas," I whispered, locking

the door. "Want some leftovers?"

The chickadee nodded and danced on my shoulder. I let the bird choose from the Tupperware in the refrigerator, then prepared it a saucer of cranberry sauce, stuffing, and green bean casserole, and set it on the kitchen counter.

I sat on a barstool as the chickadee pecked a cranberry. "I feel terrible I didn't get you a Christmas present," I said.

The chickadee made a high pitched *tee! tee! tee!* and I realized it was chuckling. "The food makes a wonderful present. I can't get this foraging in the woods." It tore off a strip of green bean and inhaled it in three swallows. "I have some good news," it said. "I learned that your guide will arrive tomorrow or early the next day."

I clicked my fingernails together. "Yeah, about that," I said. "I've decided not to meet them."

The chickadee peered up at me, cranberry sauce glinting on its beak. "You *have* to meet them! Only they can help you."

"I have a husband, you know," I said. "One who wouldn't appreciate a stranger sniffing about."

"He'd appreciate them a lot more than a darkling, I'm sure," the chickadee said, sharply.

I shook my head. "Sam is a cop; defending people is in his blood. He'll stand with me against anything. *Including* darklings."

"This isn't a common criminal, Miriam. Sam has never fought anything supernatural."

"He fought the moths and spiders," I retorted.

The chickadee snorted. "You can't stop a

darkling with a shoe. Or a gun for that matter."

"We can try."

The chickadee exhaled with frustration. "Will you at least hear me out?"

"It won't matter what you or some *guide* says. I'm staying with my husband."

The chickadee stood on the counter, glaring at me. Water dripped from the kitchen faucet with a dull *plink.* I crossed my arms defiantly over my chest. Sam's iPhone buzzed in his coat pocket on the neighboring barstool, making me jump nearly out of my skin. I rolled my eyes, embarrassed. The chickadee kept glaring up at me, unflinching. I pressed my lips tight, then tossed up my hands. "Okay, *fine.* Who is this mysterious guide and why is it so friggin' important I meet them?"

The chickadee pecked and swallowed a piece of cranberry. "They're a faerie. Think of them like a consultant of sorts."

"A *faerie?*" I snorted. "You mean like Tinkerbell, with gossamer wings and glittery dust and pom pom shoes?"

The chickadee chuckled. *Tee! Tee! Tee!* "Not exactly. Although, to be honest, I'm unsure *who* is coming. Adena passed away unexpectedly and someone new from the border sentry has been elected to take her place." The chickadee shrugged its wings. "Regardless, all they want is to give you information and options. What you do with it is your choice. And Sam will never need to be the wiser."

I lifted an eyebrow. "What kind of information?"

"That's not my place to say."

I glowered. "Why so—" Sam's iPhone buzzed. "Gah! Who friggin' calls at this time of night?" I fished the phone from the coat pocket. "Why so cryptic?" I asked the chickadee, unlocking the phone's screen. "Are the darklings some—?"

My mother's voice crowed delightedly inside my head—*I told you! I told you, I tooold youuu!*—and my heart landed in my stomach with a nauseating thump, as a stupid text message tore my life into shreds.

CHAPTER NINE

"Miriam? Are you okay?"

I stared at the phone, my mouth open, unable to find my voice.

"Miriam?" The chickadee flew onto my shoulder. "What's—? Oh!"

On Sam's iPhone was a closeup of a man's bare erection. The accompanying text read: *I already unwrapped your Xmas present. Cum & get it. ;)*

My insides were as cold and empty as an arctic canyon, echoing repressed fears, doubts, insecurities. The chickadee said something, which I ignored easily through my heart pounding in my ears. I tittered nervously and shook my head. "It's a wrong number! How embarrassing!"

Then, despite my brain and emotions screaming in unison to place the phone back in the pocket, back to where Sam and I could laugh about the silly mishap in the morning, back to where everything could be fixed, back to where my comfortable world would stay comfortably the same, my thumb scanned the conversation and revealed the text that had arrived a moment before: *Is the stupid bitch asleep yet Sammy love? I miss u.*

My chest hitched, and hitched, and hitched. I couldn't breathe. The air was gone. My *life* was gone. I sank into the stool, nerves buzzing behind my eyes. Tears scratched for release, but logic—

[denial]

—forbade them to fall, insisting they were stupid, mistaken, missing the obvious explanation.

"There must be an explanation," I whispered. My mouth tasted like cotton and my chest felt hollow, as if an undertaker had dug a grave beneath my heart to bury my marriage. The iPhone buzzed and flashed. I nearly vomited from panic. *Don't look! This is still fixable. It is all a misunderstanding. Perhaps an obsessed stalker Sam rejected, unwilling to tell you in fear of your overreaction. Don't look at the screen you stupid girl. Don't you* dare *look!*

I looked at the screen. A naked man had photographed himself in a mirror, leaning against a headboard to expose his athletic body. *Is he even old enough to drink?* I wondered, numbly. His right hand held the camera; his left hand stroked his genitals. Through the screen his smooth face leered with come-fuck-me eyes, and in that instant I realized looks *could* kill. They killed relationships, lives, futures, dreams.

"This is a mistake. Has to be a—" My face scrunched up. Water dripped from the kitchen faucet with a dull *plink.* I clenched the iPhone to my chest and ran upstairs on my tiptoes, wanting to sprint and cry and shout, but too mortified I might wake the family. My mother-in-law was right. I was unworthy of Sam's heart. I wasn't even what he *desired.* I didn't belong with him or this family. I didn't belong anywhere.

"Wait!" the chickadee pleaded from my shoulder. It flew onto the outside doorjamb as I stormed into the guest-room. I flicked on the lights and locked the door. Sam was asleep, one arm hanging off the bed. My dread and confusion flared into rage. How *dare* he lay there, peaceful and content. Ha! I'm sure he *was* content.

Did he dream of his young lover? Dream of—My insides tightened as I imagined their naked bodies pressed together, the young man's thighs squeezing Sam's head as he—

"Sam!" I hissed, marching to him. He lay motionless. I shoved his shoulder. *"Sam!"*

Sam blinked in the light. "Huh? Wha? Jesus Christ, Miriam. What time is it?"

Time for you to come clean and pack your bags you two-timing asshole! Time for you to watch my ass leave you forever! Time for you to go to hell!

All these comments raced through my head, but my tongue betrayed me. I shoved the naked photo in his face and asked only: "Why?"

He stared at the photo, stone-faced. I started to tremble. My organs felt as if they would shake apart from the anxiety buzzing inside me. I expected him to deny it, or to flip out that I had gone through his personal belongings, or to act confused about why I showed him porn, or to laugh at my stupidity as he always did. But he just stared at the phone, emotionless, as if he knew this was inevitable. As if he had pulled a paper tab at the beginning of the affair and had been merely dallying until his number was called. He showed no denial. No emotion. No *anything*. And that was the worst. Destroying our relationship, destroying *me*, meant nothing to him.

"Why?" I repeated. My voice was hoarse. Outside, a train whistle howled.

"Must we discuss this *now?*" he groaned, as if I had woke him up to discuss paint swatches for the kitchen.

Tears welled in my eyes. "Do you think

I'm unattractive? Do you not *want* me anymore?"

He flopped back onto the pillow. "I don't know."

"How can you not know?"

"Dammit, woman! Keep your voice down! People are sleeping."

"How could you *do* this?"

"We'll discuss this after we leave."

I gasped. He wanted me to pretend everything was okay for the next *two days*? He might as well have told me to wait for him in an iron maiden. "But —"

"Not *now,* Miriam," he said, then rolled his back to me.

"Sam?" I said. *"Sam!"*

He lay there motionless and refused to answer.

Saltwater trickled down the back of my throat. I thought my skull would crack from the pressure building inside my head. I wanted to rant and scream, to tear the blankets off his body and smash the clock beside the bed. I wanted him to face me, to tell me the truth no matter how ugly it was, to fight and scratch for the last piece of self respect I had, and demand the respect I knew I deserved. I didn't want to make waves; I wanted to make tsunamis. I wanted to roll over his world with all the pain and destruction he rolled over mine. I wanted him to drown in the wreckage he had caused.

Instead I slammed his iPhone onto the nightstand and stormed out of the guest room, fighting back a swell of tears.

CHAPTER TEN

I raced down the stairs two at a time. The chickadee flew after me and landed on the railing's garland as I grabbed my overcoat from the hall closet.

"Miriam—"

"Leave me alone," I said, my voice thick and wet.

"I swore to watch after you," the chickadee said.

"I don't *care!*" I threw the overcoat over my pajamas and stuffed my feet into my hiking boots, the wool socks thick inside. "I don't care about darklings or faeries or *any of it.* I just want this night to not exist." I tugged my olive knitted cap over my ears. The chickadee latched onto my shoulder as I stormed out the front door.

Entering the night felt like entering a cavern—empty and open, dark and lonely. I snuffled back a sob, gritting my teeth to prevent my grief from breaking the silence. I headed toward the train tracks at the end of the street, beelining to nowhere. Most of the houses were equipped with motion sensors. The lights sprung alive as I passed, as if the whole neighborhood was pointing and laughing, exposing me for the undesirable loser I was.

Road salt crunched beneath my boots as I veered right to parallel the tracks. Three spotlights broke the darkness in the distance, the triangular eye of a freight train watching the world.

"I don't know what to say," the chickadee said, breaking our silence.

I snorted. "Neither does Sam. But why *should* he say anything to me, right? I'm just a stupid bitch."

"Stop justifying him," the chickadee snapped. "You deserve better."

I rolled my eyes and wiped my nose on my sleeve, the wool rough against my chapped skin. "I've never felt as if I belonged anywhere, but I believed Sam was the exception. That he liked *me,* you know?" A tear rolled down my cheek. I rubbed my eyes and shook my head. "Maybe he still does. Maybe he is experimenting. Maybe I can fix this and—"

The chickadee pecked my earlobe. "Ow!" I batted it off my shoulder. It flew back and pecked my temple. "Ow! Stop!" I waved my arms, retreating. "Why are you pecking me?"

The bird buzzed my face, nipping my cheek. "Why are you flinching?"

"Because you're hurting me!"

The chickadee landed on my hat and glared down at me, its beady eye glinting in the lights of the train. "Yet you refuse to back away from the man hurting your heart."

"That's different. I can't just *leave* Sam."

"Why not?"

"Because! I have no money, no car, no one to go to, no—"

"Everything you need is inside yourself," the chickadee said.

I snorted. "Obviously you don't know me."

"Maybe I know you better than you know

yourself."

"Doubt it," I grumbled. The chickadee flitted onto my shoulder. We walked in silence for two blocks, yet I had never heard so much racket. My brain screamed *Sam is having an affair with a man! Oh my God! Sam is having an affair with a man!* and refused to shut up. Ahead, the train whistle howled. The engine groaned a hoarse *ka-chunk … ka-chunk … ka-chunk*. How people slept in the surrounding houses was beyond my understanding. Train whistles always screamed outside their windows, and wheels always clacked. The triple headlamp crept toward us, then passed. I curled my shoulders, heading in the opposite direction. A minute passed, and still the freight train trudged beside me. I numbly considered throwing myself onto the tracks.

The chickadee started lecturing about personal worth and self-respect but I ignored it. (Amazing how fast the novelty of a talking songbird wore off when it spoke truths I was afraid to hear.) Instead I focused on the train to silence the *Sam is having an affair with a man!* screams inside my head. I wondered where the train was bound for, what lifestyle the engineer left behind, what scenery awaited him, what mysteries the headlamps would reveal.

You do not belong here.

I froze mid-step. The chickadee lurched against my neck.

"What's wrong?" the chickadee asked.

I watched the graffitied cars trail past us, a shadowy parade of possibility and escape. The inner voice which always insisted I didn't belong screamed louder than my despair, and I finally interpreted the message it had been struggling to deliver all my life.

You do not belong here, Miriam. Run away. Run away and never look back.

I was wrong. Had always been wrong. The inner voice insisted I was an outsider, but it had never been an insult. It was an admission, a warning. The opening lines of my own personal fairytale. I didn't belong here. But that didn't mean I didn't belong *anywhere.* I needed to find the right place. *My* place. And maybe the train headed in the right direction.

A boxcar approached, moonlight pushing through its open center. In that instant I realized I didn't want to fix my relationship with Sam. I didn't want to save the life I had created of others expectations. I didn't want to save *any* of it. The only thing worth saving was myself.

Run away, Miriam.

The open boxcar trudged past. My heart raced toward it without me.

Dammit, Miriam. Run!

I sprinted for the boxcar. The chickadee tweeted and tumbled off my shoulder. The train trundled at the speed of a brisk walk and I gained quickly, boots crackling as they pounded the snow and gravel. Porch lights and a crisp, night sky greeted me from the other side of the boxcar's open doors. The entrance came to my chest. The chickadee zipped above my head, screeching something unintelligible against the train's clacking. I grabbed the floor with both hands, keeping pace with the train, then hoisted my body and nearly killed myself.

I had imagined it would be like hoisting myself out of a swimming pool, forgetting to consider the lack of buoyancy. I hung off the box car, stomach pressed against the door's track, my stiff arms too weak to pull myself inside. I rocked my legs to seesaw onto the floor. My elbows buckled. I clenched the door's track and two fingernails snapped back in a flash of white pain. My heels dragged in the gravel. Streetlights glinted off the massive steel wheel chomping toward my right foot. I pumped my knees like pistons, taking large sideway steps like an awkward puppet. I regained my pace and hoisted myself, this time swinging my legs over my butt and dragging myself across the floorboards like a scorpion, stomach muscles strained and burning. I collapsed against the floor, panting, and suckling fingertips tasting of blood and grime. The train's rattling chattered my teeth against the tender flesh.

I stood and stumbled to the doorway, and clenched the freezing metal frame. Wind bit the sweat on my brow. Passing porch lights glinted off the clanging wheels beneath me. If I had let go of the train when I had fallen, the wheel would have sucked me onto the tracks and ripped off my leg.

But the panic about almost becoming an amputee vanished as I whizzed through the sleeping neighborhood. I giggled nervously, then grinned and pumped my fists into the air. "*Whooohooo!*" Hopping a train would label me as irrational or impulsive or stupid or insane. But no one could ever judge me as the meek, predictable wife again. A sharp laugh escaped me. No matter the outcome of my actions, I had at least broken that stigma forever.

The chickadee zipped into the boxcar and landed on my shoulder. "I did it!" I said, clapping my hands. "I hopped a train! *I* hopped a *train!*"

"Wonderful," the chickadee grumbled. "Did you consider how you'd hop *off?*"

"No. I just did it. It was instinct."

"It was *impulse*, not instinct," the chickadee snapped. "Mixing those up will kill you."

"*You* urged me to leave," I said.

"I meant with your *guide*," the chickadee said. My eyebrows pinched. In all the drama I had forgotten that option. "They are coming to Ohio to meet you. At least they *were*. I have no idea how they will find you in ... well ... wherever you end up."

I peered down. The dark, rolling ground was impossible to discern. *Are we still passing gravel? Dirt? Pavement? Weeds?* The train's trundle seemed faster from this angle and more menacing as well. The wheels growled their metallic *ka-chunk-ka-chunk-ka-chunk*, eager to snatch me if I jumped and landed an inch in the wrong direction. I rubbed my shin on the back of my calf and shuddered.

"We won't go far," I said, reassuring myself more than reassuring the chickadee. "The train's moving slow. It's probably pulling into its destination now."

I clenched the doorframe and waited to jump to still ground. And waited. And waited. The wind grew stronger, baying in my ears. I buttoned the front of my overcoat and nestled my head into the collar. Winter numbed my nose and ears. Shrill, metallic screeches made my fillings hum and swell. The *ka-chunk-ka-chunk-ka-chunk* quickened into a *chunk-chunk-chunk*. My fingers numbed against the door's metal. Up ahead the whistle howled, then the clanging of train-crossing bells.

The chickadee pressed against my neck to hide from the wind. “The train is *not* slowing, Miriam.”

The boxcar rocked and rattled. The red crossing lights throbbed off the walls, then disappeared. Clanging, screeching, metal wheels on metal tracks, rattling metal walls. My ears rung, the racket near deafening. I crouched in an empty corner, shoving my hands in my armpits, and tucked my chin to my chest. Wind swirled inside the boxcar, throwing the floor’s dirt and grime into a windstorm. The chickadee hid inside the back of my collar as my hair whipped my bare cheeks. The train traveled at a clip now. My skin broke out in goosebumps beneath my coat’s sleeves. I coughed and sneezed and shielded my eyes as the filth pounded my face like needles.

I staggered to the boxcar’s sliding door, hacking. The train’s jostling dropped me twice to my knees before I reached the swing-handle on the outside edge of the door. I yanked on it—freezing metal burning my hands—and struggled to slide the door closed with a triumphant *clack.* The windstorm lessened. I leaned against the door, panting, grateful for a shield from the cold. Until I realized there was no inside latch. I pushed on the door but it refused to slide. The open door across from me wobbled and clanged in its track. My muscles tensed. One violent bump would close it, trapping me inside without food or water, and no knowledge of when I’d be found.

In the far corner were three pallets, stacked with plastic, woven bags—the boxcar’s sole freight. I tore open the cellophane wrapping and heaved a fifty-pound bag off the top, unable to read the contents in the dark. I dragged it to the far end of the open door. The jostling train slammed me into the doorframe. My foot slipped outside; the wind flapped my pajama pants against my leg; my cranberry coattails flailed. I clenched the doorframe until my heart steadied, then carefully pushed the bag's end onto the door's track. Fifty-pounds was too light to weigh down my paranoia, however. I heaved another bag onto the first one, forming a T. Then decided to add another. I slid the door to the stacked bags, closing off most of the wind, and propping it open to prevent accidental entrapment.

I sunk to the floor in the corner, my back against the freight. The train jumped and rattled; the floorboards jarred my rear and spine. I tried kneeling to protect myself from bruising, but the position made my knees ache. I climbed on top of the freight and laid on my stomach, protecting my face with my arms. The relief was minimal.

My fingertips throbbed. I gnawed at the broken nails, biting them to the quicks, and hoped the cargo I laid on wasn't toxic. The chickadee nestled against my nape. Soon the adrenaline rush which had numbed my anguish over Sam faded. My thoughts slunk right back to him like a mongrel eager to lick the fingers of the hand who beat it. When did he meet his lover, I wondered? Where did he meet him? How often? Was it ever in our bed? My imagination conjured up movie-quality images, which turned my entrails into water. I almost smelled the lingering cigarette smoke, the salty musk of sex, Sam's cool deodorant. Sheets on the floor, my husband on his back with his eyes rolled back, his lover's tongue wetting his—

I gritted my teeth and shoved the thoughts aside.

"How far do freight trains travel?" I asked the chickadee.

"What?"

"How far do freight trains travel?" I shouted.

"Depends on the train," the chickadee shouted in my ear. "We might be heading to Canada for all I know."

Canada? And me without a passport. I swallowed hard, and bit off the rest of my nails.

CHAPTER ELEVEN

Hours passed. I did not sleep. The train ride was freezing and jarring and miserable. As a child I had often daydreamed about hopping trains, imagining myself as an adventurous explorer in search of new wonders. Romanticized notions, I now realized. I cowered on the freight like a scared runaway, and the only thing I wondered was if it would be dehydration, starvation, exposure, or the train itself that killed me.

Gray sunlight pushed through the gap in the boxcar door, bringing no warmth. The oxidation stains on the locked door resembled melting faces, their eyes oozing, with mouths stretched and screaming. I crouched on the bags propping open the door, watching a world revealed to few. No roads. No houses. Just miles of snow covered fields, a blue haze of hills in the distance, a snaking train racing for the curve of horizon. The air seemed sterile and hollow, with whiffs of frozen snot and icy metal. The lethal scents of a savage winter. Pale yellow light stained the gray sky like an aging bruise and winked off the silver heart dangling from my wrist. The frigid wind chafed my cheeks, tangled my hair, made my nose run. It might have felt cleansing if my hands weren't caked in soot and grime, or if the polar bears on my pajama-pants didn't resemble grizzlies skiing at midnight. The scratch in my throat was worrying.

"We don't have any water," I said. We didn't have any food, either, but my stomach was thankfully still satisfied from yesterday's Christmas feast.

The chickadee clambered out from inside my collar, yanking and pecking my hair to free its feet from the knots. "I will check the rooftop for fresh snow."

The landscape streaked past us. We had to be going around 50mph, more than fast enough to whisk away a chickadee. "No. The risk is too dangerous," I said. "And you are the only friend I got."

Small piles of snow lined the closed door, melty around the edges. The snow was gray, but clean enough as long as I scraped off the top. Unfortunately, the soot and grime on my hands leeched into the snow the moment I touched it. I licked the outside; grime coated my tongue, roughening my mouth as if I had licked a chalkboard. I repressed a cough and resisted the urge to spit. I *needed* water, and this snow might melt long before the train reached its destination. *I've already sucked in a pound and a half of grime. What's a few more mouthfuls?* I took another bite, gagged, and involuntarily spat.

Maybe it'll be easier if I stop using my hands, I thought, and knelt on all fours to bite the snow like a dog. The train's jostling slammed me into the ice, ramming my nose against the floorboards. I cupped my face in my wet hands, nose throbbing; the liquid grime stung my eyes. The train jostled and sent me sprawling face-first into the ice, jabbing my nose again. I shoved my anger down into my inner tar, my body shaking, my lips pressed tight. It was like trying to cap a volcano. I thrashed my fists against the metal walls and screamed out my pain and grief, competing with the train's roar like two feuding beasts. *No wonder my husband hates me. No wonder he switched sexual tastes. I am pathetic and useless and disgusting.* I cried and wailed, cursed and yelled, wept and swore off men forever. And once I was hoarse and sore and exhausted from self-loathing, I trembled inside a rattling boxcar, all alone and lost in the world with a chickadee on my shoulder.

Hours passed. I shivered. I cried. I did not sleep. The boxcar reeked of ammonia from where I had urinated in the corner. I perched on top of the freight to avoid the yellow stream cutting lines in the floorboard's filth. In the daylight I read the bags' gray, block letters. *Soda Ash.* I had no idea what soda ash was, but it didn't *sound* toxic. One relief.

A loud metallic screech drilled into my fillings around early afternoon. Several minutes later the train seemed to hiccup, its roar softening. I leapt off the cargo and stumbled to the open door. Sure enough, the world slowed. It took nearly thirty minutes, but the train finally stopped.

I jumped off the boxcar, falling to one knee in the blessedly clean snow. I scrubbed my hands until my skin burned and a gray puddle pocketed the snow beside my feet. I shoved handfuls into my mouth, squeezing my eyes tight to the brain-freeze, making my molar's cavity scream. The train tracks steamed beneath the wheels. I huddled close to the heat to defrost myself. The chickadee popped out of my collar and flitted onto my wrist, ruffling its feathers against the warmth. The train hissed and creaked, its engine hidden beyond the railway's bend. I had expected to be dumped in a train yard or a depot or *at least* in a city somewhere. Instead, I stood stranded in the middle of God-Knew-Where, with fifteen acre fields stretching along both sides of the tracks, and nothing but woods and sky beyond.

"Maybe the engineer will help us," I said.

The chickadee fluffed its rear to the wheel's warmth. "Won't you get in trouble for hopping the train?"

My brow furrowed. I didn't know the answer. If the chickadee was right, then I had only Sam to call if I was nabbed and hauled to jail. I refused to allow him that pleasure. He would deem my plight as karma for abandoning him, despite his affair. *He will never let me ask for help*, I realized. *He will make me grovel.*

"Maybe we're near a town," the chickadee suggested. "Wait here. I'll scout the area."

The chickadee flew up and over the train. I crouched and waited beside the wheel as the heat slowly died. I scanned the length of the tracks, watching for guards or crew curious about my presence. An hour passed. Up ahead the train whistle howled. Wheels screeched, the boxcars jostled. The sky remained overcast and birdless. Clacking. Screeching. Train whistle howling. *Should I climb back into the boxcar?* It had to lead to people eventually. Without the chickadee, however, I'd still be lost.

The steel wheels rolled. I watched the train trundle past me—potentially my only means of escape—and disappear beyond the bend in the horizon.

The new silence was stark, yet ghost prints of the train's racket lingered in my ears. I hugged myself, scanning the fields, waiting. No footprints in the snow, no litter, no graffiti. It was much like my beloved mine shaft, except this place wasn't a secret. It was merely unwanted.

"Chick-a-dee-dee-dee."

"Oh thank God," I said, as the chickadee

landed on my finger. "Did you find civilization?"

"No. But I found the next best thing. Follow me."

A dull burn shot through my stiff legs as I hurried through the snowy field, pushing myself to keep on the chickadee's tail. The bird swerved around the trees, leading me deep into the woods, and stopped eventually in front of a small, tight stand of white pines.

The chickadee landed on a low branch. "Here it is."

I crept closer and realized the stand had grown in front of the narrow entrance to an abandoned mine. And like my secret place back home, it blew a constant fifty-five degrees.

"Stay in there until I return with your guide," the chickadee said.

"You're leaving me out here alone?"

"You can't keep pace with me, and I still don't know where we are or how far away your guide is. Line the inside with pine boughs for bedding. The trees will block most of the wind."

"How long will you be gone?" I asked.

"However long it takes," the chickadee said.

The mine was narrow, too low to sit up in, but long enough to stretch out straight. Flat earth stretched back into the blackness, unlike my secret spot back home, which had a stark drop at the entrance. Worry gnawed on my nerves. But, honestly, if I had never hopped the train, I would want to run away to my mine shaft anyway. I rubbed my eye. Perhaps solitude was what I needed most right now, a chance to think, to grieve, to heal.

"What about darklings?" I asked.

"I doubt they will find you before I bring your guide. They are probably still tracking you to your in-laws."

I frowned. "That's not reassuring."

"Then I'll send a protector to watch over you and keep you safe. I will return soon," the chickadee said, then flew into the woods and disappeared.

CHAPTER TWELVE

The trees were naked and as easy to see past as empty cages. Yet all I found through the bars were more bars, a never ending prison cell creaking in the wind. I strained to hear any signs of civilization—car engines, human voices, mooing cattle. Nothing but a flock of blue jays chattering in the trees, and the occasional *ploosh* of snow tumbling off the branches.

I was supposed to be at Grandma Ingrid's, but instead spent an hour collecting pine boughs from the ground and low branches, constructing a thick bed of needles inside the mine's entrance. *Did my in-laws leave without me?* I wondered. *Did Sam?* I couldn't stop yawning. My muscles felt heavy and droopy, as if they had fallen asleep without me. I worried about freezing to death if I stopped moving, though, and I worried about collapsing from exhaustion if I stayed awake. I rubbed my eye. *The mineshaft's air should be warm enough to protect me.* I buried myself between the boughs, the pine scent stirring up memories of a miserable Christmas. I curled into the fetal position, padding my body with needled branches to trap my body-heat. Pitch stuck to my fingers, my coat, my hair, its tangy scent tickling my sinuses. The train still rattled inside my bones as I drifted off to sleep; images of Sam entangled with his lover flashed behind my lids.

I woke up choking on phlegm and tears. I coughed and hacked, shuddering my chest and blowing train grime out of my sinuses, its diesel reek overpowering the pine. Pitch ripped my hair as I crawled from the shelter. My joints creaked like rusted hinges. I shoved my cramping hands into my coat pockets and marched in place, desperate to warm my muscles.

The world was dark and the moon was low. I guessed it was around eight o'clock, though it was unlike any eight o'clock I had ever known. No whirr of a washing machine starting its spin cycle. No *clink* of dirty dishes in the sink. The woodland's quiet pressed into my ears with deafening nothingness, incessantly reminding me I was alone. I buried my face in the crook of my arm to warm my nose, the wool sleeve rough against raw skin. I yearned for a week ago—a mere week—when I knew which chores needed to be done, knew the shelves were stocked with food, knew the flick of a switch chased away the cold. I wanted my dead-end job to be my biggest frustration. I wished my biggest fear was accidentally igniting Sam's temper.

Sam.

By now he must have realized only my boots and hat and overcoat were missing, and all my personal belongings—my purse, my phone, my travel bag—were in the guest room as they had been before my life disintegrated. He must have assumed something terrible had happened to me. He was a cop, after all. He knew the world was capable of evil. He knew evils happened all the time.

I felt a pang of guilt. Sam was probably sick with anguish and sleepless with worry. Then again, hadn't he done worse? My teeth chattered, but thinking of Sam and his young lover made my blood simmer. Maybe my predicament scared him, but so what? He had betrayed me, lied to me, tore out my heart and spat on my dignity. I had spent a total of thirteen years enduring the ebb and flow of his emotional tides, loving him at his worst and not causing waves. In return he had dragged me out to sea like a riptide, choking out my life. I scowled and kicked some snow. *To hell with him. He's why I am freezing to death. Some suffering of his own won't kill the bastard.*

Wind rattled the treetops. Ice creaked on the branches. My stomach growled and I had no food. I thought about the last time I had eaten. A feast of ham and cranberries and stuffing. Even my sugarless pumpkin pie sounded like heaven right now.

Peter, Peter, pumpkin eater. Had a wife and couldn't keep her. He put her in a pumpkin shell, and there he kept her very well. A train whistle shrieked in the distance. *Peter, Peter pumpkin eater. Had a wife and couldn't keep her.*

The nursery rhyme repeated in my head as I watched the darkness—a darkness which seemed solid enough to push against. Or crush me. As if it wasn't nothing, but some *thing*. An entity, its own creature. I shivered, wondering what watched me back.

Peter, Peter, pumpkin eater. Had a wife but didn't need her—

I needed light. I needed warmth. I needed fire.

I tried to remember survival techniques from my six months of Girl Scouts, but recalled only quilting, cookies, and aloof girls whispering behind my back. My knowledge gained from movies needed to suffice. I found two sticks and ripped off some hair for kindling, grimacing as I realized my survival depended on Hollywood. I matted the hair into a ball and set it on a stone outside the shelter. I placed the tip of one of the sticks into the middle and ran the other stick fervently along its side. (*Peter, Peter, pumpkin eater. Had a wife but didn't need her. He put her in a woodland hell.*) I rubbed and rubbed and rubbed and never made smoke. The sticks didn't even feel *warm*. The only fire was in my knuckles exposed to the cold. My eyes darted from the useless sticks to the darkness. Both promised death.

Cheater, cheater, marriage eater. Had a wife but didn't need her.

I growled and threw the sticks aside, then shoved my claw-like hands into my pockets and marched in place, hoping to stamp out the pain in my joints. The crunching snow sounded thunderous in the night, a signal to any predator seeking prey. I stopped, and started to shiver.

Where are you, chickadee? It had promised me help. *It promised!* I snuffled, the train's reek of dust and filth lodged in my nose. Tears chilled on my cheeks. I bit my tongue to keep from wailing, fearful of attracting predators whose teeth hadn't sank into enough meat this long winter.

Then I saw it. Greenish-gold orbs flickered in the darkness, dancing between the trees. A huge weight floated off my shoulders, and my body flushed with warmth. *The chickadee succeeded!* Two faerie protectors had arrived to save me. Two Tinkerbells lit up the gloom.

Then the lights blinked and I realized my stupidity. It wasn't dancing faeries. It was eye-shine, watching me from the darkness. My mouth went dry and tasted of fear. The hair on my arms prickled. The eyes belonged to something close. Something *big*. My first thought was wolves, but wolves had been extirpated from Ohio generations ago. Of course, I might not be *in* Ohio. I had no idea *where* I was.

Cheater, cheater, marriage eater. Had a wife but didn't need her. He forced her to a woodland hell, and that was where her cold corpse fell.

I dove into the mine, my muscles stiff and stabbing. I heard snuffing outside, and the crunching of snow beneath heavy paws. The moon lined the beast's rear haunches in silvery light. *Not a wolf*, I realized. *A coyote.*

More snuffing, then the copper scent of blood. The coyote's silhouette loomed like a sentinel in front of the mine's entrance, a gourd-shaped shadow swaying beneath its jaws. My pulse pounded in my ears. I grabbed a branch beneath my rear, knowing I was crouched too low to swing. *Should I slink deeper into the mine? Will I drop off a ledge in the dark?*

The coyote poked its head inside; a small female turkey hung limp from its teeth. I held my breath, every muscle tense. The coyote's eyes flashed green, then she dropped the turkey and wagged her tail.

A peace offering.

My fingers uncurled slowly from the branch. "Did the chickadee send you to watch out for me?" I asked. The coyote yipped and licked my face, her warm breath steaming in the cold. I wiped the slobber off my cheek with my sleeve as she nuzzled the turkey with her snout. My stomach rumbled, and although not enough to make raw turkey appetizing, I refused to waste a valuable gift. I crawled from the shelter, eyeing the coyote in fear she'd lunge for my throat. The coyote sat and watched me, tail thumping, eyes glinting green. The turkey was still warm. I buried it in a nearby snowdrift, then crawled back into the mine. The coyote crawled in after and nestled beside me. I lay stiff, breathing shallow to lessen the rise of my chest. It's not every day a wild dog beds down with you, with just their lips separating your throat from their teeth. But her body-heat soon stopped my shivering. My muscles relaxed. Both of my legs fell asleep, but the warmth was a worthy exchange. I snuggled against the coyote, resting my ear on her front paws. She approved of becoming my pillow, and lay her chin on my head to make me into her's. She smelled like every dog I ever knew, a mixture of earth and musk and adventure.

Branches snapped outside in the darkness. I stiffened. The coyote lifted her head and sniffed the air. Wind whistled through the trees.

Cheater, cheater, marriage eater. Had a wife but didn't need her.

I laid my head back on the coyote's paws. "I hope you are safe, chickadee," I whispered into the night. "Please hurry back."

The night swallowed my words and made no promise.

CHAPTER THIRTEEN

A campfire burned outside the mine's entrance. It had not been there when I fell asleep.

I lay motionless on my bed of pine boughs, watching the small flames pop and lick. The pulse in my neck fluttered nervously against the back of my hand. Whoever had laid the stone circle, piled the kindling and started the flames, had not disturbed the coyote stretched alongside my stomach, dreaming her coyote dreams. *Has my faerie guide arrived to save me?*

I crawled out of the mine, then stood up and steadied myself on the outside stone until the world stopped spinning. My hands trembled, and I long gave up debating if it was from the cold, low blood sugar, or anxiety. The coyote roused and stretched, then leapt out of the shelter. She circled the campfire, tail in the air and nose to the ground. The flames were low and the logs were graying. *It has probably been burning since dawn.* I squinted through the snow glare, scanning the woods for twinkling wands and gossamer wings, but found only prison bars guised as trees.

I huddled on a large rock beside the campfire and fed sticks into the flames. The heat on my face was exquisite. My boots squished in the mud from the melted snow, and firelight glinted off my bracelet, transforming its silver heart into gold. The weather had also warmed. Green poked from the snow in patches along the ground. Water dripped somewhere inside the mine and I wondered if it joined an orange stream somewhere to poison the world. One hour passed, then two. My fire-faerie never appeared. Snow melted off nearby branches in a steady *pip ... pip ... pip.* At my feet, a brown spider webbed the gap between two stones in the circle. *Spiders can fight wars, but are they capable of fires?*

I coughed as smoke swirled into my face. My stomach growled and my throat longed for water which didn't crunch. It had been nearly three days since the chickadee had left me in the forest, and all I had eaten were a handful of pine needles, a piece of bark (most of which I spat out), and an acorn I had found outside the mine, bitter with tannins and hard on my teeth. Now, however, I had a fire to roast a whole turkey keeping in a melting snow drift. *Thank you, spiders.*

I dug out the bird from the snow and started plucking feathers. And plucking. And plucking. *And plucking.* I never realized how many feathers a turkey had. Brown and white feathers eventually blanketed the whole front of the mine, tumbling in fluffy currents through the trees. I found a thick piece of shale to cut the body as a train howled in the distance.

The coyote munched on a patch of green grass peeking through the slush. I gutted the turkey and tried to make a decision. At night I heard a nocturnal world of yips, howls, hooting, shrieks. Creatures with teeth and talons and stomachs famished from a long, hard winter. It was possible the chickadee was like the turkey in my hands, killed for a feast. *Or maybe the chickadee has betrayed and abandoned me.* Like Sam.

Cheater, cheater, marriage eater.

I forced a thick stick through the turkey and propped it over the fire like a gruesome marshmallow.

The smoke and sunlight bounced off the snow, making my eyes water. *Should I continue waiting for the chickadee while the darkling closes in on my scent? Or should I follow the train tracks to civilization?* Maybe even hop a train again. I shuddered. Either way, I refused to wither to my death in the forest.

By the time the turkey was ready to eat it was late-afternoon. The meat was charred because I was paranoid it wouldn't cook long enough and infect me with salmonella or a parasite. I gave half of the bird to the coyote and tore off a chunk of thigh. I sighed with pleasure as the meat slid down my throat like a stick of chalk. Dry and burnt and tasting like coal, the meal was more satisfying than a thousand Thatcher Christmas dinners.

I chewed slowly and decided I needed to leave at daybreak. If the chickadee had found me once, it could find me again. If the chickadee was still alive and helping me, that was. My other choices risked my life and safety, and I had never been a gambler.

I stuffed myself with turkey and dozed off. While I slept, the sun set and darkness came. The coyote woke me with a *yip*, alerting me the fire was dying. I threw in sticks until the flames stretched, then hugged my knees to my chest, grateful for a light in the darkness. A swollen moon crept across the sky, and smoke coiled around me. I stared at the embers waving oranges and yellows and reds, but it was the charcoal I found mesmerizing. Dark and still, yet somehow as brilliant as the flame, its hidden heat capable of being as destructive as the fire illuminating its blackness. *But what if the fire* isn't *illuminating the charcoal?* I wondered. *What if the charcoal's dark shines in the light?* These ideas felt on the edge of something greater. I rubbed my eyes, too exhausted to think anymore.

Thinking was never your strongest gift, my mother clucked inside my head.

Ain't that the truth, Sam's voice agreed.

"Shut up," I mumbled and tossed a branch into the fire.

Cheater, cheater, marriage eater.

Night passed at a crawl's pace; even the bloated moon rusted. The coyote lay at my side, chewing on a turkey bone. In the distance a barred owl hooted a continuous *hoo-huh-hoo-huh-hoo-huh-huh-hoooo.* My mind clung onto Sam, asking questions with answers impossible to know. Was he late on lasagna night because of *him?* Was his continuous *forced overtime* a convenient excuse? What about all those fruitless hunting and fishing trips? The bar time with friends? Had this affair been going on for weeks? Months? The length of a marriage? Was this his only other relationship? How many were there?

Cheater, cheater, marriage eater. Had a wife but didn't need her.

My stomach tightened around my meal, sitting like a cannon ball inside my gut. The smoke stung my eyes. I watched the charcoal—watched its dark shine inside the flames—then dropped my head to my knees and cried.

The coyote nipped my calf. I sprung to my feet. "Hey! What was that for?" The coyote nipped at my ankle, then hopped back and lifted her brow as if to say: *The bastard isn't worth your tears.*

Hoo-huh-hoo-huh-hoo-huh-huh-hoooo.

I wiped my eyes on my sleeve. "It's the smoke," I said, feebly.

The coyote yipped and ran in a tight circle. I snorted, amused. "Sorry, girl. I am in no mood to play." She stomped her front paws, then lifted her head and *howled.* The hair on my arms prickled. She raised an eyebrow at me, then howled again. I snorted. "Oh, what the hell?" I lifted my head and howled with her. The coyote shifted her pitch to harmonize with mine. I howled longer, louder, my chest lightening with each note.

In the far distance her cousins answered. *"Ahhhhrrwoooooooooo!"*

Chills ran from my toes to my scalp. The coyote dropped her head and stomped her paws, enticing me to play. I flicked her ear. She batted my leg. I playfully hopped away. Bat, hop, bat, hop. Fire pumped in my blood as we leapt around the camp ring, grinning, the flames dancing just for us. Laughter replaced the hollowness inside my chest. The corners of my mouth ached from smiling. And right then, despite what the future held, despite knowing I might die alone and cold and never found, I felt happy. Genuinely *happy*. I was lost in the woods, but I had found a piece of the *real* me. It took nearly twenty-eight years to taste adult freedom, which was not flavored with peace and contentment as the self-help books had always insisted. Nor was it the calm after a dreadful struggle. Freedom was feral. And primal. And made the blood pound in my veins like a war-song about my right to exist exactly as I was created. For the first time since childhood magic buzzed along my skin. *I have no reason to suffer,* I realized, then spread my arms to embrace the world and howled like a wild woman at the moon. "Arrrrrhwooooooooooo!"

"Ahhhhrrwoooooooooo!" the coyote

responded.

"Arrrr—" A moth landed on my forefinger. I shrieked and slapped my hands together, guts and powder splattering my skin. My heartbeat raced; my body became rigid. Nothing moved in the woods but the shadows. Nothing sounded but the crackling flames.

The coyote stood stiff, eyes glinting in the firelight. She began to whine. "It was just a moth," I told her. "The weather has warmed. They are coming out now, attracted to my fire." I swallowed hard. "It-it was just a moth."

I wiped the moth's guts off on my pants, the bark of a tree, the outside wall of the mine. I scrubbed my hands with snow, but like the sap on my fingers its eyes stayed on me. Everything had changed with the flutter of its wings. *Should I flee now? Or am I being paranoid?* Night had fallen. I could trip and impale myself on a fallen branch, or break an ankle, or freeze to death. But such fates might be mercies compared with what lurked in the shadows.

The fire that had fed and warmed me now lit up my campsite like a prison spotlight, transforming me into prey. Shadows spiked up the trees from the traitorous flames. My heart jumped with them.

Stop freaking out, Miriam. It's just a stupid moth.

Branches snapped behind me; I wheeled around. The coyote's ears pricked and the barred owl quit hooting. Winter coiled up my pant legs, prickling the hairs and making me shiver. My finger-joints ached from the cold. *Will I ever know warmth again? Will I—?* My stomach jumped into my throat. *I'm beside the fire. My hands should be toasty, not covered in gooseflesh.*

The coyote crouched, hackles raised and whining. She then leapt into the woods and disappeared in the gloom. "Wait!" I pleaded. "Come back!"

In the dark crept something darker, and I knew it wasn't just a shadow. I yanked a branch from the fire and held it like a baseball bat, embers flickering on the tip. My chest heaved. Warm breath deserted my lungs. The stars paled and the flames dimmed, as if the darkness gobbled up the light. For two minutes I heard only my shallow panting and the campfire's crackle. Then snow crunched in the darkness. Sticks snapped. Yips and howls volleyed in the woods. The racket grew farther and farther away until it became a rustle, then a whisper, then nothing. The branch shook in my hands, jingling the silver heart on my bracelet. White ash fluttered around me like a swarm of moths.

My shadow danced wildly along the snow and trunks in the firelight, a demoniac possessed with fear. Wind soughed through the needles of the white pine trees. I strained to see the coyote in the forest or hear a *see-me-I'm-here* to know everything was safe. A moth flittered over the campfire, then disappeared into the darkness. A clump of spiders scurried out of the mine to chase after it.

I peered into the night, teeth chattering, eager to glimpse the darkling lurking around my campsite. Yes, it was dangerous. Yes, it could kill me. But it was also the first magical creature I knew of outside of the chickadee. Its existence proved I was not crazy or a liar or a woman lost to dreams. I had the insane urge to chase after it, to race through the woods like a barbarian, thorns tearing at my clothing, my blood pumping and my spirit free. I wanted to catch it, study it, learn its dark secrets. Whatever *it* happened to be.

My shaky breath steamed in the frigid air, abandoning me for night's siren. The branch was slippery between my palms. *How is it possible to sweat so much in this cold?* I clawed at my memory for every self-defense move Sam had taught me in our kitchen. I hoped it would not come to that. I hoped the coyote had torn the darkling's throat out. How many hours until daybreak? Would a day's worth of hiking keep me ahead of the hunt?

Ice water seeped into my marrow, welling up to fill my bones. I wheeled around to the mine and faced a solid shadow. I gasped, stumbling backwards. The shadowman stood six feet tall, its sword-like body cutting a grim silhouette in the firelight. I swung the burning branch. It whizzed through the darkling's featureless face and jarred my shoulder as it struck the ground in a flash of sparks.

Darklings aren't solid. Relief washed over me. *Whatever a darkling is, it can't hurt me physically.*

Then the darkling yanked the branch from my hand and hurled it into the trees, the embers hissing when it struck a patch of snow. Shadows coiled off its body, absorbing into the surrounding darkness like mercury. A man of starlight flesh now stood before me, his clothing and feathery hair as black as murder. I backed away, fists raised. The stranger matched my pace, moving as if he had stepped from a world of mink and violins and brimming decanters.

"Hello, Miriam." The stranger's voice was as soft and dark as murmuring owls. His eyes shone on his pale face like two blood moons. "My name is

Delano. I am excited to find you alone."

I turned and ran.

CHAPTER FOURTEEN

The woods betrayed me.

Branches scraped my clothing, grabbing at me to slow me down and sacrifice me to the night. Each breath was a stab of cold air inside my lungs. The moon was full but cloud-covered, making depth impossible to distinguish. I lifted my feet too high, stomped down too hard, jarred my knees, slammed my toes into rocks. I stumbled over roots and branches buried in the snow, scrambling to escape the shadowman with blood moon eyes. The monster darker than the darkness.

I glanced over my shoulder. Nothing followed but blackness and woodland shadows. I clambered over a steep hill to a ravine. Brambles snared my ankle and tripped me on the way down. I yanked my foot free, thorns piercing cloth and flesh. Blood bloomed against the flannel, warm and sticky, as I scrambled to my feet.

I leaned against a tree trunk and covered my mouth to quiet my panting. My ankle throbbed and stung and I tasted ash on my lip. A breeze snaked through the trees, chilling the sweat on my forehead. Ice creaked overhead on the branches. My shoulders slumped as my breathing began to steady.

Delano materialized from the tree's shadow and snatched my wrist. I screamed and thrashed as he yanked me to him, my fist pounding his chest, as cold as a corpse beneath silk as slick as ice. He clenched my forearms and shoved my back against the trunk. I shrieked as the tree's bark scraped my spine. My body-heat abandoned me for this monster, leaving me cold and alone and forsaken, just like a husband sneaking off to his leg-spread lover, like a chickadee falling to a predator of the night. *I am going to die in these woods,* I realized. For how did you defeat a shadow? How did you evade the moon?

My vision blurred. Reality became a fading background, as if only me and the darkling existed. All warmth drained to Delano with the moonlight, the starlight, the glints off the snow and ice. Did he steal them all? Or were they powerless against him, like a magnet or a black hole? "Don't kill me!" I cried. "Please don't kill me! *Please!*"

Delano tilted his head, his lips pursed. A moth fluttered onto his shoulder and stretched its wings. "*Kill* you?" He scoffed. "If I wished you dead, why would I build you a fire to warm you, feed you, and give you strength? No, no, no. I have much *grander* intentions."

I stiffened, my chin trembling, feeling like the world's biggest fool. *The fire wasn't a gift, after all. I fell for a darkling's bait.*

A coyote howled in the distance. Delano tensed; his eyes flashed like reflectors in the dim moonlight. "Did they mark you?"

"Wha-What?"

He glanced over his shoulder, his fingernails digging into my triceps. *"Did they mark you?"*

"I-I don't know what you're talking about."

"I don't have time for games!"

"I don't know! I *swear*!"

Delano yanked the overcoat off my

shoulders. I thrashed and kicked and scratched myself away from him. He snatched my coattail as I scrambled for the hill, and threw me to the ground. My palm landed on a rock; I twisted my body and hurled it at his head. He ducked, snatched my arm, pinned me in the snow.

"Stop fighting, you stupid girl!" I squirmed fruitlessly, shrieking. He flipped me onto my stomach. My face sank into the snow, and I spat out a mouthful of ice.

"Stop!" I wailed, the snow crunching loud in my ear. "Please! Stop!"

The darkling pushed my overcoat and shirt up to my neck, grinding his knee into the base of my spine. One of my arms was stuck beneath my pelvis, the other he pinned to my side. My skin tightened as the snow pressed against my stomach, but Delano's pants were just as cold. *Dear, God. Is he a demon? The Grim Reaper? Is a devil about to rape me?*

Delano brushed his fingers across my shoulders. "You are clean," he said, then hoisted me to my feet. I tugged down my clothing. Shadows uncoiled from the forest and circled us like a lightless eddy. Delano's flesh absorbed the darkness. I kicked and bucked uselessly as shadows snaked around my legs. The darkness crawled to my chest, encasing me like a frigid cocoon. I cursed myself for my stupidity, and for irrationally riding the waves I had caused. If I had never hopped the train I would be brokenhearted and miserable, but at least I wouldn't become a murder victim of night manifested. Delano squeezed me to his chest and I felt a pulling sensation, as if a black hole had burst open to suck us out of existence. I cried out and—

"ARGH!"

"Chick-a-dee-dee-dee!"

Delano staggered backward, flailing his arms as the chickadee thrashed its wings and pecked his face. The darkness fell off my body and rejoined the shadows. I scrambled away, clutching my overcoat to my chest. The chickadee dove and weaved, jabbing Delano's head with its beak, then bolted into the darkness.

I sprinted after the songbird, my ankle screaming from where the thorns had torn my skin. Delano snatched my hair. I shrieked as he whirled me to face him, his eyes blazing like two moons aflame.

Then I saw nothing.

The woods lit up like a silent flash-grenade. My eyeballs stung like thistles in their sockets; pain filled my skull as sharp and white as the light. Gigantic white blobs blotted out my vision. A warm gust whizzed beside my ear; something hard whacked Delano. He yelped and released me and stumbled away, and that was all I knew for certain. Snow cracked to my left. Then heavy breathing. The slap of flesh smacking flesh. Another light explosion. A frigid gust. A rush of heat. My heart pounding like a war drum inside my chest.

I crouched, trembling, blindly patting the snow and soggy leaves. My eyes watered, the dance with the coyote now seeming naive. I felt small, and vulnerable, and foolish. The white blobs started shrinking in my vision; a shadow flickered in my peripheral. Fingers wrapped around my wrist and I yanked myself free.

"You're safe, Miriam," the chickadee said, as it landed on my shoulder. "The darkling is gone, but we need to leave."

"I can't see," I said. "The light blinded me."

"That's why I am here," said a new man's voice, cheerful and musical. "To *guide* you." The stranger grabbed my hands and hoisted me to my feet. I realized then his flesh was hot. So unlike Delano's ice.

The white blobs in my vision shrank as the stranger and I fled through the trees. Well, more like the stranger fled. I hobbled and fell and struggled through the brush and snow. He glided through the forest as if iceskating across a frozen pond, calling out hazards we approached—Root! Rock! Dip! Puddle!—but his warnings did minimal good. The stranger caught me each stumble, wasting no time after I regained my footing. I squinted, curious to see my first faerie. All I made out was that he wore a hat and a large backpack.

We fled for nearly two hours—sometimes jogging, sometimes walking briskly, but always fleeing. The chickadee perched on the faerie's shoulder, bobbing in the darkness with his graceful stride. We had escaped the woods and now scurried through fields, but the easier terrain was still unforgiving. My ankle throbbed from where the thorns had cut me, and my chest ached from running without a bra. A stitch chewed my side, making me limp. The stranger hoisted my armpit onto his shoulder, supporting me but never stopping. I strained to hear footsteps sneaking up behind us through the crunch of weeds and snow.

"I didn't see the protector I sent," the chickadee said. "Did she ever find you?"

I nodded and spoke between puffs of breath. "Yes. She was. Helpful. And warm."

"Glad to hear it," said the chickadee. "Turkeys are hit or miss with their honor, quite frankly."

I felt a sinking sensation in my gut. "Turkey...?" My pace dwindled, then I lurched as my guide yanked me forward. "Don't you mean coyote?"

This time the stranger's pace lessened ... then his speed increased to a gallop, his arm muscles straining as if towing an anchor. I panted hard to keep up, the stitch gnashing at my side.

"Coyotes are not faerie helpers," the chickadee said, somberly. "The darkling must have sent a spy."

My stomach heaved, and I decided to never eat turkey again.

"Jump! Hole!" the stranger shouted. I jumped blindly, and puffed a relieved breath when my boots struck flat ground. "We're almost there," he said, as if enjoying some dysfunctional family vacation. He sounded hardly out of breath. Twenty minutes later we stumbled out of the snow dappled weeds, and my boots struck blacktop. I squealed as if we had stumbled upon a treasure trove glittering with diamonds. The stranger didn't pause. He hauled me along the roadway, his head swaying from side to side, scanning the darkness.

Something growled behind us. I tensed, then relaxed when I saw two headlights approaching from down the road. The stranger ordered me to stay on the shoulder, then waved his arms above his head as he entered the lane.

The chickadee landed on my shoulder. "Are you hurt?"

I shook my head, hands on my thighs,

gasping. "No. I was. Worried. About you. Though."

"Sorry it took so long. Your guide made it nearly to the farmhouse."

My heart winced. The farmhouse seemed a world away. Was Sam there now, I wondered? Was his lover nestled beside him in our bed? Or was Sam still in the city with his family, staying close to where I had disappeared?

My guide waved down a pickup truck towing a horse trailer. The headlights illuminated him briefly as the truck slowed, then stopped a few feet past. Brown tweed jacket, tattered blue jeans, red hiker's backpack with sleeping bags strapped to the top and bottom, charcoal fedora. The buckles on his chunky motorcycle boots glinted in the passing headlamps' glow. He was several inches taller than me, and svelte. Far from frail, though. He appeared strong, sturdy. Like a musclewood tree who had gone thrift shopping for clothes while drunk out of his gourd.

"*That's*—" God, I felt stupid even saying it, "—my faerie guide?"

The chickadee nodded.

My faerie guide spoke to the driver through the passenger window, then waved me over. "The driver is heading west," he said, and threw his backpack into the truck bed.

I wiped my forehead with my sleeve. "Where to?"

The faerie laughed, a sound like shell chimes tinkling in the breeze. He hopped into the bed. "No idea. But it must be better than out here, don't you think?"

I imagined Delano's blood moon eyes watching me from the darkness, his corpse-cold nails digging into my flesh. I grabbed the faerie's hand and clambered into the truck bed. We sat beside each other in the corner, our backs against the cab, the backpack and two bales of hay near our feet. The faerie tapped the window with his knuckle. The engine roared as the driver sped off.

The wind chilled the sweat on my brow. Smells of hay and horse manure wafted from the trailer, mixed with the tailpipe's exhaust. A chain clanked against the hitch. I thought about the train ride, rattling, cold, caked in grime. *It seems like months ago, not days.* My teeth chattered, and I pulled my knees to my chest.

The faerie shrugged off his tweed jacket. I tensed up when he wrapped his arm around my shoulders, splaying the jacket across us like a blanket. "The driver says we'll be driving until daylight." He slid my arm through one of the sleeves, and slid his into the other. If he noticed my unease he made no indication. "You need to rest." I watched the darkness lining the road and bit my cheek. The faerie cupped my jaw in his hand and pressed my ear to his shoulder. "Sleep. You're safe now. I promise."

Relief and exhaustion fell over me. My ankle throbbed, and every muscle ached. The faerie was warm, as if running a fever, and my head sunk onto his shoulder. He smelled like dew drenched ferns and hollow logs and early hints of spring. The edge of his hair tickled my brow in the wind. "I don't even know your name," I said with a yawn.

"Orin." He gently squeezed my side.

“Now sleep.”

CHAPTER FIFTEEN

My eyes were open, yet I questioned if I was dreaming.

Orin's chin was lifted to a salmon sky. His fedora was off and the dawn wind streaked through his hair as the pickup truck raced to the horizon. The chickadee was curled in the cup of his hand, sleeping soundly; Orin's thumb stroked the bird's head. His eyes were closed and his lips were stretched into a smile, as if he listened to a hidden symphony tucked inside the roar of wind and engine and clanging trailer. I kept my head on his shoulder, not wanting to alert him I had awakened. Not wanting to disturb his communion with morning's first light.

Orin was not the Tinkerbell I had imagined, and in the daylight all stereotypes I held about faeries melted away. He looked my age and human—very human—except for the tips of his ears which rose to dull points. Still, something was different about him, a strangeness felt before witnessed, like the tingle on your skin from a scandalous secret. What caught me first physically was his nest of hair. It glinted in the sun like mica, conjuring up memories of flip-flops and sunscreen and plastic toy buckets. Each strand was like a grain of sand, its own color of yellow or bronze or copper or tan, millions of flecks creating the illusion of a golden, sun-drenched shore. I didn't want to stop staring at it.

The truck's metal bed dug into my hip. I shifted carefully, discreetly.

"Good morning, Miriam. Did I wake you?" My breath caught in my throat when Orin looked at me. Gold speckled his eyes, dancing like coins of light on tropical waters. For some reason his smile made me think of apricots and tea glasses, tinkling with ice.

"No, no." I sat up straight and slid my arm out of his jacket. "Where do you think we are?"

Orin shrugged and put on his fedora. "Not sure. Missouri?"

Snow dappled pastures and barbwire lined the four-lane highway; the land's flatness, sparse trees, and cotton candy sky stretched beyond every horizon. An enormous truck stop waited ahead, standing alone like a blacktop oasis. *I should be at work today, at my own tiny gas station,* I thought. I doubted Sam had told my boss I was missing, meaning I had left the station shorthanded. The thought made me feel guilty, and a little ashamed.

The click of a turn-signal sounded. The chickadee woke to the bump of the truck stop's driveway. It blinked and stretched its wings, then hopped onto my wrist and bowed. "It was an honor being your watcher," the bird said.

I frowned. "You're leaving?"

"I must deliver the message that you have been reached safely. Orin will take good care of you from here. And who knows? We may meet again."

"Thank you," I said. "You are the bravest chickadee I ever met."

The chickadee puffed its chest and lifted its chin proudly. It then chirped a thank you and a goodbye before flying west over the station.

The pickup parked beside a gas pump. Orin helped me out of the bed; a horse stomped its hoof in the trailer. The driver's eyes widened when he saw us together, as if he thought he had rescued a couple of kittens, and in the daylight realized we were a couple of skunks. He mumbled incoherently to our thank yous and informed us he would take us no farther.

Warmth washed down on me as we entered the truck stop's lobby. I stopped beneath the overhead heating vent and sighed with pleasure. The hot air bounced off me, as if my skin had a layer of ice which needed to melt before reaching my core. Orin joined me without question, lifting his face like a sunflower to the outpouring warmth. We stood in silence, thawing for several minutes. Travelers darted around us to get to the travel store and diner. The air smelled of cooking grease, hash-browns, and bacon-wrapped comfort. My stomach rumbled.

"Hungry?" Orin said.

I blushed. "Starving. But I—Oh my God! *Showers!*"

Ahead of us, between an arcade and laundry room, stood a sign for private showers. Orin lifted his eyebrows, seeming to notice my filthiness for the first time. "Hm, yeah. You could use a good scrubbing." He pinched the bottom hem of my pajama top, the flannel nearly black from pitch and mud. "Better clothes, too, yes?"

I frowned. "I can't. I didn't bring any money."

Orin whipped out two fistfuls of hundred dollar bills from his jacket's pockets. "Will this cover your needs?"

"What are you doing?" I stepped up to him, chest to chest to hide the wads. "You can't go around waving cash!"

He tilted his head. "Why?"

"Because you might get robbed!"

Orin shrugged and stuffed the bills back into his pockets. "Well? Is it enough?"

"Way more. But I can't take your money."

"Of course you can. The Realm provided it to help you." He adjusted his backpack's straps and headed toward the travel store. "So you better follow me if you want any say on what you'll be wearing."

I frowned at Orin's mishmash of tattered clothing, and hurried to join him.

If Keith's Corner Shop had a beef-jerky-eating older brother with mutton chops and a doughy stomach drooping over his belt-line, I imagined this travel store would be him. It catered dominantly to male road warriors in need of comforts and supplies, and gifts for their loved ones forced to stay at home. Orin threw T-shirts of all sizes over his arm, with screen-prints of semis and NASCAR and aggressive fonts announcing the King of all Kings. I returned them as quickly as he gathered them.

He poked my nose with his pinky. "Pick something or I'll buy it all."

I bit my lip and slid hangers along metal rods. I chose a fleece lined hoodie and two black, long sleeve shirts with silver winged hearts on the front—the only women's smalls on the clearance rack. They were also the only women's wares in the travel store. I chose the smallest pair of men's jeans, a belt, fleece lined gloves, and a bag of men's one-size-fits-all socks. I debated if I could make men's briefs work too, but decided against it. Orin plopped a wool blanket, a water bottle, and a folding knife in my arms. "Keep that within reach while we're on the road," he said, pointing to the knife. "Just in case." My stomach knotted. The items in my arms felt ominous. They weren't *purchases*, I realized. It was *survival gear*, tools to keep me alive on this adventure ... whatever this adventure was.

Orin grabbed a black knapsack, toiletries and snacks, then met me at the checkout. A scrawny man complaining about the order of his lottery tickets stood in front of us. The cashier feigned sympathy—something I had done countless times in my own store—but kept glancing at me with narrowed eyes. I knew I was a fright with my filthy clothing, matted hair, grimy skin, reeking of woodsmoke and mud and sap. Still, old insecurities whispered that something was inherently wrong with me, that I didn't belong. *I left my husband, hopped a train, got lost in the woods, brawled with the supernatural, and nothing has changed.* I longed for my secret mineshaft where no one ever found me. Here (wherever *here* was) I was a freak with no sanctuary. My coping mechanisms of nature strolls and housecleaning had vanished.

Something shiny caught my eye. On the shelf beside the cash register were black velvet boxes with silver bracelets. A silver heart with an etched rose hung off the chains. The handwritten yellow sign beside it read: *Silver Bracelets for Your Loved One! Only $19.99!*

My lips pressed tight; searing tar roiled

inside my gut, making me want to wail. "I'll meet you in the lobby, okay?" I handed Orin my items, then stormed out of the store to escape the cashier's narrowed eyes and my husband's lies which followed me throughout miles of railroads and woods and highways and hell. I snapped Sam's cheap silver gift off my wrist and tossed it into a garbage can in the lobby, my blood ready to boil. *I should chuck my wedding ring in as well*, I thought, then spotted a pay phone in the corner.

My chest tightened. I could call Sam.

Did I *want* to call Sam?

I glowered. *No. I want nothing to do with the bastard*. But then again, I couldn't leave him worrying about me, wondering about me, fearing I was dead in a ditch. That would make me as bad as him. Despite everything, he was still my husband and I was still his wife. Even if he no longer loved me—even if he preferred men—I had taken a vow to honor and respect him. I needed to officially end our relationship so we could both move on with our new lives.

I wiped my sweaty palms on my overcoat. It just needed to be a quick phone call. Assure him I was safe but our marriage was over. Easy. I grabbed the receiver. *He probably won't even answer,* I thought. He might even be with his lover. My eyes narrowed. Fine. Good. Leaving a message was easier. I pressed the phone to my ear, pushed zero, and spoke the number.

The operator told me to hold. The sound of nothing hummed in my ear, telecommunication's abyss. I stared at graffiti carved into the phone's metal plate. *Gabe & Maria.* I wondered if they were still together.

"Here is your party," the operator said.

"Miriam?"

Sam's voice was tinny on the echoing connection. He sounded robotic, inhuman. I almost slammed down the phone.

I cleared my throat.

Um ... What had I planned to say again?

"Hey..."

"*Where* the *fuck* are you?"

Cheater, cheater, marriage eater.

My thumbnail slid up and down the phone-cord, clicking against the metal grooves. "I don't know. I just called to—"

"You ran away to humiliate me! How the hell do you not know where you're at?"

I clenched the phone-cord, the metal slick in my sweating palm. My husband didn't care that I had vanished. He didn't care if I was safe or what I had gone through. All he cared about was how my predicament affected *him*. Anger blazed behind my eyes. My impulse was to stamp it out as I always did, but I had been cold for far too long. I was such an *idiot.* How did I believe Sam had ever loved me, when he refused to even listen to what I said?

"Well?"

My jaw started to quake. "It's not like that."

"Miriam?" Orin stood past the phone's privacy shield, out of view. He sounded worried, almost scared. I hardly knew this stranger beyond a few spoken paragraphs, had stepped out of a convenience store for three minutes, and he already cared more about my wellbeing than the man I had shared a life with for thirteen years.

A slight pause hung on the line. "Who the fuck is that?" Sam said.

My knuckles glowed white against the black receiver, the bones ready to burst through the skin. "I gotta go."

"So help me God, if he—" I slammed down the receiver before Sam finished.

Orin's shoulders relaxed when I stepped out from behind the privacy shield. He smiled and handed me the knapsack full of my new belongings. "The cashier says we pay for the showers at the—are you okay?"

I flung the strap over my shoulder. "Yeah. I-I phoned my husband to let him know I was safe and to end our marriage. It did not go well."

Orin sighed and shook his head. I winced, expecting him to scold my stupidity for calling. "Your husband is an idiot for not appreciating your good heart," Orin said. His hug warmed me more than the overhead vents. "Come. Let's get the rest of you cleaned up."

CHAPTER SIXTEEN

I pushed quarters into a slot, then opened a door to a tiled bathroom. "Meet me in the restaurant whenever you finish," Orin said. "And leave your dirty clothes outside the door so I can start our laundry."

I spun around to face him. "*I* do the laundry."

"Don't be silly. Enjoy yourself."

"But—" I started. He waved his hand dismissively, then paid the stall across from mine and closed the door behind him.

I locked my door, then stripped out of my grimy clothing, separating my black bikini briefs from the pile. They were the only pair of underwear I had and they hadn't been washed in days. I couldn't leave them for a stranger to launder. Especially a *man.* What would my mother say?

I would say you're acting like a disgraceful slut, my mother's voice grumbled inside my head. *Have you seen my cigarettes?*

I inched the door open and slid my filthy clothes outside for Orin to wash, minus the bikini briefs. I felt guilty and vulnerable, as if I was surrendering my responsibilities and identity to a stranger. I went to hand-wash my underwear with shampoo in the sink ... then stopped. I leaned on the basin, naked, slumping deep into my shoulders. What exactly *was* my identity? Sam's wife? Gas attendant? Spineless homemaker?

I cracked open the door and slid my

underwear into the pile outside.

Shampooing my head was like shampooing a tumbleweed. Water slid off my body in black streams, making me feel like a bag lady caught in the rain. My fingernails were packed with filth, and a rotting leaf clogged the drain. I groaned. *How embarrassing.* Although I still didn't know what Orin wanted with me, I wouldn't blame him if I stepped out of the shower and discovered he had fled.

I scrubbed away the campfire and the mud and the humiliation until the water became tepid and the bathroom became claustrophobic from peach scented steam. I toweled off, shoved my wedding ring into the bottom of my backpack, brushed my teeth, and rubbed antibiotic ointment onto my ankle. The cuts were red and tender, but not infected or as deep as I had imagined, thank God. My new jeans were too baggy, the heels of my new socks rested above my ankles, I lacked underwear, and my nipples pointed through the long-sleeved shirt. Still, cashmere and silk had never felt finer.

"Miriam!" Orin stood in the back of the diner, waving me over from behind a fogged glass divider. His hair was like dry sun-kissed sand, gleaming beneath the fluorescent lighting. I sunk into my shoulders, patting down my wet tumbleweed. The shampoo had been powerless against the snarls the train and elements had created in my hair, and I felt too guilty to ask Orin to buy conditioner or a hairbrush. Although sheep shears seemed a better option. My hair was halfway to dreadlocks.

I sat in the booth seat across from Orin. A gray spider hung from a silk thread beside his ear; Orin leaned in close, his lips pursed seriously. "Uh huh. Right. Got it. Will do." The spider scurried up its line and disappeared into the overhead light fixture.

"Enjoy your shower?" Orin asked.

"I did," I said, picking at a knot in my hair the size of a newborn kitten. I glanced at the ceiling. "What was that about?"

"The chickadee is outside on the roof. He wants us to bring him some hash browns before he leaves." I blinked, unsure if Orin was pulling my leg or not. Two waitresses approached our table, their trays crowded with loaded dishes. "I hope it's okay I already ordered."

"Just as long as it's not turkey," I said, wanly.

The waitresses examined me with one narrow eye, then set down three stacks of Mickey Mouse pancakes with chocolate chip smiley faces, two orders of hash browns, two spinach omelets, a double order of bacon, cinnamon toast, a sweet roll, four mugs of hot chocolate piled high with whipped cream, two glasses of water with lemon, a pitcher of maple syrup, and eighteen packets of honey.

"Anything else?" the shorter waitresses asked me.

An insulin shot, I thought, but said: "No, thank you. This is fine."

The waitresses left. Orin tried to drown one of the Mickey Mouses with maple syrup.

"I take it faeries like sweets?" I said, pulling an omelet in front of me. The sight of it made my mouth water.

Orin peeked up at me like a kid caught with his fingers in the jam. He set the syrup aside, but Mickey was already a goner. "Not all faeries. It's been years since I've eaten Earth food. I guess I got carried away," he said, his ears' pointed tips reddening. "Of course, if I'm promoted, I'm sure I'll be sick of it soon enough."

"Promoted to what?" I asked, then bit into my omelet.

"To retriever. Currently I am a border sentry. We defend the section between the faerie Realm and Earth."

"Are they near one another?"

Orin seesawed his hand. "More like on top of each other." Apparently he saw my confusion because he added: "Think of them as two different frequencies instead of physical lands, like radio stations if you will. And, like radio stations, sometimes you can hear two stations at once. Those are the borders I patrol."

"And coming to, um, *Earth's frequency*, is part of your promotion?"

Orin grinned and puffed up his chest. "Yup! It's taken years, but the Realm *finally* allowed me this trial assignment. It's been rough since there wasn't enough time to issue me an Earth ID or driver's license, but if I succeed in their recovery mission the Realm will promote me to a retriever."

"What are you recovering?"

"You, of course," Orin said, and stuffed Mickey's ear into his mouth.

I snorted. "How can you recover something you've never lost?"

Orin chewed and swallowed, hard. "Well, ya see." He paused, shoved more pancake into his mouth, and pretended to admire the glass divider's vine etchings.

Adrenaline twinged my arms and legs. "What is it? What's wrong?"

"You're-a-changeling-the-faerie-Realm-accidentally-lost-and-we-need-to-take-you-back-before-a-darkling-kidnaps-you-first," Orin said in one breath, his mouthful of pancakes muffling the words.

"I'm sorry. Did you say I'm a *changeling?*"

Orin nodded, chewing.

"As in a *faerie* swapped for a human infant?"

Orin swallowed and wiped his mouth. "Yes. Your family isn't your real family, and humans aren't your real species. You're a faerie, like us." He gulped down some hot chocolate, then licked the dollop of whipped-cream off his upper lip. "Which is great news! Being a faerie is *much* better than being a human."

I lowered my forkful of omelet. The eggs now tasted spiced with dread. Nearly twenty-eight years ago my mother had gone into labor two weeks early, mere days before moving from California to Ohio for my father's career. She always said she knew I would be a difficult child because my birth had caused so many hardships. A birth which became the catalyst for my parents' divorce when my mother couldn't deny she had birthed a brown-eyed baby. A brown-eyed daughter born to parents whose eyes were both blue.

My stomach tightened around the omelet. My mother had lost her husband and reputation because of a faerie trick? No wonder she hated me. Although, if I *was* a changeling, then my mother wasn't my real mother. *I* also hadn't been born early. My parents' real child had. Their blue-eyed child.

I leaned back in the booth. "This is impossible."

"Nope. It is real. Rare, but real," Orin said. "Besides, why would I lie about this?"

"Maybe you're a psychopath."

"And I trained a chickadee to talk and sent a darkling after you all in the name of a sick joke?" He shook his head. "You *are* a changeling, Miriam. Look." Orin slid around the table; springs groaned as he sat in the booth beside me. He had changed into a black turtle neck and corduroy pants, the burgundy ribbing worn away on the knees. He pushed my hair back and ran his thumbs along the tips of my ears. The ridges were flat, bumpy, vaguely resembling the edge of a pie crust. Mild deformities I had spent a lifetime hiding underneath hats and headbands and hanging hair.

"See? The tips of your ears are pressed."

I patted the knotted hair over my reddening ears. "What do my deformities prove?"

"They're not deformities," Orin said. "Darklings kidnap newborn faeries. If we are unable to get our babies to the Realm's safety in time, we fold their ears and swap them with a human until it is safe to retrieve them."

A hostess seated a father and young son diagonally from our booth. They had the same deep set eyes, the same flame hair, the same cleft chin. The boy swung his feet, his sneakers knocking the bench with all the carefreeness of a child who knew he was safe and loved. His father sat tall and proud, a red bear who knew without doubt his cub was his. I felt a pang of envy. The boy's existence would never cause his parents' divorce. And he would never, ever doubt where he belonged.

"You still doubt." Orin sighed. "Humans accept you as another human because they don't know any better, but I bet they treat you differently. Standoffish? Rude? Am I right?" I bit my lip. Orin followed my eye. The waitress went out of her way to take the father and son's drink order, meandering around tables to avoid our booth. "We intimidate humans, though they don't understand why," Orin said. "They sense our magic. They fear it."

"I have no magic," I said.

"Of course you do. All faeries do."

I remembered watching Orin in the sunlight, how my skin had tingled like a scandal, how I had stared at him as if he were a secret paradise. But Orin was a jewel. I was a mouse. *Surely* I didn't cause such reactions in people because I was like him.

"Hold still," Orin said, then weaved his fingertips into the roots of my wet hair. He tugged gently against the mats, then his hands slipped to the ends. My eyes widened. Across the restaurant, the cook shouted out an order; a domed bell dinged. Orin slid his hands through the rest of my hair, tugging no harder than if dragging his fingers through flour.

Orin smiled and folded his hands in his lap. "Much better."

I slid my fingers through my wet hair. Not a single knot or tangle. "How did you...?"

"I didn't, really," Orin said. "Water *wants*

to travel in a straight line. It'll carve landscapes to do so. I just encouraged the water to follow its instincts." He smirked. "Hair tangles are easy to conquer compared to a riverbank."

"My God. You used magic. Actual *magic.*"

Orin's eyes twinkled. "Face the restaurant's entrance." He pulled my hair back when I did, as if gathering a ponytail. When I looked back his hands were cupped and full of water. I gaped at him, petting my dry hair. Orin clapped his palms closed; steam puffed out between his fingers, spiraling to the ceiling and fogging the glass divider.

"That's *amazing*!"

Orin shrugged. "It's just nature communication. Simple stuff."

"Simple?" I laughed, brushing my hair with my fingers. The steam faded off the glass. "I could never do anything like that!"

"But you *can.* Don't you see? You *are* a faerie, Miriam. And if you are strong enough to leave your husband, you are strong enough for this." Orin squeezed my hand. "*This* is why the Realm made you my first assignment. I don't think a changeling has ever been lost before, but it happened and the Realm is determined to set it right. I am here to bring you back to where you belong. Follow me. Come *home.*"

My chest tightened. I twisted a lock of hair between my fingers. With a few sentences Orin had cracked the ceiling of my reality. Its center was collapsing and sunlight rushed into the gloom. I felt dazed, squinting through the settling dust to see this new world he promised. Dare I escape my isolation through the opening

Orin offered? It was warm and exposing, a long awaited validation of my existence, my *truth*. But freedom was a lofty climb with muscles I had never used before. I might exhaust myself before I escaped, slip and plummet back to loveless isolation and break my back on the floor of my prison, only to stare at a light I was too weak to embrace.

Then again, staying would drive me crazy with questions and doubts and never ending re-evaluations of life and self. If Orin spoke truth, then my whole life had been a lie.

The waitress returned with the father and son's drinks. No glares between them. No stiffening of postures. No fidgeting or hurrying to escape. Their smiles were genuine. They were strangers, yet shared an unspoken social connection. My eyes welled with tears.

Orin pulled me to him. "Don't cry," he whispered in my ear. "This is a happy day."

Maybe it was stupid to trust the pointed-eared stranger. But a spark of hope had ignited inside me and I had nowhere else to go. Orin didn't shy from me or glare or ignore my existence. He knew where I came from. He knew how I felt in a world that felt much too big. And he wasn't the only one. A whole community awaited my return.

"The Realm wants to help you," Orin said, hugging me tight. "But faeries are not darklings. We will not kidnap you."

I crumbled against his chest like a found child who believed they had been forgotten. And I guess I was in a sense. In the span of a morning my perspective of Orin had shifted from stranger to companion to friend. Potentially my savior.

"Okay," I said, and forced a smile. "Show me the way."

CHAPTER SEVENTEEN

Orin threw his words like strips of steak and I was unable to get my fill.

Cars zipped past us on the four lane highway; an eight foot cinderblock wall blocked our view of the town to the right, confining us to the road. The snow had melted, and the moist pavement glistened with oil stains, soaked litter, broken tempered glass. My feet pointed west, but my eyes remained to the side, watching the faerie man with his thumb pointing out to the traffic. He had talked about the Realm since the truck stop, explaining festivals and commerce, deeds and politics, happiness and community, acceptance and warmth. He explained how every faerie had a purpose, whether on the Realm or on Earth. Some faeries helped plants to grow, some guided the elements, some protected faerie secrets, some encouraged nature to thrive, others worked in social and government support, and much more. Everything I had spent a lifetime seeking waited for me beyond a stone gateway in the Sierra Nevada, my personal happily-ever-after. I grinned like a child enchanted with fairytales and fantastic adventures. Only this time I didn't believe the stories Orin told me were real—I *knew* they were—and my heart practically glowed.

But every glow casts a shadow. Insecurities crept around me like swamp mist, blurring Orin's perfect illustrations. I had been born a faerie, but I was raised white trash in a midwest trailer park, and my life experiences didn't extend much further than a cash register and a kitchen. How would I ever contribute to this faerie land? Would my dullness mar its shine? Would I be a drain on its striving perfection? I tried pushing my insecurities away, but like swamp mist it swirled, recollected, lingered. I asked Orin questions to distract myself, but I never interrupted or interjected when he spoke. I remained silent, attentive, eager to snatch up the Realm's details and secrets and truths. I wanted Orin to tell me *everything*. Maybe then I would stride into his magical world and prevent myself from playing the fool.

"I do admit I prefer the Realm," Orin said. "Night and coldness are nonexistent there; it's always warm and sunny." Something red glinted on the freeway shoulder. Orin picked up a chunk of broken reflector and twisted it in the sunlight, making it flash. He licked his thumb, cleaned the dust off the surface, and placed it in his jacket pocket. "That's not to say Earth hasn't influenced our culture. Most faeries blackout their bedrooms to sleep better. The practice was once discouraged in fear of darklings murdering citizens in their beds, but with stronger security now in place it's no longer a concern. Earth-workers must still be cautious, of course."

"Do you worry about that, with becoming a retriever and all?" I asked.

"Naw. I've been trained to deal with darklings. When you get down to it, most of them are cowards. Most evil things are."

I remembered Delano's blood-moon eyes and shuddered. "Cowardly or not, I never want to face one again."

Orin chuckled. "At the rate we're going,

you'll be a darkling expert by the time we reach the Realm. Don't be surprised if the Realm offers you an Earth job because of it."

I perked. "You think the Realm will offer me a job?"

"Of course. The Realm guarantees everyone a job. Why *not* you?"

I shrugged. "I figured I'm too talentless, too long removed."

Too illegitimate.

"Nonsense," Orin said, waving his hand dismissively. "We just need to find your niche. Hmmm. You might enjoy being a taleteller."

"What's a taleteller?"

"They're faeries who spread lies to humans to protect the Realm. They're why humans believe faeries are tiny and flowery and imaginary. They often receive assignments infiltrating Earth's entertainment industry."

"Oh. I suck at lying."

Orin tapped his lip with his forefinger in thought. "Let's see, then. What abouuut..." His face brightened, blue eyes sparkling. "A healer! You'd make an *excellent* healer!"

My nose scrunched up. "I'm not into blood."

Orin chuckled. "Not *that* kind of healer. An *Earth* healer. They're faeries assigned to repairing nature. You could help heal the acid mine drainage you told me about."

I blinked. Me? *Seriously?* Repair the pollution that devastated landscapes and killed wildlife beyond count? *Me?* My insides tingled with excitement. And fear. The polluted orange waters spanned numerous states. How could a mouse like myself handle such an enormous task? Then again, how could I not? Orin insisted I had the power inside me to make such changes. If I let self-doubt block me from repairing a poisoned land, then I was no better than those who did the poisoning.

"If I healed the land ... I ... You don't know how much that would mean, Orin. The destruction is *terrible.*"

Orin nodded solemnly. "Yes. The chickadee described it to me," he said. I declined the candy cane he offered me from his inner coat pocket. He tore off the cellophane and bit the end. "Faeries left Ohio's region after it was deemed stable a few centuries ago. The Realm is probably unaware of the damage and will be thrilled to have someone knowledgeable of the area to restart the healing."

I had felt helpless along those orange banks, but if I convinced the Realm to allow me to work with those poisoned waters, heal them, help them *thrive* ... My gait became a bounce. "What do I need to do?" I asked. "Do you think the Realm will let—?"

A semi truck blew its horn—*Woooommmmp!*—its engine rumbling as it rolled ahead of us, pulling to a stop on the side of the road. We hurried to the cab and opened the passenger door. The driver peered down at us, a heavyset woman with a frizzy perm and a one-eyed toy poodle nestled in her lap. "Where you two headed?" she asked.

"West," Orin replied.

She nodded pensively, as if he had

relayed detailed instructions. "I can take you as far as The Hills. Will that do ya?"

"Sounds great," Orin said, though I doubted he had any idea where *The Hills* was.

The next several hours were torture. We traveled fast on warm leather seats, yet I had a hard time feeling grateful. To my left, the truck driver gobbled endless amounts of sunflower seeds and griped incessantly about politicians. The answers to my awaiting life sat to my right, forced into silence, his mica hair glinting against the window.

The truck driver dropped us off at a freeway exit littered with billboards and fast food marquees—our best chance to find accommodations for the night, she had said. We snacked on cinnamon toast leftover from breakfast as we walked the mile toward the motels, the town hardly more than a dingy smudge on the roadway. It was here where I realized why Orin carried so much cash. We had no identification or credit cards, but some motels took bribes. Orin said they were easy to spot —cracked paint, old signs, cigarette butts on the walkways. I doubted him, however, after the second roadside motel kicked us out, and I worried we would spend the night on the street. But Orin kept his head high, smiling brightly as we entered motel number three. The lady behind the counter glowered suspiciously at us with piggy eyes, but when Orin offered payment in full, a three-hundred dollar deposit, and a hundred dollar bribe, she asked no questions, had us sign no papers, and handed him a key card.

Our motel room was a 1970s scrap pile. Lumpy green carpet, veined mirror, golden sconces. Orin dropped his backpack to the floor and petted the peeling flocked wallpaper as if the room had come with a lapdog. "The wars lasted far too long," he said, continuing our conversation from our walk through the town. He tossed his fedora to the nearest bed. "We lost too many faeries in senseless blood. Fortunately, those days have mostly ended. The remaining darklings still cause havoc, but the Realm no longer worries. History always proves good defeats evil in the end."

"Have darklings ever tried making trees?" I asked.

Orin tilted his head. "Trees?"

"I mean peas. Gah!" I rolled my tongue with frustration. " I mean *peace!* Have darklings ever tried making *peace.* Sorry. I think my brain fell asleep without me."

Orin chuckled softly. "The only *peace* darklings attempted were lies used to kill good men foolish enough to trust their word." He ripped off a small piece of flocked wallpaper and folded it into his pocket. "Go to sleep. We have a long way to go and will talk more on the road."

Twelve hours later I woke from a bladder trying to burst its seams. Orin sat at the rickety table beside the window in his tattered jeans and tweed jacket. A daddy longlegs perched on his thumb near his face. He smirked as I shuffled out of the bathroom, yawning.

"Sleep well?" Orin asked.

I nodded groggily and rummaged through our backpacks for the remainder of our truck stop leftovers, only to find them gone. "Sorry," Orin said, sinking into his shoulders. "I woke up hungry an hour ago and figured you'd sleep until morning." My stomach growled and Orin frowned. He peeked out the curtains. The sky was tinted with navy, the first hint of the dawn.

Orin's brow wrinkled as if in deep concentration. After a few seconds he asked the spider: "What do you think?" All I heard in response was silence, but Orin sighed as if he had received an answer of little help. "Yeah, same here."

"Is that spider actually talking?" I asked.

"Of course," Orin said.

"Why can't I hear it?"

"You must strengthen your magic first." Orin set the daddy longlegs onto the table, then flipped the fedora onto his head. "We believe there is enough light, and there's a restaurant across the street. I'll bring us back some breakfast. But don't open the door for *anybody*."

Orin jiggled the doorknob after he left to make sure it was locked. I knelt beside the table, eye-level with the daddy longlegs. "Have anything to say?" I asked, and strained my ears to listen.

The daddy longlegs lifted its leg and pointed at my nose.

"Sorry. I don't understand sign language," I said. The spider scurried off the table and out of sight. "Fine. Be that way."

Every muscle in my body felt locked in a winch. I started a shower, hoping the hot water would pound away my aches and pains. I had just soaked my hair when I realized the shampoo was in my bag beside the bed. My skin broke out in gooseflesh when I stepped from the stall, the tile icy against my feet. I tied a thin towel over my chest and opened the door.

Delano stood on the other side.

I shrieked. Delano shoved his foot inside before the door slammed shut. I ducked and rushed for the gap between him and the doorjamb. His hand slid down my wet arm as I slipped through. He snatched my wrist, jerking my shoulder in the socket.

"Let go!" I shouted.

"*Quiet* you foolish girl," Delano hissed.

"Help! *Someone help me!*"

He grabbed my other wrist and shook me to face him. The towel loosened and started to slip. "Pay attention!" he snapped. I struggled and writhed as he forced my hands to his temples. My fingers brushed his ears. The tips were deformed—flat, bumpy, vaguely resembling the edge of a pie crust. I froze, wide-eyed.

"I will not hurt you," Delano said. "As I recall, *you* were the one who threw a rock at my head, scratched me, and killed my moth, all because I built you a fire, warmed the weather, and said hello."

"*You* chased me and tackled me in the snow!"

"Yes. How terrible of me," Delano sneered. "Not wanting a young woman to run off screaming into the nighttime wilderness, alone and freezing." I opened my mouth to retort; he cut-me off. "Besides, even if I *wanted* to harm you, I wouldn't dare with your faerie *guide* lurking this close. So sit down. *Quietly*. I want only to talk, all right?"

My deep breath steamed in the frigid air. I nodded and Delano released me. I noticed the upper-right of his irises were flattened, like thumbprints in balls of red clay. I clenched the towel over my dripping body and sat on the chair beside the table, the cushion scratchy against my bare thighs. My teeth started to chatter. Delano fetched my overcoat from the dresser and swirled it over me as if preparing my lap for crystal flutes and white bone china. Warily, I slid my arms into the backward sleeves. Steam billowed out the bathroom door across the room; the shower water pattered.

"Ss-so what do you want?" I asked.

"For you to listen. But I damn well know you won't. Not yet, anyway. So instead I want you to ask questions."

"Errrr. Why are you chasing me, then?"

Delano barked a laugh. "Not to *me*. To Orin." A glimpse of the bed flashed through his arm. I jerked back, startled. Delano scowled at his fingers, blipping in and out of sight as if powered on a weak circuit. "Damn. Dawn is almost here."

I lifted a mocking eyebrow. "Aww. Will you burst into flames?"

"Sadly, no." Delano smiled a strained smile, which reminded me of a war captive cursed with hope and undying faith. It made my insides curl with shame. "I will merely disappear into the darkshine until sunset."

I cleared my throat. "What's the *darkshine*?"

"Light *covers* darkness. It does not repel darkness like humans believe. The dark and its magic are always present—*darklings* are always present—beneath the sunlight's magical current, watching from the darkshine like ghosts until sunlight fades." He noticed my confusion and smiled apologetically. "It is difficult to explain and must be experienced to fully understand."

I thought about the campfire, about the charcoal shining black in the flame.

Delano knelt in front of me, the edge of his feathery hair translucent. "So listen quick. Ask Orin questions. Ask until you are satisfied, then doubt his word and ask him more."

"All I do is ask him questions!"

"You ask him about pleasantries, about pretty lands and stories that glitter and shine. Ask the ugly questions. He told you faeries flatten their infants' ears to hide them from the darklings, right? So why are Orin's ears pointed? How do faeries know which infants to hide?

"You see my ruddy eyes, my crawling shadows and world of darkness, and assume I am the bad guy. And because you assume, you believe it is truth. Yet a cute chickadee talks and you instantly assume good intentions? You place your faith in a stranger who shines?" Delano chuckled, darkly. "I hear you even feared the coyote until it licked your face. Will it help my cause to do the same?" He slid his tongue across his teeth.

"No!" I gasped, making Delano laugh. I glowered. "*You're trying to trick me.* Orin is harmless. He is like me. He's—"

"—a changeling?" Delano finished for me. His eyes twinkled like starlight. "Another question to ask." He slid a finger along the ridge of his flattened ear. "Who are you *really* like?"

The door's electronic lock clacked. "I hope you like—" Orin's eyes widened. He dropped the carryout bag in the doorway and rushed Delano, snarling.

I gasped and pulled my feet onto the chair as Orin struck the darkling's gut like a pendulum. Delano wheezed and fell to his knees.

"Orin, stop! You're hurting—" I caught my tongue. *Am I seriously defending my enemy?*

A rush of moths flew through the door and swarmed Orin's head. Orin stumbled backward, arms thrashing. Delano morphed into a shadowman and sped for the door, a silhouette blipping in and out of focus. Orin lunged for the silhouette's arm, magic shimmering like waves of heat off his skin. "I expose you, you bastard!"

Delano squealed like a fox with its foot in a trap; his face materialized in the silhouette, twisted with pain. Orin drew a knife with a six-inch blade from inside his jacket. The sun broke the horizon and Delano disappeared like a shadow in the light, his clothing falling to the floor.

"Raaaagh!" Orin yelled, and kicked Delano's pants across the room. Springtime had vanished from his face, giving way to a sweltering summer. "I know you're still here you dark*slime*!" Orin shouted to the air. Wildfires blazed in his eyes. He brandished the knife as the moths rushed out the door. "I know you hear and see me. Leave her *alone!*"

Orin threw his head back in frustration. "I am such an *idiot*." He set the knife on the table and hurried to my side. "Are you hurt?"

"No. He just wanted to talk."

"To poison your mind with *lies*, you mean," Orin spat. "I am *so sorry*. I thought we were safe with light in the sky. I should have waited until the sun fully broke the horizon, but I stupidly ate all the food and your stomach growled and—" He started collecting our belongings in a mad frenzy. "Get dressed. We must leave *immediately*. We need to—"

"Orin, relax." He wheeled around, his eyes still blazing. "Delano can't hurt us from the darkshine, right?"

"No. But the creep is *watching* us." I lifted an eyebrow, silently asking what would stop Delano from following and watching us as we headed out. Orin sighed. "Okay. Fine. But *please* let's hurry."

The shower's water had turned into glacier runoff. Although knowing Delano might be spying deterred me from finishing my shower, anyway. "You better hide your eyes," I murmured to the bathroom walls, and struggled to dress myself beneath my overcoat.

When I stepped out of the bathroom, Orin was exchanging his white T-shirt for the black turtleneck, his bare back facing me. "That's an interesting tattoo," I said.

Black lines laced down his back like wrought iron twisted into the shape of dragonfly wings. Orin glanced over his shoulder, smiling proudly. Spring had returned to his face and I saw the man of sunshine and apple blossoms and warm summer rain. "It's the design of the border sentries," he said. "But if I'm promoted to retriever the Realm will fill the gaps with—"

The daddy longlegs crawled up Orin's side and rested beside his ear. Orin's *pointed* ear. I bit my lip, my fingertips humming with the ghost print of Delano's flattened ridge.

"What is it?" I asked as the daddy longlegs scurried back to the floor.

"She says we need to watch channel three." Orin clicked on the television and switched the channel to the morning news.

My husband's face scowled on the screen.

CHAPTER EIGHTEEN

"You are such a liar!" I shouted at Sam's face.

"She loved taking walks," Sam told the news-camera. A yellow banner flashed *Christmas Abduction!* across the bottom of the screen. His lips slid into a joyless smile. "But when she didn't come home, I knew something was wrong. She would never disappear without reason."

"*Without reason?* You asshole! You—" My throat tightened, stifling my words. *You cheated on me*. My eyes watered. I couldn't say it. I couldn't hear the words aloud. I couldn't make them *true.*

Orin squeezed my shoulder gently. "Shhhhh."

I ground my teeth, my fingernails digging into my palms. Pornographic photos of Sam's secret lover had proved he didn't want me. Our phone conversation made it clear my wellbeing was outside his concerns. *So why is he trying to drag me back into his life?* It was as if he smelled my freedom, and like a missile zoomed in to destroy my happiness. *Well screw you, Sam. Screw. You. I no longer want your darkness impeding my life. For the first time in my life I am free.*

At least, I had been.

Sam's shirt collar was wrinkled and I hated myself for feeling a pang of guilt. "Fortunately we traced her phone call. I just pray she is still alive and unharmed." The bridge of his nose wrinkled as if distressed, but I knew better. Sam's eyebrows always arched when he was genuinely upset. Instead they locked in a straight line. I knew that expression as well as his barbs which had always followed throughout our marriage. Anger. Vindictiveness. I shuddered to the memories as if the past had opened before me and brought a cold wind.

"This rescue-mission will continue until she's home and her kidnapper is brought to justice."

Orin scoffed with disgust. "He thinks *I* kidnapped you? I'm not a darkling!"

"He doesn't know I'm a changeling, remember?"

"Oh." Orin smiled, his cheeks reddening. "Right."

A reporter chirped off camera: "Do you think this was done deliberately because of your candidacy for Sheriff?"

A shadow passed over Sam's face; the corner of his lip twitched. He stood before an orange brick wall, but he belonged in a dusty drinking town, boot spurs jingling as he clomped through batwing doors. "That is one theory, yes," Sam said. "And God help *any* abductor once I am elected."

So *that* was Sam's purpose—using his revenge on me to strengthen his political campaign. I scowled and briefly forgot about Delano. A new darkness had entered the motel room. Sam lacked magic, yet the power he wielded made me grow cold. Running away had humiliated him and endangered his campaign, and for retribution he would trap me, skin me alive, gut me of everything I loved and wanted and seize what he thought

I owed. He believed I belonged under his thumb, serving him. I remembered what he had told me in his mother's guest room, the meaning of his words now clear: *No one takes my girl.* The tears in my eyes felt as if they'd steam from the anger burning inside me. Confessing why I had fled was pointless; Sam would twist the story and convince his law-enforcement brethren I was brainwashed. He would lie unscrupulously to maintain his new use for me, his *publicity stunt.* An invisible noose squeezed my throat, for in the darkest most hidden chambers of my heart, I realized my husband preferred I suffer, scared and alone and without any answers, than leave without his permission.

Cheater, cheater, freedom eater. Had a wife and swore to beat her.

Sam's face scrunched up as if he would cry, but no tears were in his eyes, only tumbleweeds and six-shooters and aces under the table. His grimace was pure barbed-wire. I wiped my brow on my sleeve. *My husband doesn't want to rescue me,* I realized. *He wants a lynching.*

My mother clucked her tongue inside my head. *You should have listened to me. I told you to be a good wife, but what do I know? Now your new friend will suffer for your misbehavior. And it's all. Your. Fault.*

The curtains were open an inch, casting a beam of early light onto the table. I jumped up like a fugitive to close them. The waves I had caused in my marriage had formed a riptide; the thick curtains bunched in my fists as if capable of saving me from being dragged out to sea.

"That was Deputy Samuel Thatcher

yesterday afternoon, regarding the abduction of his wife, Miriam," a newscaster said, off-camera. A photo of my face from his birthday party last year flashed on screen. "The man who gave Miriam and her alleged kidnapper a ride to the Stop-and-Travel on the morning of December twenty-ninth reports that the alleged kidnapper is male, in his mid to late twenties—" Orin snorted at this "—light complexion, about five-ten, blond, blue-eyed, wearing tattered blue jeans, a fedora, and a brown jacket. They are believed to be heading west across the United States to California. If you have any information, please call—" Orin clicked off the television as a black widow scurried across the screen.

I flopped down onto the bed and pressed my forehead against my knees. "I hate him," I said, my thighs muffling my voice. "I don't want to go back."

"You won't."

I peered up at Orin. "But the media is sensationalizing this—this—*lie!* Soon everyone will know my face."

"We are hundreds of miles away from where they traced the phone call," Orin said. "That gives us time."

"But *how much* time? They know we're heading to California. It's a simple jump to pinpoint our destination."

Orin pinched his underlip in thought. After a moment his eyes brightened and he beamed with a toothy grin. "We'll head north!"

"Isn't everything we need west?"

"Yes!" Orin said. "So north is perfect. No one will suspect it."

"And then what? Hide out in an igloo until this blows over?"

"No, silly. We will still reach California. We'll just detour onto the ley line."

"What's the ley line?"

"It is an energy system network that crisscrosses the Earth. If we hop on at an entrance node, it will transport us along the stream. There is an exit near the Realm passage in the Sierra Nevada, but the nearest entrance for that stream is in North Dakota. Sam will never suspect it. And since the ley line is guarded and sustained with light, it will be nearly impossible for Delano to follow." Orin gnawed his underlip. "If we can't hitch to the entrance, however—or if the sentries won't let us in—it'll add several days to our journey." Orin glanced at the black widow on top of the television, as slick as a drop of oil. I thought I saw fear flash across his face. "The gamble is worth it." Orin fidgeted nervously with his sleeve's cuff, and I worried about what the black widow said.

"Is everything okay?" I asked.

Orin lifted his chin. "Of course." The cloud passed and his face gleamed with sunshine and nectar and warm golden shores. He fetched the take-out bag from the floor and set the contents on the table. "Eat," he said. "We will need our strength."

CHAPTER NINETEEN

The low hills on the horizon resembled two sleeping swans with their heads tucked behind their wings. Rounded. White. Seemingly impossible to reach. A gray, hazy sky squatted on their backs as if the sun had woken to this frozen landscape and decided: *Ugh. Sooo not dealing with this crap today.* Then pulled a blanket of clouds over its head and called in sick.

I stuck close to Orin's side to draw warmth off his faerie-fever. Our elbows were hooked, my raw nose tucked behind my coat's collar, my olive hat pulled down low. We slogged along a slushy tire-trail on a backcountry highway. Black cows gawked at us from snow filled pastures. The bare trees in the distance stood like busted capillaries against the leaden sky.

"Have you ever been on the ley line?" I asked.

"I have, but not on Earth's," Orin said. "All ley lines in the Realm are free and open for travel. Our leaders feel it encourages unity and reminds us we are all a part of something bigger than ourselves." A penny glinted in the melting slush. Orin picked it up, wiped it on his jeans, and placed it in his jacket pocket. "I pity humans and their costly inconvenient means of travel," Orin continued. "It's no wonder segregation is rampant here. I mean, how can humans connect when they are kept apart? They are left to gossip about customs they have never participated in, and despise races with whom they have never broke bread."

"Why don't faeries stop guarding Earth's entrances, then?" I asked. "If we—er, *humans*—had access, wouldn't it create a better understanding of humankind?"

"Years ago we opened Earth's lines to humans. Unfortunately, governments hid them from the common man. Militaries abused the systems, spying on governments unaware of the streams. Whispers of psychics and remote-viewers murmured within the ranks. Paranoia led to silent wars. Given the opportunity for unity, humans chose domination and control, so the Realm locked down Earth's systems again." Orin shook his head. "Pathetic, really."

Orin squeezed my elbow with his, his eyes sparkling like two pools of topaz water. "You are *so* fortunate, Miriam. Soon you will have access to a whole *world.* My favorite place is Griel. Whenever I have time off I always—"

Orin spent the next thirty minutes telling me personal stories about life in the Realm. A life I had been forced to trade for a father who had deserted his bastard daughter in a trailer park with a mother who refused to hug. I should have been greedy for any scrap of information about this new life I headed toward. I should have asked a thousand questions which glittered and shined like the man at my side. But my mind kept drifting back to Delano, his remarks about questions, and his tortured smile when I had asked if he would burst into flames.

"—absolutely perfect! Like gigantic, sparkling diamonds with—," Orin was saying, his free hand gesturing to emphasize the greatness of his descriptions about the valley of Sulare. His eyes were wide and distant, glimmering with memories.

I glowered. Delano had acted as if he wasn't the bad guy. But that was stupid. Orin was pure honey and sunshine and warm summer shores. He had shared his jacket, washed my clothes, hugged away my sorrow. Delano was cold and hollow and as dark as murder. I kicked a clump of slush. Delano had obviously been manipulating me. Trying to make me doubt—

"Are you okay?"

"Sorry?"

"You seem upset." Orin frowned. A flock of Canada geese honked in a V overhead. "Was it something I said?"

"No. I was, um, thinking about your tattoo. I thought faeries had real wings and could fly. Guess that is a lie from the taletellers. I'm a little bummed, is all."

"Oh, but we *can* fly," Orin said. "Er, well, sort of. Our tattoos symbolize that." He unhooked his elbow around mine, scanning the empty roadway. Nothing surrounded us but the cows and the frozen horizon. "Follow me."

We slipped through the barbed wire fence and into the pasture. The cows lifted their heads from the dead weeds poking out of the snow, gaping as if a traveling circus had rolled into their sleepy town. One gave a low, drawn-out *meeeeeew*.

Orin pressed his fedora down on his head, then dashed off. The cows jumped and trotted back as he sped through the field. I had just enough time to wonder if I should follow him when his feet left the snow. I gasped, delighted. He didn't fly, exactly. More like bounced across the air, as if leaping across an invisible trampoline ten feet off the ground.

I bobbed on my toes, watching, beaming, feeling seven years old again with my fingers curled around the schoolyard's chain-link fence. Back then I had watched, mesmerized, as the high schoolers across the street swarmed off grounds for lunch. Teachers had never stopped them; punishment had never loomed. They were free and they knew it. Every day I had daydreamed about joining them, knowing it would never happen. I was just a *little kid*, after all. But I also knew *little kids* eventually became *big kids*, and one day I too would know freedom.

Orin flew until he was a speck in the distance, then bounded back to me. He bounced off the air twenty feet above me, lightly whacked his head against his backpack when he summersaulted, and glided to the ground before me, as smooth as a drifting feather.

I clapped my hands, laughing. "That is amazing!"

He tugged my sleeve. "Fly with me."

"No *way* can I do that."

"Don't be silly. You're a faerie, and it's just nature communication. Run until you feel the air and light, then ask them to lift you."

I bit my lip, tingling with excitement. The thought of me flying. *Me!* "What does air and light feel like?"

"Hm." Orin twisted his mouth, thinking. "It kind of feels like a song. Now come *on.* We'll cover a lot more ground if I teach you to fly."

Hand and hand, we sprinted through the field. Orin lightened; the air tugged him on my arm like a kite in a windstorm. "You feel it first here," Orin said, patting his chest.

I was panting too hard to tell him I only felt the ground pounding my soles and a stitch in my side. Snow crunched beneath our feet. My breasts felt bruised from bouncing without a bra, making me grateful that all my adolescent wishes for a larger cup size had never been granted. With my thoughts I asked the air and light to lift me. I begged for the freedom to escape my husband, and pleaded to prove I was worth Orin's time.

"Stop!" I wheezed after a minute of nothing. Orin released my hand and flew up twenty feet; I buckled over at the waist, gasping for air. Maybe I was incapable of magic. After all, the sole evidence I had that I *was* a faerie was the conflicting statements of two strange men.

Orin glided back to me; his boot buckles jingled when they struck the ground. "Did you feel *anything?*" he asked. Was that disappointment in his voice or my insecure imagination?

"No. Nothing," I said, between puffs of breath. "I am. The worst. Faerie. Ever."

"Nonsense," he said, straightening his fedora. "You've just hit puberty. These things take time."

I snorted, rubbing beneath my ribs. "I hit puberty fifteen years ago, Orin."

"Sexually, not magically. Faeries stop aging *physically* in their mid to late twenties, *then* they develop magically."

"Whoa, wait," I said. "How long do faeries live then?"

"Typically 350 to 450 years. Some faeries

have reached 600, though."

And here I've been fretting about hitting my thirties.

"How old are you?" I asked.

"Sixty-three."

I shook my head, chuckling softly to myself. "Unbelievable. I thought I would get Tinkerbell, and instead I got Peter Pan."

"Huh?"

"Never mind."

We slipped through the barbed wire fence and continued down the slush. "Hitting puberty let the Realm find you, actually," Orin said. He picked a Miller Lite bottle cap off the roadway and placed it in his jacket pocket. "New magics release an energy pulse. The Realm didn't have any unattended pre-pubescents in Ohio, so it had to be a changeling. *Unfortunately*, darklings also feel the pulse and until your energies stabilize it's like a tracking beacon."

"Which is how Delano is following us I take it."

"Probably," Orin said. "He *could* be tailing us in the darkshine, but he needs to sleep sometime."

Is Delano asleep now, I wondered? *Or is he strolling beside me in the darkshine, laughing his ass off while I make a fool of myself?* I grimaced. More likely he was clucking his tongue, wondering why I refused to ask Orin a simple question.

I cleared my throat and pushed my hair behind my flattened ears. I didn't *have* to ask Orin anything, of course, but it *would* stop the annoying thoughts about Delano. And it wasn't as if I was asking Orin about his sex life or anything. It was a question regarding *me*, for God's sake. Totally innocent.

So why did I feel like I was about to show him a photo-text from his secret lover?

I took a deep breath, catching a whiff of rotting roadkill. "Um, Orin? May I ask you something?"

Orin smiled, his teeth a tad too big for his mouth. "Of course," he said. "You may ask me anything."

"Um, how do darklings choose which infants to steal?"

"The darkshine prevents darklings from entering the Realm, thus they steal only faeries born on Earth. That is why you being a changeling is so rare; most are born in the Realm."

Oh. That makes sense. I sighed with relief.

But a few seconds later Delano's voice barreled into my head: *Ask Orin questions. Ask until you are satisfied, then doubt his word and ask him more.*

"So you were born in the Realm?" I asked.

"Nope. I'm Earth-born." Orin picked up a pink rock and twisted it in the gray light, as if examining the quality of a diamond.

"Then why are your ears pointed?"

Orin lowered the rock. "Huh?"

"Well, if your ears are pointed and you are Earth-born, then not every infant is a target of the darklings, right? So how do faeries know which infants the darklings will steal?"

Orin nodded. "It's true. Darklings seek only some newborns." He clenched the rock in his fist and plodded onwards.

I waited for Orin to elaborate. He didn't. "So how do faeries know which ones?"

"Darklings select certain families."

I waited nearly thirty-seconds for an explanation, but Orin walked in silence, chin up, face forward. His expression was as blank as the endless horizon. His lips, which I had started to believe were frozen in a half-smile, were pulled down in a grimace.

I quickened my pace to keep at his side. "Well, *why?*" I asked.

"Because darklings are evil."

I snorted. "Surely they must have a *reason.*"

Orin wheeled on me. "Because they're *darklings*! That's what darklings *do*!" His outburst made me jump back. Orin pinched his sinuses with a sigh. "Look. Earth is the child of the Realm. When Earth was born, faeries became responsible for her care, but some families were lazy and selfish and refused to help. As punishment, the Realm stripped their day magic and imprisoned them in Earth's darkness. The darklings resent our warmth and our light and have sought revenge ever since. Since they're incapable of *physically* attacking the Realm, they kidnap our children—namely from the bloodlines responsible for their imprisonment, like *yours*—and brainwash them against us."

"So darklings are faeries," I said.

Orin's nostrils flared. "Darklings are *not* faeries!"

"But you just said—"

"Darklings are *evil!* Worse than demons!

The only good darkling is a dead darkling and the sooner they're gone the better for everyone!"

"But if they tend to Earth's nocturnal life, how—?"

"The Realm does a better job."

"But if they're stuck here, then why—?"

Orin whirled on me. *"Why are you being difficult?* We were having such a nice time and now you're ruining it with stupid questions!"

I gaped at him. A summer storm had passed over Orin's face, blocking his inner sunshine. *What secrets are hidden behind those storm clouds?* I wondered. *What does his thunder mute?* Delano had been correct and in that moment I hated him more than ever before. He was the face of every schoolmate who had laughed at my belief in magic, and every adult who had scolded my imagination. I had finally found my place in the world and in the span of a question he had ripped it away.

"I-I'm sorry," I said. "Please don't be upset. I was just curious."

Orin chucked the rock into the field and stormed down the road. A cow *meeeewed.* A few seconds later Orin stopped, his shoulders drooping. Timidly, I joined his side.

"I'm sorry, Miriam. *Really.* The darklings have caused our people so much torture and misery that the subject is difficult to speak about," Orin said, and handed me a candy cane from his jacket's inside pocket. "I know everything is new to you and difficult to understand. But trust me. The Realm can act *only* from a position of light and purity. The goodness the darklings want to destroy." He hooked my elbow with his and started down the road again. "The *only* way faeries can survive is if the darklings are eliminated."

CHAPTER TWENTY

The mold stain on the motel ceiling looked like a skull made of broccoli, and I had been staring at it for an hour. The nightmare that had woken me lingered—chaotic images of sunlight slashing Delano apart, as violently as an axe through lilies. Orin snored softly in a pile of blankets on the floor to my left, the six-inch blade tucked against his side. I watched his shoulder rise and fall beside the bed, his chin bent, eyes buried in the crook of his arm. *The sun has set,* I thought idly to myself, and for some reason felt on overwhelming sense of sadness.

The heater groaned beneath the window, straining to fight off the cold. I pushed away the sheets and padded around the room, everything wan and sallow in the dim bathroom light. I peeked into the closet, the bathroom, the rust-stained shower, expecting to find Delano's smirk, or darkness coiling along the floor like mist. Instead I found empty spaces and static shadows. But that was good, wasn't it? What girl wanted a shadowman lurking around her bed while she dreamed?

The neighbor's television jabbered through the thin motel walls. A shadow fluttered in the corner of my eye. I wheeled around to face the door and found a moth crawling along the jamb. I went to the window and cracked open the curtain.

Delano sat on a curb in the motel parking lot across from the closed office. He looked as if he had just gotten off a catering shift, in his black pants and white button-down, the sleeves rolled up to his elbows. A scrawny mongrel stood in front of him, staring intently at his hands. Even in the dim, yellow glow of the ZOOM ZOOM MOTOR INN's electric marquee (AAA & Third Night Always *Free*!), it was obviously Delano. Shadows coiled around his ankles like dry ice.

The only way faeries can survive is if the darklings are eliminated.

I gnawed on my thumbnail. Orin's statement stood out in my memory like a piano slightly off key. I didn't believe he had lied, yet something seemed hidden just the same.

Delano snapped something thin in his hands and tossed it to the dog's feet. The dog licked the pavement, and a smile touched my lips. I grabbed my overcoat off the dresser and—

And what the hell am I doing? Am I seriously about to go to him?

I needed to wake Orin, have him chase Delano out of our lives for my own protection. I went to his pile of blankets, then stopped, staring down at his mess of seashore hair. I had yet to experience Delano's supposed evil. Maybe Orin was mistaken. I turned back to the window. Maybe what I needed was Delano beside me, whispering the secrets Orin refused to tell me into my ear. My folded ear. My folded ear like his.

The overcoat bunched in my fists. *No. Orin's job is to protect me.* I needed Delano gone, to know the night was safe to wander.

I scowled. No. That was my mother's influence. I did not need a man to guide my life. Plus, what good was Orin's protection if he lured me into other dangers? I sighed, frustrated. I needed to ask Delano what was real and ... No. He was darkness manifested, surely brimmed with lies. I needed ... Dammit! I had no idea *what* I needed. But I'd never figure it out acting indecisive in a dank motel room.

I buttoned the overcoat over my pajama shirt—the polar bears permanently stained from grime and bad memories but blessedly clean. I couldn't find my pants in the dark and didn't want to risk waking Orin with the overhead light. Fortunately, the overcoat covered me to my knees. I tucked my folding knife into the pocket, slid into my hiking boots without bothering to tie the laces, and tiptoed to the door. The deadbolt peeled back with a *clack.* I stiffened. Orin did not stir. I released a long, slow breath. This felt like betrayal, but why? I had made no promises to Orin. I was not his property or his lover or his wife.

I squared my jaw and slipped outside. The moth followed and fluttered into the darkness.

My heart pounded as I crossed the parking lot. My loose shoelaces whisked against my ankles. Shadows coiled around Delano, but he did not look in my direction. He didn't seem to notice me at all. My misty breaths abandoned my lungs for the night. My bare legs broke out in gooseflesh, and every hair stood on end. Ridiculously I blushed as I realized I hadn't shaved my legs in over a week.

"Good evening, Miriam," Delano said in his murmuring owl voice. He tossed something to the dog, which ended up not being a dog but a thin, red fox. The fox snatched the tidbit with its mouth and gobbled it down. Delano peered up at me, smirking. The flatness on the right side of his irises had increased, skimming his pupils. "Have a pleasant conversation with Orin earlier?"

I crossed my arms over my chest. "Wanted to gloat, I see."

Delano chuckled, deep and low. "Not at all. I merely want what you do," he said. "For you to realize where, and with *who*, you belong."

I snorted. "What makes you think I care about your wants?"

"Considering you fled from me earlier as if I was the devil himself, and now you come to me willingly?" His eyes slid up my body. He flashed a sexy little grin. "Half dressed, no less."

"Maybe I'm just here to prove I'm not scared of you."

"Good. You shouldn't be." The fox yipped and pawed his pant leg. I heard a fibrous snap as Delano broke something in his hand and tossed it. The fox snatched it in midair.

I squinted in the dim, yellow light. "Are you feeding that fox a *stick?*"

"No. A Slim Jim I bought at the 7-11." He patted the curb beside him. "Sit. Help me feed her. She's famished."

I glanced over my shoulder to the motel room. To where Orin slept.

Delano rolled his eyes. "Oh will you just *sit.* I could have snatched you from your bed if I wanted." His sexy grin returned. "Unless, of course, you *are* scared."

"What are we, schoolchildren?" I said. Delano chuckled. I lifted an eyebrow, then cautiously sat beside him, folding my fuzzy legs to the side to prevent flashing the world. The fox darted off about ten feet and ran a nervous circle on the oil stained blacktop, her ears pricked.

"It's okay sweetheart," Delano soothed. "She won't hurt you. She's a nice lady. Like you." He made a kissing sound and tossed the remaining stub of Slim Jim halfway between them. The fox slinked forward, ears back, and snatched the morsel. Delano took another Slim Jim from the shadows beside him, ripped open the plastic wrapper, and handed it to me.

"Go ahead," he insisted.

I broke off the tip and tossed it halfway. The fox slinked forward and gobbled it down.

"Foxes are nocturnal beauties I enjoy year round," Delano said. "But since they don't hibernate, I feed them during the harsh months if they ask." I tossed another piece. The fox crept forward another foot and devoured it. "Slim Jims give them horrible gas," he added, "but I figure it helps warm them in their dens."

I laughed. I couldn't help myself. Delano smiled.

"So are these the night duties Orin says darklings are punished with?" I asked.

"Orin doesn't know what he is talking about. He repeats everything the Realm tells him, like a mockingbird incapable of individual thought. And the Realm giving him a solo mission onto Earth proves he is a dangerous mockingbird indeed." Delano noticed the irritation on my face. He shrugged as if to say *the truth is the truth.*

"Maybe you are jealous as Orin says, and trying to manipulate me out of vengeance."

Delano snorted. "Merely *listen* to him. Orin rarely uses *I* or *me*, like all the faerie slaves. It is always *we, us, the Realm.*" I bit my lip, unable to recall such details in Orin and I's conversations. "Besides, I am not being punished," Delano said. "I *chose* this life. All darklings did."

"Why would anybody choose a life of cold loneliness?"

"It wouldn't be lonely if the Realm adhered to their promises and responsibilities."

I lifted my eyebrow. He motioned for me to feed the fox.

"Earth is the Realm's child, born without caretakers," he said. "After her birth, some faeries believed it was the Realm's duty to care for her exactly as she was created. Others wanted to exploit Earth for their own personal gains. The faction favoring compassion eventually won, but unlike the Realm, night and winter energies sustain much of this planet's life and magic. A balance was needed. A guild of faeries volunteered to undertake these magics so Earth could flourish, sacrificing their light and warmth to serve the dark and cold. These *darklings* merged with Earth's darkness, quite literally, and vanished in daylight, forcing them from the Realm forever. And since new life cannot grow without warmth, they sacrificed their fertility, too. The Realm promised to replace darklings when they died with infants from preordained families. These infants were left as changelings for fifteen years to accustom them to Earth's ways, then were recollected and trained for their darkling duties. Which worked well. For a while.

"The faction of protectors made up the

majority of darkling volunteers, leaving the exploiting authoritarians unchecked in the Realm. These authoritarians have asserted themselves into positions of power and influence. They crave control, and not just in the Realm. Earth offers bountiful resources they want to exploit, but darklings are strong here and our night energies keep their light powers in check. Thus the Realm slaughtered darkling supporters and rewrote history. They lie to their people—their *slaves*—insisting darklings are evil and manipulative and will kill their children. The slaves are brainwashed to believe the Realm is pure, so they murder darklings for the *greater good* without thought or question."

Delano leaned over and bit the Slim Jim. He chewed in silent contemplation, then continued: "Some faeries stationed on Earth now realize the Realm's despotism, and a rebellion has formed. The Realm cannot afford these freethinkers to spread their dissent. It will destabilize their base of power. Thus the Realm has begun restricting the number of faeries allowed to leave the Realm and shortened the duty rotations for those on Earth assignments, all to maintain control and unquestioning submission to authority. A takeover cannot be successful as long as day and night continue. If the Realm eliminates darklings, however, Earth's environment will destabilize. Night will turn to chaos. And they will conquer it all."

Delano glanced at the moon and I realized it was the same oval-like shape as his irises. *Do the eyes of darklings wax and wane?*

"I was the last of the intentional changelings. I was born revered, but accepted my birthright as a criminal. How could I not? Faeries inadvertently ready changelings for darkling life," Delano said. "We are accustomed to loneliness and have learned to survive being different. Earth culture teaches us freewill, so when the Realm rips it from us we rebel. That's what I did when the faeries brought me back. At first I thought I had found my true place and family. Like you. But I was wrong." He gestured to the night. "Here is where I belong."

"Orin says darklings are prisoners, punished for treachery and negligence. How do I know you're not making this up?" I asked. "How do I know you are telling the truth?"

Delano shrugged. "You don't."

We sat in silence, the motel's electric marquee buzzing softly overhead. Two questions nagged me: *Where do* I *belong?* and *Who is lying?*

The fox smacked its lips and yipped.

"She likes you," Delano said.

"I'm not sure," I said. The fox ran a tight circle several feet away.

"She does. Watch." Delano cupped my hand in his—cold, cold—and placed the remaining Slim Jim in my open palm. We leaned forward, nearly cheek to cheek. The fox's ears pricked when he kissed the air.

"Do not fear, pretty lady," Delano said.

The fox slinked forward and snatched the Slim Jim, its lips tickling my hand. I gasped, delighted; Delano held me still. The fox finished her morsel, then licked my fingers. I smiled. Delano flipped his hand on top of mine, our palms down, fingers laced. I glanced at him from the corner of my eye—his slender nose and sensual lips, the tiny, triangular scar on his cheek. He smelled earthy, like clay soil after a rain.

Delano placed my hand on the fox's head and leaned back. I scratched the fox—slowly, slowly—fingers in the fur, behind her black-tipped ears. She reminded me of Delano with her harvest moon fur, her black boots like shadows crawling up her legs. *But is Delano like the fox?* I wondered. Was he a hunter? A trickster? A predator with claws and fangs, deceptively hidden in a beautiful package?

The fox leaned into my petting. "Oh wow oh wow oh wow," I whispered over and over. After a minute the fox shook her coat, then licked my hand and darted off into the streets. I hugged myself, watching where she had disappeared behind a Dumpster. Delano and I sat in silence for several minutes, my warmth fleeing to him freely. I realized I no longer feared him, and found that terrifying.

Mist escaped my lips in a trembling ribbon. "I'm sorry I threw a rock at your head. And scratched you. And killed your moth."

"You are forgiven," Delano said. "You are always forgiven."

Tears pricked my eyes and I didn't know why. I held my breath to keep them from falling, then stood up and turned my face so he would not see. Delano stood up beside me, then handed me a package no wider than a saucer, wrapped neatly in newspaper.

I rubbed my eyes with the cuff of my sleeve. "What is this?"

"A gift I believe you will appreciate. Consider it *my* apology for a rude introduction."

I didn't know what to say, so I joked to keep the tears away. "What? No ribbon and bows?"

Delano tapped the top of the package with his forefinger. A slim shadow snaked off his skin and wrapped around the present, tying a bow with black, misting edges. It hummed against my fingers, like whispered secrets inside your ear. Beyond the motel's office an engine rumbled, then a flash of headlamps lit the driveway as a pickup truck rolled into the lot. The shadows coiling around Delano's feet sped into the surrounding darkness.

A rotund man stepped out of the pickup truck, then heaved a bundle of newspapers from the bed and onto the stoop of the motel's office. He tipped us a small wave, then stopped mid-step, his eyes widening. He pulled a cell phone from his coat pocket and jumped back into the truck. Tires squealed as he peeled out into the street.

"Did you recognize him?" Delano asked.

I shook my head. "No. Why?"

"Because he recognized you."

I stiffened. I had assumed the man had reacted oddly to Delano, not myself. I followed Delano to the stack of newspapers the man had dropped, and gasped. My face was in the upper corner of the local gazette's front page. Sam's face was in a small square beside mine, sneering up at me with his six-shooter eyes. *Gotcha,* those loaded eyes said. *Come out with your hands up.*

A light popped on in the back of the motel office, the living quarters for the owner. I darted to our motel room. The doorknob rattled uselessly in my hand. *Shit.* I had forgotten to take the key. I knocked on the door. "Orin," I called. *"Orin!"*

The marquee brightened, as did the moon, the stars. The night lost some of its chill and my body flushed with warmth. I glanced over my shoulder.

Delano was gone and a bell dinged as the motel owner opened the office door.

CHAPTER TWENTY-ONE

I pounded on the door with my fist. "Orin!" I said, trying to sound urgent without waking up the whole ZOOM ZOOM MOTOR INN. *"Orin!"* I heard rustling behind the door and realized I still clenched Delano's gift. I shoved it into my overcoat pocket as the door creaked open.

Orin rubbed his eye groggily. He was in a pair of tattered blue boxers, his hair puffed out like a dandelion. "What are you doing out here?"

I pushed my way inside. "We gotta leave. I've been recognized."

He squinted when I threw on the lights. "Huh? What are you talking about?"

"The newspaper deliveryman recognized me and soon the motel owner will too," I said, tearing through the blankets. I found my pajama pants half tucked beneath Orin's pillow and yanked them on over my boots. "Trust me, okay? We need to leave, *now.*"

We collected our belongings in a mad haste. I shoved Delano's gift deep into my pack when Orin's back was turned, the shadowy bow still coiling at the edges. We fled the motel room in under two minutes, my shoelaces whipping my ankles as we scurried through the parking lot. The stack of newspapers had disappeared from the stoop, the office windows aglow. "We need to stay away from the main roads," Orin said. "Or else we risk—"

Police sirens squalled several blocks away.

Orin grabbed my hand and bolted out the motel's back driveway. The sirens grew louder as we sprinted down the sulphur-lit street, past glowing gas stations and boarded up shops. Behind us, red and blue lights throbbed off the motel's walls as we sprinted around a corner, side by side like a pair of prey animals. My hands were two clenched fists and I imagined them throttling Sam's face for making me feel like a criminal. The backstreets gave way to low income suburbs, and back toward the ZOOM ZOOM MOTOR INN the police sirens wailed. My feet pounded the blacktop. My breasts ached beneath too-large clothing. I gulped in the crisp, night air. And out of nowhere, magic came.

It wasn't a song as Orin had described—not exactly—but more like a whisper. As if the air was quietly introducing itself, making itself known. *Help me flee,* I thought, and the air obeyed. I didn't bounce as I believed Orin had when he flew across the pasture. Instead the air came beneath my feet and *heaved*. My arms flailed out, trying to find balance in the nothingness. The summoned air caught me before my feet struck the ground, then tossed me upward again.

"Miriam!" Orin shouted.

"It's as you showed me!" I squealed. We approached the end of a cul-de-sac, a house encroaching fast. I stepped, stepped, stepped up the air and over the rooftop, noticing a patch of shingles missing from its peak. I slid down the air into the backyard, hopped across the drained pool, bounced over the fence boards and into the empty lot beyond. I leapt toward the stars, arms gyrating, legs pumping as I soared up invisible stairs. Ten feet up. Twenty. Fifty. One hundred. I hardly heard Orin shout my name below as I spread my arms to embrace the moon. *Thank you for this gift,* I thought. The air parted and I slid down to the edge of the empty lot, landing gently on my knees in the dead winter weeds. Orin landed on the sidewalk beside me, his boot buckles jingling when he struck the pavement. He looked sallow beneath the street's sulphur lamppost, his eyes as wide as eggs.

"That was *amazing*!" I said, laughing and rubbing my arms. "The air is like little whispers all over my skin!"

Orin shook my shoulders. "That was *not* air," he snapped. "You summoned *darkness*!"

I stopped laughing. "I what?"

Orin's eyes narrowed. "You've been with Delano, haven't you?"

My eyes widened.

"Haven't you?"

"It-it wasn't for long. Just for a few minutes outside the motel room."

"While I slept?" Orin slid his fingers into his hair, clenched the roots. *"Do you have any idea what you have done?"*

"Nothing happened!" I said. "He just talked. Mindless chit-chat."

"You don't *get* it," Orin said. "That's what darklings *do!* He seems innocent, casual, but all the while his magic poisons you. Soon your defenses drop, then you start to believe him, then trust him, maybe even *like* him. Then when you're vulnerable his magic sucks you into the night and he goes for the *kill*."

I opened my mouth to retort, but what could I say? Orin had described mine and Delano's interaction perfectly. In fifteen minutes I had gone from fearing Delano to liking him. Even missing him. But why had my feelings toward the darkling changed? Was it because of the magic or the man?

A spider crawled out of the weeds and onto the sidewalk, a colorless creature in the sick sulphur light. Orin glanced over both of his shoulders, then crushed it with his heel.

I gaped at Orin's boot as he scraped the spider's guts across the pavement. It was then I realized they weren't spiders, but *spy*ders. Orin snatched my forearm and yanked me to my feet. "I *refuse* to lose my promotion over an innocent mistake," he whispered, our noses nearly touching. "*Never* speak of this to *anyone*. Understand me?"

"Orin, I—"

He gave me a firm shake. *"Understand me?"* I nodded. "Good. Now let's go. Quietly. And on *foot.*"

I glanced over my shoulder as we crossed the deserted street. The eyes of a fox flashed in the night, then disappeared into the shadows.

CHAPTER TWENTY-TWO

"This is ridiculous!" Orin said.

He plodded backwards along the highway shoulder, his thumb pointing out to the lanes. Cars zipped past us as they had been since we left the motel nearly twelve hours ago. We were on a major throughway with no shortage of passing vehicles to ignore us, but we had returned to farmland, leaving all signs of a city at least nine miles back. The sparse exits led to nowhere roads with factory farms and grain silos, towering above the highway like industrial palaces.

"I've never had this much trouble thumbing for a ride," Orin said. "We must have seen at *least* a bazillion cars."

My calf muscles burned like hot spurs, my lower back ached, and I was unsure if we even headed in the right direction. Ever since I summoned darkness on accident and had the cops sicced on us, the only direction Orin cared about was *away*. Stumbling across this major highway felt like a stroke of luck at first—a greater surplus of vehicles meant greater odds for catching a quick lift. Now it felt like a deadly dance with fate. More passing cars meant more passing faces, more passing eyes capable of recognizing us as the miscreants the media portrayed.

I had tucked my hair up into Orin's fedora in an attempt to fool drivers that I was male. The sun was out, but I had become so accustomed to the cold that its pale sunlight felt unnaturally hot. I tucked my cranberry overcoat into my backpack and wore just a hoodie and jeans. I wondered if the day's uncharacteristic warmth was a gift or a joke from Delano, as it was a blessing *and* a curse. The sunshine was pleasant on our faces, but it had also melted the snow, creating a sloppy mess along the roadside. Mud caked our boots and splattered our calves. Road grime darkened our jeans. I suspected our filthiness and my attempt at a disguise contributed to our lack of rides. Drivers pitied everyday strangers appearing stranded or down on their luck, especially if one of the hitchhikers was a woman. Now Orin and I resembled two, dirty male vagrants. At worst we were serial killers; at best we would stink up their cars and stain the upholstery.

A semi-truck whizzed past us, the air current pushing us aside. Orin scowled. "I give up." He stuffed his hands into his pockets and trudged forward.

"Not much is out here," I said. "Let's take the next exit. Maybe I can try to fly again and—"

"No!" Orin snapped.

I sighed and followed him in silence, my shoulders curled forward. I was stupid to suggest it. So far all I had proved was that I was a liability to Orin's promotion. My thoughts shifted back to Orin's warnings about Delano. Was the darkling trying to deceive me? A slow manipulation to trick me into his grasp? I would never see Delano again once I entered the Realm, so it didn't matter either way. Still, the knowledge failed to reduce the emotional pangs or the—.

Orin stopped abruptly; I lurched onto my toes to keep from smacking into his back. "I'm sorry for snapping," he said, and faced me. "It's not you. I'm stressed about my promotion. I thought detouring to the ley line was safer, but it's taking longer than I hoped. Now I am behind the Realm's schedule, I haven't seen a chickadee in *days*, and haven't been able to update them on our progress and setbacks. They may have fired me for all I know. That scares me. But I shouldn't take it out on you."

"It's okay. I understand," I said. "But aren't you doing what the Realm wants? Making decisions to keep me safe and get me home."

Orin shrugged. "Yes, but outside their orders. I guess we'll know if they approve soon enough."

We slogged onward. One foot, then the other. Cars zipped past. The blister on my heel's callus throbbed. I didn't even know calluses could get blisters. My soles dragged along the gravel. The billboard ahead touted the best injury lawyer in the Midwest, *guaranteed.*

I opened a candy cane and sucked on the end. "Were your parents retrievers?"

Orin shook his head. "No. Why do you ask?"

"Curiosity," I said. "You told me you were Earth-born. I thought maybe your parents were also retrievers and that's why you want this promotion. To follow in their footsteps."

"My parents are both station sentries on the southern block," Orin said. "I am proud of them, but I have always had other wants."

"Have you always wanted to be a retriever, then?" I smiled. "Was it Little Orin's dream?"

Orin seesawed his hand. "Eh. What I want is what retriever offers," he said. "It's a position with opportunity to grow. From retriever I can branch out to informant or deliverer or travel sentry. Theoretically I can even become a sniffer, though I lack the talent."

"Huh. Never took you for the career-ladder type."

"I'm not," Orin said. "I'm more of a..." He trailed off and watched his lengthening shadow.

"More of a what?"

Orin kicked a pebble down the shoulder's white line. "Never mind. It's dumb."

"Try me."

"Well, women aren't typically attracted to border sentries."

I busted out laughing. "You mean you want to become a retriever to get *laid*?"

Orin's eyes widened. "*No!* I—I want a family. You know. Wife. Kids. But border sentries are restricted to barracks. What woman wants *that* in a husband? If I become a retriever, though, the Realm will give me my own apartment. I hear sniffers receive whole *houses*." His lips twitched into a timid smile. "Stupid, huh?"

"No," I said. "It sounds like a wonderful life. One I once strived for." I shrugged. "Unfortunately I'm infertile. At least you have a chance."

Orin grew strangely quiet. Red crept up his neck.

"What's wrong?" I asked.

"Nothing's wrong," Orin said, an octave too high. "Why would anything be wrong?"

"You're as red as a beet, Orin. *What is it?*"

He sunk into his shoulders. "You're not *infertile*, Miriam. It's just, well, you and your husband aren't exactly the same species."

My face fell. "Oh my God. The faeries view my marriage as *bestiality*?"

"No!" Orin said, quickly. "Well, maybe if you *knew*." I gave a strangled cry and covered my face with my hands. "*But you didn't!* These things are expected with adult changelings."

I groaned behind my palms and felt my face flush as red as Orin's.

Orin coughed. "*Anyway*," he said, "that is why I've been nutty, even though my promotion may already be stripped." His voice lowered. "Especially if the Realm discovers I squished that spider. In which case, I better accept the idea of being a border sentry for the rest of my life. Or a toilet scrubber."

And it will be all my fault. I cringed at my foolishness—present, past, and undoubtedly future.

We trudged onward. One aching foot, then the other. My lower back was ready to snap in half as the cars zoomed uncaringly past. An hour later we approached a wooden, white cross on the side of the road with *Janie* carved into the center. The shrine was crowded with flowers, dingy stuffed animals, pinwheels, and handwritten prayers soggy from the snow and rain. Orin silently watched the pinwheels twirl and gleam. A minute later he rummaged through the roadside-treasures in his pockets, placed a heart shaped rock at the base of the cross, then walked off.

After a moment, I said: "The Realm would be stupid not to promote you."

Orin stiffened as if I had blurted a racial slur. "The Realm has high expectations, and there are also harsh repercussions in failure, but it has created a society of beauty and strength and perfection. Coal into a diamond, as the historians like to say. It's an honor to contribute to its greatness, but if I'm unworthy of a retriever position, then..." He shrugged.

We dragged our feet for several more miles, soles throbbing and calves screaming. One foot, then the other. One foot, then the other. It never seemed to end. Cars whizzed past us. The blister on my heel's callus popped and rubbed raw. We crouched in the sludge to wrap our feet with the last of our truck stop bandages, then limped onwards. The road grime darkened our shins another shade. The mud crept to our arms and waists.

A speck of blue dotted the distance, slowly taking form as we closed in. Square. Tall. A speck of yellow beneath. "Is that a...?" Orin squinted, then grinned wide. "Oh yes!" He grabbed my hand and raced down the highway. "We're saved!"

We approached a roadside assistance phone—the only one I recalled seeing during our travels. On the blue sign were white letters which read: *Emergency Call Box.* A yellow box was attached to the pole beneath it. "See that?" Orin pointed to a red dot on the lower lefthand corner. "That means this phone connects to a faerie station. I can call in and update the Realm about what's happened." Orin threw open the front of the box and picked up the black telephone inside. The metal cord swayed beneath the receiver, cut and useless. An upside-down R had been carved into the earpiece.

Orin's lips pressed into a white line as he slammed the phone back onto the receiver.

"What's wrong?" I asked.

"Rebels," he said. "They cut the line."

"Why would they do that?"

"Because they're extremists who hate the Realm and want power for themselves."

"Are they faeries or darklings?"

"Faeries," he said. "Mostly renegade Earth workers. They're trying to destroy access between the worlds so they can exterminate humans and conquer Earth for themselves. Now the Realm only sends proven adherent workers to Earth thanks to these lunatics. Which is another reason why I need to get you home, to convince them I am worthy of an Earth assignment."

Orin stuck out his thumb and continued walking.

The sun inched toward the west horizon, at that perfect angle which stings your eyes and blinds you from anything a foot above the ground. The road curved, forcing us to trudge toward the glare, our hands on our foreheads like visors. Behind us, wheels slowed.

Orin heaved a relieved sigh. "Finally."

A beige minivan approached, its windows rolled down. I smiled, opening my mouth to say thanks. *"Get a job!"* a fat middle-aged woman shouted, and chucked a pop can. Orin and I jumped backwards; Pepsi sprayed our faces, reminding me I didn't fit in with faeries *or* humans. *Maybe I have been a changeling too long.* The couple squealed with laughter and gunned the minivan down the freeway, gray puffs spewing out the tailpipe. My teeth clenched. Pepsi dripped off my trembling fists. *Me and Orin aren't bums!* I wanted to shout. *We are* good *people!* I had never picked up a hitchhiker out of safety concerns, but I had never thought ill of them; I always wished for them to find a safe ride. I wanted to chase after the minivan, lecture the people on the truth and force them to understand what was right. I felt I needed to justify my existence, and I hated myself for it.

Orin wiped the Pepsi off his cheek with his sleeve. He picked up the can, plucked the tab off with a *clink*, and placed it in his pocket.

"I doubt we will reach civilization before nightfall," Orin said, repositioning his backpack's straps. "I guess we're camping out tonight."

CHAPTER TWENTY-THREE

We had taken the closest exit off the major highway and detoured onto a country road. We managed another mile before the sky had lost its blue to purple, fading slowly toward indigo. The temperature plummeted and fat snowflakes fluttered down, as if compensating for the day's abnormally warm weather.

It was almost dark when the roadway spanned across a narrow river. A railway bridge ran alongside it. Orin stopped to stare, and for a moment I thought he intended to wait for a train to hop. I felt nauseated, my ride in the boxcar still sour in my memory. If it helped Orin's promotion, however, I'd suffer through it. Even though I preferred to wander for months on foot instead.

"This will work," Orin said. "Hope you don't mind a climb."

Orin hopped over the guardrail, dug his boot-heels into the dirt and snow, and half-slid half-ran to the river's shore fifty feet below. I followed, somehow managing to keep my footing to the wide, rocky banks. Orin set his backpack beside a cement pylon graffitied with anarchy symbols and Metallica stickers. The overhead tracks provided some relief from the falling flakes.

Orin unlatched the two sleeping-bags strapped to his backpack and handed me the flashlight he had rolled inside. I rummaged through our gear with the light; Orin rolled out our beds. Firelight sparked, then flickered across the river. Orin stiffened. Men's voices bantered incoherently, carried on a wind blowing snowflakes beneath the bridge.

"Do you think we're safe?" I whispered. "I'm sure they noticed our flashlight."

We watched the campsite across the river for nearly five minutes. At least three men were huddled around the flames, chattering and laughing.

Orin's shoulders relaxed. "A hobo camp. They would have confronted us by now if we were imposing. We will be fine as long as we stay on our side of the river. And if we *do* find ourselves with a fight on our hands, well..." Orin shrugged. "Humans are weak."

Orin collected branches from the nearby shrubs. I set out dinner. We hadn't bought any food since the last gas station, almost twenty-four hours ago. My portion consisted of a snack-bag of chips, half a ham sandwich, a candy cane, and a banana to split between the two of us. The ham sandwich worried me, but the temperature hadn't gone *that* high during the day, and my rumbling stomach insisted eating it was safe.

Orin dropped a bundle of branches beside the sleeping-bags, chunks of snow clinging to the bark.

"They look too wet to burn," I said.

"They'll burn." Orin pulled a lighter from his backpack and clicked on a flame. He grabbed the fire in his hand and threw it onto the bundle of kindling. The wood caught fire with a burst of steam; the flames shot up nearly as high as the cement pylon before steadying into a bonfire. The wind carried a whooping "Whoa!" from across the river, then the hobo camp silenced.

We huddled beside our campfire, the river rushing in the shadows. I ate the sandwich and candy cane and half a banana, but with all the calories I had burned from walking my stomach still growled. I shoved the bag of chips into my overcoat's pocket, saving them for breakfast. I found it easier to go to bed hungry than wake up without knowing when I'd eat my next meal. We finished off the water in our water bottles, then filled them with snow and placed them beside the fire to melt. It was now too dark to see the bridges overhead. Across the river, one of the men had a coughing fit and spat out his creation. I added more kindling to the flames.

"It *is* peaceful, I'll give him that."

I peered up from the campfire. Orin stood outside the bridge's shelter, gazing into the starless night. "What is?" I asked.

"The snow." Orin leaned his head back and caught a snowflake on his tongue. "It amazes me how something so beautiful is also so dangerous."

I was uncertain if he spoke of winter or Delano, and I didn't ask him to clarify.

We slipped into our sleeping bags, but the rocky shore pinched our skin and dug into our bones. We crawled out and brushed away the rocks with our feet, trying to clear away a nest like a couple of killdeer. The relief was minimal.

Orin tucked his knife inside the sleeping bag with him, and made sure I did the same with my folding knife. "I won't sleep tonight," he grumbled. "Not with strangers and darklings and rocks digging into my hips." But within an hour he was snoring, as I expected. A night owl he was not. I wondered if it was the same for all the faeries. *Since darklings fade into the darkshine during the day, it makes sense for faeries to weaken at night.*

The firelight across the river dimmed and I heard no conversations on the wind.

I lay on my stomach, my chin resting on my folded arms, and scanned the darkness for Delano. I knew I played with fire, but curiosity bested me. I had yet to see the cruelty Orin insisted darklings possessed. What I *did* see was another part of the fae, another glimpse into a magical world. The campfire crackled beside me, the flames warm against my face. Snow fell outside the bridge, reflecting the firelight like glitter floating in the night. Every shadow was in its proper place, however. I sighed and pulled the sleeping bag tight against my body. The river babbled around rocks in the dark. Perhaps Delano had fallen asleep in the darkshine and lost our trail. Or maybe he was out doing whatever it was darklings did.

My stomach clenched. I curled into the fetal position and tucked my head into the sleeping bag. My stomach clenched tighter. I ignored it. My intestines cramped and gurgled and my eyes shot open. The ham sandwich was a bad idea, after all.

I grabbed the flashlight and a wad of napkins from my backpack, then scrambled far into the bushes, out of Orin's view in case he woke. My stomach roiled, sharp with pangs. I bit my lip and pushed farther into the brush. I would die of humiliation if Orin glimpsed the mess the ham sandwich and I created should we hike past it in the morning.

Thirty minutes later my intestines were empty and sweat cooled on my brow. I knelt on the shore, my flashlight illuminating the rocks and current, and washed my hands in the freezing river.

"Got anything to eat?"

I snatched my flashlight and whipped around, illuminating a grizzled man. His face was weathered and cracked from too many hard days in the sun, his body padded with a snow jacket and a black knitted cap. *How long has he been standing in the shadows?* I wondered. *Did he watch me squat in the shrubs?*

"So sorry to scare you." Whiskey floated on the man's breath. He smiled like a jack-o-lantern, his remaining teeth stained yellow and spotted with decay. "My buddies and I lost our jobs recently and are out seeking work," he said. "I hoped maybe you had something extra to share to help us through our setback."

Seeking work, my ass. You have been slumming for years, I thought, then sucked in my lips. The woman who had chucked the pop can had accused me and Orin of being bums, too. I dried my hands on my pants and handed the man the bag of chips from my coat pocket. "Here," I said. "Take it."

His smile widened. "Thank you. Much appreciated."

"You're welcome. Goodnight." I turned back to the campsite. The man grabbed my shoulder and I squeaked with surprise.

"You sure this is all you have to give?" he asked.

"Yes," I said, my heart hammering. "I have nothing else."

"You *sure*?" The man's grip tightened; his knuckles creaked. I couldn't see our campfire around the shore's bend. Or Orin. Or my folding knife, warm and snug inside my sleeping bag. I cursed my stupidity and my bashfulness for getting me raped and killed. "I think you have *much* more," the man said. "I think you—"

"I think you need to leave the lady alone."

The temperature dropped ten degrees and my flashlight dimmed and flickered. The stranger wheeled around. *"Who's there?"*

"Me," Delano said, and somehow now loomed between us, glaring down at the stranger.

The stranger jumped back with a short cry. "How—?"

"Go back to your camp." Delano shoved the man's chest; the man tottered back a step. "And take your spying friend with you."

"No one else is—"

Delano sneered. "Fifteen feet to my left, lurking in the shadows. Green jacket. Goatee. Pony tail. Hand in an uncivilized location."

The man's eyes widened. He shot off into the darkness, shoes pounding the river stone. A second set of feet scrambled after him.

"Did he hurt you?" Delano asked. He was barefoot, dressed in worn Levis and a brown, threadbare sweatshirt two sizes too big. My flashlight lit his unshaven cheeks and the dark circles beneath his eyes. The right side of his irises had dipped past the pupils.

I let out a slow, rattling breath, unaware I had been holding it in. "No. Just shook me up." I snorted. "And now I have no breakfast. I'm such an idiot."

"You're kind, not an idiot," Delano said. A moth landed on his shoulder and climbed down his sleeve. He handed me a snack-sized Slim Jim from his rear pocket. "For breakfast."

A smile tugged at the corner of my lips. "Thanks."

"Although, I *am* curious," Delano said, snowflakes collecting in his lashes. "Why *did* you give that man what you had? Could you tell he had ill intentions?"

"No. I just—I just felt bad for him." I stared across the river. Firelight from the hobo camp skipped across the water. "And earlier, there was a woman."

"The piece of trash who threw the soda can at you."

My cheeks grew hot, and that heat abandoned me for Delano. "You saw that?"

Delano nodded solemnly. The moth crawled over his fingers, dancing like a coin across his knuckles before fluttering off into the shadows.

"I guess I wanted to prove I wasn't like her," I said.

Delano chuckled. "The fact you even care is proof you are nothing like her."

"My husband says I am too sensitive, that I need to harden up." I clicked off the flashlight to hide my face. "Maybe he's right."

"Nonsense. Sensitivity is a gift. It gives you compassion, hope in humanity, the belief in kindness. Those are *good* traits to have."

"He says it makes me weak."

"*Insensitivity* makes people weak," Delano said. "*And* selfish. It is easy to think only about yourself, without regard for how your actions will affect others.

Sensitivity, however, takes courage. It is difficult putting yourself out in the world, showing kindness when it can lead to heartache or trouble. Your husband had no right to tell you to change. Your sensitivity is needed in this world, and is the core of who you are."

I shrugged as snowflakes patted my face. "I guess."

Delano faced me and cupped my hands in his. "There is no guessing about it, Miriam. Do you honestly have no idea how beautiful a person you are?"

I groaned and pulled away. "Orin warned me you're a flatterer."

"I am being honest," Delano said, and I heard the frown in his voice. "If you saw your true self—not clouded with the judgements of cynics—you'd lose your breath."

"My lunch more like it."

Delano sighed. "You are impossible."

Something screeched like a furious kitten above the river. I flicked on the flashlight as a streak of white soared above our heads, a ghost with hollow eyes.

"Barn owl." Delano cupped his mouth with his hands and mimicked the call exactly. The owl answered. The wind of her body brushed my face as she zipped silently through the falling snow.

"Come. She has invited us to fly with her." Delano ran up the air as if on an invisible staircase. My heart swelled and I yearned to chase him, but my legs froze on the shore. He twisted in the air when he realized I had stayed behind, then landed beside me with a silent splat of shadow. *"Come with me,"* he insisted, his voice dark and sweet and painfully seductive.

"I-I can't," I said. "It's night magic. It's —"

"It is what you were born for," Delano said. He brushed the snowflakes from his hair, and I realized they didn't melt against his skin. "I saw you last night. I watched how natural you wielded darkness, unlike the day magic Orin forces onto you. *Come with me.*"

The owl dipped above us. I threw my hands to the sky. Her feathers skimmed my fingertips, and the night whispered promises on my skin. Promises of liberation and pleasure and a lightness I barely enjoyed before Orin scared it away.

Delano caressed my arm. "*Come with me*. I know you want to."

"You're right," I said. "I *do* want to. But..." *But how do I know this magic is not like heroin, with each hit taking me down the path of a demon?*

Delano sighed. "But you are not ready."

I looked at my feet.

"Then I will not force you." Delano sat with me on a log and patted my hand. "Despite what Orin says, I will not force you to do anything. Do you understand that?"

My brow furrowed. "I want to believe that. It's just..."

"Just what?"

My chest tightened. When I had met the chickadee everything seemed so simple. A darkling was an evil hunter, something to flee from and kill if necessary. But when Delano showed himself, proved he was more of a man than a monster, he became another curiosity on this curious adventure. Another glimpse at magic as I raced with Orin to a magical world. But whether Delano scared me or intrigued me, the whole time I had thought of him as an addition, a fascinating tag-along. Now he was a complication. A *choice.*

The barn owl landed in a nearby tree and *screeched*.

I could leave Orin. Right now. I could run off with Delano, embrace the night, reclaim the freedom I felt when I flew with the darkness. Night's whispers tickled my skin, enticing me to hear its secrets. Was that where I belonged? Or was it a seductive trick as Orin warned? Maybe—

"Miriam?" Orin's voice in the darkness.

I leapt to my feet. Delano's fingers tightened around my hand. "I'm safe," I called back. "I needed to go to the bathroom." I turned to Delano and frowned. "I'm sorry," I said, even though I had no reason to apologize.

Delano kissed my wrist. Shivers rushed through my body. "Sleep. You need it," he said. "I will stand guard tonight."

Across the river, the hobos' campfire was nearly black. "Do you think they'll return?"

"Doubtful," Delano said. "I am more worried about the darkling whose territory I am trespassing on." He rubbed his jaw gingerly. "She's furious I warmed the day while she slept, and packs quite a punch."

I blanched. Delano smiled, his teeth flashing white in the darkness. "Do not worry. I can handle Amaya. Though you will suffer her snowy night in return."

"Miriam?" Orin called.

"Go," Delano whispered.

I started back to the campsite.

"And Miriam?"

I glanced over my shoulder.

Delano's ruddy eyes glinted and I heard the smile in his voice. "Remember to open my present."

CHAPTER TWENTY-FOUR

My heart raced and my legs trembled, but from anxiety or exhaustion I had no idea. I dropped my backpack to the tile and leaned my forehead against the door, forcing myself to breathe deeply. The public bathroom smelled like most cleaned public bathrooms, a mixture of synthetic cherries and disinfectants. I latched the lock with a gratifying *clack.* This was not how I had intended to welcome in the New Year.

We had woke and left our camp hours ago. Orin was across the street at a rundown gas station, begging for a ride. I had told him I wanted to change into fresh clothes at the McDonald's instead of at the gas station since it was probably cleaner. Which was true. But I also wanted the familiarity. My life was spiraling out of control and the McDonald's reminded me some things in the world remained the same.

I scrubbed my face with soap and water at the sink. The paper towels were rough against my wind-chapped cheeks.

I had regretted my decision to use the McDonald's as soon as I entered, however. A dozen customers—including two highway patrol officers—ate breakfast at the tables, most of them reading newspapers with my photo tucked inside. I had kept my head down and zipped into the bathroom, making my best impression of a sick woman in desperate need of a toilet. And now that I was locked in the bathroom, I felt I *would* be sick.

All this anxiety and struggle isn't worth it. Even

if I wasn't the worst faerie to exist—even if I hadn't channeled the wrong energies—all the dangers and unknowns of this trip frayed my last nerve. Gazing into Orin's eyes, with all the warmth and promise of spring, made it easy to believe in impossibilities. But I had fooled myself. I wasn't adventurous or daring or worthy or strong. I was just me. Plain, boring, insignificant Miriam. And I yearned for my plain, boring, insignificant life back. It sounded like a fairytale.

I dried my hands with paper towels and sat on the sink's counter—the cleanest area in the bathroom, I assumed—and tried to steady my nerves. *I should call Sam.* I knew he would never stop chasing me, and at least crawling back to him would give my life some stability. Sam's lies were known and familiar. Infidelity was a story told countless times. At worst it would lead me to a divorce, probably an apartment somewhere to live out my average, predictable life. I might manage a grant, go back to school, recreate a life strictly on my terms. Orin and Delano, on the other hand, promised only unknowns. One of them was a liar. If I picked the wrong one, I might end up abused, murdered, or enslaved in ... well, I had no idea *where* I would end up. A new world. A new existence. Living with a new *species*.

Of course, just because Sam stopped chasing me didn't mean Delano would. And what would Orin do if I ran off and further threatened his promotion?

Someone knocked on the door. I jumped off the counter without thinking, my muscles programed to flee at the slightest disturbance. I stood motionless, poised like a rabbit at the first whiff of danger.

Knock. Knock. Knock.

Three firm knocks. Not Orin. He had promised two quick, three slow. I backed into the corner, pressed my palms against the wall. *It's the highway patrol officers. They recognized me.* "It-It's gonna be awhile," I said. "Sick."

A woman mumbled something incoherently on the other side of the door and left. I let out a long breath and rubbed my face.

I opened my backpack and groped for fresh clothing. Newspaper crinkled against my fingers. *Delano's present.* I lifted it out, the ribbon of shadow now gone. I slid my thumb beneath the piece of tape—protecting the newsprint from ripping as if it were fine parchment—and peeled back the wrapping.

It took me a heartbeat to realize what I saw. I then squeaked with surprise and slapped the paper against the gift. I glanced over my shoulder, as if I was sixteen and my mother lingered in the doorway, ready to ground me the instant she assumed I had done something wrong. She wasn't there, of course. The one place she lingered was inside my head.

Why on Earth did Delano give you a gift like that? I'll tell you why. It's because he knows you are a—

I pushed her voice out of my thoughts, then scanned the bathroom for spiders who would tattle to Orin. I checked the stall, the sink, the wastebasket, the hand dryer, the changing table with a picture of an excited koala. No spiders. Only a moth nestled in the corner above the door, nearly invisible against the beige wall.

Delano? Are you here?

My insides buzzed with that naughty

sixteen-year-old tingle. I peeled back the newspaper, exposing a bra and three matching panties, each made of fine, indigo lace. I was clueless as to where Delano had found them. Orin and I had passed mainly truck stops, convenience stores, and rural shops on our trek. This lingerie belonged in a Paris boutique.

I stroked a satin strap, smooth beneath my finger. Maybe I should have been offended and listened to Orin's warnings—that Delano was a seducer and a trickster. Which was believable, considering his kiss from last night still tingled on my wrist, and I yearned to thrust my body against his in thanks. Did that prove Orin's warning had merit, however? I thought about the chickadee's lecture in the boxcar, scolding me for confusing impulse with instinct. Was my desire for Delano impulse? Were lies tangled in these designer threads, his bait gift-wrapped in newspaper and lace? Maybe that was Delano's scheme. Intrigue me, love me, lure me. Then crush me when I let him close. *Or maybe what I feel is instinct.* Maybe I was so broken, so discarded, that I saw demons in kindness, crimes in compassion, and believed all the negatives even if they were lies.

I pulled out a small white card tucked between two of the panties. In perfect black cursive it read: *I thought you might appreciate some security during unstable times. —D*

I snorted, then giggled, then couldn't stop. Perverted or not, lingerie was what I had been pining for the past week. I buried my mouth into the crook of my elbow, biting my overcoat's sleeve to muffle my laughter. In the mirror my cheeks flushed as red as pomegranates, and the ache in my chest was the best sensation I had felt since ... when? Before being lost in the woods? Before jumping the train? Before my loveless marriage?

Of course, if Orin was right about Delano, this sensation was incredibly dangerous. I glanced at the trash bin, knowing I needed to throw Delano's gift inside. Instead I tore the tags off with my teeth and untied my boot laces. *Just trying them on won't harm anything*, I reasoned. The moth wiggled its rear against the wall as if settling in for a movie-night.

"You better close your eyes," I told the moth, then stripped naked and changed into my new pretties. I pivoted on my toes in front of the mirror, beaming like a supermodel. The bra and panties fit perfectly, as if the lace were indigo vines which had crept onto my skin. *Okay, you had your fun. Now throw them away.* Covering the lingerie with truck stop clothing felt insulting, but I did so anyway, hyperaware of the indigo secrets pressed against my skin. I slid my hands over my hips, buzzing inside and yearning to be reckless. *Be calm. Be calm. Be calm.* I took a deep breath and forced my composure, like an injured bird fearing the flock would kill them the instant its weakness was discovered.

Knock-Knock. Knock ... Knock ... Knock.

Orin.

"Miriam! You will never believe the ride I found! Hurry up before they change their mind!"

"Be right there." I glanced in the mirror before leaving the bathroom. My face was neutral. The face of a bird too afraid to sing.

CHAPTER TWENTY-FIVE

"*That's* our ride?"

Orin nodded enthusiastically. "Great, huh? They're heading to Montana, so they will take us most of our way. All it cost was groceries and my fedora." Orin bounded off to the gigantic RV at the gas pump, his boot buckles jingling. The RV must have been the top of the line in its heyday, which I assumed was somewhere around the early eighties. Rust spots now dotted the mustard stripe highlighting its center, and tie-dye curtains hung in windows crowded with decals of hearts and stars. Each hubcap was painted yellow with a black smiley face. The eye of the rear had been chipped, making the wheel look as if it was winking.

A young man, no older than twenty-two, in patched jeans and a stitched suede coat popped out of the RV's side door. His short, dark dreadlocks poked out of Orin's fedora like a squid who'd been crushed with a conch-shell. "Aaaaallll aaaabooooard," he called out, then disappeared inside, cackling as if he had told the wittiest of jokes.

A chubby brunette in a tropical wrap-skirt and a puffy ski jacket crushed her cigarette with a Doc Martin before climbing into the RV. A brown Volvo pulled up to the neighboring gas pump. I hid my face from the driver and followed Orin into the RV.

The interior reminded me of a grizzled man unable to let go of his younger, protesting days. The brown carpet and plaid upholstery were worn and ripped, the couch brightened with paisley throw pillows and a fuzzy black blanket with a huge marijuana leaf in the center—the kind sold on roadsides, strung up on chain-link fences. The cupboard above the brown stove and refrigerator had no doors, displaying an impressive stash of boxed macaroni and cheese. To the left was the bathroom and a bare mattress peeking out beyond an open accordion doorway. A multicolored glass pipe sat on the tabletop behind the passenger seat, along with a box of matches, an orange highlighter, an empty wine bottle caked in candle wax, and a kingsize bag of Skittles. The RV couldn't scream "drugs on board" any louder if it had a gigantic bong strapped to the fender.

I leaned into Orin's ear. "Are you sure this is a good idea?" I was debating going back to Sam, but I wanted to on *my* terms, not handcuffed in the back of a cop car with a felony charge.

Orin grinned. "It sure beats walking."

Or accidentally summoning darkness to fly. I frowned. *I should run away right now. Call Sam from a pay phone and end it all here.*

Orin squeezed me to his side. "Everyone, this is Miriam." I stiffened to the sound of my name. My photo was flying across the country faster than I was, riding on articles full of betrayal and lies. *It's stupid not using aliases,* I thought. For all I knew, Sam might have offered a reward by now, changing my rescue mission into a manhunt.

No one seemed to notice who I was though. They merely smiled, said some hellos, and wished us a happy New Year.

"That's Clayton," Orin said, pointing to

the dreadlocked man in the fedora. "Hannah and her sister, Kayla, and Sean behind the wheel."

"Nice to meet ya," Sean said, and cranked the ignition. He was in his early twenties with the red mutton chops of an eighteenth-century politician. "Better get comfortable. This moose is about to roll."

Clayton buckled himself into the passenger seat. Kayla, the chubby girl from outside, passed everyone a can of generic root beer from the fridge before locking the door and joining Hannah at the table behind him. Hannah was the youngest of the group; I guessed she was about sixteen. The beads in her dirty blond cornrows swayed and clicked as we rolled out of the gas station. Orin and I curled up on the couch across the way, our backpacks clenched between our feet.

"Hope you don't mind a rocky ride," Sean said. He set his root beer in the cup holder and slipped a hand-rolled cigarette between his lips. Clayton flipped open his Zippo—*clink*—and lit its tip. The walls rattled as the RV accelerated onto the freeway at about the speed of a tortoise drunk on gin. Glassware tinkled in the kitchen cabinets, and tie-dye curtains swayed against the back of my head. Orin cracked open his root beer and lifted an eyebrow as he sniffed the can's outpouring mist. He sipped. His eyes sparkled and he chugged the rest. I handed him mine when he finished.

Sean rolled his window down an inch as skunk smoke coiled through the RV. *Oh my God.* I thought. *Is he smoking a freakin'* joint*?* I pinched my sinuses. *Dammit, Orin! What the hell did you get us into?* I nudged his side. Orin smiled and wiped his mouth with the back of his hand.

Sean passed the joint to Clayton, who

sucked on it so hard I thought he'd turn inside out. My head started to pound. I pressed my hands against my temples. *Please let me get out of this safely and with dignity. Please, oh please, oh please.*

Police sirens screamed behind us. I jerked up as straight as a groundhog to peer out the window. "Suuuuuu-*eeeeeeet!*" Sean hollered as the flashing red and blues zoomed past. "Go get your sweet fried slop!"

I collapsed back against the couch cushions, heart and head hammering. Orin pulled a box of candy canes with a clearance sticker from his backpack and passed them around. "Sweet!" Sean said, and hung one off his ear. "Literally," Clayton said, and cackled. Hannah's hair beads swayed and clicked.

"So why are ya heading to North Dakota?" Kayla asked, peeling off a candy cane wrapper. She had brown braided hair and a freckled pug nose. Each of her fingernails were painted a different color of the rainbow, just like the bag of Skittles.

Orin coughed into his elbow, then cracked my root beer open. "We're gonna hitch a ride to the Realm on the ley line."

My eyebrows jumped. *Is Orin seriously talking about faerie stuff?* I didn't know if he was allowed to or not; I hadn't seen him interact with humans outside of a few clerks and a self-absorbed trucker. *Is he suffering a contact-high?*

"What's the Realm?" Kayla asked.

"It's where I am from," Orin said.

"Where's that?"

"Fiji," I said, without thinking. Orin eyed me curiously, but only smiled.

"You're from *Fiji?*" Hannah said. A candy cane crunched between her teeth. "That is so *cool!*"

Clayton sniggered. "Gonna be hard to drive to Fiji."

"Why? Is it far?" Sean asked.

Clayton inhaled another hit, then passed the joint to Hannah. "It's in the fucking ocean, brainiac."

Orin opened his mouth to speak but I cut him off. "Orin has a pilot friend named Ley in North Dakota who is taking us." I was impressed how smoothly I lied. Of course, they probably would have believed me if I said we were heading to the desert to wait for the mothership.

Hannah puffed a ring of smoke, then stretched the joint to us. "Wanna hit offa this?"

I smacked Orin's hand away. "No, thank you," I said.

Orin looked puzzled. "What is it?"

"Mary Jane," Hannah said, and passed it to Kayla.

"Huh?"

"Drugs," I whispered in Orin's ear, making his eyes widen.

"Oh. Oh, no. I can't," Orin said. He coughed into his elbow. "The Realm will know."

"Why does Fiji care about what you do in America?" Kayla asked, and blew smoke behind her shoulder.

"He works for their government," I said.

Clayton leaned around the passenger seat. "There's some clean piss in the fridge if you need it, man."

Orin shook his head, tousling his beach sand hair. "The Realm will know."

"Fuckin' governments!" Sean bellowed, and blared the RV's horn with indignation. An Accord cruising beside us swayed in surprise, then floored it to pass. "They're all the same! Restricting our universal given right to what Mother Nature *gifted* us and—" A metallic *clang-tink-tink* rang outside as a smiley face wheeled across three lanes of traffic. "Shit! Lost another one."

"It doesn't bother me," Orin said. "I'd gladly trade in any high for the Realm."

"Why? What's so great about it?" Hannah asked.

"Well, it's warm all the time and sunny," Orin said. "Once upon a time, it was war-torn. But the Realm cleaned it up and now it is the safest place to live. There's never any darkness and no unemployment and everyone is cared for and supported."

I groaned inside my head as Orin inadvertently filled the next generation with lies about what they believed was Fiji. They listened, starry-eyed (although that might have been the pot), enthralled with the parts about nonviolence and caring for each other, despite the lack of drug usage. After twenty minutes I started to worry they would try to tag along.

I stood up to toss Orin's empty pop cans into the kitchen garbage. The RV bumped and swayed. I lurched to the right, then step step step, braced myself on the wall to keep from falling. Kayla joined me as I tossed the cans into a plastic bag hanging off the oven door.

"You're her, aren't you? The Christmas-abduction woman," Kayla whispered behind my shoulder. I froze. *I knew this ride was a bad idea. I knew I should have ran.* She took my silence as acknowledgement. "Thought so. Don't worry, I won't say anything." She paused. "Unless, of course, you *want* me to. But you don't *look* like you are in any danger. Are you?"

Danger? My eyebrows pinched together. I felt split between two magic-wielding beings, clueless about which of them to trust or what plight awaited if I chose wrong. I had started developing my own magic, which the man of sunshine told me was evil and wrong and would consume my soul, while the man of shadow insisted following the light would lead me to my doom. I was lost on this world and about to be lost on another world where I had no idea how to behave or what to expect. A foreign world I couldn't call up on the internet to learn about customs or climates or *anything* before devoting my abnormally long life. That was, *if* my enraged husband didn't hunt me down first. So, yes. I was in danger. I was in a *boatload* of danger and uncertain about what to do or where to go or who to trust. I wanted out of this mess. I wanted to go *home.* But I didn't even know where home was anymore.

I watched Orin smiling on the couch, blathering about the Realm he loved. "No," I sighed. "I'm not in danger."

"I didn't think so," Kayla said. "You and Orin click too well. And your husband seems a bit *off.*"

I snorted, partly from amusement, but mostly because someone else, a *stoned stranger* no less, saw what I did about my husband. It made me feel less crazy.

Kayla motioned to Orin with her chin,

her voice low. "Did you two run off together?"

"Huh? Oh! No! Orin ... Well, we met along the way. My husband assumes he kidnapped me since he can't own up to the reality that I left him. Sam doesn't care about the truth, especially if that truth can damage his political campaign."

"Why *did* you leave, then? Did he abuse you?"

Abuse me? I bit my lip. Another simple question I was unsure how to answer. Did Sam leave me wounded and scared and hopeless and alone? Yes, all the time. But he never left bruises and believed any man who struck a woman was a coward. *You are too damn sensitive, Miriam,* my mother sneered inside my head. *Suck it up and be grateful he never struck you.* For that was all that *really* mattered, right? Society deemed a woman cowering beneath a fist a victim, but if she cowered beneath harsh words she was a doormat.

Cheater, cheater, confidence eater. Hurts his wife, but prove he beats her.

"Not *physically,*" I said. "I found out ... on Christmas ... I found out ..." I swallowed hard. "I found out he cheated on me. With a younger *guy*." There. I said it. The words left my throat like a spiked ball, loath to admit what had happened, afraid to make it *true.* I didn't realize how scared I had been to say it aloud. *He cheated on me.* I rubbed my forearm, feeling very small. Feeling very *exposed.* As if my confession encapsulated me like a gigantic snow globe, magnifying my failure at keeping my husband happy. I winced, expecting disgust or horror in Kayla's eyes, as if all men were loyal except to vile women. She would realize I was ugly and insignificant and unlovable, just as my mother had always insisted. Then, once the initial shock had settled, she would laugh thinly at herself and realize *of course* my husband cheated on me, for anyone who glimpsed me would recognize my worthlessness.

Instead, Kayla raised her eyebrows and said: "What a *fucker!* I hope his dick rots off."

Him. She placed it all on *him*. And why not? It was Sam's choices, Sam's actions, Sam's betrayal. *I* was the victim.

Yet that realization didn't make it hurt any less.

Cheater, cheater, confidence eater. Hurts his wife, but prove he beats her.

Tears clouded my vision. Kayla pulled me into her arms and squeezed, smelling of smoke and potato chips and stale patchouli oil. The boys gabbed with Hannah near the windshield, their attention focused on the road and each other. Marijuana thickened the air, making my head throb. Kayla patted my shoulder, then led me into the bedroom and locked the accordion door behind us.

"I'm sorry," I said, rubbing my eyes as we sat on the edge of the bare mattress. The closet's mirrored doors rattled in their track. "I guess all the stress is getting to me."

"Do *not* apologize." Kayla handed me a Subway napkin from her jacket pocket. "You're *supposed* to cry when you've been hurt."

I snuffled and dabbed my eyes with the napkin. "Everything feels out of control. This morning I actually debated going back to my husband."

Kayla scooted closer to me. "I'm glad you came with us instead," she said, and patted my knee. "But why were you considering that?"

"Because I know Sam won't stop chasing me unless I do. And he's not *that bad.* I mean, he always remembers my birthday and he sometimes brings me flowers for no reason at all."

"Do you *want* to go back?"

"No," I admitted. "I can't remember the last time we were happy together. But if I break my marriage vows by just leaving, then I am no better than him."

Kayla skewed her lips. "Your husband breaking his vows frees you from yours."

I stared at her, startled by the simplistic truth in her words.

"Why did you marry him?" she asked. Her tone of voice was curious, not cruel.

I shrugged and stared out the window, watching the heads of telephone poles streak past. The RV swayed and clattered. Kayla sat in silence, squeezing my knee reassuringly, waiting patiently until my thoughts collected. "I guess I married him because he paid attention to me and promised a home not propped up on cinder blocks." I laughed a sad little laugh. "Pathetic, huh?"

Kayla shook her head. "No. Human."

My brow furrowed. *Then what's my excuse? I'm not even that.*

"If you're miserable with Sam, then why not stick this out with Orin a bit longer? If your husband catches you, well, you debated going back anyway. But if you make it to Fiji, then he can't easily chase you across international borders, right?"

"No," I said, realizing chasing me across *magical* borders was impossible. And wasn't magic why I chose this adventure? *Am I willing to turncoat on my beliefs and dreams because Sam is* easy*?*

"Plus you're almost there," Kayla added.

"Yes, but, I don't even *know* Orin that well. I mean, I can't deny we have a connection, but he acts weird sometimes."

"Weird how?"

"Well, he hates being questioned."

Kayla chuckled. "Every man hates being questioned."

"And his mannerisms are sometimes odd."

"Cultural differences?" she asked. I blinked, confused. "I mean, I don't know Fijian customs or anything. Maybe he is acting normal where he's from."

"I never considered that." I scratched the bridge of my nose. "But how do I even know he's telling the truth about ... Fiji?"

"He *lives* there, doesn't he? Besides, if you hate it, leave like you left your husband."

"I guess so. But there's also..." I bit my lip. "There's another."

Kayla's face brightened. "A love triangle after all!"

"No!" I said. "We're not lovers. We just have another connection. But there are odd things about *him* too." I groaned and flopped back onto the bed. "I don't know what to do."

"Sounds like you are afraid of being betrayed again," Kayla said. I turned my face to her. She shrugged. "Your asshole husband shook you up and now you're *super* terrified of abandonment since you're in new territory. So the question becomes, out of the three men, who is always there for you?"

I thought about the forest, the hitchhiking, the coldness and the fights, and realized both Orin and Delano had risked themselves for me. Why would either betray me now? "Orin," I said, after a moment. "But that is because *I* am with *him*. Delano would do the same if I let him."

"Well, whatever you decide, you need to decide," Kayla said. "Your life is too complicated, and things get worse the longer you wait."

I gnawed my lip, staring at the yellow water stains on the ceiling, unknowing who to trust. *Magic, magic everywhere and not a crystal ball to tell me.* I *did* know, however, that Kayla was right. It wasn't the adventure I wanted to flee from; it was the risk of betrayal. And what had been my solution? To crawl back to the betrayer who had started the fear, all because his abuse was familiar, even though the familiarity would undoubtedly leave me desolate and deserted, brokenhearted and alone. I needed to simplify my life, but not with Sam. That narrowed my choices down to two: Follow my head or follow my heart. Orin or Delano.

I sat up and took a deep breath. "You are right," I said. "I need to pick one. And I know who I'm going to choose."

CHAPTER TWENTY-SIX

"Crank the heat," Clayton said. "It's cold."

"It *is* cranked," Kayla said from the driver's seat. "Welcome to the frozen north."

Me, Orin, Hannah, and Sean had been squished together on the couch for the last three hours, watching comedies on the flat screen TV. Clayton sat cross-legged beside us on the floor. Fuzzy blankets. Popcorn. Leftover pizza. It was like a traveling sleepover, but without curfews or chaperones or truths and dares. My eyes watched the television with the others, but my thoughts circled around Orin and Delano, the possibilities each promised, their potential lies and hidden secrets. Orin sat at the end of the couch with an ingenuous grin, gripping a can of root beer and a half-eaten candy cane. I was squished against him, head on his shoulder, enjoying the warmth of his faerie fever like I had in the truck bed when we first met. He still smelled of dew drenched ferns and hollow logs, only now it was familiar. *He* was familiar. And my heart ached as I realized how scared I was to lose any familiarity, no matter how small or new.

Orin sipped his soda, eyes never blinking. On the television Lars Lindstrom introduced his family to his new girlfriend. Beyond the windshield the sun set in a splash of orange and gray, and a faint *thud* sounded from the bathroom. I lifted my head from Orin's shoulder. It was most likely something tumbling off a counter from the RV's continuous bumps and trundle. *But maybe...*

I excused myself and tottered to the bathroom, bracing myself on the hallway walls for support. I paused outside the door, fingers on the latch. To my right, everyone laughed. Orin sounded above them all, like wind chimes over rain.

I slipped into the bathroom and locked the door. A man's silhouette stood behind the shower's opaque curtain.

"Delano?" I whispered.

"A little help, please," Delano whispered back.

I peeked behind the curtain. "What—? Oh!"

Delano stood naked in the stall, his back to the wall, hands splayed to hide his genitals. "I normally have clothing waiting for me when I leave the darkshine," he said, grimacing, "but I am a bit restricted tonight."

I found a pink and white striped beach towel beneath the sink and passed it to him, shielding my eyes with a hand. Delano tied the towel around his waist, then slid open the curtain.

"This moment feels oppositely familiar," he said.

I smirked. "Consider it payback, with interest."

Delano glanced at his bare torso, then waggled his eyebrows at me. "You're interested?"

"That is *not* what I meant," I said. "What are you doing in here, anyway?"

He placed the fallen shampoo bottle back on the shelf. "I fell asleep."

"In the shower? That sounds

uncomfortable."

"I figured it was out of the way, so if the sun fell before I woke I wouldn't be caught. Besides, I slept well." Delano's eyes twinkled. "I dreamt of you."

I dropped my gaze to the floor. "Um, why don't you merge with shadow?"

"Too intense. Orin will sense the magic this close, and I'd rather not fight the mockingbird."

"Well, you'll be caught the next time he relieves all the root beer he's chugging." I frowned, then a thought hit me. "Hold on. I have an idea."

I peeked my head around the bathroom door. "Hey, guys? May I take a nap in the bedroom? I feel ill."

"You're sick?" Orin leapt to his feet. I'd seen smaller eyes on an owl. "How can I help? Water? Tea? Wet rag? Med—?"

"No!" I took a deep breath "No. I just need to lay down for a bit. Car sickness."

"Go ahead." Kayla glanced over her shoulder from the driver's seat, her eyebrows lifted, silently asking if I needed another talk. I smiled and shook my head, then swung the bathroom door open to block everyone's view of the hall. I motioned Delano into the bedroom. He obeyed, staggering when the RV hit a dip in the road.

I followed him and locked the bedroom's accordion door behind us. "Now, maybe we—Oh my God! *What happened?"*

Silver scars crisscrossed from Delano's shoulders to his hips, slicing apart the tribal wings on his back as if he had been flogged. Unlike Orin's tattoo,

Delano's black lines were thick and crude, perfunctory instead of ornate, the puckered scars making them resemble puzzle pieces with the cracks in-between. I slid my hand down his spine without thinking, as if my fingers were erasers capable of healing the past.

Delano turned to me with a wan smile. "Freedom happened. But don't you worry. It was many years ago and worth all the pain." He hitched the sliding towel up on his hips. "I am more concerned about making it to morning unnoticed. I doubt the bed is less conspicuous than the shower."

"I meant the closet," I said, and slid open its mirrored door. The narrow floor was crammed with sleeping bags and comforters and stuffed plastic bags.

Delano frowned. "Not quite how I imagined spending my night."

"Do you have a better idea?"

"Maybe." Delano placed a cold hand on the crook of my neck. My breath caught in my throat as his finger slid down the back of my shoulder, tracing the bra strap beneath my black shirt. "You know," he said, "you never did thank me for the present."

The closet's mirrored doors rattled, reflecting the bare chested man behind me. I cleared my throat and said: "We haven't seen each other since I opened it."

Delano slid his hand under my shirt's collar, his cold fingertips slipping beneath the strap. My skin broke out in goosebumps. "*I* saw *you*."

I wheeled on him, trying to appear indignant. His grin told me I was a terrible liar. He pushed my hair behind my ears. Folded ears, just like his.

Whispers danced across my skin. Was it Delano's magic or mine? Or were we pulling together like moon and tide? Outside the bedroom, the men hollered at the television. Inside, the thin carpet hummed beneath our feet. Delano stepped closer. My back pressed against the mirrored door; our chests nearly touched. He leaned over me, the tip of his nose caressing my neck. His stomach muscles clenched when my fingers brushed his skin.

"Was the gift a poor choice?" Delano asked. He hesitated, then kissed my throat, soft and cautious.

"Terrible," I said, my pulse throbbing against his lips.

"Mmm. You better tell me what you want instead, then."

I closed my eyes and clasped Delano's sides, his skin icy beneath my hands. The RV rocked our bodies together, and I realized I knew exactly what I wanted. I wanted his towel to drop. I wanted his lips on my lips, his body against mine. Skin on skin, and sin on sin. I wanted to throw him onto the bed and try to make his cold flesh sweat, see how deep his shadows stretched. His hand cupped my lower back and pressed my pelvis against his. The hair on my arms prickled, as if I stood beneath the thunder of a midnight storm.

"Tell me what you want, changeling," he whispered, and brushed his mouth over mine.

I inhaled his breath, cold and filling, a deep sigh on an icy, winter night. I closed my eyes and felt my words vibrate against his lips. "I want you to leave."

He chuckled. "Back to the shower so soon? How dirty do you plan to get?"

I twisted my head; his lips struck my jaw. My knees weakened and I pushed him away. "I mean for good. I need you to leave me alone, Delano."

The corner of his mouth twitched. "You don't mean that."

"Wh-what I want is unhealthy. I have made my decision. I am going to the Realm. I am going to become a healer and help—"

"A *healer?*" Delano barked a laugh. I glanced at the door, fearing the others had heard. "The Realm will *never* let you become a healer. Human life made you too independent, a *liability*. They will force you into the mining pits as they forced me. Anything to control you."

"You lie."

"*I do not lie!* Which is why I haven't made any happy promises like the idiot mockingbird outside."

My fists balled. "Leave Orin out of this."

"Orin *is* this!" Delano said, his teeth clenched to keep from shouting. "You have been forced into stormy times and feel the only escape is to follow the sunshine. But you cannot deny our connection. For God's sake, you wielded darkness! I saw you *freed* through it."

"Only because you infected me with your magic. Your sly, *seductive* magic."

Delano stepped away from me, his eyebrows raised. "Oh-ho. Is *that* what the mockingbird now sings?" He motioned his hands down his body. "Are shadows coiling around me? Do you see anything other than flesh and blood?"

"No," I said, cautiously.

"No. You don't. And that is my proof. I

am not using magic right now, as I told you in the shower. This is me. Stripped and vulnerable." He unballed my fists and laced his fingers together with mine. "Do you still feel nothing between us?"

Whispers tingled my skin; I felt the pulling sensation like moon and tide. I wanted to say to hell with the Realm and a promising life. I wanted to sneak off into the night with Delano's arm around my waist. I wanted to take on the world with him at my side. The chickadee had told me to follow my instincts, not my impulses. Which was this? *Maybe my heart has pointed the way all along.* I stepped closer to Delano and peered into his eyes.

Delano's ruddy eyes.

Delano's ruddy eyes which still waxed and waned.

My heart hardened. No magic? Here he was, caught in a lie.

"How stupid do you think I am?" I snapped. Delano recoiled, as if my words had struck. "Are you trying to tell me your eyes followed the moon before you became a darkling?"

His brow wrinkled. "I am confined to the night. My eyes are a reflection of my existence. I cannot help that."

I yanked my hands away from his. "So magic *is* still working within you. *Dark* magic. *Seductive* magic. Just as Orin said."

Delano's chin quivered, then his nostrils flared. "I am a *darkling*, not an incubus! What the hell do I have to do to prove myself to you?"

"Nothing." I turned my back on him and

unlocked the accordion door. “If you want what is best for me, then leave me alone.”

CHAPTER TWENTY-SEVEN

"Stop! Stop! Stop!" Orin said.

"What? Why?" Clayton asked. We had stopped for the night at a rest stop, and a late lunch at a greasy spoon. We had just finished refilling the RV's gas tank and now passed a city welcome sign as we trundled back toward the freeway onramp.

"I know someone in this town," Orin said. "They will give us a ride straight to our destination."

"You got it, man." Clayton pulled the RV over, idling in a red zone and blocking half an intersection. A Civic blared its horn as it darted around us, the driver's middle finger pointing to the roof.

Orin grabbed his backpack; I did the same. Kayla threw her arms around me. "I am *so glad* the Universe crossed our paths," Kayla said. "Best of luck to both of you." She leaned back, giving my upper arms a firm squeeze. "Stay true."

I watched Orin hop from the RV to the sidewalk. "Already am." I smiled, then joined him.

Hugs and goodbyes and no-thank-yous for marijuana made the rounds. Then Orin and I stood on the side of the street, waving to our road warrior friends as they disappeared into their adventure without us.

"Who do you know here?" I asked as we headed back toward the gas station.

Orin picked up a glinting bottle cap from the sidewalk and placed it in his pocket. "I don't know yet."

"That's a bit disconcerting. Care to explain?"

He pointed to the community display beside the town's welcome sign. It was a typical community display, with brown boards forming a mount to display the town's local organizations, churches, clubs, and societies. Between the emblems for the Free Masons and the Girl Scouts was a white, round medallion, smaller than the others, with a red cursive R in its center.

"That's the Realm's traveler symbol," Orin said. "It means a faerie lodge is near." He twisted the medallion, popping its face off the board. On the back was an address with a simplistic map and a warning which read: Level Two Rebel Threat.

Orin twisted the emblem back into place. "This way."

The sky was slate-blue and cloudless, but the air had bitter teeth. Giant wreaths hung from lampposts wrapped in silver garland, twinkling in the late winter sun. The snow had been cleared through downtown, the uneven sidewalks busy with pedestrians. *Am I walking among faeries*? I wondered. I kept my face down and scanned the streets from the corner of my eyes for hidden magic. People bundled in coats and scarves meandered between brick cafes and antique stores, emptying their wallets on post-holiday sales, cups of coffee, and steaming fresh baked goods. Every exposed ear was curved, however. And none of them were folded.

Then we rounded the corner and found an image straight from a child's popup book. A white Victorian styled home, three stories high with a rounded tower, a blue slate roof, and glittering icicles hanging off its gingerbread trim. Beside a three tiered fountain stood a Christmas tree half the height of the house, bedecked in frosted garland and crystal orbs so clear they looked like bubbles floating on the boughs. A golden winged angel perched on top of the tree's crown, her trumpet pointing straight to the heavens.

"Wow," I said. "That *has* to be the faerie lodge."

"Huh?" Orin followed my eyes to the house. His nose wrinkled. "No," he said. "Absolutely not."

We strolled past several more blocks, away from the festive downtown, away from the Victorian and craftsman houses, away from the humans and their shops with painted windows and after-holiday sales. The lampposts' lights popped on. We stopped only when Orin picked up an earring from the gutter, its orange glass bead glinting in the dying sun before he slipped it into his pocket. We trudged through unplowed grimy snow, past mechanic shops and warehouses, and cut through unfenced empty lots.

Orin pointed ahead. "There it is."

At the end of an industrial cul-de-sac was *Bob's Mini Storage*. Several long buildings with blue corrugated roofs and rollup doors stood behind a ten-foot chain-link fence topped with spirals of razor wire. A small office with an *Open* sign blinking in the window stood beside an electronic gate. To the left of *Bob's Mini Storage* was an abandoned towing company. To the right was *Bob's Pick-N-Pull*, with a huge vinyl sign hanging on the front gate stating they were closed until further notice.

"Are you sure this is the right place?" I

asked.

Orin grinned a big-tooth grin. "Oh, yes. Definitely. I hope they have a room for the night."

My nerves started to fray as we approached *Bob's Mini Storage.* Orin was the only faerie I knew and I was uncertain if he was an accurate representation. All of my previous knowledge of faeries came from fairytales, movies, and cartoons. Lies of the taletellers. If we *were* in a fairytale, we would approach a castle or a house made of candy, most likely in a glen inside an enchanted forest. Not a storage unit in Anywhere, USA. What if I didn't fit in? What if the other faeries thought I was *too changeling*? I swallowed, and wished for all the rooms to be full.

A buzzer sounded when Orin opened the office door, and the scent of new carpet struck, hard. There were no candy walls or gingerbread trim, no enchanted castle that appeared to unlucky travelers who stumbled into a ring of toadstools. The left wall was crammed with moving boxes, packaging tape, and bubble-wrap for sale. An electric heater whirred in the corner with a glowing orange face. To our right was a long desk with a credit card reader, a single paperclip, and a computer. A daddy longlegs sat on top of the monitor; a young woman sat behind it, her nose buried in a newspaper. My muscles tensed.

"No new rentals. All storage units are full," the woman said, her eyes on the paper.

"We were more interested in room and board," Orin said.

The woman's head jerked up, striking me with that familiar faerie-tingle. She was around my age.

(*No*, I reminded myself. *She could be older than this country. She might have even watched the Mayflower set anchor.*) Her ears were pointed and her eyes gleamed like beads of amber. "Och! Of course!" She smiled, whipped a huge leather bound book up from beneath the desk, and dropped it on the desktop with a startling *whap*. "Names. Divisions. Purposes."

"Orin Grian. Border sentry," Orin said, and passed the woman a paper card from his pocket. "On a probationary retriever assignment for changeling recovery."

The woman read the card and handed it back to him. Her eyes shifted to me. "I take it this is the changeling?"

Orin nodded. "This is Miriam Thatcher. Realm name Aluala Liath. Awaiting placement."

I blinked. "Aluala Liath?"

"That's what your parents named you and what is recorded officially," Orin said. "The Realm will make you change your family name to keep the generation-records consistent, but you can keep your first if you prefer."

Miriam Liath. Not bad. The thought of shedding my married *and* maiden name felt surprisingly freeing.

"Please remove your jacket," the woman told me.

"Why?"

"This is Miriam's first visit to a faerie establishment," Orin said, quickly. "She is unfamiliar with procedure."

"I understand," the woman said as she

came around the counter, yet her amber eyes were hardened with irritation. "Due to elevated rebel threats in the area, I must check your wings to ensure you are allied with the Realm."

"But I don't have wings yet," I said.

She shrugged. "Procedure is procedure. Take off your coat. It just takes a second to see if your back is scarred."

I hesitated, then complied. She lifted the tail of my shirt, then Orin's, sparing us hardly a glance. She then scurried back around the counter and studied the book. "We have two singles left with a shared bathroom," the woman said.

Orin groaned. "No doubles?"

Orin and the woman turned to the daddy-longlegs on the monitor. I strained to hear what it said, but heard only the whir of the heater. "It's not that!" Orin blurted, blushing. "I've been sworn to protect her and must remain nearby."

A darkness entered the woman's stare. "We are fully Realm protected," she said. The last word came out in harsh chunks. *Pro-tec-ted.*

Orin's spine stiffened, like a soldier in front of a commander. "Of course. It has been a wearisome travel. Two singles are fine. Thank you."

"Back building. Use the red doors on the ends." The woman handed us each a key, our room numbers burned into their leather tags. My stomach churned and I wanted to flee, but I convinced myself what I felt was merely nerves—impulse, not instinct—and that I was at the start of something wonderful. Something *magical.*

“Meals are held in the restaurant at the end of the hallway.” The amber-eyed faerie smiled sweetly. “Please enjoy your stay.”

CHAPTER TWENTY-EIGHT

Heat struck like a sauna when the red door opened and I instantly started to sweat. The hallway was long and dim and lined with locked doors, springing unearthly images to mind. Secret vaults. Long lost tombs. Treasures hidden in the dust. I clenched the straps of my backpack as Orin and I searched for our rooms, the canvas moistening beneath my palms.

Beyond the narrow entryway at the end of the hall a guitar trilled and an unseen applause erupted.

We found our rooms halfway down the hall—numbers twenty-three and twenty-four—and separated to store our belongings. I clicked on the light and was surprised with what was revealed. My room was tiny, barely large enough for a twin bed and a four drawer dresser, but other than the size it was nothing like a storage unit. The walls and ceiling were white plaster, the beige carpet thin but clean. A sachet of red tulle dangled above the doorway and scented the room with mothballs.

I set my backpack on the bed, shed my clothing to a long sleeve tee and jeans, and ran my fingers through my hair. Orin was waiting for me when I reentered the hall. He had changed into blue cargo shorts with a pocket half-torn off and a tight-fitting, faded yellow tank top which dipped to his sacrum, fully exposing his tattoo wings. All he needed was a surfboard to be ready for sand and waves.

I pushed my sleeves up to my elbows and pulled the shirt off the sweat at the base of my spine. *It's gotta be ninety degrees in here,* I imagined. "I feel improperly dressed."

"Nonsense. You look great," Orin insisted, as he always did, whether I was freshly showered or caked in mud with sticks and leaves in my tangles. I smoothed out my hair as we headed down the dim hallway to the restaurant's blaring light.

How fitting, I thought, my chest fluttering. *What better way to leave one existence behind and begin another than through a light at the end of a tunnel?*

I halted, realizing I was steps away from my whole life changing. Again. "Um, Orin?" He stopped and turned, his eyes on mine as if I were the only thing in the world. At the end of the hallway a guitar hummed and a cymbal started to *ching*. "I realized I haven't thanked you and I want to. For watching out for me. For your truthfulness. For your kindness. For *everything.* Thank you."

"Of course. I *am* your guide, after all."

I hooked my arm around his. "And my friend."

Orin grinned his contagious grin and squeezed my elbow with his. "Yes. And *you* are *my* friend. Are you ready to meet your people?"

I smoothed out my hair. "Yes. I am," I said. Then bit my lip to keep it from shaking.

The restaurant's atmosphere crackled like the blast of a shotgun. On the surface was that magical buzz, the vibrating powers of the fifty-something faeries inside. At a glance it was like any human establishment. Some of the faeries mingled around the bandstand, some ate meals at the tables, others drank at the bar, some swayed on the dance floor. All were willowy and wore clothing which dipped low on their backs, displaying the differing artwork of their tattoo wings. The restaurant could easily seat a hundred, but unlike humans the faeries did not spread themselves throughout the tables or floor, creating distance between themselves and the other guests. Instead they stayed close to one another, as if an unseen nucleus drew them in.

Except for the man alone in the corner, scanning the restaurant with flat, granite eyes. He stood opposite the bandstand with a brindled, hunchbacked greyhound at his side, his steely face as expressive as a corpse. His tailored knee-length coat and pants were the color of cinnamon, and yet he still felt *gray*.

"Who is that?"

Orin's eyes followed mine. His face brightened. "That's a sniffer," he said. "They hunt darklings and rebels and criminals who escape the Realm. Sniffers are the most honorable of professions and the bravest of all faeries."

The sniffer blinked slowly and watched the crowd. A whip hung coiled off the right side of his belt; a knife hung off the left. His hair was so blond it reminded me of a glare off a windshield. *Snow blindness,* I thought. *If snow was gray.* The hunchbacked greyhound stood stiff, and licked its chops.

Orin and I meandered through the tables, arm in arm. Faeries smiled politely as we passed, each of their ears pointed. Beneath the atmosphere's magical crackling I felt another hum in the air. It was faint. Soft. Rising from the mortar in the flagstone, from the plaster of the plain, white walls. I realized it was the restaurant's own magical buzz, a feeling of community and friendships, and a vow to protect all secrets. It was the sensation of collapsing onto your bed after traveling too long, the sigh in your ear that reminded you were home.

"This next one is for all you hard working men and the ladies who love you," the singer said into his microphone. I sat with Orin on the edge of a crowded bench. Red and white roses bloomed in small copper buckets along the center of the table. Steak kabobs sizzled on a grill behind the oak bar, but through its savory smoke I still caught whiffs of mothballs. On stage, a violinist dragged out three long notes, sad and low. Hardworking men escorted their ladies to the floor.

I smoothed out my hair. Nine spiders squatted on a yellow sponge across the table from us—four wolf spiders, four daddy long legs, and one black widow. Behind us, three chickadees chattered and ate seed from a glass bowl on the bar. All around us faeries started to stare.

I smoothed out my hair. *Don't let their open stares frighten you. Kayla was right. Nothing is wrong. It's just cultural differences.*

A waitress with a pinched face and a stained apron filled the spiders' sponge with bourbon from a decanter. "Tonight's meal is Dorwian kabobs," she told us. "Can I bring you two some drinks to start?"

"You must try rose mead," Orin told me. "It's a Realm specialty."

The waitress leaned over to peer at my ear. "My goodness. You are a *changeling*?"

I sunk into my shoulders. "Yes."

She grabbed my arm and yanked me from the bench to my feet. "Everybody!" she shouted to the room. "The Realm found their lost changeling!"

The band stopped playing mid-note and every head in the room—faeries', spiders', chickadees', and the greyhound's—turned to me. The waitress yanked me back up when I tried to retake my seat.

"Well?" the singer said through his microphone. "Say your name, girl!"

I cleared my throat. "Mir-Miriam. But I guess it used to be Aluala?"

I smoothed out my hair as a rumble rolled through the crowd. A man with a shaved head approached from several seats over. His tan shorts were frayed at the edges, his green tank-top as faded as Orin's. "I can't believe it! Conley and Makeena's daughter! Lordy, child! We all thought ya were dead!"

"You knew my parents?"

He laughed and slapped me drunkenly on the back. "*Knew em?* I worked with em on Earth's calvary for nearly a century. Good faeries. Devastated when they couldn't find ya. My name's Alston. Praise the Realm! They will be thrilled!"

More faeries approached, friendly and curious. They asked where I had been (Ohio), what I had been doing (oh, nothing much), what living with humans was like (lonely), how I felt to finally go home (overwhelmed but excited). I felt claustrophobic with questions, unsure which to answer first, not wanting to be rude to those I passed over.

A woman with apricot hair and a splattering of freckles across her button nose barged through the crowd. She plopped herself beside me and introduced herself as Shea. "I wondered why you were dressed strangely," she said. "You must be *dying*. Come with me. I'll find you something more befitting."

I followed Shea to the end of the long hall and into a room as small and plain as mine. She dug through a dresser drawer and tossed me a short lavender dress. "Try this on," she said, then sat cross-legged on the bed.

"Um, *here*?" I asked.

"Where else?"

I felt awkward changing in front of a stranger (it brought up all that stomach-swirling anxiety from my high school locker room days), but Shea acted as if I was merely about to wash my hands at a sink. I bit my lower lip and pulled my shirt over my head. Shea jumped to her feet with a soft laugh. "Take that off, too," she said, and unlatched my bra. I stiffened and she noticed my unease. She smiled gently and squeezed my shoulder. "Such garments are prohibited. For within the Realm faeries must always display their wings."

The dress fit well, formfitting on top with short bell sleeves. The back dipped to my sacrum, exposing my naked skin, and flailed into a skirt which brushed the middle of my thighs. I tugged on the hem to increase the length, but the fabric refused to give.

Shea smirked at my mud splattered boots. "Not what I would choose, but they will have to do."

I padded back to the restaurant, skulking behind Shea and tugging on the dress's hem. The band had increased their tempo, singing about honor and duty and a war called Quarin, and how the blood of the righteous will never spill again.

"The dress has heliofiber woven into the

fabric," Shea said as we meandered through the tables.

I smoothed out my hair. "What's heliofiber?"

"A Realm grass used in embroidery. It glows when you add magic."

I frowned. "Oh. Well. I'm not good with magic."

Shea shrugged. "You are young. You'll develop your skills with time. But until then ... Orin!" Orin turned away from a group of faeries near the bar, a glass of mead in hand. "Come take our changeling for a spin. Show her how heliofiber works."

Orin's face lit up. He set his mead on a table, then dragged me toward the dance floor.

I dug my heels into the flagstone. "No! I can't dance!"

"So? Neither can I. What does that matter?" He clenched my wrists and whipped me into a circle. I squealed as he spun us around like a demented game of ring around the rosy. My stomach flopped. Around and around, one direction, then the other. He added a hop to his step. Hop, hop. Skip, skip. Halfway through the song he granted me mercy and settled into a simple sway. I still followed his lead terribly, but laughed too hard to care.

"You're right," I said. "You can't dance."

He grinned. "Neither can you. Told you it doesn't matter."

My body swayed with Orin's, both of us unable to match the band's rhythm. He slid his hands down my back and cupped the base of my spine. The dress flickered beneath me. Gold glowed in the fabric in the shape of intricate knot-work, the fabric's secret embroidery. I squeaked with excitement. Orin twirled me away from him, my fingers sliding off his as I let go and spun. The dress flailed out and the gold light disintegrated. I clapped my hands, bouncing on my toes. Orin started towards me, but Alston stepped between us, cutting him off.

"Will ya give the honor of an old fart such as myself a dance?" he asked.

"Of course," I said. He didn't look a day past twenty-five.

Alston took my hand and around and around we went, my dress glowing gold. His hands slid off me and the light faded until another man snatched me away, lighting up my dress again. My cheeks flushed from laughter and heat; sweat dripped down my back. The dress shone and twirled as I passed from hand to hand, each man another glimpse into an enchanted world.

The sniffer blinked slowly in the corner.

Three songs and seven men later (or was it eight?), a woman cut in, thrusting her butt to push away a dark-haired man who already had a turn. She pulled me in, our noses so close I went cross-eyed. The lavender dress flared gold. "Hi! I'm Breena." Her spiky hair blazed like autumn vineyards and her eyes gleamed like fine brandy. She had a body which belonged on stage in a tutu dancing the dance of sugarplums, not sporting the frayed hot pink and black checkered minidress she wore. Silver studs cuffed her wrist; the belts on her scuffed boots wrapped from her ankles to her knees and jingled as she whirled. She seemed like a girl who would kick your ass for teasing her, then bake you a cake to say she was sorry for losing her temper.

"I hear you need a ride to the ley line to shake your psycho husband's tail," Breena said. "I am heading out early. Sunrise. Don't be late, kay?" She spun me away from her, then skipped off into the hallway, her wings a coiling of spirals and polka dots.

Orin snatched me before the swarm of faeries waiting on the sidelines descended. He twirled me against his chest, then dipped me low enough that my hair swept the floor. Gold light reflected off the flagstone. "You're flushed," he said.

"I'm *dying*. I need air."

Orin returned me to my feet. I wiped the sweat off my brow as we headed toward the door.

"Miriam!" Orin said. "Your dress!"

The fabric glowed its gold knot-work, yet Orin stood six inches away. "How are you doing that without touching me?" I asked.

Orin grinned. "I'm not. That's all you."

I gaped at my dress. "Impossible. I suck at magic."

Orin dragged me to the nearest table, then tore a rose petal on a centerpiece. "Heal the flower," he said.

"I can't—"

"You *can*." He pushed me down onto the bench.

I took a deep breath and hovered my hand above the flower. *Heal*, I commanded with my thoughts. *Heal. Heal. Heal.* Several faeries gathered around to watch. Then several more. The sniffer stayed in his corner, yet his eyes felt heaviest of all.

Nothing happened.

My shoulders slumped. "Told you I suck."

"Keep trying. *I know* you can do this. You feel it *here*," Orin said, and poked my sternum.

I concentrated harder. *Heal. Heal.* A bead of sweat slipped off my jaw, and my hand started trembling. *Please, heal. Please!* Several faeries sniggered and whispered. My heart hammered as the light on my dress disappeared. *Oh for the love of God you stupid rose,* heal*!*

Music hummed on my skin, then unfurled from my chest and through my fingers. My ears grew hot and the restaurant's murmur seemed to double. I caught snippets about crevices and insects, cobwebs and silk, and realized I was eavesdropping on a conversation of spiders. The music on my skin shifted from a hum to a symphony. My dress flared gold, warm and blinding. The rose petal quivered. Then the tear shone a brilliant white and mended.

The faeries raised their glasses and cheered. Alston clapped my back. "Get this girl some wings!" he bellowed.

"I *told* you you'll make a good healer." Orin squeezed my shoulders. "Now come on. Let's get some fresh air before you pass out."

Faeries beamed and patted my back, congratulating me as Orin escorted me to the restaurant's door. No one shied away from me, no one sneered. I was *present* for the first time in my life. I had finally found my community. I finally belonged.

Winter bit my skin when I stepped outside, and every hair on my arms and legs stood on end.

I never thought I would yearn for the cold after the train ride and the woods and wandering miles of endless slushy roads. Yet I sighed with relief as iciness filled my lungs and left again in misty ribbons. It felt like the first time I could breathe for the last hour.

Orin handed me his key. "You need water. I'll be right back."

The restaurant's door closed behind him; the celebration inside became a whisper. I hugged myself, beaming. Gold light flickered on the hem of my dress. Magic's buzz sang on my skin, lingering like a lover's embrace. I leaned back against the storage unit that wasn't a storage unit, and gazed up at a million stars.

A shadow fluttered in my peripheral. My muscles tensed.

Delano stood twenty feet away. He stepped towards me when he realized I had noticed him, his palms open in a gesture of surrender. "Please," he said. "Hear me out."

I bit my lip. Then turned my back on him and opened the restaurant's door.

Orin exited before I crossed the threshold, a glass of water in his hand. When he saw Delano his eyes widened, as large and explosive as two live grenades.

"Go back," I said, trying to push him inside.

Instead, Orin held his ground and shouted: *"Darkling!"* for all the faeries to hear.

CHAPTER TWENTY-NINE

The sniffer fled through the door with Orin's shout still hanging in the air. Delano took a step back, his eyes huge. The building's shadows rolled toward him, lapping against his ankles like the waters of the Styx.

The sniffer strutted forward, his hunchbacked greyhound growling at his side. His lips curled into a murderous grin. "Delano *darkling*," the sniffer said. For such a stony appearance, his voice was soft, almost musical. It reminded me of Orin's. "You are guilty of treason, kidnapping, murder, embracing dark magic—"

"I am guilty of many things," Delano said, "but none of those Realm *lies*."

Faeries piled out of the restaurant door, gathering behind the sniffer. Rage twisted their faces when they noticed the darkling in their lot. "Kidnapper!" "Baby killer!" "Demon!" "Manipulator!" "Liar!" they shouted.

The sniffer shrugged off his coat and tossed it to Breena, and only then did I realize he was the only faerie whose wings had been concealed. His back was an elaborate snarl of scimitars and claws, darkening most of his skin. "Any last words?" the sniffer asked. The greyhound pawed his foot against the pavement like a bull, hackles raised, and slavering.

Delano stood alone in the shadows, outnumbered at least twenty to one. I had to force my feet to stay still. Delano had shown me only kindness, and I didn't want him hurt no matter the allegations against him. But the eyes of the faeries burned with hatred and rage, their anger radiating off them as intense as their magic. My heart raced with fear and guilt and shame, as if whatever happened next would be all my fault. I glared at Delano. *Why didn't you listen to me you stupid man? Why didn't you stay away?*

Delano's hands curled into fists. "I do not want to fight."

The sniffer smirked. "Then surrender willingly."

Delano chuckled and shook his head. He shifted his weight as if to turn his back on them, then he vanished in a burst of shadow and appeared an inch from my face. I yelped with surprise; Delano seized my arm, shadows racing up our bodies. Coldness filled my marrow and I felt a sucking sensation, as if a black-hole had burst open behind me. My head swam. My consciousness started to slip. Then Delano flew off of me in a silent explosion of light.

Orin caught me one-handed before I fell to my knees, water from his drinking glass splashing onto my shoulder. I was lightheaded, nauseated, as if I had jumped out of a sauna and into a pool of glacier runoff. I staggered to my feet, swaying.

The sniffer blasted Delano with another burst of white light, slamming him into the chain-link fence. Wire cut Delano's ear; blood streaked a fence pole as he fell to his knees. Instinctively I darted to help him, but Orin yanked me back and forced me to the restaurant wall. Delano seemed to melt into the shadows, then materialized on his feet. Darkness slithered off his body like the skin off a snake.

"What did you do with the human baby once you realized it wasn't a faerie?" the sniffer sneered. "Torture it? Broil it?"

"I tried to return her," Delano said. "But the parents—"

The sniffer scoffed. "*Liar*. The Realm found its corpse, the flesh torn from the bones, the eyes plucked from its sockets."

I gaped at Delano, revolted.

"*Lies*," Delano sneered.

The sniffer flung his arm at him as if catching an invisible ball; Delano did the same. Light and heat exploded from the sniffer, colliding with Delano's cold burst of shadow. The two forces wavered and shot up three stories; the air between them seemed to split. Light infiltrated the darkness like illuminated icicles, pulverized by the darkling's gloom. Delano leaned into the sniffer's magic, grinning wide, his eyes almost euphoric. My bones hummed and static prickled my skin. Delano shoved harder and the sniffer's light folded backwards like softened, white gold.

If this had been a movie the speakers would boom with whooshing or crashing or screeches or bangs. But the only sounds were heavy breathing, the insults and shouts from the faerie crowd, the crunching of gravel beneath Delano's shoes as he closed in on the sniffer.

"You *must* realize I can destroy you," Delano said. Droplets beaded on the sniffer's forehead—the first time I saw a faerie sweat. "But I do not want to fight. No darkling wants to fight."

The sniffer scoffed. "If you think we will

lay down and let you destroy us, you are sorely mistaken."

"Kill him!" the crowd cried. *"Kill him!"*

"Stay back!" the sniffer shouted as the faeries started to rush the darkling. Shadow and light danced in their eyes. Their teeth were bared and thirsty for vengeance.

"Is this what you want?" Delano shouted at me. "A brainless mob demanding the execution of innocent men, all to protect their own enslavement?"

"Ignore him, Miriam," Orin said, poised to lunge beside the sniffer. "Darklings murder and torture faeries and exploit changelings for their own sick desires. He is trying to trick you."

"Miriam—" Delano started.

"Darklings are outlaws," the sniffer said. "Prisoners who stole their power from their punishment."

"Lies!"

"He is darkness manifested. A *demon,*" Alston added. "And you are another victim he wants to enslave and devour. Don't trust him if you value your life!"

Delano's irises burned like hellfire, half eaten by the moon. *"Lies! You* must *come with me!"*

My brow furrowed, and I stepped toward Orin.

"No! Come with *me!"* Delano screamed. He disappeared in a burst of shadow and reappeared in my face, nearly jerking my arm from its socket. I screeched as shadows raced up my legs, my body, covering me like a pall. "I *tried* being polite," Delano snarled, his fingernails digging into my arm and his shadows shrouding my throat. "But I *refuse to lose you—*"

Orin smashed the glass of water into Delano's cheek. A glass shard sliced his skin, but Delano's grip and shadows tightened around me. Then steam burst in his face and he stumbled backwards, yowling. I broke through the shadows, gasping, and scrambled behind Orin.

"Leave her alone!" Orin shouted. Magic shimmied around his hand like heat off blacktop. Delano cursed, pawing frantically at his eyes and cheeks. His flesh looked bubbly, and I realized Orin's magic boiled the water on his face.

The sniffer's light plowed into Delano. The darkling flew six feet into the air and landed on his back. The sniffer whipped a knife from his belt and lunged. Delano rolled, merging with shadow. A spark leapt as the sniffer's blade struck pavement. Delano emerged as a shadowman beside the fence. Darkness dripped off his body like when he had first introduced himself in the woods. But he snarled instead of smiled and the shadows did not melt into the surrounding darkness. Blackness whirled around him in thin strips, as if he stood amid a swarm of bats.

The sniffer launched a blast of light at Delano. It hit the black whirlwind and ricocheted back into the crowd, slamming three faeries into the side of the restaurant. Delano grinned as sly and malicious as a necromancer. The water on his cheek froze into a starburst pattern. Faster and faster the shadows whirled around him. Delano threw his head back and screamed. At first I thought it was pain, that Orin had made the water boil again. Then Delano's voice became the wind, strong and howling. Everyone skidded backwards; I leaned into the gales to hold my footing. Clouds raced overhead and blocked the starlight, the moonlight. Ice pelted the world. The chain-link fence waved and clinked as the wind tried to tear it free from its posts. All warmth drained into the darkling inside the shadowy whirlwind, who grinned like a devil with blood moon eyes. Alston lost his footing and flipped backwards, feet over head. The lamplights illuminating *Bob's Mini Storage* exploded; bursts of glass tinkled against the pavement. A woman screamed as shrapnel tore into her arm. Snow formed miniature drifts against the faeries' feet; snowflakes caught and melted in the folds of their clothing, their eyelashes, their brows. Every body shivered. Every jaw quaked, the chattering teeth unheard in the screeching gales.

The sniffer circled his hand above his head, a silent command which made all the faeries tense to attack. They shimmered in unison, their combined magic making my skin crawl. But in a blink Delano and his whirlwind disappeared into the shadows, leaving a raging blizzard in his wake.

The faeries cursed and split to search the lot, leaning into the gales, shouting to be heard above winter's screeching. The sniffer's greyhound paced where Delano had stood, its nose to the ground and ears pressed against its skull. The pelting ice stung my skin like needles. *No wonder meteorologists never make accurate predictions*, I thought.

Orin squeezed my shoulder. "Are you hurt?"

I shook my head, a silent lie. My heart had been ripped in half and left sputtering inside my chest. Who was that monster in the shadowy whirlwind?

Where was the gentleman with the starving fox? Or the passion I had snuck into my arms? I shuddered, thinking of Delano's blazing eyes, the bloodlust grin as the faeries fell before him, his screams that I belonged with him as if I were a piece of property, a *thing* to do with as he pleased, just as Orin had warned. Delano had feigned defenselessness. He had feigned weakness and sympathies, and for what? To gain my trust? To lower my guard? Orin had been right. Delano was a manipulator, an incubus, a liar who used compassion and seduction as bait. Delano was the fox, after all. And God help me, I was the fool.

The sniffer yanked me from Orin and slammed my back against the wall. His pant legs flapped in the wind. "Supporting *darklings?*" he spat in my face.

"*What*? I—"

"You tried to aid Delano," the sniffer snarled. "Supporting darklings is a slight against the Realm." His eyes pierced like steel as he whipped the knife from his belt.

Orin pushed himself between us, his arms out and chest forward like a shield. "It's not her fault!" The sniffer's knife tapped his jugular, the blade pressing a white line in his skin. Orin held his ground, unflinching. "Miriam's a changeling," Orin said. "And the whole drive of a darkling is to manipulate and confuse changelings. *It's not her fault.* Blame Delano."

The sniffer's lip curled, exposing teeth and gums. A drop of blood slid down Orin's throat. For a terrifying moment I thought the sniffer would slit Orin's throat right there and let him bleed out in the falling snow. The sniffer's eyes then narrowed. He stepped back and sheathed his knife. "Watch her," he grumbled, then slinked back into the restaurant with his greyhound at his heels.

Orin released a shaky breath and wiped the blood off his throat with a tissue from his pocket. "Are you okay?"

I nodded, squeezing my lips tight, trying to act brave. Orin pulled me into a hug anyway. "I am so, so *sorry*," I said, and buried my eyes against his trembling shoulder. "Delano tried to *kidnap me!* He was more concerned about losing, as if this is all some sort of sick game." I snuffled. "You were right. The whole time he used me, tried to trick me. I am such an *idiot*."

Orin stroked my hair. "You are not an idiot. I hate that it came to this, but at least you now see the truth." I nodded against his shoulder. My teeth chattered. "You're freezing," he said. "Let's go inside."

Orin escorted me into the restaurant. I let the door close on the darkness behind us, and readily embraced the light.

CHAPTER THIRTY

Morning inched toward the horizon, illuminating my insecurities. I held my breath as I headed to the restaurant. Yesterday felt like a fading dream, the evening a lingering nightmare. *The faeries were kind to you because they pitied you,* my old insecurities said. *They don't* really *like you. How could they after the havoc Delano caused because of you?*

As I approached the crowded table, however, I realized my old insecurities were just that. Old. Seven faeries smiled as I approached, and enthusiastically waved me over to join their meal. Orin scooted over on the bench, allowing me into the clique as if I had joined them every breakfast since birth. As if the whole changeling fiasco had never happened. Our driver, Breena, was seated across the table adding honey to her teacup. Alston was also there, his nose red. I smiled, wondering if he had ever gone to bed. Orin wrapped his arm around me in a good-morning hug, then poured me a cup of tea from the table's kettle. A waitress brought me a plate of fried eggs.

Breena handed me a burgundy sweater. "Put this on when we leave," she said. "It's Realm wool. Finest wool in all the worlds. You will need it. The weather is terrible."

"Thank you," I said, and ran my fingers along the sweater's braided front. *Realm sheep must be made of velvet.*

Alston chuckled. He had a goose egg on

top of his bald head where he had whacked it on the pavement. "That was some excitement last night, eh? I haven't had a good fight in decades. I'm surprised Delano had the balls to show up here."

Orin stabbed his eggs with a fork. "He's been troubling us the whole trip."

Breena snorted. "No wonder California is having a heatwave in January."

"What do you mean?" I said.

"Darklings keep territories," Alston said, rubbing his goose egg gingerly. "Delano's territory is near the Realm entrance in central California. But since he is chasing you all the way out here, their winter has gone crazy."

I shouldn't ask prying questions, I thought, a heartbeat before one blurted out of me: "But why would winter change if darklings have no *true* powers on Earth, only stolen?"

"Earth has been manipulated and abused for so long that she becomes confused when darkling magic is ripped away." Alston chuckled. "Global warming, anyone?"

"But won't that still cause major environmental problems if the darklings are killed off?"

"When. Not if. There may be some minor issues at first, but the Realm has all the means for a speedy repair." Alston smiled amiably. "Who knows! That might be your first healing assignment, little changeling."

The restaurant's red door flew open with a bang. A frigid wind gusted through the heat, and the faeries genially griped. A hooded man in an oversized coat entered. He scanned the room as if expecting a friend, then skulked to the bar and plopped himself onto a stool. Snow melted off his shoes in falling clumps. He clenched his coat to his chest, demanded hot mead, and slumped deep into his shoulders.

Breena turned to me, using the pause to change the topic. "Excited about the ley line?"

I washed down a mouthful of eggs with some tea. "More nervous than anything."

Alston waved his hand. "Nonsense. Makes you a bit disoriented the first time, but it cuts lots of time. You will be in California before you know it."

"And unfortunately miss the heatwave if Delano tails in fast," Orin said. The front door opened with another gust of frigid wind. The clerk who had checked us in—the faerie woman with the amber eyes—darted across the restaurant and disappeared into the hallway.

"You showed lots of guts last night," Alston told Orin. "If you want a *great* promotion, kill that dark*slime* bastard. *That* will speed you through the ranks."

Orin smirked. "I'll leave Delano's death to the sniffers," he said. "Unless, of course he—"

A piercing roar came from the hallway. I threw my hands over my ears, thinking a rabid bobcat had somehow snuck inside. A streak of brindle flashed in my peripheral. The stranger at the bar dashed for the door, toppling over the barstool. The teeth of the sniffer's greyhound tore into his calf. The stranger fell, screaming. The greyhound shook his leg like a game of tug-o-war, blood splattering its narrow snout. The man's shoe flew across the room and bounced off a tabletop. Red soaked through his cargo pants and sprayed the bar and flagstones.

The sniffer strode across the restaurant from the hallway, his cinnamon coat flailing behind him, and crushed his boot heel into the stranger's sternum. He made a cutting motion with his fist; the greyhound backed off, hackles raised and growling.

"Durin Reimse," the sniffer said in his melodious voice. "You are guilty of treason against the Realm. Any last words?"

Durin Reimse spat on the sniffer's shin. "Fuck the Realm."

The sniffer whipped the blade from his belt, then yanked Durin's tongue from his mouth and sliced it off. Durin screamed a tongueless scream, blood gurgling inside his throat like mouthwash. The sniffer tossed his tongue to the floor with a wet *smack*, and watched his victim writhe. I clutched the edge of the bench, my flesh crawling. The faeries huddled together, silent and wide-eyed. The amber-eyed clerk hovered in the hallway's entrance, chewing her lip.

"We are as strong as our weakest link," the sniffer said, and slit Durin Reimse's throat. Blood gushed in torrents; his body bucked against the flagstone. The sniffer yanked Durin's coat-collar with both hands, making his victim stare into his flat, granite eyes as he died.

The sniffer dropped Durin's corpse to the floor, then slammed his boot into the ribs. The body jolted, as if startled by the loud bone-breaking snap. The faeries leapt from their seats and cheered. I shrieked and jumped nearly out of my skin. The faeries then rushed the sniffer, vying to touch him, praise him, thank him for keeping them safe. The dead man's blood passed from palm to palm as he shook each of their hands. Red footprints danced around the floor as the faeries treaded through the expanding puddle.

Fried eggs crept up my throat. *Holy hell. My desperation for community has made me blindly embrace the faerie Mansons.* I grabbed the clerk's wrist as she dashed for the sniffer. She turned, her amber eyes gleaming.

"What was that man's crime?" I asked.

"Sedition."

I imagined suicide bombers and gun-wielding rebels and streets full of dead civilians. "He was a terrorist?"

The clerk nodded gravely. "I recognized his face from an alert the Realm released last week. He was caught distributing fliers questioning the Realm's work conditions in the mines."

"The sniffer killed him because of *fliers*?"

She lowered her voice and leaned in close, like a sinner confiding a terrible secret to a priest. "Notice how he doesn't have that warm glow like the rest of us?" I forced my eyes to the corpse. He wasn't as pale as Delano, but he didn't have the other faeries' radiance, either. I swallowed audibly. *He looks like me.* "That means he started using night magic," the clerk continued. "Only a matter of time before he joined the darklings."

When she realized I had nothing else to say (what *could* I say?), she hurried off to shake the sniffer's bloodstained hand. The sniffer glared at me from over her shoulder. His lip curled and my insides curled with it. Durin Reimse's blood pooled against the side of the sniffer's boots. Orin stood in the puddle with him, hands in his jeans pockets, rocking on his heels like a child in a playground talking to the school's most popular kid.

The room started to spin. The blood's cloying, copper reek mixed with the taste of eggs in my throat. I cupped my hand over my mouth and sprinted outside.

The restaurant door slammed behind me. I vomited up my fried eggs and tea and all the bile in my stomach, the mess steaming in a snowdrift. I leaned over my knees for nearly a minute in the falling snow, gasping, making sure everything was out. A gale sprayed me with snowflakes and chilled my clammy brow; the tastes of acid and sulphur burned my mouth and throat. When I looked up my heart quickened. The sky was still dark.

Delano.

Maybe he hadn't tried to kidnap me. Maybe he had tried to save me from a sniffer's blade. I paced the length of the building, muscles taut, boots crunching in snow past my ankles. I squinted through the haze, eyes scanning the walls, the rooftops, the lot, as if I was speed-reading the world. "Delano?" I whispered, snowflakes melting in my hair. I was too afraid to shout, too afraid my tongue would end up on the flagstone. Too afraid to flee, fearful the fangs of a blood-crazed hound would drag me back, screaming. "Delano!" I whispered louder, almost whimpered. "*Delano!* If you're there, please come out. *Please!*"

In the dark crept nothing darker.

Wind whipped across my cheeks. The chain-link fence clinked. I leaned against the storage wall and slid to my knees in the snow, the tears sliding down my cheeks feeling as fat as pearls. Did the sniffer keep glaring at me because three nights ago *I* had summoned darkness? Maybe he sensed it. Maybe he was waiting—*yearning*—for me to slip, for his greyhound's teeth to rip my flesh, for my changeling blood to soak the floor.

The door creaked beside me. I tensed, fists raised.

"Breena is ready to leave." Orin's voice was upbeat, cheerful. A red fingerprint dirtied the back of his hand. "I need to change clothes and then—*What's wrong?*"

Snowflakes snaked across the lot. I wiped my tears on my sleeve. "Tha-that man."

Orin dropped to his knees in the snow and threw his arms around me. "It's okay. He's gone now. We're safe."

"The sniffer *killed* him!" I snapped, and slammed my hand into his chest.

Orin fell to his backside, recoiling at my rage. "Y-yes. For the good of everyone."

"And what about *me?* If the sniffer discovers I summoned darkness, will he slash my throat *for the good of everyone?*"

Orin blanched. "That's different. You were ignorant. It's not as if you used it for evil."

"Does the Realm care *what* I used it for?"

Orin watched the snowflakes melt on his knees and said nothing. *At least I have my answer.*

"Maybe that man was like me," I said. "Maybe he was—"

"No! He was *bad.* If the Realm unleashed a sniffer on him they had a *good* reason. *Understand*?" His outburst made me flinch and nod without thought. Orin stood up. "Get ready to leave." He peered over his shoulder at me before opening the door, tears shimmering in his eyes. "And don't mention this to *anyone*."

Orin disappeared back into the restaurant. I stood up and hugged myself, scanning the lot for ruddy eyes and starlight flesh, for any misplaced shadow. Instead I found snow covered pavement and a lightening sky, and an old, familiar loneliness creeping back into my life.

CHAPTER THIRTY-ONE

After witnessing night magic capable of flattening a crowd, and murderers disguised as saints, the ley line no longer seemed so scary.

I followed Breena and Orin to a locked storage unit at the end of the lot. The soles of their boots were wet with blood, and left pink prints in the snow. The pelting ice had become quarter-sized snowflakes during the night, thick enough to hide the rest of the storage complex in a gray, winter haze. Breena shimmered with magic, which melted a path in the snow as we approached.

My heart sank when Breena rolled up the storage unit's door. Inside waited a rusting, red Jeep Wrangler. Its plastic windows were yellowed and cracked, offering shoddy protection from the raging blizzard. The seats were torn, the floorboards filthy with dirt and trash. A loop of wooden beads hung from the rearview mirror. I buttoned my overcoat and climbed into the backseat. Orin took the front, with Breena behind the wheel. The two of them chitchatted about the weather, plans for an upcoming holiday, and advancements in Realm security. The reek of the dead man's blood lingered in my nose.

The Jeep crawled through downtown, slush splattering up to the windows. Lamplights glowed in the haze like drifting jellyfish—the only objects visible more than twenty feet away. The morning cold pushed through the cracks in the rear window, prickling the hair on my nape. I slid on my gloves and nestled deep into my coat, tucking my nose behind the collar.

"Am I even on the road?" Breena asked, right before the Jeep lurched onto the sidewalk. She plopped back off the curb. "Guess I am now," she said with a laugh, and switched to four-wheel-drive. She noticed my unease in the rearview mirror. "Oh, relax. Once we make it to the ley line all your struggles are over."

If we make it to the ley line.

The interstate was as bad as downtown. A sprinkling of cars and semi-trucks trundled along at a snail's pace. Oncoming traffic followed a snowplow scraping white clouds to the shoulder. A FedEx Freight truck rolled past us, spraying the Jeep's plastic windows with slush, its headlights bouncing off the black ice in glaring streaks. I leaned my head back and stared at the roof. The fabric sagged in the middle and swayed. Breena had told us the ley line was about two hundred-and-fifty miles away. At this rate we'd be there in seventeen hours.

"This is some snowstorm," Breena said. "I can't remember the last time a darkling was so pissed." The windshield wipers squealed, smearing filthy arches across the glass as snow snakes slithered across the roadway. Breena snorted as if she remembered a dirty joke. "Delano must be extra hormonal."

I blinked. "Why do you say that?"

"You saw past his lies and refused your betrothal." She laughed. "He knows he'll never get laid again."

"*Betrothal*?" I shoved Orin's shoulder. "You never said anything about a *betrothal*."

"Because you're *not* betrothed," Orin said,

defensively. "I *told* you darklings are demented and evil. They spin lies to justify stealing our children for their own disgusting wants. He believes you are *owed* to him, to do with as he will. All because you were born to one of the families darklings blame for their imprisonment."

Breena made a gagging sound. "Can you imagine coupling with that *thing*. All shadowy and *cold*."

I thought about Delano's lips brushing my throat and remembered only heat.

"You are fortunate the Realm found you first," Breena said. "You will *love* it there. No coldness or darkness, and you'll never want for anything."

"Yeah. Great," I grumbled.

"What's wrong?" she asked. "Was it something I said?"

"She's upset with the sniffer execution." Orin said this hushed, as if admitting he wet the bed every night.

Breena glanced over her shoulder at me. "Really?" She shrugged and faced the road. "Yeah. I guess if you're used to human customs it would seem severe."

I scowled out the side window, gnawing my cheek.

"*But*," Breena continued. "Such incidents are rare and *always* on Earth. The Realm has almost zero crime. Can Earth say the same?"

"No. But at least in the United States the citizens are free."

Breena's eyebrows lifted in the rearview mirror. "Free, huh? So everyone you know takes shortcuts through alleys in the middle of the night? Or leaves their valuables unlocked? Trust their children to strangers?"

"Of course not. That's dangerous."

"It is dangerous because humans have dangers. Fear restricts them. Unlike us. The Realm's punishments are severe but justified. I'd rather my child always be happy and safe, than read a stupid flier."

"Even if it's *your* child handing them out for something they believe in?"

Orin's head sunk beneath the headrest.

Breena's eyes narrowed. "That will *never* happen. My daughter is a good girl."

So was I. And what the hell has that brought me? A mother who hasn't met or spoken with me since I was eighteen, a loveless marriage I'm unable to escape, and the inability to belong anywhere.

"These harsh punishments protect humans, too," Breena continued. "The Realm *must* be strict on Earth or else sloppiness breeds. Imagine if someone revealed to humans they shared a planet with magical beings. What would happen?"

"Chaos," I said, after a moment.

"Exactly. Chaos." Breena tucked a hair-spike behind her ear. "Soon you'll understand the joys you've been missing. Although, as a healer, you won't deal with the Realm much after training." Her voice lowered into a sneer. "But it sounds as if *you'll* appreciate that."

Breena pulled off at the next exit and I felt a wave of relief. Maybe she had enough sense to return to the storage lodge to wait out this storm. I didn't want to have this conversation for the next seventeen hours. I didn't want to be out in the cold. I wanted to crawl beneath the blankets and sleep until I was dead.

Instead, Breena parked on the side of a rural backroad and stepped out of the Jeep. She unsnapped the roof and tugged the canvas back to where I sat. Snowflakes fell on the dash and melted in Orin's eyelashes. The wind spiraled inside, crackling the paper trash on the back floorboards. Gooseflesh crawled up my neck and tingled my scalp. I tugged my knitted cap toward my shoulders, the olive yarn creaking to the strain. "What are you doing?" I asked.

"Getting us to the ley line." Breena climbed behind the wheel and slammed the Jeep door shut. "Which do you prefer, Orin? Road or flakes?"

Orin licked a snowflake on his lip. "Road."

The Jeep fishtailed as Breena peeled out onto a backroad, thick with snow. I clenched the side of the roll-bar, fingernails digging into the foam. Orin unlatched his seatbelt and stood up, his hands gripping the top of the windshield, his body against the dashboard.

"Nobody out on these roads," Breena said. "Including cops."

"No traction, either," I said, then shrieked as we slid sideways. Orin's hip slapped the plastic passenger window. We almost clipped a fencepost before straightening. I squeezed my fists against my eyes as we slid into the other lane.

Please let me live through this! Please let me live through this! Please let me—

The tires steadied with a jolt, as if catching dry blacktop. I peeked up from my fists. Orin's arms were stretched over the windshield, his palms facing the road. The snow ahead of the Jeep fell and flattened as we approached, hardening like sheets of smooth, thick ice. But we never slid. The Jeep held straight and true.

Orin laughed. "Take that, dark*slime*!"

An aura of heat shimmered around Orin and Breena. The snowflakes melted into rain and diverted before the windshield like a curtain opening to pass. I shrugged off my overcoat and pushed the sweater's sleeves to my elbows. The snowflakes above us vanished in puffs of steam. Behind us, the road returned to slush with hardly a tire-track to mark our way.

"See?" Breena said. "Easy-peasy. Fast passage to the Realm from here on out."

"Are you both doing this?" I asked, shouting over wind and the roar of the soft top flapping. The Jeep was flying at 70MPH.

Orin nodded, peering over his shoulder at me. The gold in his eyes blazed, like tiny suns reflecting in tropical pools. His hair whirled in the wind like a sandstorm. "Help us," he said.

"I'd rather not endanger our lives with my shoddy magic," I replied.

"Then be our navigator. Tell us where the ley linc is." Orin tapped his heart. "You'll feel it here. The musical feeling, except entering instead of leaving."

I closed my eyes to concentrate, but I didn't need to. The feeling came fast, as if waiting to be asked. I pointed ahead to the left. "There," I said. It sounded more like a question.

"Told you you're a natural." Orin winked at me, and I smiled.

A break in the fence-line approached fast. Breena cranked the wheel to the left. I shrieked; the Jeep almost clipped the fencepost as it skidded into a snow-filled pasture. The wooden beads clicked against the windshield and made me think of Hannah's cornrows in the RV, and all her pot smoking friends. *I never thought I would feel safer driving with them,* I thought. The Jeep's rear waggled, then straightened. My stomach flopped. "Is this a bad time to mention I get carsick?" I said, right before the snow flattened before Orin's hands like a white sheet, shifting to fill the uneven pasture. We sped through the empty field without dips or jostling or bumps. A Lamborghini would have had no trouble zipping through farmlands with Breena and Orin behind the wheel.

Breena pumped her fist into the air. "Screw the darklings and their winter and their cold and their storms!" She and Orin laughed and bumped each other's forearms together—the faerie equivalent of a high-five, I assumed. A flock of Canada geese honked and flapped into the air as the Jeep sped toward them like a cue ball aiming for the break.

I slipped the sweater over my head and used the sleeve to wipe the sweat off my brow. The snowdrifts flattened to Orin's will. Steam wrote cursive in the air. *What would humans do with such powers?* I wondered. Would they all use it with integrity and empower their communities? Would they use it *for the good of everyone?* I doubted it. I thought about the sniffer and the criminal he had killed. The criminal who shouldn't have been a criminal. But maybe that was the point. Maybe that was what Breena had been trying to tell me, and why the Realm survived. If Earth was the lesser child of the Realm, then humans were the lesser children of the fae. Maybe faeries were as selfish and egocentric and cruel as the species I had spent a lifetime coexisting with. Maybe faeries needed harsh controls to prevent their own destruction.

Or maybe I was making excuses because I had nowhere else to go.

CHAPTER THIRTY-TWO

We had crept back onto a freeway, and cold seeped in through the walls.

Sleet pelted the Jeep's windshield incessantly. Traffic crawled and slid, headlights glowing like lost spirits in the oppressive gray haze. Snow plows were out in vain, slush and ice filling their paths behind them. I had tried to sleep for the past hour to escape this winter caravan, but no luck. Breena dominated the conversation like a warlord, every word grinding. I would have enjoyed it if she babbled about her life and family, her work as a deliverer, places she had visited or heard of, ideas and dreams. But no. All she ranted about for hours and hours and *hours* was of rebel forces, their warfare, the Realm's advancements against their movement on Earth. She detailed rebel guerrilla tactics, faerie outposts they ransacked, murders, torture, thievings and rape, and how she *personally* knew the loss and pain of someone who knew someone who had heard from someone else. She had angered when I laughed because she had insisted the Realm had no crime. "The *Realm* doesn't," Breena had sniffed, while Orin hid his face behind his hand. "Faeries would have complete peace if not for these rebels and darklings. Besides, goodness can be achieved only through the blood of the wicked. Every fairytale tells you that."

I suspected Breena was trying to scare me for the jab I made earlier regarding her daughter. *You will be at the mercy of these rebel savages once you are working alone on Earth*, the undercurrent of her words seemed to whisper.

But her threat felt more like an award. I'd gladly confront an infantry of rebels if it meant escaping this cold, rattling Jeep, and Breena's constant bitching.

Our exit dumped us onto an icy street paralleling the freeway, eventually leading to a barred service road. Orin hopped out of the Jeep and opened the gate for us to pass. Scrubby trees and tangled brush encroached on the snow laden road, blocking the surroundings. The land was uncared for, long forgotten and allowed to grow wild. Until we rounded the first corner, anyway. The roadway cleared before us, black and wet and glistening. The snow and sleet melted the moment it struck the pavement as we sped along for nearly three miles, curving through the gently rolling thicket.

"There's the ley line entrance," Breena said, as we crested the highest hill.

I leaned between her and Orin to peer out the windshield. I expected to find a monolith or a volcano or a million-year old crater, something tourists traveled to from across the world to photograph, something spiritualists gathered around to energize their souls, something anthropologists flocked toward to study the dead civilizations who had once worshiped the holy site. Instead, I peered down at an old barn in a twenty acre snowy field, surrounded in snarls of bare trees and brush. The paint had weathered away decades ago; the storm's gray light bled into the colorless boards. Its sagging roof seemed unfit to handle the piling snow and ice.

We zigged down the hill and zagged through the brush. The snowfall had lessened, but the wind remained strong, making the snowflakes appear to be falling up. Breena sped around the final curve and slammed on the breaks. The Jeep lurched forward; the seatbelt jarred my shoulder. Two brand new, black SUVs blocked the road in front of us. Seven faeries—six men and one woman—stood in front of them, arms crossed over their chests, eyes glaring. They were dressed in formfitting, high-button white suits, with red peeking out from beneath their collars and cuffs. Sleet evaporated around them in a dome of steam. The leader lifted his palm in a stop gesture. His chin was sharp and long, his mahogany hair lashing in the wind.

"Are those rebels?" I asked.

Orin shook his head. "No. Ley sentries."

Ley sentries? I wondered if they were similar to border sentries, but couldn't imagine Orin in those white uniforms. They were too sterile, too stiff, too cold.

The mahogany-haired sentry strutted toward the Jeep and peered through the driver's window, his eyes small and suspicious. His magic made my skin tingle. "I need you to shut off the engine and step outside the vehicle," he said through the plastic. *Sacire* was stitched in red across his heart.

Breena killed the Jeep's engine. The other sentries approached. "What's the problem?" she asked.

"This is a checkpoint for your safety," Sacire said. "Rebels murdered a family nearby, parents and two children. They attempted to use the family's stolen ley cards to gain access, most likely to attack the ley line itself."

"How *terrible*," Breena cried as she exited

the Jeep. Orin hopped out, then pushed the seat forward so I could too. Wind tousled my hair and I had to squint to keep the sleet from stinging my eyes. Four of the sentries surrounded us, their bodies tense as if ready for battle.

"Please provide your ley cards and state your positions and purposes," one of the four said, facing Breena as she rounded the Jeep to join us. His face and scruffy hair reminded me of a badger. The back of his jacket was open, the lower hem and collar holding it together in thick white bands. His wings were similar to Orin's, but the lines thinner and more jagged.

"Breena Urith," Breena said. She handed a paper the size of an index card to the sentry. "Deliverer, returning to the Realm on schedule."

The badger-faced sentry studied her paperwork, then glared at us. *Tura* was stitched across his heart in red thread. "And you two?"

"Orin Grian. Border sentry. On a probationary retriever assignment for changeling recovery of Aluala Liath, human name Miriam Thatcher." Orin handed the sentry a paper card. "Here's my Realm card, but we don't have ley cards. We were supposed to land travel along central country, but diverted to the ley system for safety concerns."

Sacire pushed his way in front of Orin. "You don't have *ley cards*?"

"I called in last night from faerie station nineteen," Orin said, standing as tall and stiff as a soldier. "The clerk told me she'd issue an emergency travel-291B form once authorized."

"*Once authorized*," Sacire repeated harshly.

"And how long has it been since you diverted, *borderer*?"

"Four or five days," Orin said, then quickly added: "But I couldn't get through earlier. I sent a spider, but never received confirmation. And rebels cut a road call box."

Tura lifted a thick eyebrow. "Rebels vandalized Realm infrastructure?"

Orin nodded enthusiastically.

"Frad, run a check for Orin Griath," Sacire said. "See if he was authorized for travel since this morning." A dark-haired faerie with eyes like espresso nodded, then bounced onto the air and flew off towards the barn.

Orin relayed detailed directions to the cut phone cord while we waited for Frad to return.

"She is your assignment, I take it," Sacire said, pointing at me with his thumb. Orin nodded. "Has she left your sight at all?"

Orin paused. "No."

Sacire narrowed his puny eyes. "Why the hesitation? Are you *unsure*?"

"I'm sure," Orin said. "It's been a long journey. I needed to make certain before responding."

Sacire nodded, seeming almost proud of this answer. His glare shifted to me. "It is rare to meet a changeling. You are my first."

I didn't know what to say, so I forced a smile.

Frad returned with two paper cards in hand. "They're clear," he said, handing Sacire the information. "The Realm authorizes them to use the ley system." He turned to Orin. "They also said you have two days left. Then you're fired."

Orin paled.

Sacire studied the cards, then handed them to us. "Here. Keep these with you."

"Thank you." I slipped the card into my rear pocket and started back to the Jeep.

Tura grabbed my shoulder. "*Stop*. You are not done here."

"But I thought—"

"We need to perform a strip search."

My hair whipped across my face. "Sorry?"

"Strip search for your safety," Sacire said, having to holler above a gust of wind. "We need to check your wings."

"I don't *have* wings yet," I said, my coattails thrashing against my legs.

Sacire glowered. "*And* we need to check for weapons. Please take off your clothing."

I laughed "You're joking, right?"

Orin gritted his teeth. "Miriam."

"We do not joke. It is for your safety," Tura said. "If you have nothing to hide, then you should have no issue."

"Just because I don't have anything to hide doesn't mean I should make myself vulnerable and at the mercy of *strangers*," I snapped.

"So you think you are better than everyone else, huh?" Tura snapped back.

Sacire squared his shoulders and leaned into my face. "We are *ley sentries.*"

Orin jumped between us. "Please!" he

pleaded. "Humans raised her, remember? She has been taught to be ashamed of nudity."

Sacire clenched his jaw. He gave a curt nod. "I understand. We will allow her to strip behind the Jeep."

"What?"

Sacire crossed his arms over his chest. "No strip search. No ley line access."

I wheeled on Orin, sleet pounding my face like beestings. "Can't we hitchhike the rest of the way?" I asked, trying not to beg.

"I got only *two days*," Orin said.

"We can't be *too* far away," I said. "Maybe we can take the Jeep? Return it later?"

"I'm not licensed yet," Orin said.

"I am!"

"Even if we drove straight there, it will take at *least* twenty-four hours, *without* bad weather or problems." Orin said this gently, but his eyes pleaded: *Please don't force me to choose between you and my promotion.*

Breena rolled her eyes. "Oh for God's sake, Miriam. It's just *procedure.* Ley sentries care about protecting the Realm, not the oh-so-precious goods you hide beneath your clothing." She pulled her shirt over her head, exposing her small triangular breasts to the world.

How does she not notice the sentries leering? Orin then shrugged apologetically at me and yanked his shirt off. Frad, and a brunette with a stern face suggesting she had something to prove, crowded to examine Orin's wings.

It's just cultural differences. I crept behind the Jeep, hugging myself, feeling out of my body. All I had wanted was to get out of this blizzard, away from Sam's trail and Breena's griping, start my new life. Now I wanted to flee the ley line I had struggled to reach. I'd plod through a thousand miles of snowstorms if needed, but I couldn't do that to Orin. Not when I risked his career and potentially cost him his dreams, all because I refused to follow customs he had adhered to all his life.

Just get it done with, I told myself. *You lose some privacy, but so what? Focus on Orin and the freedoms you'll gain.* My brow furrowed, the last thought ringing false in my head.

I turned my back to the sentries, set my cranberry overcoat on the Jeep's roof, then pulled my sweater and T-shirt off in a single movement. My flesh tightened and my nipples hardened to the wind. Somewhere in the storm I heard a faint *chick-a-dee-dee-dee.*

Tura chuckled. "Look at *this,*" he said, and snapped my bra strap. My spine stiffened with a jolt as the other sentries chuckled and crowded around. "Take off that ridiculous thing."

I unhooked my bra with trembling hands and let it fall to the ground. A pale sentry snatched it and squeezed the cups, as if the indigo lace hid blades and bombs. Sleet melted on my skin and dripped off my elbows. Tura barked at me to hurry. I kicked off my hiking boots and socks, and stood on tiptoe. Even with magic melting the snow, my feet numbed against the pavement. The sentries examined my articles of clothing as they fell.

"Hands on the Jeep," Sacire said, after I stripped naked.

The Jeep's plastic window creaked

beneath my sweating palms; my whole body prickled with goosebumps. Through the plastic I watched two sentries lackadaisically search Orin and Breena. *Two sentries,* I thought, bitterly. I had *five*, all men, even though Orin and Breena were the ones capable of wielding magic. Every muscle in me felt tense enough to snap. Acid crept up my throat. I swallowed it down and forced myself to focus on a gray stone wedged in the Jeep's rear tire tread.

Two sentries rustled through my clothing, pulling out the pockets, turning everything inside-out. A third searched through our belongings inside the Jeep, but I caught him glancing through the window, peeking glimpses of my bare breasts. Sacire slid his hand down my back and lingered on my hips. His thumbs caressed the dip at the base of my spine. "Strange to see a wingless adult," he said. "Never have I seen a woman so nude."

He crouched—his bare hands sliding slowly down my rear—and spread my cheeks apart. *No gloves,* I thought, and started to tremble.

"Cold?" Sacire asked, caressing inside my thighs. I clenched my teeth and refused to answer. A drop of sleet dripped off my nose. Steam coiled around me. As Sacire stood up, he slid a single finger up my leg, my torso, my neck, my jaw. He caressed the folded ridge of my right ear and leaned in close. His mahogany hair lashed my cheek in the wind. "I hear changelings are immoral," he murmured, his breath hot inside my ear. "Is it true?"

"*No*," I snapped.

I heard the *snik-beep* of a digital camera. I spun around, but Sacire shoved me back against the Jeep before I saw who had snapped the photo. "Just a precaution. For your *protection*," Sacire said, his words as slick as grease. "I assure you it's for official purposes only." He chuckled, then patted my rear and stepped away. " Now dress yourself," he commanded as if I was his whore. "You're clean."

What an odd statement, I thought, numbly, fumbling into jeans which clung to my moist skin. *I can't recall the last time I felt so dirty.*

I rushed to dress, then rejoined Orin and Breena. "See?" Orin said with an ignorant smile. "Easy." I crawled into the backseat and said nothing.

Our belongings had been dumped unceremoniously along the Jeep's seats and floorboard. I shoved my belongings back into my knapsack; Orin and Breena organized theirs in the front. My fingers clutched something hard and cold. I stiffened. *How safe are these checkpoints if they missed my folding knife?* I wondered if Orin's knife was still tucked inside his jacket, but didn't dare ask.

"You will be grateful to know that, because of these searches, the ley system is free from rebels and dangers," Tura said outside Breena's window as we latched our seat-belts. He handed us each a copper token with an R engraved in the middle. "These tokens prove you have undergone our search. Give them to the sentry at the ley entrance."

Sacire leered at me. "Unless, of course, you wish us to search you again."

I cast my eyes to my toes, which ached with cold inside my boots. *More sentries are inside the barn?* If these men stripped us *outside* the ley line, what safety precautions were done *inside*? Blood draws? Cavity searches? Electro-collars?

Breena thanked the sentries and drove off toward the barn.

CHAPTER THIRTY-THREE

"Never had a changeling in the ley line before."

"Will it cause problems?"

The man on the stool smiled amiably. "No idea. Never had a changeling in the ley line before."

Mice scuttled in the rafters. I had expected the barn to be a repeat of the storage unit, its outside a ruse. But the barn lacked plaster walls and counters and, thankfully, checkpoints. Inside were just rotting stables, dirt packed floors, and a man on a wooden stool in front of a closed plank-door. The barn was just a barn. And yet it wasn't. It felt warm, despite only decaying boards shielding us from Delano's blizzard. The air was thick, but it wasn't the thickness of dusty attics or humid summer days. It contained a stillness, as if the barn held its breath, waiting for an unseen predator to pass.

The man on the stool lurched to his feet, his joints creaking like the barn's rotting rafters. Ginger-haired and smooth-skinned, the man's brown eyes were weathered, as if exposed to too many rains. He seemed not only *in* the barn, but a part of it—the wood, the rot, the dull, wild-smell of long-ago animals. He appeared younger than Orin—twenty-three or twenty-four—yet he held a sense of timelessness. I expected if you sawed his bones in half you'd find more rings inside than inside any towering redwood.

The man pocketed our tokens and chatted familiarly with Breena as he lifted our shirts to inspect our backs. His own wings resembled gnarled tree roots, with more skin than ink—the mark (or non-mark, if you will) of lower rank. *How many centuries has he sat on that stool?* I wondered. He probably had assisted in the barn's raising *and* had planted the seeds for the timber.

The man shuffled to the closed plank-door. "Have *you* been in the ley line?" he asked Orin.

"Just the Realm's," Orin said.

The man nodded sagely. "Very similar." The plank-door creaked open on rusty hinges. "Just opposite flow and different scenery."

The man led the three of us down a long, narrow staircase. Roots poked from the dirt walls and ceiling; the wood creaked beneath our weight. At the bottom was a pale pink light, its shine seeming to hum in the gloom. *Just another light at the end of another tunnel,* I thought, wryly, then realized I was holding my breath like the barn. At the base of the staircase was a wooden deck, like a pier, but instead of an ocean it jutted into a pink haze, as if someone had lit a fire deep inside a nighttime fog.

"Happy travels," the man said, and stepped to the side.

I blinked. "We just jump *into* it?"

The man nodded.

My brow furrowed. I had expected a carrier. A car or a boat or *something*. "How fast is it moving?"

The man scratched his cheek. "Oh, about the speed of spirits."

"How fast is *that*?" I asked.

The man shrugged. "About the speed of

spirits."

"Oookaaay. How long will it take us to reach California?"

"About the length of a dream."

I scowled. Orin cupped my shoulder. "It's not a physical thing," he said. "It's the Earth's life force. Its blood. Its *magic*. It moves between the frequencies, as will *you* when you jump in. We will reach California in roughly six *physical* hours. But time feels distorted inside the ley line, like a dream."

I stared at the flowing pink mass. *If air flowed like a pink river, this is what it would look like.* "I dunno about this. The last time I hopped blindly into something it whisked me away hundreds of miles and dumped me into a forest to die."

Breena sneered. "Changelings are worse than children."

"Ease off," Orin said. "Everything is new to her."

"Whatever," Breena grumbled. "I don't have time for fearful crap." She glared at Orin from over her shoulder. "And neither do you," she said, then jumped into the stream.

Her body's image hung on the current, like a bright light lingering in your vision after a camera flash. Then the stream pulled her apart like cotton candy and she was swept away.

I gasped. "It-it *disintegrated* her!"

"Just an illusion," Orin said. "Are you ready?"

All my blood fell to my feet. "I-I dunno about this." Although, if I *didn't* jump into the ley line, I'd have to face the ley sentries again. I swallowed, hard, unsure which fate sounded worse.

"I'm your *guide*, Miriam. I'll never let anything hurt you." Orin weaved his fingers with mine and squeezed. "Hold onto me tight. Good." He smiled. "Now we'll face everything together."

Orin's warm index-finger caressed mine, and my heart started to steady. Nobody had ever been committed to my well-being before. Not my mother, not my husband. I waited for the catch, for the "I'll love you *if...*" But there was only Orin and his backpack waiting patiently on an underground pier, his hand clasping mine.

I nodded. "Okay. Together."

On three we jumped into the stream.

The ley line whisked us west as gentle as a warm breeze. It felt sort of like an airport's moving walkway, if you had been wrapped in a comforter right out of the dryer before being carted along. A continuous soft *whoosh* filled our ears, as if they were pressed against a seashell. White light streamed behind us, marking our trail.

"See? Easy. The rest of our journey will be fast now." Orin's words came out seconds after his lips stopped moving, as if video and audio were out of sync. "As fast as a dream."

And the ley line was dreamlike, indeed. I clenched Orin's hand, seeming to clench it *and* clench *through* it. *This must be what the darkshine is like*, I thought. *Except here it is light and warmth instead of cold and darkness.* Moving inside the ley line was a little like walking, a little like swimming, and a little like nothing at all. Sometimes everything was sharp and in focus. I could make out every fiber of Orin's tweed jacket and each shade of sand in his hair. Other times I seemed to lose myself, as if I had become one with the warm, foggy sea.

We also weren't alone.

When Orin had said the ley line flowed on a frequency between the worlds, I assumed he meant the Realm and Earth, like his border sentry post. But now, peering into a pulsing pink abyss, I caught glimpses of other beings, sometimes other *lives*. Some were unclear images, like nebulous strangers strolling deep in a mist. Others were like watching a television in short blips. Lanky, ash-skinned men in rough-spun robes with knobby elbows and faces impossible to see. Spiraling smoke serpents. A vibrating child with the eyes of a lemur and the energy of addiction. A dome house with a small garden growing stalks of meat. Colorful giants crawling along adobe walls. Some of the entities seemed to stare right at us. Others seemed unaware, like amoebas.

I shuddered. "What are they? *Who* are they?"

"Other travelers. Glimpses of other frequencies we're streaming through," Orin said, his words still delayed.

"There are more worlds than Earth and the Realm?"

"Many more. But very few are accessible."

"Can they see us?"

Orin shrugged, his shoulders leaving white trails. "I imagine so. Who can say?"

Squat men with pointed hats scurried past us with leather satchels under their arms. A glass of iced tea tumbled off a tabletop into the lap of a woman and disappeared in a puff of air.

I closed my eyes and breathed in the Earth's magic, cozy and sweet and filling, like the feeling of fresh baked bread in your nose or of gratitude warming your heart. My eyelids glowed pink inside, as if me and the ley line had merged. I could lose myself to its gentle security, like a pocket of warmth beneath a quilt on a cold, winter night. My forehead was lax, my muscles as fluid as bath oils. Orin's fingers caressed mine. I squeezed his hand and brought it to my chest.

Then the ley line *screeched* and ripped us violently apart. I spiraled upwards, out of control, thrashing, writhing, losing Orin in the warm, pink abyss. I screamed, but sound never left my lips. My flesh pressed against my bones; my teeth clenched and creaked, making my jaw tremble. I whirled and whirled and whirled until the pink warmth became black ice and my skin scraped along something as rough and stinging as salt. The light died and darkness flooded as the dream booted me out into a nightmare, leaving me cold and forsaken and gagging on my desertion.

CHAPTER THIRTY-FOUR

I flew up several feet into the air in a burst of grit, then crashed onto my left biceps and rolled onto my backpack, gasping. I curled up and threw my arms over my face as dirt showered down upon me. The air tasted harsh, like ammonia or chlorine or bleach. I sat up, nauseated, my head spinning. A star speckled sky stared down at me, witnessing my confusion. "What the—?" Wind roared. Sand pattered my face. The ley line's magic dripped off my body like invisible rain. "Orin?" I called. "Or—?" I gagged on fumes and nearly retched. My eyes watered and burned.

Metal clanged. Voices hollered, distressed. I wiped my eyes, hacked my throat raw. Behind me, spotlights flooded a quarantined interstate. Men in orange jumpsuits and respirators scurried around an overturned tanker truck, clear liquid gushing from its side. The headlights of stopped cars stretched beyond the wreckage, like an audience of wraiths applauding the destruction.

The wind wailed; fumes smacked my face. The ground beneath me was damp, as if the ley line was bleeding. I dug frantically with my hands, pushing aside rocks and sand to get back into the stream. "*Orin*?" I croaked. I coughed and hacked on air as harsh as embers.

"You! *What are you doing there*?"

Two men in orange jumpsuits and respirators lumbered toward me. I leapt up, gagging, and dashed into the darkness, my wobbly knees smacking together. The world spun. Dirt fell off my backpack, my coat, my hair. Sand pounded my treads, and a tumbleweed brushed past me in a gust. *I'm in the desert,* I realized. *How* the hell *did I wind up in the* desert*?*

Outcroppings jutted from the earth—looming, dark monstrosities which blotted out the stars in jagged silhouettes. I glanced over my shoulder. The men in orange had abandoned the chase and were scurrying back to their disaster. I dodged into a wide fissure, wove between two rock walls, and fell to my knees in the sand, dry-heaving.

I rummaged through my backpack, my arm throbbing from where I had struck the ground. I tucked my knife into my pocket, then pulled out the flashlight and clicked it on. The expansive darkness gobbled up the beam. Beige rock seemed to stretch into eternity, its surface as rough and pocked as an elephant's hide. Wind moaned and rushed through the hidden stone valley. I buttoned my overcoat and shivered. Unlike Ohio, winter here didn't harden the air to drill inside your chest, jabbing icicles into your bones and lungs. The desert's cold was open and sweeping, an all encompassing ocean rolling over the crags and dunes to drown all warmth.

I tucked myself into a shadowy crook in the rock and leaned my head back. The sky was cloudless, as clear as glass. The Milky Way slashed the heavens like a splattering of diamond dust. "What do I do now?" I asked the stars. Millions were present, but none had an answer. Wind moaned. The temperature seemed to plummet another ten degrees. I rubbed my face wearily. Somewhere I had lost my hat. Orin was miles away by now and I was lost and alone, dumped in God knew where. *It* is *the damn boxcar again.* Was it best to stay put or to continue toward the Realm? I didn't know where I needed to go, exactly, but I had a general idea. I chewed my lip. Of course, if I arrived at the Realm's entrance alone, Orin could kiss his promotion goodbye and—

My heart jumped into my throat. *Did I fall into another world? Can—?*

"Changeling?"

I straightened with a jolt. "*Delano*?" My voice came out in a strained sigh, a mixture of relief and fright. A puff of breath escaped my lips, then bolted for the darkness.

"Oh this is bad," said a woman's voice. "Bad, bad, *bad*. Why is *she* here?"

I wheeled toward the voices. My flashlight illuminated two darklings. But not Delano. The man was lean, with a long, chestnut pony tail, his hair shaved on the sides. The woman's hair was short, layered, and as ruddy as their eyes. The man stood before her, his head tilted inquisitively. His black pants, tan sweater, and gray smoking jacket suggested he was on his way to a poetry reading, not a midnight wander through the desert. As he stepped toward me the stars dimmed and my warmth fled to feel his embrace. His eyes studied me—two half-moons on a long, pale face. The woman clenched his right arm, grimacing. Her almond eyes glanced back and forth from me to the darkling man. Her burnt orange cocktail dress rippled against her knees. Her bare toes curled in the sand.

The man leaned in to sniff me, then recoiled. "Woo! She reeks of the ley line. She must have gotten ensnared in the bleed from the chemical tanker."

The woman glared at me. One eye wide, the other squint, giving her an air of lunacy. "We need to get rid of her, Gethen."

I heaved the backpack onto my shoulder and slid my back against the rock. "No need," I said with a nervous laugh, sidestepping. "I was just leaving."

Gethen appeared in front of me in a burst of shadow, shoved me back into the crook. "*Tisk.* You leave when *I* say. Comprende, *changeling*?"

The woman crept to his side, her lips pressed tight. Her ears were pointed, I realized, but the man's were folded like mine. "That's Delano's changeling, that is," she said. "And if Delano comes here, a horde of sniffers will follow."

"Sweetling, sweetling," Gethen soothed. He kissed the top of her head. "We *need* Delano to come. If the *Realm* catches the changeling, more darkling blood will flow."

"I don't *care* about the other darklings!" The woman's shout echoed in the canyon, *darklings-lings-lings-lings* dying slowly in the stones. "I don't want war on our turf!"

"Then we *need* to keep her," Gethen said. The woman snorted. "Really! Look at her, Melinda! She is weak, her magic underdeveloped. It will take her forever to leave here alone. Delano has undoubtedly sensed her location. He will find her and whisk her away as fast as shadow, bringing the fight to *his* territory, not ours."

"And the Realm will follow as fast as sunlight." Tears shimmered in Melinda's eyes. Her shoulders fell and I wondered if she wasn't a creature incensed from insanity, but lashing out from fear. "Why don't they leave us *alone?* All I want are my stars and my rabbits and my pretty desert flowers."

"I want you to have those things, too, my love," Gethen said. "But contributing to the darklings' demise will not protect them."

Melinda scoffed. "She's not even a darkling! She's just a—" Her eyes brightened. "Oh! Oh! I know! Let's *kill* her!"

"What?" I gasped.

"It's a great idea!" Melinda said, bouncing on her toes. "If she's dead, Delano and the Realm won't come here since a *new* faerie will be targeted as a darkling replacement. Everyone will ignore us to find her."

Gethen chuckled and stroked Melinda's hair. "My sweetling is so clever."

"*Clever?* It's a *terrible* idea!" I said. Melinda tightened her fists, grinning murderously. I brandished my knife in her face. "Back off, psycho! Or I'll—" Gethen snapped his fingers and a shadow jumped from the rock face, knocking the blade from my hand. I squeaked with surprise, then froze. Gethen smiled at me from behind Melinda's back, then lifted a finger to his lips and winked as if we shared some important secret known only to us.

Gethen hugged Melinda, squeezing her back to his chest. "*However,* sweetling," he said, "Murdering Delano's changeling probably isn't the best tactic."

"Of course it is. It solves everything," Melinda said.

"But isn't she how *I* came to *you*?" Gethen asked. "Scared, abandoned, confused. How would *you* have felt if another darkling killed me just to be left alone?" Melinda's face fell, and I thought I saw guilt budding in her half-moon eyes. He sighed dramatically, then dropped his arms from her waist and gazed woefully at the stars. "I know your Gethen has been a nuisance this last century, but—"

"*No*!" Melinda spun around and threw her arms around his neck. "I *love* my Gethen! I couldn't *bare* life without him!"

"Then hear me out," he said, and cupped her face in his hands. "Let's take her into Mountain Heart."

Melinda pulled back with a gasp. "*Mountain Heart?*"

"Faeries can't enter and she will never escape."

"But that is *our* place." Melinda stepped away from him, her eyes now slits. "First you want to risk my rabbits and flowers. Now you want to imprison a *changeling* in our *home*?"

"Only until Delano arrives," Gethen said, quickly. His ponytail lashed in the wind. "Then we will ransom her. Will my sweetling like some gold? Perhaps new jewelry?"

Melinda stomped her foot. "I don't want any stupid gold or jewelry."

"Some fancy artwork?"

"No."

"Hmm. Cash?"

"No."

"You little minx. You're going to force me into it, aren't you?"

Melinda lifted her nose to the sky.

Gethen groaned as if he had just suffered an embarrassing defeat. But he smiled when her back was turned and gave me another wink. "All right. You win. If you let her into Mountain Heart, you may get a kitten."

Melinda squealed and spun to face him, her orange skirt twirling. "*Really*?"

Gethen grimaced. "Yes. But you must promise to feed it."

"Oh I will!" Melinda said, clapping her hands.

"And change its litter."

"I will! I will!"

"And not kill Delano's changeling."

Melinda's shoulders slumped. "Fiiiine." She gazed up at the dark rock face. "Who knows how long it will take Delano to find her, though. We might need to hole up for *nights*."

Gethen pulled her close, smiled lovingly into her eyes. "Holed up with a beautiful sweetling. Oh my. *Whatever* shall we do with ourselves?"

Melinda giggled. The desert wind howled. They leaned in for a kiss. Gethen's eyes widened an inch from her lips.

Melinda's brow furrowed. "What's wrong?" she asked, right before he coughed a mouthful of blood in her face.

"Gethen!" Melinda shrieked.

Gethen-then-then-then... the rocks shrieked back.

Gethen collapsed as Orin yanked a knife out of his back.

Melinda fell to her knees, screaming her lover's name. Orin lunged for Melinda's chest. She shrieked and recoiled; the blade sunk into her side and she disappeared in a puff of darkness. Orin wheeled. The wind howled. Melinda reappeared beside Gethen's sightless face, bawling, tried to wrap his corpse in shadow. Orin lunged, moonlight glinting on the blade. Melinda vanished without her lover's body, her final wail hanging on the stones.

I stood as stiff as a board, gaping. "Wha-what—"

"The chemical spill caused a wound in the Earth and we bled out of the ley line." Orin squeezed my arms, my legs, checking for injuries. "I was dumped on the other side of the interstate. We need to hike a few miles, but we might catch an easy hitch. Are you hurt?"

I shook my head, staring at Gethen's corpse. Blood streamed out of his back. If I hadn't witnessed Delano bleed red in the lamplight, I would have believed darklings bled shadow. "Nn-n-no. They-they—"

"They were deciding whether to murder or kidnap you." Orin sneered at the dead darkling, then knifed a button off the smoking jacket and tucked it into his pocket. "Sorry to ruin your plans, dark*slime.* Miriam is going home."

CHAPTER THIRTY-FIVE

I had traveled nearly three thousand miles and now found myself unable to climb seven stone steps.

The two-storied log mansion was the work of a craftsman. Each log was cocoa streaked umber, the timber exquisite and sanded to perfection, as if the selection and preparation of trees had taken years through painstaking precision and ritual. The mansion's face was mirrored windows, each framed in thick, twisting tree branches. The Sierra Nevada wilderness reflected in the glass, along with the river stone courtyard, Orin's relief, and my pale and anxious face.

The semi-truck we had hitched a ride on in the desert was completing an interstate delivery to Sacramento, and once we were on the California roadways the rest of our travel was cake. Roadside call boxes were everywhere, and the first one we reached had its cord intact. A faerie driver in a Bronco retrieved us at the nearest exit an hour after Orin's phone call. A few hours and a nap later we stood outside the Realm's main Earth station.

My heart fluttered as I realized our struggles were ending.

"This place was once heavily guarded," Orin had said as we sauntered up a river stone pathway. "But it attracted too much attention from the humans. Forty years ago the feds raided, believing it a cult." He shook his head at the absurdity. "Thankfully, we haven't had any problems since the Realm decided to keep the grounds low key."

Low key wasn't how I would describe it. The vine-covered stone wall encompassing the eighty-two acres seemed like it could reflect cannon fire with hardly a chip to its face. The only noticeable entry was the solid, six-inch thick oak and iron gate where our driver had dropped us off. A single guard had answered when we knocked, and granted us passage without a sentence of conversation. I had expected an embassy of sorts, with barred windows, razor wire, video surveillance, and roaming sentries like at the ley line. Instead, the Realm's station looked more like a private vineyard, an aspect which blended in with the quaint, artsy villages and ski resorts we had passed on the way to here.

"What if the rebels raid?" I asked, as we passed a limestone fountain with water trickling from a mermaid's upturned hands. "Or the darklings? How will the Realm defend themselves?"

"There are sniffers and a scattering of roaming patrols," Orin said. "Besides, the entrance *to* the Realm is on the grounds. Border sentries can flood the compound in under two minutes. And neither rebels or darklings are stupid enough to face an entire faerie army."

I suspected such measures were rarely needed, if ever. The grounds reeked of power and defense, a locked chest booby-trapped to explode if ever cracked. Chickadees—*the bravest spirits in the woods*—darted between the trees, and I caught glimpses of spiders scurrying along ornamental fences and garden pathways. *Hidden eyes lurk everywhere here.* And those were just the ones I noticed.

Orin started up the log mansion's front

steps—large, stone things with rippled edges like oak leaves. My legs turned to marble.

"What's wrong?" he asked, as he trotted back to me.

"I—I'm scared. What if the Realm hates me? What if they don't let me become a healer? What *then*?"

"No one will hate you," Orin said. "And at worst they will recruit you into infantry." He shrugged. "Who knows? We might both be border sentries at the end of today."

I lowered my voice. "But Delano said the Realm forced him into the mining pits."

Orin drew back, his eyebrows raised. "Of course they did. Delano is a criminal, a con-artist. A faerie gone bad."

I eyed the windows, my hunched reflection staring back. "Delano told me he *chose* to be a darkling."

Orin laughed. "Yeah. He chose it over a *prison sentence*." Orin squeezed my shoulder. "*You*, however, have nothing to worry about. You are a good person, kind and brave. The traits the Realm embraces. They will provide everything you want."

We plodded up the giant stone steps. The front door flew open when we reached the landing; a sniffer loomed on the other side. He was tall and trim with a chin like a cleaver. His hair was combed-back jet, his eyes two chips of sapphire. A white greyhound stood stiff beside his knee, a chickadee on his shoulder. Like the sniffer at the faerie lodge, he wore tailored clothing the color of cinnamon, a knife and coiled whip on his belt.

And like the sniffer at the faerie lodge, he felt just as gray.

"Name and business," the sniffer said.

"Orin Grian," Orin said, as I skulked behind him. "Here to report off to Raina for successful probationary retriever assignment of adult changeling, Aluala Liath."

The chickadee puffed its feathers. "You are late," it said.

Orin shrugged. "We had setbacks."

The sniffer stood aside to let us into the mansion's foyer, his greyhound sniffing our legs as we strode past.

"Inform Raina her guests have arrived," the sniffer said, locking the door behind us. The chickadee chirped and flew off through a side doorway.

The log mansion's foyer was the size of a small ballroom. Two large doorways yawned along the sides, with red walls beyond them to conceal their secrets. The rear wall had a single closed door, carved intricately with vines and birds and bunches of grapes. A wood stove stood in the foyer's center, fire crackling behind its glass doors, its smoke stack engraved with roses which disappeared into planked, vaulted ceilings. Plush throw rugs with differing designs covered the floorboards. The room had no furniture. Instead, colorful pillows of velvet and suede the size of large dog beds circled the wood burning stove, inviting repose and casual conversations. The place reminded me of an opium den of some obscure, millionaire woodsman.

"There's my new retriever!" A woman glided out of the doorway the chickadee had flown through, her arms outstretched. Long, curly hair bounced against her back in varying hues of the desert—yucca, peyote, and mesquite, all tucked inside the sand. Her slinky dress slid to her ankles like liquid jade, flashing a milky thigh with each step. A dozen gold bangles jangled on her wrists. The pink diamond on her choker was the size of a quail egg and gleamed as bright as her smile.

A hunched, flaxen haired man in a gray suit and a yellow and white striped vest scurried behind her. He had the small eyes and long face of a ferret, and clenched a thick book and clipboard to his chest.

The woman squeezed Orin's shoulders and kissed each cheek. "I thought you'd *never* get here," she said, then hugged me as if I were her daughter, her hair smelling like sunlight and blooming wisteria. Her eyes widened like rings of smoking sage. "And *you* must be Miriam." She squealed, delighted. "Our Aluala has finally come home! Come. Sit. You two must be exhausted from your travels. Do you like champagne? Kegan, bring us champagne."

"Yes, Raina." The ferrety man set his book and clipboard beside the wood burning stove, then scurried out of the foyer. Raina stepped out of her golden high heels and plopped onto a peach cushion beside the fire. Orin and I sat on yellow and baby-blue cushions across from her.

"So, retriever...?" Orin asked, his eyebrows raised.

"Of course, silly," Raina said, then wagged her finger at him. "I admit I was skeptical when I heard you detoured to the ley line. But then you killed not one but *two darklings*." She giggled and pushed his knee with her bare foot, the rhinestones on her toenails sparkling. "I knew then I had made the right decision."

Orin grinned at his lap, red creeping up his neck. "Thank you, Raina. But there has been a mistake. I killed only one. Melinda escaped."

Kegan scurried back into the great room with a bottle of champagne and three flutes. He filled the glasses, handed us each one, then settled into a lavender cushion beside Raina.

Raina sipped her champagne. "There is no mistake. Melinda is dead. The wound you inflicted proved fatal. The lunatic probably died in a pit somewhere, singing her stupid Gethen's praises. And with you killing *both* of them, there's no longer a darkling in that region to kidnap a so-called replacement. For once the Realm doesn't need to scramble to protect any infants." Raina sipped her champagne, radiating pride. "All because of *you*, Orin. I sense a sniffer career in your future. Won't our Orin make a wonderful sniffer, Fino?"

The sniffer blinked slowly beside the front door. "Superb."

Orin was a beet. "Oh, I dunno," he said with a nervous laugh. "It was all just dumb luck."

"Orin," Raina said firmly, and lowered her flute. "Most heroes I know are built on accidents, coincidence, good timing, or someone else's misfortune. The difference is they know how to play off the truth and twist it to their advantage. Why, take Fino. He would have never slain his first darkling if a moving van didn't plow into it first. Right, Fino?"

"My lady is mistaken," the sniffer said. "I chased down that darkling on foot and popped its head off with my bare hands."

Raina laughed and clapped her hands together, her gold bangles jangling. "You see? *That's* how reputations are created. Boast your accomplishments, Orin. They will take you farther than you ever imagined." She drained her flute. "And what about *you* my changeling? Has my new retriever described the Realm's systems? How everyone plays a part?"

I nodded. "Yes. I hoped..." I gulped a mouthful of champagne and winced as it slid down my throat. "I hoped to become a healer. On Earth, I mean, that is." My voice sounded weak beneath the foyer's tall ceilings.

Raina lifted an eyebrow. "A healer? Why, that is a large commitment."

"I know she'd be great," Orin said. "She is kind and calm and compassionate. Her first magics even healed a rose petal I tore, and she has knowledge of damage in a region unknown to us."

Raina straightened as if Orin's words were sobering. "Damage? What kind of damage?"

I took a deep breath and told Raina about the devastation in Appalachia. My voice shook, then strengthened, as I described the abandoned coal mines slashing the scenery, the yellow streams that murdered habitats, the slag piles altering the landscape, the ponds with water like battery acid which bleached dead leaves, and remained as clear as gasoline year-round.

When I finished, Raina leaned back in her cushion and released a long, slow breath. Her face had paled. "Thank you for bringing this to our attention," she said. "The destruction sounds *dreadful.* And frankly it is embarrassing the Realm has allowed this poison to seep for so long. The faerie stations in that region have long been abandoned. I suspect most are in desperate need of repair. Am I wrong, Kegan?"

"No," Kegan said, scratching his cheek. "Green Valley in West Virginia is probably the closest to acceptable."

"West Virginia, you say? Hmmm. It's not Ohio, but do you believe your first healer assignment will benefit there, Miriam?"

"My first...?" I beamed. "Yes! Yes, of course!"

"Kegan, make a note. Send a builder with Miriam to West Virginia to repair the station, along with two other healers to start the work and train her."

"Noted," Kegan said, scribbling. "Anything else?"

"Yes. Send for the tattooists so these two can get winged and purged."

My brow furrowed. "Purged?"

"Didn't Orin tell you?" Raina shrugged. "No matter. It is tradition. We burn purium during your tattooing."

"What's purium?" I asked.

"A Realm herb to induce visions of those things which hold you back," Raina said, and stood up. "It provides a safe space to confront them so you can move freely into your new life."

I blinked, startled. "A *hallucinogen*?"

We followed her to the closed, carved door in the back of the foyer. "Purium isn't a *hallucinogen*, exactly. The herb gives images to our hurts so we may heal them," Raina said. "As a changeling, your mother will inevitably make an appearance. It is a miracle she didn't drown you in a bathtub when you were an infant, quite frankly. And I hear you are married."

"Yes," I said with a cringe. "I'm sorry. I didn't know faeries and humans are not supposed to—"

Raina laughed, as sharp and sudden as a soap bubble popping. "Don't *even* worry about that," she said, flapping her hand dismissively. "The Realm will never hold you accountable. I suspect, however, your relationship with him was lousy, so expect his appearance as well. Is there anyone else significant in your past? Siblings, perhaps? A father? So-called friends?"

"No," I said. "Well, maybe my mother-in-law. I haven't really had anyone in my life except my mother and Sam. Until Orin, anyway."

"Two people." Raina shook her head and gripped my shoulders in front of the doorway. Her eyes were glassy as if she might cry. "A changeling's life is terribly lonely. I am *so sorry* for everything you were forced through." She wrapped her arms around me and hugged me tight. "I don't care of the circumstances, it is inexcusable for the Realm to lose a changeling. But everything will be different now." She pulled back and kissed my cheek. "I *promise* the Realm will give you a life you deserve," Raina said, and pushed open the carved door. "Starting now."

I expected a tattoo parlor to be behind the door, with pleather recliners and the tang of adrenaline in the air. Instead the room seemed to expand, as if opening its arms to welcome us, embrace us, as calm and gentle as a goodnight kiss. Two massage tables stood in the room's center like cushioned altars, a large copper cauldron filled with dried, grassy herbs between them. Beeswax candles lined the walls on low, narrow shelves, waiting patiently for anointment and flame. My voice softened naturally to a whisper as we padded inside, as if we had passed through the doorway of some holy temple.

Painted wings filled the walls like foreign scripture. Their black lines ranged from swooping to jagged to coiling to narrow to thick to sharp to curved to harsh to winsome to everything in between. Some were plain, with wide empty spaces between their veins. Others were so intricate and ornate that the white paint beneath appeared gray. Hundreds of wings stretched from the candles to the ceiling, the occupation they represented written in cursive at their tips.

Raina brushed her hand across a set of wings between two closed doors. "I hope you like this design, Orin," she said with a giggle.

Orin puffed out his chest. "Best in the room," he said, then pulled me to the picture to point out the painting's details. "The base of this image is inner sentry wings, so my tattoo will look different overall. But see these details? They are the retriever's and will be incorporated into the empty spaces of my wings."

The retriever's lines were thin and wavy, like ripples of water and wind. "It's beautiful," I said.

"And here is the healer tattoo," Raina said, pointing above a looking glass in the corner. "Details will be added as you acquire specialties or if you progress into apothecary."

My future tattoo was more feminine than I had expected. Its delicate, swooping lines and spirals reminded me of unravelling ferns, with tiny, heart-shaped leaves branching off the curls. The wingtips coiled, like trailing coattails. I couldn't have designed it better.

Raina fluffed her ringlets in the looking glass. "A healer is a tedious life and isolates faeries from the Realm for months to years. Are you *sure* you want this? You cannot go back once the ink is in your skin."

"Yes." I admired my future tattoo and grinned. "It is *perfect*."

"Leave your belongings in the corner. The tattooists will attend to them," Raina said. "There are showers behind these two doors. Scrub yourselves clean and I'll have garments left for you to change into. Do you require anything else?"

"This is more than I wanted already," I said, as Orin shook his head.

Raina smiled with all the warmth of desert dunes. "Welcome home, Aluala. I sincerely hope you love your new life."

CHAPTER THIRTY-SIX

I wrapped my wet hair in a towel and stepped into the dress waiting for me outside the shower door. It was as formfitting as river water, the plum silk so light I still felt nude. Dainty jeweled straps traced my shoulders, glittering tiny rainbows beneath the bathroom lights. The back dipped to my sacrum in an artistic bunching of rippled fabric, exposing my hips from the rear, and resting a mere foot above the hem on my thighs. I owned pillowcases with more fabric, and yet I had never worn a dress so exquisite.

I pivoted in front of a full length mirror in the small, marble bathroom, and grimaced. *This cannot be what a faerie healer looks like.* Every faerie I met had a subtle brilliance about them, a vision of nature in bodily form. All I saw in the glass was a scrawny midwest housewife with a pasty complexion and scabs on her ankle. I pulled the towel off my head, let my damp hair tumble. I rolled my shoulders back, lifted my chin, stuck out my hip, smiled, rotated to hide the purple bruise on my biceps. The midwest housewife refused to leave.

I sighed. *Maybe adding wings will help.*

Or if you saw your true *self, not clouded with the judgements of cynics.*

I bit my lip. *Am I seeing the reflection of insecurities? The judgements of those who had never loved me?* Maybe once I confronted the visions of those who held me back, they would take their damage with them. I stepped from the bathroom, the purium now seeming less frightening.

The overhead lights in the tattoo room were off and all the candles burned, illuminating hundreds of painted wings in a bronze and holy hue. Meditational music played from overhead speakers, a mixture of pattering rain and trilling flutes. Orin stood between the tables, chin up and chest bare, his hands clasped behind his back like a soldier. He had changed into pants the color of gunmetal, the front buckled with two bronze oak leaves.

He smiled when I joined his side, then ran his fingers through my hair. His cupped palms filled with water, and we giggled when he clapped them together in a puff of steam.

I smoothed my tresses. "Soon I will be able to dry my own hair," I said.

"And much more." Orin grabbed an unlabeled wine bottle that had been left on his table and pulled the cork out with a *pop.* "Here."

"A toast?"

He chuckled. "No. It is an oil which makes the skin absorb more ink. You rub it onto your back." He poured some into my cupped hand, then into his. It had a warm, medicinal scent. Not quite eucalyptus, not quite clove. Orin reached over his shoulder and showered the floor with golden droplets.

"Here. Let me. You are making a mess." My hands slid down the curve of his neck, his shoulder blades, spreading oil across his border sentry wings. His back was lean muscle, as taut as a bowstring. "My God. You are as tense as a brick."

"Well, yeah," he said. "I'm terrified."

This surprised me. I poured more oil into my hands, worked it down his spine, his hips, kneading the flesh with my fingers. "Why are you afraid?" I asked. "You succeeded. We both did. We are getting everything we wanted."

"Yes. And I am grateful." Orin winced as my thumb worked a knot beneath his scapula. "But you were a great first assignment. What if my next assignments are different? What if I do a horrible job?"

"You won't," I said, my fingers tracing the tips of his wings. "You were *meant* to be a retriever."

"I guess we'll see." Orin turned to me, his eyes almost violet in the candlelight. He took the bottle and poured oil into his palm. "Your turn."

I pulled my hair in front of my shoulders and tensed beneath his grip.

Orin snorted, amused. "You think *I'm* tense? Your shoulder has ribs."

"I'm scared, too," I said. He pressed my shoulders down when they hunched, warmed them with his hands. "I have a new world waiting for me, a new community, a new *career*. I've never even had any formal schooling. Sam said the money would be a waste."

I winced as Orin's grip tightened. "Your husband is a fool."

My knees weakened as Orin's knuckles rocked along the top of my shoulders. My chin dipped to my chest. "You know," I gasped, bracing myself on the table's edge, "they're tattooing my *back*, not my neck and shoulders."

"I know," he said, then massaged my neck and shoulders until the flesh moved beneath his palms like softened butter.

He dribbled more oil onto my back, traced it with a finger as it dripped down my spine. A candle flame popped on its wick in the corner, sending long shadows shivering up the wall. The heels of Orin's palms pressed into my lower back, then slid up to my neck and back to my pelvis, his fingertips slipping beneath the plum silk. From the speakers, rain pattered and flutes sang. I leaned heavier on the table. Orin stepped closer, drizzled more oil. My tensions melted away as his hands slid down my neck, my shoulders, each dip of my spine, tracing the healer's tattoo yet to be. The edge of his pants tickled my bare calves. His slick hands slipped across my hips and caressed them until they gleamed.

Orin corked the bottle and set it on the floor. "That should do it," he said.

"Thanks," I said, breathlessly, turning to him on legs of jelly.

Orin dropped his eyes from mine and cleared his throat. "You know, um, I was *thinking*. We both have Earth jobs now, which means we can still see each other." He tucked a thumb behind his oak-leaf buckle and sunk into his shoulders. "That is, if you *want* to be friends."

"Of *course* I want to. You *are* my only friend." I smirked. "Although, I'll probably just bring you more trouble."

Orin clasped my hands and rubbed his thumb across my knuckles. "Good. I like your trouble," he said. Then the carved door opened and he pulled away.

Three faeries entered the room, each carrying a stool and pushing a thin metal cart toting tattoo guns, ink bottles, towels, bottled water, closed wooden boxes. I assumed the faeries were female, but wasn't certain. Each wore a shapeless white robe, like a nun's. Scarlet veils concealed their heads and faces, their eyes shrouded behind black gauze. One lit the herbs inside the giant, copper cauldron. White smoke started to coil through the room. The tattooists stood like blood-faced phantoms in the firelight and pointed to the massage tables without a word.

Orin and I crawled onto our stomachs. I lowered my cheek to the face-rest, my heart jackhammering against the tabletop.

"Hey."

I turned my head to Orin. He smiled at me, his hand outstretched. I clasped it, our arms bridging the two tables. "Everything will be over before you know it," he said. "Just tell the visions what is needed to move on."

"How will I know what to say?"

"You'll know," he said, then squeezed my hand and released.

The tattooists seated themselves on their stools. One sat near Orin. Two sat near me—one on each side, one for each wing. The music shifted from rain and flutes to harps. I breathed in the white smoke. It smelled faint but clean, vaguely like cucumbers. The painted wings before me seemed to flutter on the wall in the candlelight.

This is it. No going back now. I closed my eyes as two metal guns buzzed behind my ears. *Let my new life begin.*

CHAPTER THIRTY-SEVEN

The needles jabbed my scapulas, but the vibration bit deep into my spine. I hissed and winced and ground my teeth to absorb the pain. *I'll* never *enter a trance. My back feels assaulted by a swarm of frigging yellow jackets.*

White smoke drifted to the ceiling, snaked along the floor. I inhaled its faint cucumber scent, and the warm medicinal oil which wasn't quite eucalyptus, wasn't quite clove. I gritted my teeth to keep from whining. Orin looked asleep on his table, the needle jabbing ink into his flesh. *How is he doing that? Is he faking? Is this a test?*

The smoking herbs burned my sinuses. My brain fuzzed. I watched Orin across from me, his head facing away. His hair glinted like mica in the candlelight, the countless sands of some foreign shore. I blinked. Time jumped. The tattooist on my left had been inking me, then they fussed with a cloth. My head jerked up; the tattooist on my right pushed it back to the table. The harps were now xylophones. Guns buzzed. Needles jabbed my skin. Orin seemed to flatten before me, as if transforming from a sculpture into a photograph. I breathed deeper, coughed gently. The photograph became a watercolor, then the watercolor bled to the edges of my vision. I blinked. Time jumped. Guns buzzed. Nothing bit my back. The xylophones were now Native American drums, deep and thumping. They seemed to grumble: "*Doom. Doom. Doom-Doom-Doom.*" The cucumber smoke had faded. I tried to remember who had extinguished the herbs, when black ink spilled over the watercolor and swallowed the world.

Doom. Doom. Doom-Doom-Doom.

My body floated up from the table and drifted into the vast nothingness. Embers sizzled somewhere outside my vision. I felt no jabbing needle, no pain. The tattooists must have left. *Weird. You'd think I would remember them leaving.* Footsteps clomped somewhere in the darkness. "Hello?" I called. "*Hello*?"

A figure stepped from the gloom.

Sam.

He rushed at me, screaming: "Look at the trouble you caused! What is *wrong* with you? Are you *stupid?*"

I recoiled with a gasp and shrunk down, as if I were a wad of wet wool, withering in the heat of his rage. I wanted to hide inside myself, go numb. *No. I must tell him what he needs to hear so I can move on to my new life.*

"I-I'm sorry, Sam. I didn't mean to upset you," I said, as I had a million times during our marriage to calm his storms.

Instead, he screamed louder: "Well you *did* upset me! *And* embarrass me. *And*—"

I glanced around, my heart racing. *What do I do?* I couldn't appease him through cooking or chores. I had no bedroom to hide in until his storm had passed, or a secret mineshaft to run to and pretend everything was fine. Only darkness existed, and Sam's anger which filled the void. My breathing quickened. I had spent years tiptoeing so as not to wake his anger, had scurried when it stirred, had hid and cowered when it rampaged. In the vision, Sam's fury almost had a face, all murderous eyes and scales and snapping jaws. But hadn't that monster always been there? Hadn't our whole marriage served its swells and falls? I had sacrificed oil painting for a tidy house. I had sacrificed school for avoiding debt. I had sacrificed personal preferences—from meals to television shows to weekend activities—all to keep the invisible monster asleep. I had. I had. I had.

"I work my ass off to give you a nice home," Sam screamed. Spittle struck my cheek and I smelled stale Camels on his breath. "And you repay me with *abandonment*? Doesn't our marriage *mean* anything to you?"

Thick worms wriggled inside me; my pulse thumped dully, deep inside my gut. I pressed my lips tight. We were married, but I realized our marriage wasn't free. A slave master named Rage owned the whole illusion—the love, the companionship, the home in the woods—and it all bowed to its whip. *I* bowed to its whip. Rage was Sam's problem, but his problem was my problem because I was the good little wife who never caused waves, yet was somehow guilty of being unable to control an ocean.

My eyes widened as realization dawned on me. This purging wasn't about what *Sam* needed to hear, but what *I* needed to admit and say. Sam refused to take responsibility for his emotions. Instead, he used them as an excuse to belittle me, *correct* me, indulge in behaviors despite who it hurt. My eyes narrowed. Sam believed all of his actions were justifiable since they made *him* feel good, God dammit! And didn't he fucking *deserve* it? For only one crisis existed. *His* crisis. Which everything and everyone miraculously caused, but him.

I lifted my chin, stared him square in the

face. "Your choices are not my fault."

Sam sneered. "You're pissing me off, woman."

"No, *I'm* not!" I shouted. "*I* don't control your anger. And you no longer control me. I don't need you, Sam. *Go away!*"

His face turned purple. But the insults he screamed in my face became jumbled sounds, like some fitful rainforest bird.

"Go away!" I slammed my hands on his chest, but the moment we touched he faded from my vision, like steam on glass.

I stood alone in the darkness. A cold wind ruffled my hair, and my lips twitched into a smile. "I did it."

"All my problems are *your* fault!"

My mother staggered out of the shadows, her hair and blouse in disarray, a glass of scotch sloshing in her thick hand. She hadn't aged a day in a decade, and I went rigid as if I was still a teenager surviving beneath her roof.

"You ran my husband off, made me miserable and alone!" she shrieked. I spun away from her, but she materialized in my face like an apparition. My impulse was to flee like I did in the past, to escape her through painting and books and daydreams, to try to sleep her off like a drunk which never went away. But each way I spun she was in my face, screaming.

"You are *not* of my womb. You're not even of this *world*. You are an evil imp sent to destroy my life! I should have drowned you in the bathtub. You owe me. *You owe me!*"

"Stop it!" My shout echoed in the gloom. My mother faded, then snapped back into focus, her lips pouted, blue eyes glaring. "You are not a victim!" I snapped. "And I am not your abuser. I'm sorry for your pain and losses, but we did the best with what we had."

"*We* did nothing! *I* put up with *you*! You think being a changeling is the only reason why I hate you? I hate you because you are horrible, Miriam. You alone ruined my life. You! You! *You*!"

I bit back tears, but no longer felt the sunken-chest pain of failure. I realized this woman was incapable of love, and nothing I did could change that. I never failed her as a daughter; she had failed me as a mother. The mother I had yearned for all my life was a delusion.

"*I* do not inhibit you," I said. "*You* do. You are free, like me. Go find your happiness."

I expected her to go ballistic, smack me and insist I created all of her woes, as if I was some unstoppable force of misery. Instead, she fell to her knees, wailing, and melted into her tears.

"Ha!" My joyful bark echoed in the empty darkness. "This is easier than I thought. Bring on my monster-in-law!"

Harps strummed. I winced as something pricked my back. *I must be coming out of it.* I beamed. *Thank God. My tattoo is almost finished. I will finally go home.*

A hand fell on my shoulder from the darkness, the skin as warm as sunlit shores. I tensed, knowing it was Orin.

Oh, God. How do I handle this one*? I don't* want *him to leave. Is* that *what I say?*

His warm fingers caressed my neck. "Orin. I—"

But when I turned I found Delano.

His irises had disappeared, his pupils as black as two new moons. "You are forgiven," he said, in his low, owlish voice. "You've always been forgiven."

I choked back tears, unknowing why they had sprung. "I have nothing to be sorry for."

His face fell, as if he stood before someone who suffered an unspeakable tragedy. "Yet."

"I need you to go away," I said, my voice hardly above a whisper. I expected him to fade like the other phantoms, but he lingered, tears dripping down his starlight face. He nuzzled my palm when I caressed his cheek, then grabbed my hand and pressed it to lips as warm as an Indian summer. I slid my fingers through his midnight hair, smelled the earth on his skin. He seemed more real than Sam somehow, more solid than my mother. "Are you really here?" I asked.

"No," he whispered, his teardrops beading along my finger. "I am merely a chance to cleanse yourself."

"Delano. I..." *What do I say to him? Do I thank him for making me feel special and beautiful and wanted? Do I apologize things couldn't be different? Do I admit I still crave him beside me?* Warm medicinal oils tickled my nose. Not quite eucalyptus, not quite clove. Needles pricked my sacrum, and the words leapt out of me without thought: "I'm sorry I can't see in the dark," I said, and threw myself into his arms.

Delano caught me, squeezed me to his chest. "I see *you*," he said, and disappeared the moment our lips touched.

I stumbled forward as if falling through a shadow. "Delano?" I said, almost cried. I wheeled around, trembling. I broke out in gooseflesh, shivering alone in the black nothingness. *"Delano! Come back!"* I called, standing on my toes as if I could peer over the darkness. Bells chimed. Harps strummed. Light crept into the blackness and I knew my eyes were opening. I fought it, tried to remain in the dreamscape, searching for a darkling in the gloom. "Delano! *Delano!*"

I smelled oils, warm and medicinal. Not quite eucalyptus, not quite clove. My eyes opened to Orin sleeping, bleary with tears. I sat up. My head felt three feet above my shoulders; my back ached like a third-degree sunburn. The veiled tattooists and their guns were gone, the embers in the copper cauldron now white ash. I stepped into a pair of slipper-shoes waiting for me and practically slid off the table from the slick oils gleaming on my skin.

Monks and their singing bowls hummed from the overhead speakers. The candles had melted almost to the shelves; some had begun to gutter. I shuffled to the looking glass in the corner, rubbing away sleep and visions from my eyes. I still felt Delano's tears on my fingers, the brush of his lips on mine. Then I yawned and he slid from my consciousness like any other dream. My past was cleansed. No more manipulative darklings or cheating husbands or belittling mothers. I admired the vine-like quality of the healer's tattoo painted above the looking glass and smiled. *This is your fate now*, the picture promised. *It is time to start anew.*

I turned my back to the mirror and

glanced over my shoulder. Delano stood with me in the glass. I gasped and jumped to face him, but found only flames dancing on candle wicks, Orin snoring softly on his table, walls full of painted wings. My heart started to pound. *If Delano's not here, then...*

I twisted my rear to the mirror, and nearly fainted when Delano's miner tattoo reflected back.

CHAPTER THIRTY-EIGHT

I gawked at my reflection's missing spirals and swooping strokes, as if staring long enough would make them appear, fresh and black and fern-like on my skin. But my new tattoo remained as harsh and crude as the isolation and enslavement it promised. *A miner tattoo.* I swallowed hard. *A miner's fate.*

My breathing shallowed, fast and stabbing. I spun away from my reflection, the long shadows from the candles flickering like prison bars along the walls. My insides felt hollow, empty, except for the increasing nausea bubbling inside my gut. *Is this the tattooists' mistake? A sick joke?* My eyes shifted to Orin, sleeping peacefully on his table. *Is* he *somehow behind it?*

I shook my head. *Nonsense.* Orin was my friend, my protector, my personal guide. He would never deceive me. But then again, hadn't I thought the same about my husband? Didn't I sit on a barstool in my mother-in-law's kitchen and deny his actions, despite the truth staring me in the face? I sunk to my knees, my heart pounding, reliving that night's hopelessness, the heartbreak, the gut-wrenching betrayal. Only this time the image screaming treachery was tattooed on my flesh. This time the naked proof was me.

I slid my hands through my hair, gripped the roots. *There* must *be a mistake. Raina arranged a builder to accompany me to West Virginia. Two healers will join us, train me, heal the poisoned landscape.* Orin's oiled back shimmered in the soft candlelight, ripples of bronze and gold. His freshly tattooed lines were the retriever details without question. *I'm still reacting from the herbs, visualizing my sorrows and fears. That* must *be it,* I rationalized, and ignored the coals in the copper cauldron which were now snuffed and cold.

I twisted my back to the mirror. The miner tattoo glared at me, raw and indelible and mocking. I waited for its crude black lines to fade like the hallucinations, but they lingered like the consequences of a terrible decision. My entrails turned to water. I started to hyperventilate, the smoky air making my head pound. Overhead the monks continued chanting; their singing bowls hummed. I tried calling Orin's name but managed only a strangled cry. A cry much like a fox with its leg in a trap.

This is really happening. Oh my God. I forced three deep breaths. The room was windowless, and outside the door was the murmur of lighthearted conversation. The genial voices of those who had doomed me.

I found my backpack and coat in a closet and dumped the contents onto the floor, desperately searching for my knife, but finding only clothing, toiletries, leftover snacks. *Where did it go? I specifically remember packing it in the desert.* I yanked Orin's jacket and backpack from the closet and dumped his belongings. A shard of reflector, bottle caps, odd shaped pebbles, a scrap of flocked wallpaper, a rusted earring, a pop tab, a darkling's button. But no knife. My face fell. *Our knives are gone.* Long, thin shadows wavered on the walls. *They took our knives while we were unconscious. Why would they take our weapons? Unless—*

Orin mumbled sleepily and stretched his legs.

"Orin!" I leapt to my feet and shook his shoulder. "Orin! Wake up!"

Orin lifted his head from the table, blinking in the candlelight. "Miriam? Wow. I had the weirdest vision. I saw—"

"*Help me!* They gave me a miner tattoo!"

Orin sat up and rubbed his eyes, like a child stirring from nap-time. "Don't be silly," he said with a yawn. "You are reacting from the purium still."

I wheeled my back to him. "*Look* at it," I snapped.

Orin lowered his hands from his eyes. He stared silently, as if mesmerized. He then chuckled and scanned the paintings on the walls. "We must have interpreted the pictures wrong."

"We didn't interpret the pictures wrong," I said through gritted teeth. "Raina lied. *The Realm doomed me to the pits.*"

Orin slid into boots and tottered to the looking glass. "Impossible. The Realm wouldn't lie." His voice was stern with confidence, yet his shoulders relaxed when his retriever wings reflected in the glass. He went for the carved door.

"What are you doing?" I hissed, smacking his hand off the knob.

"We have obviously misunderstood the procedure. I am going to clarify," Orin said, and threw open the door.

I hid in the room's flickering shadows, peering outside. Raina lounged on a floor pillow beside the wood-burning stove, her legs folded to her side, a teacup in hand. Kegan sipped tea across from her, a plate of scones and strawberry jam between them, as if enjoying a picnic in some royal garden. The sniffer stood guard at the front door, as straight as a pillar. His sapphire eyes tracked the Realm's new retriever as he approached Raina. His white greyhound tensed at his side.

"Ah, Orin. You have awakened." Raina smiled sweetly as Orin knelt on one knee before her. "You must be famished. Have a scone."

"Thank you for offering, but no. I believe there has been a misunderstanding."

Raina sipped her tea. "Oh?"

"Miriam *might* have been given the wrong tattoo." Orin lowered his voice and I had to strain to hear. "It appears to be a miner tattoo."

Raina's teacup clinked against the saucer as she set it on the floor. "There is no mistake. Just as there is no damage in Appalachia and no need to send labor better served in the Realm."

What? I stormed into the foyer, my fists clenched. "There *is* damage! I have *lived* in it!" Orin jumped to his feet, blocking my path with his body. I stood on my toes, glaring at Raina over Orin's shoulder. The sniffer tensed beside the door, ready to lunge. His greyhound's curved back bristled.

"With great respect, Raina," Orin started, "I believe there has been a mistake. Miriam—"

"Miriam is an adult changeling," Raina said. She stood up and sighed, like a surgeon informing a husband his wife had died on the table. "Adult changelings are dangerous creatures. They hate our ways and seek to destroy them. Sometimes through rebellions, sometimes through *lies*. I am sorry we didn't inform you earlier. You were on probation and we questioned your trustworthiness."

Orin's eyes widened. *Is he actually believing this crap?* I thought, horrified. "Why *the hell* would I lie about acid mine drainage?" I snapped. "What could I possibly gain?"

"We received intel about rebels in Appalachia positioned to murder healers and builders." Raina smirked. "Thankfully the report arrived before our healer infrastructure was severely damaged."

"That is a ridiculous *lie*!" I shouted, my fists trembling with fury. "If you believe me a traitor then why not order me killed, you conniving *bitch*?"

Raina giggled. "*Kill* you? Why, what will killing you *accomplish?*"

Her words struck me like a cold wind, and the night outside the motel room slid into my memory, when Delano had fed a starving fox and warned me of my fate. *And he forgave me. Remember that. He knew all along what I'd do.*

My mouth went dry; swallowing felt like pinpricks. "Delano told me the truth, didn't he?" Raina watched me, her eyebrows raised. "The darklings are innocent. If you kill me, another faerie infant will take my place to become a darkling. But if you keep me alive and buried..."

Raina's head was down, but her sage eyes peered up at me, twinkling like the pink diamond on her throat. A smile touched the corner of her mouth, agendas and secrets hidden behind her lips. My skin crawled. It was the smile of a sociopath. The smile of a changeling's mother. "Why, I have *no idea* what you are talking about,

Miriam," Raina said, then turned her back to me. "My patience is waning. Bring her to the mines, Orin. Use force if necessary."

"Mm-Me? But I—"

"You are a retriever and you will complete your assignment." Raina glared over her shoulder. "Unless, of course, you want your promotion lashed off your back."

"No!" Orin said. "It's just that—"

"Retrievers understand changelings have been corrupted with human evil, but corrupted changelings still contribute in the pits and benefit the good of the Realm."

"Evil?" Orin blinked. "Since when are humans *evil*? Our ancestors promised to protect them since—"

Raina wheeled on him. "You *question* me?" A darkness passed over her face. "You swore you were strong enough for a retriever position, Orin."

"*I am.* It's just—"

"You swore you were devoted to the Realm. Are *you* a liar as well?"

"No!"

Raina thrust a finger at his face. *"Then bring Miriam to the pits or my sniffer will bring you* both*!"*

Raina's scream lingered on the logs. Her face was red, her sage eyes smoldering. Orin's brow furrowed. The sniffer tensed in the corner; his greyhound bared its teeth. Kegan cleared his throat from a floor pillow, and sipped his tea.

Orin sighed and grabbed my wrist. "Let's go."

My lip twitched. "Orin, you know I'm telling the truth. The chickadee *saw* the acid mine drainage. It told you—"

Orin yanked me towards him. "Let's *go!*"

I dug my heels into the floor. "No! This is wrong! I'm not a liar or a—*Ow*!" Orin swept my feet out from under me. My teeth clacked when my head whacked the floor; white stars burst in my vision and I tasted blood on my tongue. Orin cranked my arm behind my back. I cried out and writhed, pain shooting through my shoulder, twisting the raw tattoo. The sniffer stormed toward me, blade in hand. I remembered the fugitive's tongue sliced from his mouth at the faerie lodge, the wet smack it made as it struck the flagstone. I pressed my forehead against the floor and wailed.

Orin crammed his knee against the base of my spine. "Shut *up*, Miriam! You are being *selfish*."

The sniffer's greyhound snarled inches from my face, slaver soaking into a throw rug. I saw the tartar on its teeth and the brown spot on its gums, smelled the reek of old bones on its breath. "Here," the sniffer said, and handed Orin something from outside my vision.

I winced as thin wire tightened around my wrists and cut into my skin.

Raina giggled. "Oh, Orin. I know you will make an excellent sniffer someday."

"Thank you."

The pride in Orin's voice made me want to puke. Blood wetted the wire and trickled into my palm. Raina glared down at me. I remembered her on the cushions when we arrived, telling Orin how greatness was created. *Play off what* really *happened and twist it to your advantage.* Lie, in other words. The truth was not important, just the perception of truth. The *truth* the Realm wanted their public to believe to maintain their greatness, their agenda.

Raina slid a finger up Orin's arm, traced a circle around his shoulder. She cupped his ear with her hand and whispered, then smacked his ass before returning to her tea.

Orin yanked me to my feet as easy as yanking up a fallen broom. He clenched my forearm, forcing me ahead. "*Move,*" he commanded, then opened the front door and shoved me out into the cold.

CHAPTER THIRTY-NINE

"Orin, *please* don't do this."

"This is the way it must be."

"No. It *isn't.*" My head pounded. We had left the garden pathways and followed a wide woodland trail carpeted in pine needles. Venus peeked out above us. The log mansion had disappeared behind the trees, leaving us surrounded in granite outcroppings and conifers, their shadows stretched in the dying light.

"Only the Realm knows how to keep the whole happy and safe," Orin said, then stopped short to pick up a pinecone with hardened amber on its spines. His fist clenched above it, as if he suddenly realized such interests were unsuitable for an official Realm retriever. He pushed me forward down the dirt path. "It is honorable to contribute to our community, even if it is not how you had hoped." He then added beneath his breath: "I'm sorry it can't be like how we discussed. I truly am. But I have no choice."

"Bullshit," I snapped. "You always have a choice. Just admit I'm not worth the consequence."

Orin's grip on my forearm weakened. "It's not *that.* I must do what the Realm says."

"Why?"

"Because the Realm is why faeries have peace. They want what is best for us."

"*Peace?* By threatening their people and punishing them with violence?" I scoffed. "Yeah, some peace. Do *you* think I lied?"

"I don't know what I think."

I glanced over my shoulder, gaping at him. "Are you *serious?*" Orin avoided my eye. "Jesus Christ, Orin! They're acting like I am a terrorist plotting for months to destroy an infrastructure I didn't even know *existed* two weeks ago. Isn't the more obvious explanation the *Realm* is lying? Using this for their own purp—?"

"No!" Orin wrenched my wrists over my spine; I cried out as pain tore into my shoulder. My legs buckled and a stone cut my knee as I struck the ground. A jay squawked in the pines as Orin yanked me to my feet and shoved me forward. Blood trickled down my shin as I stumbled along the trail.

"Asshole." Hot tears stung my eyes. "I thought you were my friend."

"I *am* your friend," Orin said. "That's why I didn't tell them about your use of night magic or your meetings with Delano or criticizing the Realm. Otherwise we'd be heading to your execution."

"*Don't you get it?* They will *never* execute me, no matter how much they have against me. If they do, this whole thing starts over. My death triggers the next changeling and another chance for darklings to increase their numbers. The Realm will eradicate the darklings faster if I'm kept alive, sentenced to life in the pits." My face scrunched up as truth fell into my stomach, like the thud of dirt on a coffin lid. "A *faerie* life sentence. Five hundred years. Holy shit."

Orin shook his head wearily. "I don't understand why the Realm chose you for the mines, but —"

"Because the darklings—"

"But it doesn't matter. The Realm will still care for you and provide everything you need."

I scoffed. "As what? Muddy water and gruel? Hovels? Free shackles and chains?"

"No!"

"How do you know?" I stopped short; Orin bumped into my damning tattoo, rocketing a flare of pain up my back. "Maybe *this* is why the man in the restaurant was murdered for fliers. Have you *seen* the conditions the miners work in? Or are you repeating what the Realm tells you like a—like a—" My throat was wet and thick and I nearly vomited up my words: "Like a *mockingbird.*"

"I don't need to see the conditions," Orin said. "I know the Realm loves and cares for the miners."

"How do you know?"

"Because the Realm says so."

I scowled and marched forward. "Yeah. That's what I thought."

We hiked in silence, our heads down. A chickadee darted between two conifers; I glowered and wished for it to drop dead. A chilling wind cut through the trees and ruffled the flimsy skirt against my thighs. Gooseflesh covered my skin; my teeth clattered louder than a typewriter. *How much light-magic will I need to wield before I grow warm like Orin?* I wondered. *Will I even have the opportunity?* I imagined the mines as dark and dank, boundless beasts impossible to overpower, the epitome of helplessness. Orin joined my side and wrapped his arm around my shoulders to quell my shivers. I shrugged him off and stormed ahead. He reached for my forearm, then decided against it. His pace matched mine, but he kept his hands to himself.

"There's the entrance," Orin said.

Two rectangular stones dominated a clearing fifty feet away, the space between them large enough for two men to pass through, shoulder to shoulder. They stood half the size of the surrounding pine trees and loomed above the clearing like grave-markers for twin giants.

"So that's what I've been striving to reach, huh?" I said. "I expected something grander. Some banners and lights, or at least guards to protect the infallible holy land."

"Guards patrol past the gateway," Orin said. "Border sentries, like me, remember?"

"Oh no," I sneered. "You are a grand and noble retriever now. And I'm a miner." My anger died then, as fast and brutal as a neck being snapped. It sank into the inner tar inside me—the pit of repressed sorrow and hatred—and left me feeling numb and distant. *I haven't felt like this since I left Sam,* I realized, and wondered if the mines would drown me in my inner misery, leaving me with nothing but darkness.

"Tell me," I said, hoarsely. "Does the Realm's eternal sunshine reach inside the mines?"

"Some," Orin said, behind my shoulder. "Just enough to..."

"To what?"

He stared at the standing stones for several heartbeats. "To prevent harnessing dark magic," he said, then clutched my arm. I took this as a signal and stepped toward the opening. I held my breath, as if readying to plunge into deep and murky waters.

Orin yanked me backwards, pinned me to

his chest. I cried out: "Ori-*ack!*" His forearm hooked my throat; the oak-leaf buckle ground against my sacrum. I writhed, blood pounding in my ears. His grip tightened. Dread sunk into my gut. *I'm such an idiot.* Raina had never intended to let me into the Realm intact; even in the pits I'd still have a mouth. This was Orin's final test, his chance to show the Realm the depths of his devotion. What had Raina whispered in his ear? To torture me into silence? Slice out my tongue? Beat me into a coma?

I tried to wheel on Orin. His elbow thrusted into my chin, clicking my teeth. He squeezed me against him; I winced as my tattoo pressed against his chest. Orin's free hand slid my hair behind my shoulders. His hot whisper tickled my ear: "Run away, Miriam." I tried to face him. He clenched the roots of my hair and forced my face forward. His throat clicked as the wire slipped off my wrists, wet and sticky with blood. "You don't belong here. Run away. Run away and *never* look back."

Orin released me. I hesitated for hardly a moment and he shoved me forward. I stumbled, then sprinted into the woods. Needled branches slapped my face. My heart galloped with me. I didn't know where the nearest town was and doubted I could survive a winter night in a thin, skimpy dress. But I knew I needed to run until I found civilization or my muscles exhausted or my lungs exploded or I died of exposure. I needed to run until I met my fate. *Any* fate, except for the one behind me.

Twilight shadows reached across the ground, like fingers clawing their way out of an early grave. I gasped huge gulps of sterile air. The compound's wall loomed ahead. Behind me branches crashed and a hound's bark carried on a breeze. A thin creek approached. I made to jump, then stopped short, my hair standing on end when I heard Orin screaming.

CHAPTER FORTY

I wheeled toward Orin's scream and pushed through the brush, twigs and pine cones cracking beneath my feet, then stopped with a jolt. Orin had risked his life for mine, had told me to flee and never look back. I was too weak to fight a sniffer or his greyhound. And even if we somehow escaped these woods alive, the Realm would hunt us down until the end of days. Returning for Orin was suicide.

Orin's screams filled the forest and I sprinted back toward the standing stones.

I crept along the lengthening shadows encompassing the clearing, cupping my hand over my mouth to silence my panting. The clearing seemed wider from this angle, like an overgrown gladiator stadium, a place for games and death. The sniffer pinned Orin's throat to a standing stone; I winced, imagining the grit grating Orin's raw tattoo. The greyhound crouched beside his master, its white hair bristled and teeth gnashing. Orin's left pant-leg was shredded. Blood dripped down his shin like chocolate syrup in the twilight.

My fingers wrapped around a fallen branch.

"There's been a mistake," Orin said. "Miriam isn't a—"

The sniffer tightened his grip. "Changelings pit faeries against the Realm."

"*How?*" Orin croaked. "I don't understand."

The sniffer's eyes narrowed. "You question the Realm." He slipped the whip off his belt and slapped the coiled leather against his calf. "Retrievers must be devoted. Doubt collapses the whole."

Orin's eyes widened. "I *am* devoted! I swear! I love the Realm! I *serve* the Realm!" The sniffer spun Orin around and rammed his chest against the stone. He stepped back and brought the whip behind his head. "No! Stop! *Please!*" Orin pleaded. "I *love* the Realm! *I love—!*"

The sniffer thrashed the whip across Orin's back; his wings exploded in a burst of flesh. Orin collapsed onto his side, wailing. I recoiled, muffling a cry with my hand. The greyhound's eyes flashed in the dying light. Its ears pricked as its stare turned to where I hid.

"Get up," the sniffer shouted. Orin heaved himself to all fours, his arms trembling. Blood dripped off his sides, dirt and pine needles clinging to the gaping skin. "Get *up!*" The sniffer rammed his boot into Orin's rear, plunging him face-first into the ground. The whip cracked twice and Orin screamed as his blood flew into the air.

"Get up!" The sniffer brought the whip behind his head. Orin rolled onto his side and threw back a shimmering hand. His magic slammed the sniffer's chest, hurling him spine-first into a tree at the edge of the clearing. The whip tumbled to the fallen needles. The greyhound lunged. It sunk its teeth into Orin's shoe and dragged him across the ground, screaming. I leapt from the tree-line and swung the branch, bashing the greyhound's head like a grand slam in a summer game. The greyhound reeled sideways, yowling. I pounded the

back of its skull with the butt of the branch until it collapsed into a pile of pinecones, its paws and eyelids twitching.

I rushed to Orin's side. He shoved me away with the heel of his palm. "I told you to *go*," he snapped. "I can't protect you. I—"

Heat slammed our backs like a tsunami of fire. Orin struck the dirt and rolled; I crashed onto my butt twenty feet away. The sniffer flew in from the shadows in a shimmering aura. Orin struck out with his magic. The sniffer dodged, and whammed his boot across Orin's chin, flinging him to his stomach.

"Attacking a sniffer is *treason*." The sniffer ground his boot into Orin's gashes, as if stubbing out a cigarette. Orin wailed and retched from pain. The sniffer whipped the knife from his belt and yanked Orin's hair to expose his throat.

"Stop!" I screamed. Night's whispers filled me like a wind, the strength of glaciers on its gusts. Twilight's glow drained into me, lending its light to illuminate the threats of the world. My night-vision intensified—the trees, the stones, the sniffer lowering his blade—and everything became as distinct as a photograph in blues and grays. I stood up, my heartbeat slowing despite my nerves. Shadows dripped off my fingertips like smoke.

The sniffer wheeled on me, wide-eyed. His body-heat flew into me like a fever. The whispers inside me ravaged it, froze it, energized me like a battery. My muscles flexed; my veins bulged as if flooded with ice water. Orin shivered as snowflakes began to fall.

The sniffer sneered. "Darkling," he said,

then blasted me with magic.

Darkness exploded out of me in a silent burst of shadow. The sniffer's magic struck mine, then drained into me. The frigidness inside me gobbled up his warm energy, like a blood sacrifice to some chilling Creator. Shadows curled around my ankles, but it wasn't like dry ice as I had thought with Delano. Darkness was an *entity,* a living, breathing being, forced to obey me. *Protect Orin*, I commanded. The sniffer yelped as shadows raced up his legs and encased him like a body-bag. His teeth started to chatter as his warmth flowed into me, energized me, froze. His faerie-fever was supercharging, making the Realm's hallucinogen seem weak and trivial. My eyes rolled. Never had I felt so high.

I twisted my fingers, and the darkness slammed the sniffer to the ground. Orin's tortured screams still hung in my ears, but Delano hung in my heart. I flushed with shame at the thought of the darkling. I had strung him along, made him believe he had found a shard of goodness in his dark, lonely world. Then I had stabbed him in the back, abandoned him, told him to go to hell. The magic Delano wielded coursed through my body and I *knew* he could crush me, Orin, and any sniffer who stood in his way. Delano didn't spare the faeries at the lodge out of inability. He spared them out of *mercy*, despite the atrocities the Realm inflicted on his kind. Yet the Realm—the *tin predators*—abused their authority on a population of duped faeries who believed they did good. My temper boiled; the sniffer wailed as my shadows tightened. The Realm had manipulated their people's kindness into a covert hatred, a weapon to be pointed at whomever they deemed with no more justification than a convenient lie.

I gnashed my teeth. *Stop him,* I commanded the darkness. Shadows crushed the sniffer against the ground. His screams gurgled, as if drowning in a pool of tar. His heat flowing into me weakened, but anger still blazed behind my eyes. *Stop him. Stop him. Stop—*

"Stop!" Orin said. "You're killing him!"

I recoiled with a jolt and the night magic slithered back into the shadows. The sniffer and his greyhound lay on the ground, snowflakes pattering their still bodies.

Orin staggered to the sniffer, picked his pockets, stole his coat. "Hurry," he said, hissing as the coat slid across his mangled back. "We need to fly past the walls, *now.* They will kill us when they wake, if the Realm hasn't sent guards after us already."

CHAPTER FORTY-ONE

I dumped a pharmacy bag to the floor and slammed the hotel door behind us. Orin snuffled, his teeth chattering. He leaned heavily on my shoulder, my knees aching from supporting his weight for the last several hours. He felt warm but clammy, as if a film of humidity had settled across his skin. His complexion was as pale as bleached bone.

"Sit here and take off the coat," I said, easing Orin onto the bed. I cranked up the heat and inventoried our room—wood paneling, queen bed, coffee pot, ice bucket, hangers, towels, shampoo, soap, extra bedding in the closet. I slid my hand down my face and groaned. We needed the smells of rubbing alcohol and latex, not cedar and Pledge.

Be grateful for what you have, Miriam. Be grateful for what you have.

Even though the room wasn't the hospital we needed, it was far more than I had dared hoped. I had darted into the first hotel we spotted—a Swedish style lodge with a gigantic crackling hearth surrounded in antlers and bricks. I didn't expect to stay at a place this upscale with only three-hundred dollars in the sniffer's coat pocket and no identification. But I had strutted into the foyer and lied to the innkeeper with all the finesse of a seasoned actor. The innkeeper readily believed my story about a blown radiator and two teenage punks mugging us on the road. With a nonexistent ski season (thanks to Delano's abandonment of the area), the innkeeper folded our cash into her pocket and slid a key across the desk.

I latched the door's deadbolt. Any moment a greyhound's teeth could tear into our flesh, or a sniffer's whip snap out of the shadows. I shuddered. *I can't think about that now. I'll freeze up. Focus on Orin.*

Water gushed into the bathtub; I tossed a hand towel inside. I felt robotic, concentrating on every movement of my body to prevent myself from becoming frantic. *Breathe in. Breathe out. Breathe in. Breathe out. Don't run. Stay calm. Stay calm. Stay—*

I glimpsed myself in the mirror above the sink and gasped. My eyes were red. Not bloodshot or rubbed raw, but *red.* As if the irises had rusted. I pulled down my lower eyelid to expose the trick, but found only the whites. My eyes were not as ruddy as Delano's, but I knew they would be if I continued using night magic. *How long until my irises also wax and wane?* I swallowed, hard. *How long until I disappear into the darkshine?*

Stay calm. Stay calm. Stay calm.

The bathtub steamed. I rung out the hand towel and filled the room's ice bucket with hot water and shampoo, mixing it with my hand until it sudsed.

Orin sat bare chested on the edge of the bed, staring at his palms as if wondering how something precious had slipped through his fingers. He hissed and winced as I eased the wet towel onto his back to soften the crusting gashes. "Sorry," I said, "but we can't afford an infection." I paused. "Faeries do get infections, right?" Orin nodded.

I peeled back the towel and shuddered. Three slashes sliced across his back from his right shoulder to his left hip. His tattoo looked as if it had exploded. I dipped the washcloth into the soapy water and dabbed his wounds. Orin flinched, but otherwise stared silently at his fingers.

When I finished, the water was as red as my irises; a film of pink soap bubbles floated on top. I started a pot of coffee and fetched the pharmacy bag I had picked up from the outskirts of town. Inside were two chocolate bars, a tube of generic antiseptic ointment, a roll of gauze. I sat cross-legged on the bed and smeared the ointment gingerly on Orin's back. The bedside lamp flickered and my heart sunk. Even used sparingly the ointment barely coated his gaping wounds. And none remained for the dog bites on his shin. My hands trembled as I wrapped Orin's torso with gauze, the effort seeming as ludicrous as attempting to conquer tyranny with only teardrops and hope.

The coffee pot clicked and hissed. I tied off the bandage on Orin's hip, then helped him slip into the sniffer's coat and buttoned the front. "We need to find a hospital," I said, kneeling before him. I dabbed the dog bites with the wet towel. His shin and calf were red, but the torn flesh was white and jagged. "We don't know if—"

Orin snuffled; his whole body twitched, the veins on his neck bulging like ropes.

I dropped the towel. "*What's wrong*?" I cried, fearing he was having a seizure.

Orin covered his face with his hands, and wailed.

My shoulders slumped with relief. *Not a seizure. Fear.* "Okay, we won't go to the hospital," I said, rubbing his knee. Orin sobbed. I bit my lip. "But we *will* make it through this. Understand me? We *will.*"

Orin peered up from his hands. His face crumpled and my heart broke. A light somewhere inside him had died. Tears dripped from his eyes like droplets in empty caves. He wasn't sobbing out of fear or pain or of not knowing what came next in his life. He had walked the length of the universe seeking God, and at the end found only a void.

"I loved the Realm," he whispered, then dropped his head and bawled.

I wanted to embrace him, hold his body against mine as he trembled from grief. But the gashes on his back—first from tattoo, then from whip—isolated him from comfort, compassion, the Realm, a future family, everything he wanted, everything he loved. My Peter Pan had grown up in the span of a whip-crack, and slammed the door on NeverNeverLand forever. I crawled onto the bed and pulled him toward me. He capitulated like a scared child, shaken awake by a terrible nightmare. We laid on our sides with our foreheads touching, our hands clasped between our chests, ankles entwined. I smelled the blood in his wounds, the inflamed open flesh, the lingering medicinal oil which wasn't quite eucalyptus, wasn't quite clove. Orin cried himself to exhaustion, and we fell asleep caressing each other's fingers, saltwater drying on our cheeks.

And that was how the cops found us when they stormed the room, guns drawn and ready to shoot.

CHAPTER FORTY-TWO

"Police! Don't move!"

For a split second I thought I dreamt of the sniffer, his whip lashing my shoulder to the bone. Then someone hurled me off the bed and slammed me into a wall. I shrieked as two burly men in musky, blue polyester corralled me in the corner. Four other police officers swarmed the bed, screaming incoherent commands. Two of them aimed their guns at Orin's head; the other two grabbed his arms and dragged him face-first onto the floor.

"What's your name?" the officer demanded. His hand jabbed my clavicle, shoving my back against the wall.

"Miriam Thatcher. But—"

"Get the legs!"

Orin writhed in agony as the officers wrenched his arms up over his spine. "Quit resisting!" Another officer struggled to trap Orin's flailing legs in a figure four. Orin's screams sounded too big for the room, as if they could burst through the walls and crush us all in the wreckage.

"Stop it!" I lunged for Orin. The police officer shoved me back into the corner; another pointed a Taser at my torso. My fingernails dug into my palms; adrenaline shook my fists. "He's not resisting! He's *injured*!"

Handcuffs clicked. The bedside lamp flickered. Orin wailed as hands grabbed at his back, his fresh tattoo, the lacerations which shredded his wings and life apart. The cops tugged his clothing—searching for weapons, drugs, needles—then wrenched him to his feet. Orin's knees buckled. The cops slammed him against the wall to keep him from falling, shouting in his ear to stop resisting. Orin wailed, his voice gurgling, tears streaming down his cheeks.

"*Please* let him go," I pleaded. The officer yanked me away from the wall, squeezing my wrists behind my back; his other hand probed the hem of my dress. I shook with rage. The officer had a baby face and I resisted the urge to ask if he was out past his bedtime. "Orin didn't do anything wrong. I *swear*!"

The officers forced Orin toward the door, his face twisted with pain. "There's been a mistake." Orin's voice cracked like breaking shells. He shuffled in a dipping gait, as if the floor was rotten ice beneath his feet. "It's just a mistake," Orin repeated. "It's just a mistake. It's just a mistake. It's just a mistake."

"Miriam." The baby-faced officer had released my hands. He gazed into my eyes with an odd mixture of sympathy and pride. "You are safe now."

"I *was* safe," I snapped, then clenched my jaw to keep from yelling. With the click of Orin's handcuffs the police had exposed us to the Realm more than ever before. I watched the door, my heart pounding, expecting a sniffer to charge past the threshold, whip cracking, and exploit our vulnerability.

The officer's expression of pride faltered. He straightened his back and lowered his tone—a boy trying to convince the world he was a man—and in that moment I realized it didn't matter what I said. It didn't matter I had lived my experiences, breathed them, struggled through and nearly died for them. It didn't matter I knew the facts. The police believed Orin was a threat. They believed I needed saving. And because they believed it, they accepted it as truth. They didn't realize they were abusing me instead of saving me, forcing me to watch helplessly as the innocent was tortured for my choices. I wanted to rebel, demand the facts be heard. But what did that matter? *Orin will get a jail cell. Orin will suffer for my faults and I can't do anything to help him.*

"Is there anybody nearby we can call for you?" the officer asked.

"No." I wiped my eyes with the back of my hand. I had never felt like such a failure. "Orin is my only friend."

"All right. Let's get you to the station and figure this all out," he said, then escorted me out of the room.

The innkeeper waited outside the door, a room key dangling off her finger. She looked smug, as if she had single-handedly gotten a bad man off the streets, and seemed surprised when the damsel in distress cast her the glare of death. *No wonder she gave me a room,* I thought, bitterly. *It was merely a trap.* Orin stood beside the patrol cars, hands cuffed behind his back. Two officers searched every thread of his clothing for contraband. A third officer clutched Orin's wrists behind his back and pushed his body forward, as if preventing him from plunging off an invisible diving board. Except the swimming pool was empty. If the officer let go, Orin would face-plant onto the concrete.

The contents in Orin's pockets were

spread out on the hood of a patrol car—a folding knife, Rayban sunglasses, loose change, dog biscuits, a small spool of wire, a ring of keys—a sniffer's odds and ends, glinting in the spinning red and blues.

The baby-faced officer seated me in the back of his patrol car as a passenger. I pressed my forehead against the glass and watched Orin be manhandled into another vehicle as a prisoner.

CHAPTER FORTY-THREE

The bagel with cream cheese made my stomach growl, but I refused to eat it. *It might be bait.* And I was sick of falling for traps.

I sat at a large folding table, a wool blanket around my shoulders, a lukewarm cup of coffee in my hands. I had hoped my use of night magic against the sniffer was enough to make me disappear into the darkshine upon daybreak, but no such luck. Across from me sat two middle-aged men with opposite complexions and identical fake smiles, both in suits without ties and perfectly creased collars. They had told me their names were detectives something-or-other, but I thought of them as Huey and Dewy, and wondered if Louie watched us from behind the gigantic mirror on the wall to my left. I wondered if this interrogation was going as he hoped.

"I want to see Orin," I told Huey and Dewy (and Louie if he played spy as I thought).

Huey shook his head. "Not possible."

"Why?"

"He's still at the emergency department for medical clearance."

"When will I see him?" I said.

"Why do you care to?"

"Because he's my *friend*."

I caught a whiff of Old Spice as Dewy's sausage-like fingers scribbled something on a yellow pad. "Strange term to call your abductor."

"For the thousandth time, *he didn't kidnap*

me," I said. "What do I have to do to convince you people?"

"The ER doctor says it looks like he was whipped. Know anything about that?"

"He was attacked."

Huey lifted a bushy eyebrow. He reminded me of an anorexic walrus. "By *you*? Were you fighting him off?"

"Don't be stupid. He's my *friend*."

"Then how did he get them?"

I thumbed the bite marks on the rim of my polystyrene cup. "I don't know. I wasn't there. He came to me afterwards, but didn't say anything."

"So you didn't see anything, didn't hear anything, he didn't talk to you, and you didn't ask him about it." Dewy went back to scribbling. "Uh-huh. You two sound like the bestest of friends."

I shrugged. "Can I go now? I've done nothing wrong."

A wedge-shaped man with a hawklike face entered the room, carrying a laptop. My eyes narrowed. *Louie, I presume.* Louie set the laptop on the table, then slipped out of the room as silently as he had entered. Dewy pulled the laptop to him and started tapping buttons.

"We are concerned about your safety, Miriam. And we'd hate for a bad man to go back on the streets to hurt others."

"Oh, please. Orin is the sweetest guy I ever met."

"Then why did he kidnap you?"

I slumped into my chair. "He didn't

kidnap me! As I've been telling you for *hours.* I ran away from my jerk of a husband because he cheated on me. I just met Orin along the way."

"Then what's with those cuts on your wrists? It appears you were tied up, detained."

"Kinky sex," I said.

Dewy lifted an eyebrow. "I thought you were *just friends.*"

"We are. Can I go now?"

Huey scratched his thick mustache, then folded his hands on the table. "We fear you are under the influence of Stockholm syndrome, Miriam. Have you heard of it?" I shook my head. "It is common in kidnapping and hostage situations. The victims become attached to their abductors. They trust them, sometimes even fall in love, and will do anything to protect them."

"But Orin didn't abduct me." The fear of Orin being incarcerated for a psychosis I didn't have made my words come out in a whine.

"We have evidence that leads us to believe otherwise." Dewy turned the laptop around. On screen was security camera footage from the truck-stop where I had called Sam. I was at the pay-phone, shoulders slumped, in my pajamas, and noticeably filthy even through the grainy imaging.

"You took no money or belongings, left no note, used no vehicle. Just *poof!* Disappeared," Huey said. "And here you are in this footage, about four days later, in the same pajamas you were last seen in, obviously in distress."

I rubbed my eye, my brain fuzzy with exhaustion. "I hopped a freight train, then later met Orin *randomly* and hitchhiked with him."

"You hopped a *train?*" Dewy chuckled. "Sam says you are withdrawn and conservative and you prefer your life predictable. He says you are a girl who doesn't change things, not even your brand of laundry detergent. Yet you want me to believe you *hopped a train*? Just like that? That's a whopper if I ever heard one."

"Well I never expected my husband to play the skin flute with some college kid," I snapped.

Huey stared at me, confused. Then his eyes widened. An awkward silence settled in the room. Dewy sucked in his lips to keep from smiling. Onscreen, Orin entered the picture and I slammed down the receiver. He handed me my new knapsack, then embraced me and led me out of view. Huey cleared his throat and paused the footage. "You hung up fast and seem distressed when Orin enters the picture."

"Of course I was distressed. I just had a fight with my husband."

"Your husband says otherwise," Dewy said. "He says you sounded confused, that you didn't know where you were, and you hung up mid-sentence as if cut off. Is he lying?"

"No," I said, slowly. "But—"

Louie popped back into the room. He whispered into Dewy's ear. Dewy nodded grimly, then Louie left.

"Has Orin been slipping you drugs, Miriam?" Dewy asked.

"What? *No!*"

"Your eyes are very red," Huey said.

"I haven't slept much. Can I go now?"

"I mean, why else would a sweet, quiet, small town girl like yourself wear a skimpy dress in winter and get tattoos with a guy she barely knows?"

"That is none of your—"

"Orin popped positive for meth and ecstasy," Dewy said.

I blinked. "What?"

"Did he encourage you to eat or drink from containers you didn't see him open? Generous with snacks or candy? Have things happening around you felt unreal? Maybe felt better than they should?"

I opened my mouth but could not speak. I thought about Orin's candy canes and all the food he had ordered without me present. I thought about the chickadee and how I had convinced myself I had eaten a hallucinogenic mold in the carrot cake. Had I been right? Had everything I experienced been a bad trip?

A memory hit me: Sam and his buddies in the living room during half-time on Superbowl Sunday. Empty beer cans filled the trash; Cheetos were scattered across the floor. Sam bragged about a recent arrest where he had tricked some poor sucker into believing his brother had betrayed him. Sam told the sucker the district attorney had promised a reduced sentence if he ratted out his brother and friends. The sucker accepted Sam's deal and ratted out everyone. In truth, however, the sucker's brother had never squealed. Everyone was convicted, Sam never involved the district attorney, and the sucker received a full-term prison sentence. *"For some reason everyone thinks it is illegal for cops to lie,"* Sam had said. *"I swear. The public's ignorance is a better weapon than the gun."*

My eyes narrowed. "You're lying."

"No," Dewy said. "Orin popped positive. They even—"

"Drug test me."

Huey and Dewy exchanged a glance.

"Drug test me," I said. "I will prove I'm clean. Then you can let me and Orin go."

"Excuse us for a moment."

Huey and Dewy left the interrogation room. I glared at Louie hiding behind my reflection in the mirror, then set my coffee cup on the table and listened to the wall clock. Tick … tick … tick … tick … My stomach growled. The bagel would have won the battle of wills if I didn't fear the cream cheese had developed salmonella from sitting out for so long.

Tick … tick … tick … tick … Nearly an hour passed. I remained alone. Were Huey and Dewy interrogating Orin? Maybe they were drug testing him, after all. *Hopefully the Realm's herb doesn't pop up. Or the pot smoke from the RV.* My brow furrowed. *Maybe goading them was a bad idea.* I gnawed on the stub I had left for a thumbnail, tasting the bitter dirt of the Sierra Nevada. *God. Orin is probably scared out of his wits.* But at least he was safe behind bars. The Realm guarded their secrets from humans, so I doubted they would attack us here. I relaxed some and wondered what Orin had told the detectives. How much did he divulge? Did he—?

My spine straightened with a jolt. I glanced nervously at the mirror. *What if Orin snapped?* What if he had decided he had no friends, only enemies—faeries and darklings and humans alike. Maybe he had used magic on them all, went on a rampage of heat and wind. Maybe he summoned water from the pipes in the walls and boiled everyone alive. *Maybe Huey and Dewy haven't returned because the entire police station is a unit of steaming corpses.*

I jumped from my chair and banged my fist on the mirror. "Hey!" I shouted. I made a visor with my hand and tried to peer through the glass. My rusted eyes peered back. "Is anybody in there? I'm not pressing charges and I've done nothing wrong. You can't detain me forever!"

The door creaked. I spun around. Louie beckoned me outside with his finger.

"It's about time." I followed Louie down the hallway, but we never made it to the exit sign. "I want to see Orin."

"Can't right now. They're talking to him in one of the other rooms. It's an investigations thing. Anytime a possible state-crossed crime occurs with an officer's family member they gotta dot every I and cross every T. Sometimes the FBI pokes around too."

"But I *told* you he is innocent."

"Stop worrying yourself. If what you said matches up we will release Orin soon. Besides, I found you a distraction."

Louie opened another door and directed me inside. This interrogation room was smaller than the last and lacked a one-way window. There were just four white walls, a table with three folding chairs, and my husband standing in the corner.

CHAPTER FORTY-FOUR

"Miriam!"

Sam threw his arms around me and squeezed—a lasso ensnaring its target at last. I bit my tongue to keep from crying out as he pinched my tattooed skin.

"Thank *God* you're alive," he said, his voice muffled in my hair. "I've been so *worried*." He smelled of cigarettes and dirty laundry, as if he'd been chain-smoking for days without a break for a shower. Yet when he pulled back to kiss my lax lips, I noticed his face was clean shaven and no dark circles hung beneath his eyes.

"I'll give you two a few minutes," Louie said, then closed the door behind him.

Sam dropped his arms and stepped back. His eyes narrowed and a shadow passed over his face. "You wanna tell me what the fuck has gotten into you?" he snapped. "Explain why you've been gallivanting all around the country with that blond-haired faggot."

I scoffed. "Like you should talk."

Sam's eyes widened, then creased with rage. "*Sit your ass down*," he shouted, and thrusted a finger at the table.

A lifetime of repressed rage fought to explode out of me, but I swallowed it with my pride. *Pick your battles*, I told myself. *You are in no position to be reckless.*

I clenched my jaw and sat.

He pulled the blanket away from my

back. "So it's true," he sneered. "Jesus. If you are going to tattoo half your body you could at least get something attractive."

I stared at the wall and said nothing.

"The silent treatment, is it?" Sam towered over me, his fists on the tabletop like a territorial gorilla. "I've been tailing your ass all across the country to bring you home safely."

I rolled my eyes. "Oh please. You didn't do this for me. Our community will never elect a cock-sucking sheriff, or one unable to control his wife."

"Is *that* what this is about? *Revenge?*"

I threw my hands into the air. "It's not always about *you*, Sam! *I* don't want to be with you. *I* needed to leave."

"After everything I have done, a divorce will be *terrible* to my candidacy."

"Infidelity is a lot worse!" I snapped.

He slammed his fists against the tabletop; a vein throbbed in his forehead. I clenched the blanket tight around my shoulders. The gray wool was rough against my raw skin, but Sam's gray-green eyes were rougher. *How can this be the same man I had fallen in love with in high school?* My heart had always fluttered when he winked across the classroom, but gazing into Sam's eyes now felt like smut or car accidents or gore—everything that made me recoil. My lips had tingled when his mouth brushed mine in the hallways, but his lips now left the stain of every kiss he had stolen behind my back, and the bitter aftertaste of every lie. At 6'5" my husband made an impressive figure, but standing there in the interrogation room he had never seemed so small.

Sam flopped into the chair across from me with a groan. After a moment he said: "What the hell do you want from me?"

"All I want is for you to leave me alone."

"And what am I supposed to tell the media, *huh?*"

"Tell them whatever you want. Say I got amnesia. Say *you* left *me*. Say I need an extended vacation to heal from all the trauma. *I. Don't. Care.* I promise to say whatever you want if you just *leave me alone*."

Sam clasped his hands in front of his face, concealing his mouth in concentration. "The vacation idea might actually work." He trailed off, then leaned back. "Is there any way I can persuade you to come home with me?"

I shook my head. "No"

"Where will you go?"

"I don't know." I smoothed my plum silk skirt. "Me and Orin will figure that out later."

Sam's eyes narrowed. "You intend to stick with the faggot?"

"Stop calling him that!"

He rolled his eyes. "Why? That's what he *is*. For God's sake, Miriam, stop being so damn sensitive."

"No!" I shouted, and slammed my fist on the table. Sam's eyebrows jumped with surprise. "Sensitivity gives me empathy and gratitude and the belief in something bigger than myself. I will lie to save your career and I will hide to protect your pride. But I *refuse* to sacrifice the goodness in me because it makes your bitterness uncomfortable!"

Sam stared at me, dumbstruck. As if a

mouse had leapt from the brush to rip out the lion's throat. I half expected him to vanish like vapor as he did in my purium vision. Instead, he leaned back in his chair with scrutinizing eyes. I folded my arms over my chest and stared him down.

After a minute of silence he sighed, then said: "Let's make a deal. If you don't speak to the media, I'll house you and Orin at a motel until you figure out where to go *on vacation*. I will even set aside finances for your *vacation* from my account, for as long as you stay quiet."

The hair on my neck prickled. *This is too good to be true.* Was there a catch, or had the Realm made me paranoid? I had lived with Sam since I was eighteen, shared his home and shared his bed. Once he had been my universe, my knight in shining armor. I tapped my thumb on the tabletop. He had never hurt me. Not *physically*, anyway. And he could distance us quickly from the Realm. Sam would undoubtably give Orin hell, but gibes were pleasant compared to a sniffer's blade.

I snickered.

"What's so funny?" Sam asked.

"This whole situation. I've been so desperate to stay ahead of you and now I'm considering going *with* you."

Sam shrugged. "At least it got us out of visiting Grandma Ingrid."

Our eyes met, and we burst into laughter.

Sam reached across the table, cupped my hands. "*Please*. Let me do this for you, okay?" His smile faded. "You're right; I know it. It will never work between us. I did ya wrong. I know *that*, too." He leaned back in his chair and rubbed his eyes with a groan, and I glimpsed the exhaustion he carried. The weight of his career, the election, the fear of failure, a marriage built around lies and aversion, the inability to openly express a personal truth his family and community would never accept. I pitied him then, and realized he wasn't the powerful force I once thought he was. He was dark and dominating but otherwise harmless. A shadow shrinking in the light.

"I don't want you unhappy, Miriam. You are a *good* person." Sam lowered his hands to the table, his chin trembling. "I loved you once, you know."

My throat clicked. "I know. I loved you, too."

"Then let's help each other out. I'll fund what you want, if you don't damage what I want. Deal?

"Deal," I said. We shook on it. "Now, will you *please* get Orin and I out of here?"

"That I will."

I followed Sam out of the interrogation room, his car keys jingling like boot spurs in his hand.

CHAPTER FORTY-FIVE

I squinted as Sam and I trotted down the steps of the police station, the sun glaring into my eyes. The air had become crisp since we were detained. Wisps of clouds cut through a powder-blue sky.

Sam's rental car—a brand new, white Nissan Maxima—was parked near the police station's front door. He leaned against the driver's window and lit a Camel. A brisk wind circled around me, rippling my hair and the hem of my skirt. A dirty receipt tumbled into the hedges. The detectives had let me keep the blanket; I hugged myself for warmth and focused on the police station's door. Sam sucked on his cigarette, the soft crackling the sole conversation between us. His silver belt buckle glinted against his faded blue jeans. I ground my teeth. *What is taking Orin so long?* Every second that passed was another second closer to the sniffer tracking us, the Realm imprisoning us, a knife sliding across our throats.

A spider scurried across the trunk of the car. My breath caught. Was it a spider or a *spyder*? I flicked it to the ground and crushed it with my foot, twisting my toe until a stain remained. I had forgotten about spies. How did you hide from an army of spyders, lurking in spaces too small to see?

Sam smoked almost to the filter, then threw the butt on the ground and let it burn.

"Are you sure they're releasing him?" I asked.

Louie opened the station's door as if I had

uttered the magic words, and Orin skulked down the steps. Never had I seen his gait so heavy. His shredded pant-leg had been cut to the knee, and his calf was freshly bandaged. His hands were shoved deep into the sniffer's coat pockets, his shoulders curled forward as if ducking from the world. He scanned the parking lot, his eyes darting to the trees lining the street, to the Crown Victorias behind the chain link fence.

I met Orin halfway to the Nissan and threw my arms around his neck. He hugged me low on the waist, both of us avoiding the rawness on each other's backs. He tucked his face into my hair and whispered hoarsely: "I'm sorry."

"You have nothing to apologize for," I said. "How is your back?"

Orin pulled away and shrugged. "Painful. The doctors re-bandaged it. They wanted to stitch it, but I refused."

"Why did you refuse?"

Orin nearly spat his words: "Because I am sick of *lies*."

I sighed, unsure what to say. "We got a ride."

Orin glanced at Sam—who glared at him—then back to me. His brow furrowed. "You want to do that?"

"We are otherwise stranded," I said, then lowered my voice so Sam wouldn't hear. "*And* it's safer than trying to outrun the Realm on foot, right? It'll also get us cash and time until we decide what to do next."

Orin blinked. "You're not returning to Ohio with Sam?"

My back straightened. Orin had spoken much louder than my whisper. I sensed Sam's eyes boring into the back of my head. "No," I said, slowly. "That has not changed."

My husband's footsteps clomped behind me. Dread filled my bones.

Sam extended his hand to Orin. "I guess I ought to thank you for protecting my wife." He forced a smile which did not meet his eyes. "God knows what would've happened if she attempted this harebrained adventure on her own, ya know?"

Orin shook his hand. "Oh, I wouldn't worry. She is stronger than she appears."

I doubted Sam noticed the sly smile tugging at Orin's lips before he turned to unlock the car.

Orin slid into the back behind the driver and leaned forward to keep his gashes off the seat. Sam walked around to open the front door for me. "I think I should sit in the back," I said.

Sam's eyes hardened—two six shooters cocked and aiming. I recoiled. My instincts (*or is this impulse?*) told me to grab Orin and flee. *But flee where?* The sniffer would track us on foot. Sam sighed deeply; his tension released on the exhale and returned the husband I knew. His eyes softened and my shoulders relaxed. Those bullets I had imagined were blanks.

"Whatever you feel is best," Sam said, then left me for the steering wheel.

In-N-Out wrappers and Redbull cans littered the rear floorboard, yet the whole car reeked of newness, making my stomach clench. New-car-smell always shoved me toward the edge of carsickness. So did backseats on windy, mountain roads, come to think of it. For a brief moment I thought the front seat *was* the better option. Then I realized sitting beside Sam would cause more nausea than any swaying car.

The ride was quiet. No music, no conversation. Just breathing, the occasional cough, and the engine's trundle. I tucked my hands between my knees, sitting in a triangle with my adulterer husband and my outlaw faerie friend. I gritted my teeth and reminded myself that every tick of the odometer brought us farther from Raina, farther from the sniffer, farther from the Realm. Orin leaned his forehead against the window and closed his eyes. His shallow breath fogged the glass in two patches, growing and shrinking like the tide. I wondered if he regarded this car ride as I did. Was he grateful for the quick escape? Or had his devotion been so deep that fleeing the Realm felt like abandonment, despite their lies and torture? I frowned. *Maybe Orin knows fleeing is pointless, merely killing time before the sniffers inevitably kill us.*

I reached over and patted Orin's thigh. Orin's fingers found mine and squeezed. His forehead never left the glass and his eyes never opened. My thumb rubbed his, a pathetic attempt at comfort, but the one comfort I had to give.

Sam glared at me from the rearview mirror. I met his eyes and felt ... nothing. I had suffered too many real threats to shrink away from Sam's empty ones. The realization would have felt liberating if it wasn't so depressing.

My stomach spun as Sam raced along the curvy, mountain roads. Flip flop. Flip flop. Around and around. My sinuses burned with nauseating newness.

What made new-car-stench, anyway? Freshly molded plastics? Gassing upholstery chemicals? Metal coatings burning off? Flip flop. I cracked open my window and leaned my forehead against the cool glass, mimicking Orin. Maybe he was carsick as well.

Winter whistled through the window. I closed my eyes and dozed.

The crunch of tires on dirt and gravel woke me. Sam parked in a turnout on the side of the road, the engine running.

"Where are we?" I asked, rubbing my right eye. An overgrown field, fenced in barbed wire, formed a valley between two forested hills. The sun had dipped behind the peaks, sending a burst of vermillion across the sky.

"No idea," Sam said with a groan. "I must have taken a wrong turn somewhere." He pulled a map from the console and opened his door. "Stretch your legs and piss if ya gotta. I need to figure out where I got lost."

Orin and I climbed out of the car and stretched gingerly, our backs too raw to pull taut. I circled my head to get the crick out of my neck. Orin limped to a fencepost and took a leak.

"Hold this down for me, will ya, Mir?" Sam tried to spread a roadmap across the car's hood, but the wind kept flipping up the paper. I pressed one side down, the warm engine vibrating beneath my palms. "See highway thirty-nine?" he asked.

I scanned the roadways, the wind trying to tug the map from my hand. "No." Branches snapped behind us in a thick tangle of brush. I wheeled around with a start.

"Dammit, Miriam! Hold it *down,*" Sam said, trying to tame the map. "I can't do this alone."

"Sorry," I said, and pressed the map to the hood. I glanced over my shoulder. "I thought I saw eye-shine in the bushes."

Sam's finger traced a paper highway. "Probably a cat or a raccoon or something."

Or a hunchbacked greyhound.

Orin joined us, peeking over my shoulder. The map rattled, fighting Sam and my's grip.

"I don't think there *is* a highway thirty-nine," I said, after a moment.

"There is. It's what I came here on," Sam said.

"Well, I don't see it," I said. "Maybe you drove off the map."

Sam groaned. "Guess I should have paid extra for GPS."

More branches snapped. Orin stiffened with me; we glanced at each other, then to the brush.

"Let's keep driving," I said.

"Do I look made of gas money?" Sam said. "Keep searching. I think the rental company gave me an atlas."

The map snapped up when Sam let go, crinkling against my chest in the wind. Sam ducked into the car; Orin grabbed the map's wild side and pinned it to the hood. I squinted in the day's dying light, desperately trying to find highway thirty-nine. But I was convinced highway thirty-nine didn't exist. Sam probably mistook what road he arrived on and his ego now hampered his judgement. It happened frequently during our marriage, but usually lead to delays and arguments. Now it would lead to a sniffer slitting our throats if we kept dawdling. *But how do I tell him* that*?*

"Found the atlas," Sam said as he rejoined us. A single snowflake drifted onto the map and melted. "Hey, Orin. Do me a solid and hold this a sec, will ya?"

Orin's eyebrows pinched together. "What do you want me to do with this?" he asked, awkwardly holding the grip of Sam's Glock.

"Nothing. Thanks for the fingerprints," Sam said, and slammed his fist into Orin's face.

CHAPTER FORTY-SIX

Orin staggered backwards, blood gushing from his nose, but before he brought his hands to his face Sam nailed him in the temple and dropped him like a stone.

I gawked as Sam yanked the gun from Orin's hand. I knew I needed to do something—rush to Orin's aid, attack Sam, run away, *something!*—but my brain and body refused to connect. I stood aside, useless, mute.

Sam snatched a fistful of Orin's hair and wrenched back his head. Orin hung, insensible, making Sam look like a headhunter claiming his prize. Orin's eyelids fluttered; his whites rolled. Blood streamed out of his nose and spotted the dirt.

I flew at Sam, dug my nails into his forearm, and *yanked. "Are you insane?"*

"Do you take me for an idiot?" Sam shouted, shoving me off him. "Do you think I can't smell a setup?"

"*What* are you talking about?"

"I was on the other side of the mirror, Miriam." His fingers curled in Orin's hair, straining his knuckles white. "I heard you tell the detectives about Mark and those photos, and I *know* you will tell others!"

Mark. The name of my husband's lover is Mark.

"If you didn't want anyone to know you were gay you shouldn't have screwed a man!" I snapped.

"*I am not gay!* If you were capable of

satisfying me, my tastes would have never changed. This is all *your* fault! And I'll be damned if you'll blackmail me for *your* inabilities."

"You're blaming *me* for your *betrayal*?"

"*You* are the adulterer," Sam said, and thrusted his finger at Orin. "Running off with *him!*"

I gaped at Sam, dumbfounded. "Orin is *not* my lover!"

"The police found you two *in bed* together!"

"We were sleeping!"

"Oh yeah?" He dropped Orin to grab my arm and waggled my cut wrist in my face. "Kinky sex, was it?"

My jaw fell. "No," I spluttered. "I didn't mean—"

"Not so tough when caught in your lies, are you, you stupid slut? You will *not* ruin the future I have sacrificed for, *understand me*?" He glared at Orin and shook his head. "A pity Orin fooled the detectives. I tried to fend him off, but he snatched my gun and murdered you. It's a goddamn miracle I killed him before he killed me." He gestured at Orin with the gun barrel.

I lunged on Sam. Comical, really. Like a gnat attacking a gorilla. But after surviving trains and magic and the elements and rebels and homeless lunatics and blizzards and perverted guards and ley lines and darklings and bloodthirsty greyhounds and sniffers and the Realm and the police, I'd be damned if Orin and I lost our lives to the bastard who drove me into it all. My shoulder rammed Sam's arm; he staggered and stumbled over Orin's body. I pounded my fists on his chest as if he were a door I was desperate to have answered. He sneered and shoved me to my ass, then pointed the Glock at my face. My heart hammered. I remembered the torn rose petal in the restaurant and the heliofiber glowing gold in a twirling dress. I tried calling in that sensation to protect me, straining to hear sunlight's song. But the only answer was winter whistling through the valley, and a rattling map ensnared in barbed wire.

I scrambled to my hands and knees. Sam lunged, caught my skirt. He dragged me towards Orin, my fingertips gouging claw marks in the ground. The wind swallowed my screams, killing them in the valley. I twisted onto my side and chucked a handful of gravel into Sam's face. Sam cursed, dropping me to shield his eyes. I sprung to my feet and bit his wrist, prying the Glock from his hand. Sam snatched my hair. I crammed the barrel against his chin and pulled the trigger.

Click.

Sam sneered. "You think I'm stupid enough to hand that faggot a loaded gun?"

My blood dropped to my stomach. "Sam," I squeaked. "I—" Sam clenched my hair and yanked me to his eye level. His pupils were huge, like two empty casings in a six-shooter gun. He swatted the Glock from my fist.

"I can't believe you tried to kill me, you bitch!"

"Sam! *Please*! I'm sorry! I-I—!" I shrieked as he swung me in a semicircle, hair ripping from my scalp. My shoulder whacked the rear passenger window. Sam clenched my throat and rammed my back against the door. I squirmed and tugged on his fingers, nails digging into his flesh. I might as well have been trying to pry apart a mountain.

My body bucked beneath Sam's grip, as useless as a flag trying to tear itself from the pole. His hands squeezed tighter. My eyes bulged and I heard a breathless hiccup, startled when I realized it escaped from me. Blood throbbed in my ears, and my tongue became a gelatinous glob inside my mouth. I tried gasping for air, but none flowed in. Sam's face was lax, watching me with the soft, sinister promise of a noose swaying beneath the branches. My hands slipped off his. Once upon a time I had found safety in these arms. *How was I so blind?* Sam had never been my knight in shining armor. He had never been my protector. Sam was a mole, a hidden enemy armed with broken hearts, betrayal, lies.

Cheater, cheater, marriage eater. Lured his wife just to deceive her.

The sun crept slowly behind the hills, bruising the sky. Sam licked his lip, his eyes fixed on mine. I tried calling in night's whispers, begging the shadows to protect me, pleading for them to force my husband away. My skin prickled. Was it from magic or lack of oxygen? Just a few more seconds...

White and gray stars bloomed in my vision, scattering across a darkening sky which didn't darken quick enough. Sam's wedding ring dug into my throat, keeping its promise of until death do us part. My extremities numbed, and somehow my body lightened and floated past the panic and pain.

"You brought this on yourself," Sam said, as blackness crept into my vision.

Then a naked man materialized behind

him in a puff of shadow, his fingers arched like claws and ready for murder.

CHAPTER FORTY-SEVEN

Delano's fingers dug into Sam's eye-sockets; his pinky hooked a nostril and yanked backwards, as if trying to rip off a Halloween mask. Sam cried out, releasing my throat. I collapsed to my knees, gasping and coughing, stars popping black and gray in my sight. Sam flailed. His heels dug into the gravel as Delano dragged him backward by his armpit and face.

"I'm gonna *fuck you up*, blondie," Sam shouted. He bucked Delano off his back and spun around. "I'm gonna—" Sam jumped back with a start when he realized it wasn't Orin who had attacked him, but a naked man with eyes like bloodstained scythes. *"Who the hell are you?"*

"Blast him, Delano!" I croaked.

Sam gaped at me from over his shoulder. *"You* know *this crackhead?"*

Delano grinned and licked his teeth. "I'm keeping this old-school," he said. Both men circled each other, fists up. "I *want* to feel this wife-beater's blood on my hands."

Sam whipped a folding knife from his pant pocket, flicked the blade open with a *snap*. "Oh, there will be blood, motherfucker. Just not mine." He flipped the knife blade-down and lashed out for Delano's throat.

Delano threw up his arms to shield himself, yelped when the blade struck his wrist. Sam ducked down and left, dragging the knife across Delano's forearm, then swung backward, aiming to impale the darkling's kidney. Delano rammed his bleeding elbow down onto Sam's ribs before the blade found its mark, then hooked Sam's shoulder and used the momentum to hurl him to the ground. Sam's hands opened to catch his fall, dropping the knife as he rolled onto his ass. Delano seized the weapon and brought the blade behind his head, ready to plunge it into Sam's heart. "Not such a tough-guy now, *are you*?"

"You dumb-ass." Sam snatched a small revolver from an ankle-holster beneath his pant-leg and fired.

"*No!*" The gunshot echoed in the valley; a murder of crows screamed from the hills as Delano collapsed to his side. My magic blasted Sam as he pulled the trigger, hurling him sideways in a wave of darkness. His head whammed against a fence post and knocked him out cold.

"Oh my God oh my God oh my God." I staggered to Delano and rolled him onto his back. His forearm was gashed from wrist to elbow, oozing dark blood; bright blood dribbled from the gunshot wound above his left hip.

Delano sat up with a grunt, curling his legs to hide his nudity. "I'm okay," he said, clutching his side. "The bullet just clipped me. It didn't go in, see? But *you*." He lifted my chin with his thumb, examining my throat.

"I'm fine," I said, then burst into tears. "You were right about *everything*. I should have trusted you. I am so *sorry*."

Delano cradled my face in his palm. He tilted his head and smiled, his ruddy eyes on mine. "You used night magic."

I snuffled. "*Of course.* I-I couldn't let Sam hurt you. I couldn't—"

Delano crushed his lips against mine. I jerked with surprise, but he pressed firmer, held my face against his. I felt night's magic hum on Delano's body, tasted winter on his lips. Whispers caressed my skin and called me home. I tensed, then cupped Delano's face in my hands, opened his lips with my tongue. I gave my warmth to him freely, shivered to his chill. Venus's brilliance paled above us and the dying light dimmed. But for once neither glow seemed to lessen. Instead, my darkling shined.

Orin whimpered in the dirt behind me.

I jerked away from Delano, my heart racing. "Orin?" I crawled to him and shook his shoulder. His nose was swollen and becoming purple; the tip jutted to the side. "Come *on*, Orin. I need you to wake up." His head rolled feebly; his eyelids hardly twitched.

"They marked you."

Delano stared at the miner tattoo on my back, his face heavy with sorrow. I dropped my eyes and curled my shoulders forward, as if doing so would somehow hide my foolishness, make the ink slide off my back like tears. "Yes, they did. And not as a healer," I mumbled. "Just like you warned."

"I should have found you sooner. Maybe I could have stopped it." Delano lurched to his feet, grimacing. He pulled the blanket from the car's backseat and wrapped it around his waist.

"How long have you been following us?" I asked.

"I lost you in South Dakota." Delano kicked Sam to assure he was unconscious, then emptied the revolver and chucked it into the field. "I headed for the Realm entrance in hopes of catching you and heard a news report in a cafe that you had been detained. I found you as Orin came out of the police station."

I snorted. "And snuck into the car."

"Thanks for giving up shotgun." Delano popped open the car's trunk, rummaged through Sam's luggage. He slid on a pair of Carhartt pants, which hung loose on his hips and bunched at his ankles. He then grabbed a bottle of Aquafina and ripped two undershirts into strips for bandages.

The knife blade glinted in the twilight. I watched Orin and Sam breathe shallowly in the gravel, smelled the blood dripping off Delano's arm. "This is all my fault," I said.

Delano sat beside me and patted my thigh. "Tell me what happened."

I washed and bandaged Delano's wounds and told him everything. The sniffer slicing off the man's tongue. The guards. The ley line. The desert. The darklings. Raina's lies. Delano's tears beading in my vision. Waking up to the wrong tattoo. The Realm forcing Orin against me. Orin defying the Realm and sacrificing his freedom to save my life. Me running away. Orin's flogging. Fleeing through the wilderness. The hotel. The police. The interrogation. Sam's promises. My stupidity.

Delano sat in silence while I spoke, then said: "I'm surprised the mockingbird had it in him to stand up to the Realm."

"And now they want us dead." I finished

cleaning the blood off Orin's face with a scrap of undershirt. A shard of broken reflector winked in the gravel beside his ear. I wiped it with my thumb and tucked it into his pocket. "What do we do now?"

"That depends on—"

Orin groaned. His head rocked in the dirt.

"Orin?" I nudged his shoulder. "Orin! Can you hear me? *Wake up.*"

Orin's eyes fluttered, then widened on the darkling.

CHAPTER FORTY-EIGHT

"*Darkling!*" Orin tried to lurch to his feet but fell backwards onto his ass.

"Stay down! You're hurt," I said.

"Kidnapping her in a moment of weakness, *huh*?" Orin spat on Delano's face as he staggered to his feet. Heat shimmered around his fists.

"*Kidnapping her?*" Delano leapt up, wiping his cheek. His nostrils flared with rage. "This from the *murdering coward* who stabbed Gethen and Melinda in the back!" Shadows coiled around him. "I should return the *favor!*"

"Stop it!" I pressed a hand on each of their chests, hot and cold against my palms. "Sam would have murdered us if Delano hadn't arrived when he did."

"Sam...?" The blood drained from Orin's face. He touched his nose and winced. "What—?" Orin's eyes widened. "Your throat!"

"I'm okay," I said, and quickly recapped what had happened. "Delano saved my life," I said, after I was done. "*And* yours, Orin."

Delano hitched up the Carhartts, smirking. "You're welcome."

"Did you hear me thank you, dark*slime*?" Orin snapped.

"Truce you two. Okay?" I said. "The *Realm* is our enemy. Not each other. So let's figure a way out of this mess. *Please.*"

Orin took a deep breath. "It's simple. We

need to run and hide, far from the Realm's entrance."

"*That* is your plan?" Delano laughed. "A sniffer will slit your throat the moment something shiny distracts you, mockingbird."

"Don't call me that!" I squeezed Orin's shoulder. Orin scowled and took another deep breath.

I turned to Delano. "What do you suggest?"

Delano pursed his lips and tapped his chin. After a moment he said: "I see four options. One: Flee, as the mock—er, as *Orin* suggests. Which means blending with humans or embracing magic in solitude. Either way, the Realm will hunt you down and kill you.

"Two: Crawl to the Realm on your knees and grovel for a life-sentence in the pits. The Realm will agree so they can lure you into a public execution and make you an example."

I wrinkled my nose. "No to both of those."

"Wise," Delano said. "Three: Embrace night magic and join the darklings."

Orin recoiled as if he whiffed a rotting corpse. "Ugh! Never!"

"Is it even possible for a faerie?" I asked.

"Yes," Delano said. "But once you go past the darkshine, you are in the darkshine forever. It is impossible to return to the light."

"I would die from disgust before I made it into the darkshine," Orin said. "I prefer to grovel for the pits."

Delano's lip curled. "Figures. Lashing off a bigot's wings is much easier than lashing off his prejudices."

"*I am not a bigot!* I merely believe in *virtue* and *principles*."

Delano lifted an eyebrow. "Mmm. The same virtue and principals the Realm inflicted on your back?"

"*Stop it,*" I said. Although, honestly, I was relieved Orin adamantly refused to join the darklings. It hurt my heart to imagine Orin's warm glow fading into cold, pale moonlight, his tropical eyes filling with blood. That wasn't the faerie I knew. But then, who was he now? Did Orin even know? The Realm had stolen his identity to mold him into one of theirs. He had submitted to their propaganda and in exchange had never developed his truth. Now he was no longer blind, but was still a shell filled with knee jerk reactions to well designed lies. If Orin chose the darklings, he was programmed to feel as if he rejected purity. Going solo went against the hive mentality he always knew. Groveling to the Realm—those who pretended to love him only to torture him—went against sanity. I bit my lip, worrying he'd still choose the last. For Orin not only loved the Realm, but was *in love*. And how many tales had been written about fools killing themselves for an unhealthy lover?

"What's number four?" I asked Delano.

"Join the rebels."

Orin's brow lifted and an uncomfortable silence lingered. Shadows drifted around Delano's feet, curling like a beckoning finger.

"The rebels are terrorists," Orin said.

"No. The Realm *wants* you to believe they are terrorists," Delano said. "And now the Realm says *you* are a terrorist. Do you believe that as well?"

Orin's eyes narrowed. "I did what was *right.*"

"Same as the rebels," Delano said. Orin glared at him, silent. "They have a camp a few miles from my home. We're not friends, but we're not enemies." Delano eyed Orin. "I know they will take you in. They will heal you, feed and shelter you, give you work. The rebels *need* soldiers to free the faeries. However, I doubt *you* have the strength to swear against the Realm, mockingbird."

"I am *not* a *mockingbird*!"

"Time to prove it." Delano eyed me. "You, on the other hand, the rebels will refuse. Even if they trusted changelings, your wings are intact. They will assume you are a spy."

I frowned. After fighting to keep Orin safe I didn't want him out of my sight, let alone out of my life. The rebels weren't a glamorous option, but his other options guaranteed death, whether of his body or his spirit or both. I cupped his shoulder with my hand. "The rebels sound like the safest place for you. And the smartest."

"But what about you?" Orin asked.

Yes. What about me?

"You must choose," Delano said. "We can lash off your wings and attempt to join you to the rebels without guarantee and possible execution. *Or* you can come with me."

"Force her into the darklings?" Orin gasped. "You tricking son of a—!"

"I will force her into nothing," Delano shouted, his blood eyes blazing. "I will protect her

whether she joins the darklings or not."

Orin grabbed my hand. "*Miriam.*" I thought he would scold me, beg me to flee the shadowy monster. But when I faced him, his eyes were glassy, his underlip lax. He looked worried, sad. A young man afraid of losing his friend forever.

"I just want you safe," I told him.

Orin snorted; a smile touched the corner of his lips. "That's supposed to be *my* job."

"Is there a safer option for me?" I asked. Orin frowned. "Delano has never hurt me, you know."

Orin's mouth opened and closed, like a fish gasping for breath. I could almost see his logic fighting the Realm's propaganda of why darklings needed to be killed and never trusted. "I know. But. I. But." He sighed, then nodded in defeat.

I pulled him close and we squeezed each other's waists. He tucked his eyes against my shoulder and I breathed him in. He still smelled of hollow logs and dew drenched ferns and early hints of spring, but beneath these familiarities lurked something sinister. The stink of dried blood and raw open flesh, the first reek of infection. My face scrunched up; I pressed my cheek against his neck. Orin needed help, something impossible for me to give.

Delano tapped our shoulders. My throat clenched, fearing Sam had awakened. Instead, he pointed to the car. A wolf spider dropped from the rear wheel well and scurried toward the field.

"Realm spyders lurk everywhere," Delano said. "You must choose."

Orin clasped my hands. "Rebels," he

said.

My fingers curled around his. "Delano."

Orin's face crumpled. He dropped my hands and turned away with a sob.

"I must protect you first," Delano told me. "For neither of us will relax until you are safe. Agreed, Orin?"

Orin's shoulders quivered. The back of his head nodded.

"You promise to return for him?" I asked.

"I promise. He saved your life. I *owe* him." Delano pulled the car keys out of the ignition and tucked them into his pocket. "Sam, however, can suffer a long walk home."

Shadows curled around my feet and climbed my legs. "I apologize now," Delano said, hitching up the Carhartts. "You lack the night magic needed to make this trip comfortable." Cold shadows slithered along my hips, my torso, my shoulders, coating me like a cocoon. I felt a sucking sensation, as if I wobbled on the edge of a black hole. Orin darkened in front of me, the shadows inhaling his sunlight, gobbling him up. He faced me as the fake night engulfed the world. *The sun is setting,* I thought, and my heart started to race. *This is happening too fast! I might never see Orin again, this might be our forever-goodbye.* I wanted to shout to him. Tell him how much he meant to me, how he was more than a guide, more than a friend. I wanted to embrace him, fold his sunshine into my pocket. I wanted to keep him always at my side, even if it meant a lifetime of fear and struggling and uncertainty. Anything to keep his warmth in my life, anything to keep basking in his glow.

Orin's eyes glimmered in the gloom like the waters of a lost paradise. Then the black hole sucked me in and there was only darkness.

CHAPTER FORTY-NINE

Water woke me from somewhere in the distance, dripping slow and steady onto stone.

Pip ... pip ... pip ... pip ...

I stretched in the warm nest of quilts and comforters; my hands wormed beneath a heavy pile of feather pillows. My neck was swollen and tender; swallowing made me wince. An oil-lamp hung off a bedside hook. I blinked in its soft light and tried to gather my bearings. Dirt walls touched three sides of the four-post bed, planked sparsely with rotting boards. Timber beams were lain like picket fencing to hold the seven-foot earthen ceiling. The air was stale, with a cool hollowness which reminded me of sweaters and late October nights. Beyond the foot of the bed loomed a wall of darkness.

I sat upright in a gray, plush bathrobe. I pressed the thick collar to my nose, smelled Delano in the threads. The oil-light flickered, scurrying shadows along the walls like mice. Shelves were carved into the dirt, lined with fur and crammed with books, papers, bundles of ribbon-bound photographs, a scattering of gold nuggets. But despite the soil and rotting boards, the bedroom lacked the dankness of dungeons and basements. The walls whispered about aging wines, hidden treasures, secret societies. Its coziness kept claustrophobia away.

The oil-lamp cast a halo around the bed then gave up, its wick no match for the gloom. My skin tingled. The light hinted of mysteries inside the darkness, of magic and new beginnings. I stood up and held the lamp out toward the boundless darkness. Railroad tracks led from beneath the bed, cutting straight into the black. Bricks had been laid between the rails, creating a pathway, cold and rough beneath my bare soles.

I found a kitchen several feet to the left, hardly bigger than a cubbyhole, with two rickety cupboards, a sink, and a one burner camp-stove. Shelves were dug into the wall, lined in clay tiles and stacked with mismatched mugs and dishes. A tiny, round table stood in the corner, set with a single, woven placemat and an empty bud-vase. A mobile of antique keys and locks hung above, its silver teeth casting orange stars in the lamplight.

The bricked railroad led me to an open roll top desk, teeming with journals and books, a laptop, Sam's car keys sealed in a jelly jar. Delano slept in an office chair beside the desk, his legs curled up onto the seat, a rolled towel pressed between his ear and shoulder for a pillow. The sleeves of his burgundy dress-shirt were rolled up, exposing blue stitches on his left forearm. He blinked awake when the light passed over his face.

"Hello, changeling." Delano smiled and stretched his legs. When I had first met him, his eyes had been two full moons. Now they were clipped red fingernails, nearing the end of a cycle, readying for a new phase.

"Where are we?" I asked, my voice raspy.

"An abandoned gold mine." Delano winced when he stood up, clenching his side. "It's not much, admittedly. But it is home."

I remembered the abandoned coal mine back in Ohio. My safe haven when the world felt too threatening. I snorted, amused. "A *mine*?"

Delano blanched; his scythe eyes widened. "I know it seems in bad taste because of the Realm," he blurted. "But it's safe from faeries and deep enough in the Earth to keep the darkshine away." He scowled as he rolled down his sleeves. "*Tsk!* It's a damn mess, too. I—"

"Stop!" I set the lamp on the desktop, then clasped his wrist and pulled him to face me. Water pipped in the dark. "You misunderstand. I love it. *Really.*" Delano's shoulders relaxed. "How long have I been unconscious?"

"A day," he said. His nose wrinkled. "But at least you fared shadow-transport better than the mockingbird. He had way too much light."

My heart winced. "How is Orin?"

"He will wake up, eventually. Fortunately, the rebels accepted him eagerly." Delano shrugged. "At least he was unconscious when they reset his nose."

"Do you think he'll be safe?"

Delano tapped his fingertips together. "Well, he will be healed, fed, and strengthened. Given work, security, and purpose. But *safe*?" Delano shook his head. "None of us are safe. War is coming. I smell it like rot in the walls. And the Realm *will* triumph if the rebels don't organize, or if the darklings refuse to fight as Gethen and Melinda proved with their lives."

I frowned. "You sound as if we have already lost."

"No," Delano said. "Darklings are angering. Mockingbirds are starting to find their voices, sing their own songs. We have a chance."

Water dripped in the darkness. *Pip ... pip ... pip ... pip ...* I rubbed my arms.

"But never mind what may come," he said. "I have more pressing matters right now."

"Such as?"

"*Such as* I need to get thousands of bats back into hibernation." Delano chuckled, bitterly. "That ... will be difficult."

"Can I help?"

His eyebrow raised. "Do you want to?"

I nodded, smiling.

His face lit up with joy. Then fell. "If you use night magic, you will slip further toward the darkshine and will never return should you cross."

"I know."

"Your life will be dark and cold and thankless. You will never have children or feel the sunlight on your face. You will be hunted relentlessly, and if I should die, an army will do whatever is necessary to assure you remain alone." Delano smiled, both loving and sad, and brushed his fingers through my hair. "A darkling's path does not lead to the happily-ever-after of fairytales."

"No, but it is the path I was intended for." I clasped his hand, and together we stepped toward the darkness. "And I'm ready to see where that path leads."

ACKNOWLEDGEMENTS

I started Darkshine in 2009 and finished it in 2012, where it then sat for four years while I figured out what the heck to do with it. Many people helped and offered support during that time, but I feel a few need special acknowledgement. In alphabetical order:

Anastasia: You are proof genetics mean nothing when it comes to sisterhood. Thank you for your love, your creativity, your intelligence, your honest encouragement, and for a crazy and authentic twenty years. **Dennis:** Thank you for teaching me the language of Appalachia's birds, and for helping me fall in love with its streams and trees. R.I.P. Rock-Step. **Joshua**: There are many reasons why I dedicated this book and my life to you, but they are far too vast—and far too intimate—to list here. You are both my rock and my heart-song. Thank you. For *everything*. **My Early Readers**: Thank you for taking time out of your world to help me out in mine! **Nikki**: Your enthusiasm carried me through many rough spots. Thank you for believing in this book. It means more to me than you probably know. **Nora**:

You have put up with my neuroses with the patience and solicitude of a saint. Thank you for your help as I muddled through this process, and for sticking with me through all of my freak-outs. I'm sure more will come. **Rowan**: You weren't born yet when this book was completed, but you are a huge reason on why I am doing something with it now. I love you so much, my little amazing. Thank you for being you.

Miriam's story continues!

To get an e-mail about new releases, please sign up here:

http://eepurl.com/bXKmnH

*

Please consider leaving an honest review. Even one worded reviews help new authors tremendously! Thank you!

ABOUT THE AUTHOR

R.D. Vallier is an explorer, a storyteller, a dancer, a lover of all things shiny or grimy or bizarre. If she is not traveling dirt or blacktop roads, then she is in the wilderness handcrafting an off-grid homestead with straw and mud and, at times, crossed fingers.

You can peek into her life at: www.rdvallier.com

And if you feel like chatting with R.D., she'd love it if you dropped her a line at: RD@rdvallier.com

CPSIA information can be obtained
at www.ICGtesting.com
Printed in the USA
FSOW01n0105270716
23017FS